I0642981

ICARUS ASCENDING

BY
JACKSON PEOPLES-ROSENBLATT

Copyright 2017 Jackson Peoples-Rosenblatt
All rights reserved.

ISBN: 0692614168
ISBN 13: 9780692614167
Library of Congress Control Number: 2017909112
ESC Press, San Diego, CA

Once again for Cap,
And, as always, for L.C.

Author's Note

Icarus Ascending continues the story lines of many characters from my earlier novels. To help readers keep track of how this volume is related to the others, a **Directory of Recurring Characters** appears at the end of the book.

DANIEL KMETKO: 1967

I

Daniel folds himself into the driver's seat of the Fiat. He is six feet tall and extremely broad shouldered. The joke around town is that the car could fit neatly in his pocket, or, alternatively, it could be a mascot for his key ring. Left foot on the clutch, two quick dabs on the gas pedal, turn the key. The starter makes a noise like a coffee grinder. The engine coughs twice as if clearing its throat and then sputters into a kind of irritable wakefulness. The sound calls to mind an overgrown lawnmower. He lets the engine warm until it settles into a steady but slightly uneven idle.

He rescued the tiny car from a barn in Elfrida. The day after he got his driver's license he drove out there in Dad's GMC to inspect it. Beneath the grime it was immaculate. The odometer read less than eight thousand, and the rest of the markings on the instrument panel turned out to be calibrated in metric units. So less than five thousand miles. The widow who sold the car to him for thirty-five dollars knew nothing about it except that it had been parked there by her nephew on a brief visit home from the army. She said he had won it in a game of poker, which seemed likely. Daniel knew about the nephew. He'd been a senior the year Daniel was in seventh grade. He wasn't the type to mess around with tiny foreign cars. The Fiat's inclusion among his belongings had to have been accidental. He was famous all over the county for his Harley and his Corvette. They were also parked in that barn, and the widow wanted a lot more than thirty-five dollars to part with them. What she really wanted was her nephew back. The story around the county was that the Viet Cong booby trap had blown him so completely to smithereens that his flag draped coffin contained only a few bloody shreds of what he was wearing at the time of the detonation.

When Daniel bought the car and towed it home, it bore expired license plates that proclaimed "Beautiful British Columbia". Daniel wondered how the tiny car got from Canada to wherever the fateful hand of cards had been played. During Daniel's labors to bring the Fiat back to running condition, this mystery took a back seat to a more pressing one, how to get the engine to idle smoothly. It wasn't what you could accurately describe as a rough idle. It just wasn't a smooth one, and Daniel feared that this betokened some internal imbalance which would eventually result in a loud and smoky cataclysm followed by immobility, with an oily puddle under the car as testimony to its misery. The mechanics of the town refused to discuss the matter. As far as they were concerned he should have left the Fiat rotting in that barn. Better yet, it should never have been imported. Even a Canadian should have known better than to waste money on it. Best of all, the Italians should never have built it in the first place. Obviously they knew nothing about cars. They should have stuck to the production of wine, pizzas, and large busted actresses, things they clearly excelled at.

Daniel bought a second hand set of shop manuals that he had seen advertised in the classified section of a magazine devoted to imported cars. When they arrived, it turned out the seller had neglected to mention that they were in Italian. Visits to a couple of war bride mothers of Daniel's classmates were unavailing. The text was too technical for them to decipher. The shop manuals, the ladies implied, would be better employed as doorstops. Or, properly shredded, their pages might provide an effective mulch for use in their vegetable gardens.

Finally, sitting in the kitchen at Christopher Melendez-Greene's house and eating tortas prepared by Esmeralda, the housekeeper, Daniel learned the secret. Once every three months, a mechanic came the hundred miles from Tucson to perform routine maintenance on Graciela Melendez-Greene's Alfa-Romeo 2600. An Italian mechanic, a young man with fastidiously pomaded hair, a tattooed left forearm, and shoulders even broader than Daniel's, explained that the Fiat's uneven idle was as natural as the earth's imperceptible wobble on its axis.

"The two cylinders are in line," the mechanic explained through crooked, nicotine stained teeth that for some reason made Daniel think of the Parthenon.

"The pistons move in unison. Their forces do not oppose each other as you might expect or even hope for since that would bring everything inside the engine into balance, but reinforce each other so that the little engine constantly rocks in its mountings."

The mechanic's English was heavily accented and surreally inexact, but that's how Daniel's brain translated it into knowledge that allayed his anxieties, and he thanked his lucky stars for the overheard snatch of conversation which had alerted him to the mechanic's scheduled visit that day, his own determination in risking a visit to forbidden territory, and last but not least Esmeralda's hospitality. Finding Daniel in the garage with the mechanic when she went out to announce lunch, she immediately invited him inside as well. Her tortas were legendary.

Since then, Daniel never worries about the Fiat's idle any more, nor does he worry about the slight crunch he hears—more feels, really—through the lever each time he shifts gears. Enzo cleared that up, too, the mystery of the non-synchromesh gearbox, grinning at Daniel through those ravaged teeth. With a better set of teeth, Enzo could have been a movie star. The toast of Rome. Daniel could imagine it all too well, and it made him sad to think of the random unfairness of life. At any rate, the car's symptoms are no longer causes for anxiety, just charming idiosyncrasies—part of the romance of driving a foreign make.

After slathering himself with tanning butter, Daniel ascends. It's the hottest day of the summer so far, and the municipal pool is packed. It's as if every soul between the ages of six and eighteen in the whole town is there. Daniel's sister, Athena, is on the gate. Athena hates gate duty, and her fury at being given the assignment makes her implacable in performing it. Nobody can snarl at a cute eight-year-old or his whiny mother like Athena. The male lifeguards are too tenderhearted. They barely manage to keep order when the crowd is half this large. When the right cheerleaders are on the scene, they're completely useless. Of all Daniel's assistants, only Athena can be depended on to keep anarchy at bay. Daniel's father often jokes that Athena should have been named Hippolita instead, after the queen of the Amazons.

Daniel remembers being a small boy staring up at the bronzed giants on their high perches overlooking the pool. They seemed like the heroes of the chapters someone had inadvertently left out of the books of mythology in the public library. With their strong, shining bodies, eyes like those of birds of prey, and robust baritone laughter, they reminded him of gods. They possessed magic which could only be guessed at. Eventually he grew up to be one of them, the most giant, most golden one of his generation, and he realized that all those idols he had stared at so breathlessly were just guys. None of them had any magic, regardless of the impression they gave. They wore their mystique like Halloween costumes and shed it as thoroughly and immediately. You only had to pay attention to realize the truth, something he suspected most of his peers couldn't be bothered with.

He watches Christopher Melendez-Greene come in, trailing his friends, Patrick Jenkins and Jeremy Pryce. Daniel wonders why on earth Patrick, his second-in-command, would want to spend his only day off this week at the pool. Somehow the threesome successfully stood up to the fearsome Athena. Quite a feat, since when Patrick is off duty she insists on treating him like any other member of the public ("civilians", she calls them) and Jeremy is her ex though that situation will soon correct itself if Jeremy has his way. Half the girls in their class are Jeremy's exes as are an equal number of girls in the class just behind them. The girls of the town seem to think Jeremy has magic, though Daniel assumes they define the term differently than he does.

Christopher, Patrick, and Jeremy will be seniors this fall. Next summer, Patrick will be the ranking lifeguard because the idiots at City Hall will bypass Athena based on their belief that a penis is the most important qualification for the position. Patrick won't have any more magic then than he does now, yet someone will gaze up at him in wonder. There is always someone susceptible to the allure of a lifeguard, even the most lackluster of examples of the breed. Daniel doesn't allow himself to think about who may be staring up at him. In a few more weeks he'll be off to basic training and nothing about this place will ever matter again.

Daniel arrives at the opera house early. Miss Du Plein has given him his own set of keys. She had to clear this with Mayor Whitelaw's office. *Daniel Kmetko needs keys to the opera house? Why, of course. That Daniel—he's quite a boy, isn't he? Such a fine young man, rather. You certainly are fortunate to have him for a lighting technician.* The discussion must have gone pretty much like that, as they always seem to when the subject is Daniel. He'll never stop being amazed at how people believe in him so fervently. In their idea of him, at least. Their faith in him, their simple, abundant faith, ought to make him happy. He used to think it did until one day he realized he never had been happy. Not one time in his whole life. He wasn't sad. He wouldn't say that. At least not sad very much. Just not happy. Not like they all thought he must be. Because he must be, mustn't he? How could Daniel Kmetko not be happy? That wouldn't make sense. It would be like a world where the sky was green or a solar system where everything revolved around Uranus.

Daniel Kmetko—not happy. He's pondered the matter sufficiently that there's no longer any doubt about it. He is not happy. Worse than that, he has no magic, regardless of what everyone thinks. If there is cause and effect at work here, he is not aware of it. He doesn't really spend much time on the question of causality. He won't allow himself to think about why he prefers not to ponder it. He's much too busy for that. He hardly ever rests. Rewarding the faith of his fellow citizens with appropriate displays of exuberance, or at least contentment, is how he prefers to exert himself. His *not happiness* is a secret he will take with him when he leaves town. In years to come, if people around here remember him at all, his intention is that they remember him happy. Though he may have no magic, he'd just as soon they all continue to believe that he does. It's not that difficult to maintain the illusion. He has passed his life up to now being told he is good looking. He is popular. He's good at everything he turns his hands to. Like this current task, getting ready for tonight's final dress rehearsal. Tomorrow night, Friday, is opening night for the Red Dog Summer Theatre production of *Little Mary Sunshine*. The summer theatre is a long-standing town tradition. Framed posters hanging in the lobby of the opera house testify to productions stretching back decades. One of the early owners of the mine married a minor Broadway luminary. Bringing her back to the town, he set her up as the supreme local arbiter on all matters relating to the arts. She decreed that the town must enjoy a rich diet of culture, and almost immediately the opera house rose on its site directly across the square from the courthouse and set at ninety degrees from city hall. The giant, bare chested, heroically muscled art deco statue of a miner set at the exact center of the square gazes like an Olympian god at the frieze on the courthouse, but consequently displays its Herculean buttocks to the opera house. This has occasioned great mirth among generations of the townspeople. That sculpture was a later arrival, a product of the WPA. By the time of its advent, the mine owner and his lady were long gone. Their legacy that brought orchestras, touring virtuosi, out of work repertory companies, and associated charlatans and loonies to the stage of the opera house survived in a radically truncated form after the Depression and World War II transformed the town's fortunes. The endowment the mine owner provided was now only enough to support one major production a year, the summer musical. Originally these extravaganzas were directed and starred in by the mine owner's wife. For decades now, generations of high school drama teachers have put on the show with their students as the cast.

Athena had been drafted into one of those productions right out of sixth grade. At that age she was already an Amazon—of an unmistakably Viking Princess type. Eighteen months older, Daniel was encouraged to accompany her on this exotic new endeavor. Daniel's protests that he had no interest in singing and dancing met with their father's perennial good humor and steely determination. Stagecraft, he suggested, was a pursuit sufficiently manly for anyone. Athena graduated from chorus member to ingénue with astonishing rapidity. Then, growing bored, she set her sight on character roles. She was physically unsuited for them, but this only served to increase her determination. Her Lady Bracknell back in April had been a *tour de force* lauded by newspaper reviewers as far away as Tucson. University drama programs were recruiting her.

For his part, Daniel applied himself to the less glamorous theatre arts. He displayed a remarkable aptitude for scenery painting, and his dexterity and powerful build were greatly prized by stage managers. But what finally turned a more or less accidental off season hobby into a holy calling was the divine mystery of the light booth. Once initiated into its priesthood by a moody Mexican senior who left for New York the morning after graduation never to return, Daniel didn't look back. "Let there be light", he would murmur as he bent over the dimmer board, and there would be light in an infinity of shades and hues and at any imaginable level of intensity from barely perceptible to blinding. It fired his imagination as few things ever had.

The Kmetko siblings came by their theatrical bent honestly, though this was not something they were especially proud of, preferring that it never be mentioned. Their mother had been a Hollywood starlet, a contract player at Fox, when she met their father. He had just finished law school and moved to Los Angeles to take a position at a prestigious Wilshire Boulevard firm. With his handsome face and athletic physique, he looked, in his snappy new suits, more like an actor playing an attorney than a real one. They met at a party in Malibu and got married in Vegas two weeks later. Being married bored Estelle, and motherhood was even less to her taste. Three months after Athena was born, Estelle died in an automobile accident. The man at the wheel was a small time producer. His secretary testified at the inquest that he'd been in "heavy negotiations" with Mrs. Kmetko on the subject of a "comeback vehicle". She hadn't been home to her husband and babies in nearly a week when the tragedy occurred.

Soon after the funeral, Tad Kmetko brought Athena and Daniel to this remote copper mining town about as far off the beaten track as it was possible to go. He had given up his job as a rising young corporate lawyer and taken a position as assistant county attorney in a place that offered little or no opportunity for advancement. They moved into a ramshackle hacienda high in the pass overlooking the town and the mine. The structure predated the founding of either. With its narrow slit windows, eight foot thick adobe walls, and commanding views to both east and west, it was more like a fortress than a dwelling.

As Daniel labors in the light booth, he hears the opera house coming to life. Other crew members arrive. Next come the cast and musicians. In the isolation of his aerie, he registers their sounds but doesn't allow himself to be distracted. He focuses on his work, checking and double checking every item on his list, ritualistic in his devotion. His concentration remains undisturbed until he hears the footsteps of his nemesis on the stairs.

Athena gets roles in every local production, but Daniel has only acted once. That was in response to a challenge posed by his father, who suggested that there might be certain nuances involved in stage lighting which could only be appreciated by someone with acting experience. Daniel accepted this proposition readily enough but considered it an academic question. Dad, however, wouldn't let it go at that. "How will you know what kind of insights you've been missing all this time if you don't try it?" he asked, and overhearing that discussion, Athena became more insistent than ever in her campaign to get Daniel onstage.

Knowing they would give him no peace otherwise, Daniel auditioned. Miss Du Plein had every reason to cast him. He would look superb on stage. This and his notoriety as an athlete would pack in audiences. She would have the satisfaction of pleasing Athena, whom she depended on as a leading light of the Thespian Society. It might conceivably ingratiate her with Tad Kmetko, whom she adored passionately if secretly, her adoration tempered by her certainty that he wouldn't recognize her if he ran into her on the street. Finally, the more she considered it, the more she convinced herself that in the halls of Reg Dog High School there walked no better possible foil for Christopher Melendez-Greene, whom she had already cast in her mind as Algernon Moncrieff in her upcoming production of *The Importance of Being Earnest*. So Daniel became Jack Worthing for six weeks of rehearsals and the three weekends of the run. He had actually aspired to the role of Lane, the butler. Looking back on it, he sees the experience as a dream, pleasant for the most part, but with certain nightmarish aspects.

Christopher enters the light booth, wearing, Daniel notes, that smarmy Algernon grin he hasn't yet been able to banish entirely in the four months since *Earnest* closed. He's whistling an approximation of the organ introduction to "Whiter Shade of Pale." Daniel has no idea why he can't stand Christopher. There is no rational basis for it. It's like the instinctive hatred of snakes some people have, Athena for instance. Christopher has never done anything to deserve his rancor. Daniel understands that perfectly. Daniel is a year ahead in school, and Christopher invariably shows appropriate deference. Then, too, Daniel is a star athlete while Christopher is no athlete of any kind, and once again, Christopher's acknowledgement of his inferiority is always perfectly appropriate. There is nothing notably objectionable about Christopher's appearance, the smooth black hair, pale, clear skin, and bright eyes, except that taken all together it's just a little too perfect. The girls of Red Dog consider him cute, but since he has no discernable personality and apparently lacks the requisite motivation nothing ever comes of the attraction, the girls finding nothing sufficiently compelling about him to spur their own aggressive impulses. He's unnervingly talented as an actor, but Daniel has no aspirations in that direction. He is, except for his appearance and the star turns he achieves onstage, so nondescript as to be downright invisible and he manages at all times to be completely unobjectionable unless you're obsessed with nitpicking. Despite all this, Daniel despises him.

He knows it's his own fault. It is without doubt a sign of some grievous flaw in his character. Had his upbringing been more conventionally religious he might have consulted a priest or minister about it, but he supposes that such a person would find the whole thing as incomprehensible as he does. The best solution he has ever been able to come up with is to ignore it. This hasn't been difficult at all as long as they're not in rehearsal for a production. But all that changed last spring when they were cast in *Earnest* together. Their proximity was too close and persisted for too long. There were moments on stage when it was all Daniel could do not to grab Christopher and strangle him. Closing night came as a blessed relief.

And then Christopher, damn him, insisted on being Daniel's assistant in the light booth for this production. Everything was wrong with the plan. Miss Du Plein had already mentally cast Christopher as the male second lead—Patrick was to play the principal lead, Captain Jim—and this alteration had a domino effect, impacting casting for every male role. Not to mention that for the life of him Daniel couldn't imagine what he would do with an assistant. Any assistant. There was no possible point to it, and this was enough, apparently, to transform it from a harebrained scheme to an imperative. That's Daniel's karma.

As they work through their pre-performance checklist, Daniel hears arriving cast members greeting each other, the stage crew practicing a particularly tricky scene change, instrumentalists tuning up, Miss Du Plein giving instructions to her assistant director in an especially histrionic tone. Closer to hand, he hears Christopher still whistling "Whiter Shade of Pale" just on the cusp of audibility. Telling Christopher to stop it would necessitate speaking to him, so Daniel bears it. When that song first came out, he really liked it. He doesn't know if he'll ever be able to forgive Christopher for spoiling it for him. He's still pondering this when the overture begins and he has to give his full attention to the task at hand.

They work like they share the same brain, Daniel on the follow spot, Christopher on the dimmer board. Not a single cue is bungled. The fades up and down are perfect. They are as professional as can be. Daniel would give anything to have something to blame Christopher for, if only silently.

The rest of the dress rehearsal is about as bad as it's possible for a dress rehearsal to be. Not counting Athena, that is, who as always has been perfect in every way, and a couple other members of the cast. Maria DeGaetano, Athena's best friend/spiritual doppelganger, for instance. And Greg Yates. He's Patrick, Jeremy, and Christopher's fourth musketeer, though, due to the influence of his cheerleader girlfriend, a little erratic in their orbit. He's just out of tenth grade, shy and awkward offstage but nearly as dazzling as Athena in front of an audience, which makes Miss DuPlein's casting of him somewhat inscrutable as far as Daniel's concerned. He, too, has been perfect in tonight's rehearsal in a character part. Should Patrick happen to falter in the male lead, Greg's his understudy. Daniel would like to see the turmoil that would set off among their crew. He'd like to see Greg in the role, just once. He has a hunch about Greg. He sees something there, though he's not sure what. But something that, like the voices in his own head and heart, lives to leave Red Dog behind.

Overall, it's been the kind of dress rehearsal referred to by that old theatrical saying, "terrible dress rehearsal; great opening night". Daniel takes no pleasure in that. Miss Du Plein doesn't subscribe to the superstition. To her, a bad dress rehearsal can only be a sign of the end of the world, and she reacts accordingly. Her notes will be copious and trenchant (thanks, Mrs. Miller, Daniel's senior English teacher, for that collegiate vocabulary) and they will culminate in an orgy of emotional blackmail. The company won't clear the opera house until late, which will delay Daniel in his final preparations for opening night.

"Christopher," he says, hating the way the name feels in his mouth, "need you to tell Patrick and Jeremy you won't be riding home with them. I've got to have your help here. I'll give you a lift when we're finished."

"*Oui, oui, mon capitaine*," Christopher answers, punctuating it with a snappy little gesture that might actually be the way Frenchmen salute but almost certainly isn't. It at least clears up the question of Christopher's current identity. Apparently he and his friends are in the throes of some elaborate Foreign Legion fantasy.

The opera house finally empties and Daniel and Christopher set to work. They replace gels in every lighting instrument. They snug the instruments in their mountings. They check every receptacle. They remove tape, clean, and re-tape every connection. There isn't a piece of equipment or associated wiring that they leave untouched.

To Daniel's astonishment and relief, Christopher has been the ideal assistant all through rehearsals, and tonight is no exception. There's not a wasted word or motion. There's not a hint of clumsiness. The right tool appears in Daniel's hand almost before he asks for it. Nothing is forgotten. Nothing gets dropped. And the French accent has been jettisoned like excess ballast in a storm at sea. They finish hours earlier than Daniel anticipated due to Christopher's efficiency. It's a miracle. One he would never have asked for and wishes he hadn't witnessed. He adds it to the list of Christopher's sublime but reprehensible acts, like a religious writer chalking up another miracle to the credit of St. Somebody of Somewhere, who, before beginning to perform miracles had been a whore and never entirely gave up the trade.

The worst ten minutes of the whole night come during the drive to Christopher's house. The vibrations he gives off dissipate sufficiently in the expanses of the opera house that they're hardly noticeable. Even the confines of the light booth are spacious enough to keep them from becoming too obtrusive. Daniel can close his eyes and it might be anybody at all working alongside him. He might even be alone. But in the tiny car, Christopher's presence is intolerable. Daniel can't shift gears without touching Christopher's denim clad thigh, can't turn the wheel without his shoulder brushing against Christopher's. And there's a smell. Not an unpleasant smell. Just a smell that says unmistakably that someone else is present and it's Christopher.

They pull up in front of the house. It's one of the largest in town—a Craftsman Style monster. Now Daniel has to speak.

"Thanks for everything."

"*De nada*."

He'll take it. It's not an act—it's widely rumored that Christopher's mother doesn't speak a word of English and that Christopher himself didn't start learning it until beginning first grade.

When Daniel gets home, Athena is pulling a sheet of chocolate chip cookies out of the oven. Baking is how she unwinds from any particularly stressful experience.

"Want one?"

"I'll split one with you," Daniel says.

"Nobody eats half a cookie."

"Guys who are serious about their abdominal muscles do," he says.

"You're crazy."

"What's new? Other than the discovery that insanity runs in families?"

"Idiot," she laughs.

"Idiocy is hereditary, too. Who gave you a ride home? Not Jeremy, I hope. You know I hate his driving."

"Nancy."

"No, Athena, no" he moans. "That's even worse."

"She's a very careful driver."

"Not talking about her driving."

Nancy misses no opportunity to lobby Athena. Her goal is for Daniel to agree to write to her at Arizona State. That will signify that they're an item. He hates the idea of encouraging her even that remotely.

"I didn't promise her anything."

"You didn't try to talk her out of it, either."

"It would just make her more determined."

"Jeez, sis."

"You know I'm right."

She finishes placing the cookies on a rack to cool and starts tidying the kitchen.

"Leave that," he says. "You cook, I clean."

"You don't have to."

"Yes, I do. It's part of your training. So some guy won't take advantage of you. Repeat after me, 'I cook, you clean'. That's your mantra."

"Idiot."

"Say it."

Athena has made a spectacular mess. If he leaves things in this state Mrs. Robek will have a stroke when she arrives in the morning and Athena and he will be banned from the kitchen except under her supervision. He can't have his dietary regimen disrupted that way. He washes and dries the cooking things, wipes down the countertop, scrubs out the sinks, and sweeps and mops the floor. By then the cookies are cool and ready to be put in a tin. He inhales deep draughts of fresh baked but puts them away without eating anything. He's worked too hard to let it all go that way.

Daniel showers. He combs his hair somewhat obsessively. He's always been very particular about his hair. He thinks it must go back to the first time he heard the story of Samson in Sunday School. It's going to be a real adjustment in a few weeks when a military barber shears it off.

He walks through the silent house to his bedroom. He stands at the window staring into the darkness. He knows exactly where to look. Christopher's out there, just like almost every night. Daniel has no idea when it started. Years ago, at least. Probably as far back as grade school, though it was no more than once a week then. It's only during the last couple of months that it has become this frequent. He doesn't know why somebody doesn't stop it. Surely Christopher's mother and father must know what's going on. What kind of parents wouldn't know that their son leaves the house almost every night to go stare at the bedroom window of the girl he thinks he's in love with?

II

The applause dies away and Daniel cuts the follow spot. An instant later, as the curtain begins to close, the stage lights go out, too. Christopher's timing is impeccable. Daniel hears the curtains swish into place and a two count later the house manager has the auditorium lights up. Closing night—the last performance. It's all over. Daniel's brilliant career. Daniel the wizard, the bringer of light. He hunches over the dimmer board, runs his fingertips across the pages of the script, exhales slowly and feels the tension starting to ooze out of him. Farewell to the life of the theatre.

The cast party is at Christopher's house. It is forbidden territory, but Daniel can't not go. Just days away from his departure, he's more conspicuous than ever. He drives home, takes a quick shower, changes into fresh jeans and a white t-shirt. The canyon is chilly at night even in late August, but the white t-shirt is his signature. He combs his hair obsessively, staring at its silken gleam in the mirror. He wills himself to leave the house. He won't stay any longer at the party than he has to. He won't get involved in any discussions. He'll describe his plans in only the most cursory manner. What don't people already know about the Marine Corps? Not a damn thing. And everything.

"See here, Womblesleigh," Patrick says in an accent meant to be Veddy British and Upper Crust.

"Yes, Brigadier Shaggington," Jeremy answers. His fake accent matches Patrick's

"The situation is intolerable."

"Agreed, sir."

"See to it man, I say, see to it."

"I'm afraid I don't follow you, sir."

"Don't follow me? Sort of bloody rubbish is that? As my adjutant, it's your bloody job to bloody well follow me."

"Understood, sir. What I meant to say was I didn't follow your argument."

"Truly?"

"Sorry, sir. But what does the situation have to do with me?"

"Remaining single in the current circumstances is far too dangerous. It's a downright provocation, I tell you. The whole city is a tinderbox. Anything might set those hordes off."

"But sir, I really don't see what I can do about that."

"Nonsense, my boy. I believe there are some excellent purveyors of quite lovely young English brides located in Bloomsbury and Mayfair these days. Totally reliable firms. Absolute discretion. Offering top drawer young ladies. Bishops' daughters and such. Even an Honourable or two. Swiss finishing school kind of product. Positively ripping girls. That's how Templeton got his wife. Absolute corker. She's the youngest sister of a baronet and second cousin by marriage to one of those Yank millionaires. Just have Sparks wire your requirements to London on the Marconi set, don't you know?"

"That sounds so. . ."

"What, Womblesleigh?" Patrick demands. "What does it sound? Bloody cat got your bloody tongue, man?"

"No, sir," Jeremy says, voice trembling ever so slightly.

"Well then, out with it, man."

"I suppose I'd hoped to arrange things in a somewhat more conventional fashion. On my return home."

"Can't allow that, I'm afraid," Patrick insists. "No time for such niceties. The current situation is far too perilous. An unmarried British officer is nothing more than a perpetual temptation. Drives the memsahibs out of their minds with absolutely uncontrollable passions. Can't really blame them. Local product doesn't hold a candle to the Cream of British Manhood, what? Still, we can't have the same thing happening to you as happened to young Winklebottom here. Can we, Winklebottom?"

"No sir," Christopher says, sounding like Oliver Twist after having been refused that bowl of gruel.

"It's all right, my boy, you needn't speak of it. I shall do that for you. We all understand it was horrific. Being abducted in that manner, ripped from your bed without a stitch of clothing upon your person. Those hordes of howling women with their paws all over your satiny smooth boy skin, subjecting you to the most exquisite and degrading tortures the Hindoo mind is capable of devising until you moaned with pleasure and sobbed for mercy with one and the same breath. Hours and days and weeks of that unspeakable torture. A lesser man than you, one not quite so athletically constructed, so to speak, might well have died from the ordeal. Doctor Armitage assures me that your rescue was just in the nick of time. Another day of that, and you'd have been a broken man. Can't say I'm surprised that you've complained to him of nightmares. All things considered, it's no wonder you go around thinking you've been transformed into a Welshman, singing "Men of Harlech" at the top of your lungs during dress parade and asking cook to serve you leeks for brekkie. No, Womblesleigh, we can't have any more episodes of that nature. It simply won't do. I can't have another of my men used in such a barbaric manner. It's a reflection on the empire, don't you see? On the Empress Herself. So see to it, man. I say, see to it."

"Sir," Jeremy says, "consider it done."

"Good man."

So much for the patio. Daniel wanders inside. In the living room, Nancy Miller, vice president of their graduating class and breathless aspirant to his very own athletically constructed person, is playing the *Warsaw Concerto* on the

Melendez-Greene Steinway. Daniel loves the *Warsaw Concerto* and would like to stay and listen, but it's too risky. Nancy can't be encouraged.

Greg Yates, PatrickJeremyChristopher's D'Artagnan, sits on the bottom step of the house's main staircase with his girlfriend, Rosalie Bonner. Last year she was captain of the JV cheerleading squad. Her amiable ruthlessness will probably ensure her elevation to varsity co-captain this coming fall. Rosalie and Greg are known as the school's odd couple. By rights, she should be dating a varsity athlete rather than this artist/intellectual, and, conversely, Greg should go after one of the girls in the Thespian Society. Daniel admires their serenely subversive nonconformity. They break off their conversation and watch him pass, feeding his paranoia.

Rosalie reminds Daniel of Athena. It's not just that she's another Viking princess. He thinks of her as dangerous in the same way Athena is dangerous—the way all women with minds of their own are dangerous. Like Athena, Rosalie will get what she wants regardless of what efforts or strategies that requires. And all these years she's wanted Greg Yates. Athena must want somebody, but Daniel has no idea who that might be. He suspects that such a creature is hypothetical at this point and that he'll never be found in Red Dog.

The buffet is full of things Daniel won't eat because of his abdominals. He nibbles on a carrot stick and wonders if he's put in enough of an appearance. He'd really like to leave. Through the open windows he hears Jeremy and company starting up again. They're always at it. Thursday afternoon at the pool they were anarchists in pre-revolutionary Russia, rioting in the streets to the sound of balalaikas and throwing bombs indiscriminately. All went well with their plot to detonate a bomb in the middle of the Czarina's spring cotillion at Tsarskoe Selo until the character played by Christopher was abducted by rampaging daughters of the aristocracy who sneaked into the servants' quarters during a particularly stimulating gavotte. They ripped him from his humble cot without a stitch of clothing on his body and dragged him through the streets of St. Petersburg to the Winter Palace, where under the direction of the evil dwarf Kaspustin they subjected him to the most degrading and exquisite tortures the Imperial Russian mind was capable of devising until the satiny smooth boy skin of his exquisitely sculpted young body was helpless with unspeakable sensations.

It's harmless enough, Daniel supposes, these little improvisations of Patrick and Jeremy's. Or would be, if so many of them didn't include characters who were such obvious references to Athena. This month alone she has been Hippolyta, Queen of the Amazons, commanding her she-warriors to abduct the beautiful young Spartan, Hilarophon and then hold him captive and subject his satiny boy skinned wrestler's body to the most degrading and exquisite tortures the Amazon mind was capable of conceiving; Rotunda Aggravatrix, mistress of Caesar Disgustus, who, with the aid of her handmaidens abducted the beautiful young charioteer, Julius Augustus, ripping him from his bed without a stitch of clothing on his person and subjecting him to the most degrading and exquisite tortures the entire Roman Empire was capable of devising; and Helga, the Nazi She-Devil of Berchtesgaden, who howled at her underlings, Ursula and Babette, *"you're being too easy on him, you must milk him and milk him and milk him; force it from him—force it until he has no seed left to bestow on the womenfolk of our enemies",* whereupon they subjected him to the most degrading and exquisite tortures the Nazi mind was capable of imagining until he was a Mere Shadow of His Former Self. And those are just the episodes of their ongoing "radio theatre" production Daniel has been present to overhear and silently deplore.

Daniel has tried his best to protect Athena and, more important, teach her to protect herself. Because Jeremy, Patrick, and Christopher are just the tip of the iceberg. The universe, apparently, is full of guys intent on—well, exactly what guys their age are intent on, and Daniel won't be around much longer to fend them off on her behalf. Dad will do his best, of course. But in another year she'll be off to college, where the men will be older, more experienced, more insistent, and even less inclined to treat her respectfully. Daniel lies awake at night worrying about his sister's honor. When he tries to talk with her about it, she laughs at him. There's more than one way to skin a cat, she insists. She doesn't have to be stronger than they are, just smarter.

Which is some comfort at least, because he's never met a guy yet who's as smart as Athena.

Expectancy crackles in the air like static electricity. It occupies the rooms of the house like an invisible, silent guest. It hangs like an unseen fog over the back yard and clings wisplike to tree branches and the eaves of the house. Tonight, Daniel knows, he is expected at long last to declare himself. He is supposed to walk up to some girl—he knows who leads the betting and who's a close second and who's breathing down her neck—and ask her to write to him while he's gone. To wait patiently and faithfully through the weeks of basic training, the months of his inevitable tour in Southeast Asia, the years of his hitch in the Corps. To be waiting still and greet him with open arms and a tear-blurred smile on the day of his heroic return. He knows that more than one girl here at the party is avidly watching his every move for a sign that she's the one and the moment is imminent.

It's a fairy tale, no more real than "Jack and the Beanstalk" or "Rumplestiltskin". Nevertheless, everyone is frantically maintaining the fantasy, adapting it to changing circumstances and new situations but fanatic in its defense, its sustenance, its perpetuation. So far, he has done the bare minimum required of him in this regard to remain a member of the community in good standing. You're varsity quarterback: you take the head cheerleader to the homecoming dance. You're class president: you take the vice president to the winter formal. Or the secretary if the vice president is a boy. You don't even think about skipping prom. You make all the right appearances with all the right young ladies on your arm. You pose for yearbook photos, give interviews to nervous girls who write for the school newspaper, flirt with girls in the hallways, the serving line at the cafeteria, the library. You do what must be done. But because Daniel clearly understands the depth and breadth of the abyss between his classmates' expectations and his own intentions, he treads oh, so carefully. He's a lone infantryman trapped in the middle of a minefield on a moonless night. Any move he makes is potentially fatal—to his integrity if nothing else—so he makes them with the greatest deliberateness.

Tonight he'll do nothing. Everyone will think whatever they think. Mostly they'll suppose they've misjudged the timing. It's still over a week until he leaves for basic training. There's always the Very Last Party of the Summer next Saturday. Not as appropriate an occasion as this, since it's far less intimate a gathering and potentially pretty rowdy, but Daniel can pull anything off. At least that's the myth. The delay might signify nothing more than that his selection isn't present or hasn't yet been finalized. This possibility will throw the betting off.

Nancy Miller believes that she's just the girl for Daniel. She believes this with the same simple faith with which she believes in Father, Son, and Holy Ghost. She knows she is not beautiful, but she's pretty enough. She is smart and hard working. She is dependable and well organized. She is talented. Her piano playing speaks for itself, though she's no Maria De Gaetano. And while she's no Athena, either, she has a tuneful, though small, voice. Most of all, she is good. Overall, there are certainly more attractive girls in Red Dog. There are girls with more vibrant personalities, girls who are far more popular. She understands how Daniel might find any one of them more desirable. But she truly is a virtuous young woman, and thus her price is above rubies. Simply put, she's more worthy than any of the others. She might not make the best girlfriend for a boy like Daniel, but that's not the point. A girlfriend is someone a boy wants and needs for a very short time, but a man needs a wife. And she'll make a far better wife for Daniel than any of the others could. She'll make the kind of mother his children deserve to have. Daniel is smart enough and good enough himself to figure all this out. And if somehow, inexplicably—because men are inexplicable most of the time—he fails to, Athena will set him straight. Everyone knows Athena wears the pants in that family. And a good thing, too. The Kmetko men are strong and handsome but helpless when it comes to practical and domestic matters, to be quite honest.

So it's a foregone conclusion, really. Nancy simply has to be patient and pray faithfully for God's Will to be Done in This as in All Things. She will attend Arizona State. She's leaving just a few days after Daniel goes to boot camp. She will get her degree in elementary education. By the time she graduates and gets a teaching job, Daniel will be out of the service. She will support him while he attends school himself. He will major in secondary education. When he gradu-ates, they will come back here and he will get a job at Red Dog High School. He will coach football and baseball and wrestling and he will teach Social Studies, because that is what all the coaches teach at Red Dog High School.

Nancy will stay at home raising their children, Robert and Daisy. Robert will come first, because every girl should have an older brother. Nancy is sure her life would have been very different if she had had an older brother. She has not enjoyed being an only child. She has had to look out for herself in ways no girl should be forced to. It has been a bitter and lonely experience. It's the one thing about her that Athena doesn't understand. She knows it has made her stronger, but she will do anything to spare her own daughter similar confusion and heartbreak, so her firstborn will be a boy. She prays for this regularly and is certain God sees the matter as she does. When Daisy starts first grade, Nancy will go back to work. She will teach second grade, but at a different school than the children attend. Meanwhile, she and Daniel will have taken over as sponsors of the Methodist youth group. Daniel will teach the boys to be sober and responsible and to treat the girls with respect. She will teach the girls to be virtuous women, industrious and God fearing.

Daniel knows all this because Athena reports faithfully on her discussions with Nancy. Athena keeps no secrets but her own. He returns the favor, though the young men of Red Dog are surprisingly reticent in his presence. He assumes that they find him too intimidating to confide in. They've never asked for his help in getting close to Athena. Guys don't work that way. This means he has nothing to share with her but advice. She's obviously coming out worse off in the bargain. But he has to know everything she hears, because forewarned is forearmed. In high school romance a good defense is the most critical thing. In some ways, it's the only thing that matters. Nancy's plan reminds Daniel of one of the horror movies his mother appeared in. The one where the newlyweds move into the beautiful suburb only to learn, when it's too late, that all their neighbors are zombies. The shot of his mother, the palms of her hands pressed to the sides of her face, eyes wide with terror, mouth open in an unending scream, sums up his feelings perfectly.

As head cheerleader, Lucy Balich has more to offer Daniel than any other girl in Red Dog. Her extravagant physical charms and scintillating personality—she loves the word scintillating, especially when applied to her—are just the tip of the iceberg. She has no brothers, and due to a series of deaths and other mishaps in World War II and Korea, no boy cousins either. Her father, Big Louie, owns and operates the largest Ford dealership from Red Dog to Tucson, and there is no one for him to hand it over to when the time comes.

The Kmetkos are Protestant, while the Baliches are Serbian Orthodox. But that's no problem, really. Lucy hates her church. It will be a pleasure to convert. There are no pews in the sanctuary. You have to stand all through Mass, except when it's time to kneel. She's not sure what she dislikes most, the standing or the kneeling. Still, it could be worse. The Baliches only attend on Easter and Christmas Eve. And for weddings. But for weddings, folding chairs are brought in. She won't convert until after the wedding, however, because the sanctuary at St. Cyril's is much prettier than the one at St. Mark's Presbyterian where the Kmetkos attend.

After Lucy and Daniel return from their honeymoon on Waikiki, he will report to work at the dealership. He will be spectacularly successful. Who wouldn't want to buy a car from a guy like that? By the time he is thirty he'll be general manager. She'll get a new Thunderbird convertible every year. Everybody in town will know it's her when she drives to the country club.

She'll have a couple of babies because all men want sons, but she's not really interested in motherhood, which, she believes, is what transformed her mother into a bloated, drunken, complaining hag with roots constantly in need of touching up. The real reason for her to have children is that on the day his first grandson is born, Big Louie will finally stop favoring her sister Janice over her. Janice has been his favorite for as long as Lucy can remember. Big Louie is forever pulling Janice into his lap for a cuddle or tickling Janice until she nearly pees herself or leaning in to whisper little things into Janice's ears that make her blush. Janice is not at all scintillating. Lucy can't understand for the life of her why their father has always ignored her. But once he has a grandson, he'll have to pay her more attention.

Daniel will work long hours at the dealership, which will leave Lucy free to go on weekly shopping trips to Tucson with her friends. When the weather is nice she'll lie out beside their pool, and the housekeeper—Maria-Alma Consuelos, recovering slowly and painfully from that hideous, disfiguring accident—will bring her drinks and snacks, and, when it rings and it isn't her mother on the line, her telephone on a long, long cord.

Nancy is not the only girl at Red Dog High who confides in Athena.

This isn't a horror movie. It's film noir. It will end, Daniel suspects, with someone floating face down in the pool.

Maria-Alma Consuelos realizes that hers is an uphill struggle. Anglo boys have sex with Mexican girls all the time, but they hardly ever marry them. Hardly ever isn't the same as never, though, as Christopher Melendez-Greene's parents prove. And if any Mexican girl in the county is going to marry an Anglo boy it's Maria-Alma, three times runner up in the county beauty pageant. If America really was a land of liberty and justice for all, she'd have won the damn trophy already. And she's not going to marry just any Anglo boy. She's going to marry the Anglo boy of all Anglo boys and put these snooty Gringa bitches in their place forever.

When they get married, Daniel will get a job at the mine. Dad and Uncle Chuy will get him onto the right crew and right shift. By the time he's thirty he'll be a shift foreman. She'll have a baby every year for a while, but small ones that won't ruin her figure. When she pushes the stroller through the aisles at the supermarket, the Gringa bitches will be unable to contain their jealousy.

The list goes on and on. Daniel knows these girls' intentions like he knows the fifty states and their capitals. Things couldn't be any clearer if the girls' already composed wedding announcements were posted on billboards all over town. Their fantasies are like a stack of unread screen treatments languishing in the in-tray of some two-bit Hollywood producer. As varied as they are, they all have one thing in common. Each and every one of them represents a death sentence, as far as Daniel is concerned. Death is death, whether it's fast or slow.

As he passes the kitchen doorway he sees Nancy and Athena huddled in conversation. Nancy is emphatic, Athena serenely placating. As he passes the doorway into the dining room, he sees Jeremy's Cousin Suzette and her friends looking at him and giggling. As he passes the doorway into the conservatory, he sees Helen, Miss Du Plein's assistant director who graduated with him last May, and Ellen, who will be Miss Du Plein's new assistant director next school year, whispering behind hands raised to their cheeks in a gesture so timeless that it can probably be found on a Greek vase in a museum somewhere. Really—everywhere he looks. He would be thrilled if someone were to sit him down and explain to him that nothing he sees tonight means what he thinks it does and he's just being paranoid.

But really—everywhere he looks.

There's commotion in the back yard. He moves to one of the French windows in Dr. Greene's study for a look. Several dozen kids have arranged themselves in a three quarter circle around Patrick, who stands, looking soulful and serious, waiting for them to settle down.

"'O, what a rogue and peasant slave am I. . .'"

Daniel nods. Monologue time. He's yet to attend a gathering of thespians without observing this ritual. They're like druids at Stonehenge on the eve of the summer solstice. No surprise that Patrick identifies with the tragically misunder-stood Prince of Denmark. He aspires to exactly such a mystique. This is bizarre, because Daniel doesn't think Patrick literally wants to be bloody, dispossessed, and dead at the end of Act V. Nevertheless, Patrick gives it his all and the crowd is suitably appreciative. Daniel wonders which one of the underclass boys in the circle considers himself the pre-eminent Hamlet-in-waiting, ready to step into the role the minute Patrick graduates and leaves for college. There has to be such a boy. There's one of everything in this crowd, except, perhaps, one of Daniel.

It's probably that Greg Yates, now that Daniel thinks of it. For some reason, Greg never participates in these little extravaganzas. Daniel senses they're too impromptu for Greg's comfort. Greg gives the impression that every word com-ing out of his mouth has been rehearsed. Considering the nature of their friends and associates, it's a perfectly reasonable strategy as far as Daniel's concerned.

Next it's Jeremy's turn.

"'Is this a dagger that I see before me?'"

Macbeth. If that's not typecasting, Daniel doesn't know what is. Ambitious, ruthless, amoral—Jeremy's intentions ought to be prosecutable. Daniel fully expects to hear, not that many years from now, of his arrest for something fairly exotic. Some non-violent crime such as smuggling or fraud. That's the kind of guy he is. The garden variety thugs of the town have nothing on him. Jeremy struts and frets and then is heard no more. Until next time.

Christopher steps into the circle, and Daniel holds his breath. Yes, it's Christopher's signature piece, Mercutio's Queen Mab speech. He performed it at state festival last fall and won a medal. Patrick and Jeremy enunciated, emoted, *acted*. Christopher simply is. Shakespeare must have imagined it exactly this way. As always, Christopher steals the scene. And what Christopher is in this instance is barking mad, mad as a hatter, mad as those crazy ladies in the operas Dad listens to on Saturday mornings on the radio live from the Metropolitan Opera in New York. Sanity gushes out of Christopher like blood gushing from gaping wounds. Before his speech is half over, he's partway up one of the oak trees, hanging from a branch one-handed like a monkey, his immaculate white t-shirt blazing in the hot moonlight. Daniel can almost hear, somewhere far away, The Bard laughing.

Someone has put Daniel's beloved *Fantasia on a Theme of Thomas Tallis* on the stereo. Why would anyone do that? It's as if someone knows of his passionate attachment to this music and is trying to send him a message. But he refuses to entertain that possibility. It must be a coincidence. He doesn't want to know about it if it's not. It's hardly appropriate music for a cast party. They should be listening to—well, just about anything else. He recalls a cast party last winter at which, despite all protests, Patrick commandeered the turntable for a full hour. He played "Along Comes Mary" over and over without a break until Jeremy threatened to smack him over the head with a cast iron skillet he'd found in Maria DeGaetano's mom's kitchen cabinet. While they were arguing, Christopher snatched the 45 off the turntable and ran outside with it. He tossed it into the dark canyon like it was a Frisbee and that was that. "Along Comes Mary" is the kind of thing that gets played at these cast parties. Not the *Tallis Fantasia,* which, if Daniel didn't know better, he would think the composer, Ralph Vaughan Williams, composed especially for him. Not anything classical, really, except once when Jeremy insisted on "Ride of the Valkyries." Daniel suspects that the "Along Comes Mary" episode was retaliation for the "Ride of the Valkyries" episode. For best friends, Patrick and Jeremy seem to carry around lots of mutual hostility. Daniel stands just outside an open window to listen, head tilted exactly like in that picture of the terrier listening to the gramophone. This music is soul stirring. Listening to it is what church should be like. If it were, Daniel could probably believe in God.

All around, competing with the music, he hears laughter, gossip, lies, boasts, complaints, hopes. The dialogue of futility, in other words. *Existentialism, thy name is Daniel.* He couldn't look any less like an alienated beatnik from New York, but his fervent devotion to irony, he feels certain, is more authentic to that philosophy than black clothing, bongo drums, and silly configurations of facial hair

The *Tallis Fantasia* ends and is replaced by something Daniel doesn't recognize though he knows he's supposed to. "Not Joni Mitchell," he hears Jeremy complain, and the music changes once again. Back inside the teeming house, resuming his assigned role, he moves through the rooms like a prince visiting the provinces. His hair is shining, sun bleached, and perfect; his tan is smooth and golden; his immaculate white t-shirt clings to his satiny boy skin—damn that Patrick and Jeremy, the way those phrases of theirs get into the brain and won't be banished. Damn them. The flimsy fabric follows the contours of Daniel's body like a Labrador on the scent, the wide, square shoulders, the broad, flaring back, the swelling curves he's worked endless hours in the gym to bring to their current magnitude and opulence. He has never looked better than he does tonight, except maybe when he won the Teen Mr. Arizona bodybuilding title back in May. He is an icon. He knows it. He enthralls. He glories in and despises the power of his own beauty. The adoration it brings him comes too easy. His classmates sell themselves into the slavery of its worship far too cheap. It means nothing, this splendor that they indenture themselves to so mindlessly. Could anything be more superficial? He is a shining collection of gaudy surfaces when what he craves is true significance.

They will all remember this. The girls will talk about him, giggling nervously. The boys won't say anything, but each will measure himself against this ideal and come up short. It's so shallow that it makes him want to cry.

"Got the keys to the Fiat with you?" he asks Athena.

"Why? Can't find yours? You must be slipping. Old age setting in, I guess."

He waves his set at her.

"I'm heading home. Bring the car when you come."

"Drive it yourself," she says. "I'll get a ride."

"No. I'm walking."

"Really, Daniel, I'm ready to leave."

"No," he says. "Your people, your party. Stay. Bring the Fiat home when you come. And if it's a minute before two a.m., I'll send you back down here."

At home, he takes his fifth shower of the day. Here as at the pool, water is his sanctuary. Water is the hands of his dreamed-of lover, caressing, soothing, and ravishing him. It is the arms of his dreamed-of lover, embracing him, bearing him up, giving him wings. Water glides across him, clings to him, polishes him like he's living statuary, comforts and redeems him.

Until he turns it off and he's just Daniel again. Soggy Daniel, hair plastered to his scalp. In his room, towel cinched at his waist, lights out, he sits in a straight backed chair listening to time pass and waiting for his present and his future to intersect, waiting to step off of one and onto the other.

He hears the Fiat drive up, hears Athena come inside and lock the front door. He moves to the window, pulls back the drape, looks out into the darkness. It's only a few minutes before he catches sight of the white t-shirt glowing in the moonlight like ectoplasm as Christopher saunters the last few yards up the hill.

Daniel watches as he settles himself at the base of a huge tree and begins his vigil. Really, Daniel should tell somebody about this. Christopher is obviously crazy. Perhaps crazy enough to be dangerous. But Daniel would have to explain why it has taken him so long to come forward, why he didn't talk about it the first time it happened, or the tenth or the hundredth. And what explanation could he offer? He has no idea why all he's ever done about it is look out the window and see Christopher down there staring up at Athena's window right next to his own and turn back away and go to bed, so whatever explanation he gave would be a lie.

III

With the city pool closed, Monday is a perfect day to strike the set. Closing night, Miss Du Plein begged for helpers, but it isn't a glamorous task. Daniel isn't surprised when fewer than ten people show up. Actually, he's relieved. It is easier to organize the effort with fewer people present. They may be a handful but they're the right handful, all clear on their tasks and competent to perform them with little or no supervision. Athena and Nancy are in the lobby sorting and inventorying costumes prior to bundling them for transport to the laundry. Backstage, Aaron and Darren Garza are taking the set apart flat by flat, cleaning them, and readying them for storage. Beside Daniel on the high catwalk, Christopher hums the inevitable "Whiter Shade of Pale" under his breath. And directly below them on the auditorium floor, Patrick and Jeremy have laid out all the props. Miss Du Plein is a fanatic about taking inventory, and that's what they're doing.

". . .it was that infernal woman, Admiral Ramsbottom," Jeremy says, "the one the natives call the 'Pearl Queen'. She whipped the village women into a frenzy with her hideous promises of the forbidden delights they would experience. They massed their dugout canoes in the mouth of the River Oomfalloo by moonlight. It was a full moon that night according to our astronomical charts and only partially obscured by clouds. When *H.M.S. Recalcitrant* anchored in the offing, the fiends gave her crew ample time to settle for the night. They boarded just after midnight and the fighting was savage, according to the dispatches. Those hordes of Malays were eventually beaten off, but they took one of the crew with them in their howling retreat."

"One man?" Patrick asks. "That's not so bad, Muswell."

"Ah, Admiral, there's the rub."

"What do you mean, Muswell?"

"The man they took was young Lord Codpiece. He had lashed himself to the helm in a valiant but perhaps misguided attempt to keep the Malays from taking control of the ship. When they left, they took him with them in chains."

"Codpiece, by Jove," Patrick marvels. "I was at school with his Great-Uncle Willie. Devil with the ladies he was, that Willie Codpiece."

"Indeed, sir. The ship's company gave chase, of course. But it was no good. Those she-demons disappeared into the jungles. Leaving behind not a sign of young Codpiece."

"But my God, man. Wasn't there anything else they could have done?"

"Not with that typhoon bearing down, sir. You know those eastern typhoons. Devils, they are. *Recalcitrant's* crew had to pull her right out into open water. They were forced to abandon the chase, um, er, search."

"Dash it all, Muswell, this is intolerable."

"Indeed, sir. But it seems we've had a stroke of luck."

"How so?"

"One of our informants tells us that young Codpiece has been seen in Hong Kong. Apparently there's a very special establishment there."

"Establishment?"

"A brothel of sorts, sir. Catering to the wives and mistresses of the Chinese merchants and warlords, from what I'm told. Exclusively manned, if you'll pardon the expression, by virile young European abductees and the odd Englishman."

"What do you mean, odd Englishman?"

"Not that kind of odd, sir, just an odd lot in that company."

"Right. Proceed."

"Well, I mean, sir. Young Codpiece, held captive and forced to serve as male concubine to the entire Orient."

"I get your drift, Muswell. It's monstrous."

"Indeed, sir."

"The Codpieces are one of the most revered, most respected, most refractory families in all of English history."

"Refractory, sir?"

"Yes, Muswell, refractory. You show me a Codpiece and I'll show you a creature with a mind of its own."

"Sir."

"When I think of that fine young officer. . ."

"Just down from Oxford, he was, sir. Took a double first in Histrionics and Cryptoglossia. Wrote a monograph on the history of spontaneous conjugation that totally revolutionized the discipline. At age twenty. I mean, I ask you. A true Renaissance man, they say."

"Yes, yes, Muswell. And quite the physical specimen, from what I've been told. Of course he'd have to be, coming from a tribe like the Codpieces."

"Sir."

"Something must be done, Muswell. When I think of that stalwart young man, the veritable flower of English masculinity, his satiny boy skin being mauled by the claws of those dusky. . ."

Daniel steals a quick glance at Christopher, who has spent the last twenty minutes removing bulbs from the long line of fresnels hanging above the stage apron. Handling the bulbs with gloved hands as Daniel had shown him, he holds each one up to the light to check the filaments before wrapping it in cotton wool and placing it into the storage case. He doesn't seem to be paying a bit of attention to Patrick and Jeremy. Daniel finds himself almost on the point of asking Christopher what he thinks when his friends start in like that, basically talking about him being raped. But he can't imagine how he could even begin to speak of it. And besides, doing so would require addressing Christopher directly.

Tuesday, Daniel meets Miss Du Plein at *Tia Elena's* for a farewell lunch. She will fly to New York on Wednesday for a family wedding, and by the time she returns on Monday he'll be gone. Miss Du Plein is in her mid-thirties, a tall, pretty woman with questionable taste in clothes. At least by local standards. For all Daniel knows, she might be considered extremely fashionable in New York or Paris. Her wardrobe features scarves galore, chunky bracelets and necklaces that look like something Wilma Flintstone and Betty Rubble might wear for a night at the opera, and skirts made of rough fabrics that remind him of the bags live-stock feed is packed in. Her personality is equally eccentric. She seems to aspire to membership in that great sisterhood that includes Isadora Duncan, Virginia Woolf, and Amelia Earhart—larger than life, vivid, and individualistic. Athena's pantheon, in other words.

The young women of Red Dog are both fascinated and repelled by her. Many would like to emulate her but don't dare. Because as they see it, the other side of her individuality is her spinsterhood, a fate worse than death. Every year when some young, single male teacher joins the faculty at Red Dog High School, ears prick up and noses twitch at the prospect that this time, finally—but of course it never happens. Those young men are starkly conventional. What would they be doing here in Red Dog if they weren't? And starkly conventional young men are as fascinated and repelled by Miss Du Plein as are all those teenage girls. She might be fun to have drinks and shoot the breeze with when the moon is full, but at Red Dog High School football games she sticks out like sore thumb. Or any-where else, really, that it might occur to those young male teachers to invite her. Deer hunting in the Chiracahuas? Fishing at Rucker Lake? The county rodeo?

If ever there were a fish out of water, Daniel thinks.

Why the hell does she stay, year after year, when her marital prospects wither and her eccentricity seems less and less picturesque and more and more bizarre?

It's Dad. Miss Du Plein would never say so, of course. And Daniel missed the signs at first. But Athena clued him in, and since then he has to admit it's pretty unmistakable. Miss Du Plein is in love with Dad. Athena and Daniel aren't sure whether Dad is aware of the torch she's carrying. Probably not, since he has a preoccupation of his own. It's certainly not something either of them would discuss with him. The Kmetkos have a healthy respect for each other's privacy, thank God. And there'd be no point in it anyway. Dad, really, is no more suit-able a match for Miss Du Plein than any of those young male teachers, who almost invariably either move away after a couple of years or disappear for a week or two some June and come back to Red Dog with a young woman in tow that they intro-duce, grinning sheepishly, as "the new Mrs. so-and-so".

In the four years Daniel has known her well enough to observe it, the gleam in Miss Du Plein's eyes has grown dimmer and dimmer. It's a lesson to him.

Don't try to live where you don't really belong. She has no idea how profoundly her example has influenced him. Once upon a time, he might have. . .

Miss Du Plein eats her *chimichanga* and he eats his *tostada grande,* and she speaks of the shows she's scheduled for the coming season. A vehicle each for Athena and Christopher because the university recruiters might come, there might be scholarships for the two of them, and wouldn't that be remarkable? Juicy parts for Patrick and Jeremy as well, and she's so excited at the prospect of more awards at the all-state drama festival next April. Really, this senior class will be the crowning achievement of her career to date. Doesn't Daniel think that a *Godot* with an all-female cast is a brilliant idea? She's not sure it's ever been done anywhere. She'll use Athena, of course, and, well, maybe the younger Balich girl, Janice. Very, very talented. A little erratic, and not as disciplined as Miss Du Plein would like. But working alongside Athena will whip her into shape. No question about it, there's something intriguing about Janice Balich, doesn't Daniel agree?

Nobody finds Janice Balich more intriguing than her own father, Big Louie, and the whole town understands the reason why. With, apparently, the exception of Miss Du Plein. Daniel wonders if he should clue her in, but it's not his secret to tell. And what difference does it make whether or not Miss Du Plein knows about it? Perhaps Janice will call on that secret as she prepares to portray Estragon and the result will be exactly the kind of theatrical event that Miss Du Plein glories in. How many times has Miss Du Plein insisted to her students that the theatre is about them, their lives, their experiences?

Miss Du Plein orders flan for dessert and insists that Daniel share it with her. He savors a single spoonful.

"Time for your final exam," Daniel says.

"I have to get ready for work," Athena says.

"The pool doesn't open until eleven on Wednesdays. We've got all morning."

"We can't do it tomorrow?"

"You're working double shift tomorrow. And I still have to pack."

"Daniel."

"Hey, if you'd rather I sold it back to the widow," Daniel shrugs. "All it would take is one phone call."

"Don't you dare."

"Then meet me out front in five minutes. And wear something you don't mind getting dirty."

"Other girls don't have to put up with this kind of abuse."

"Since when do you want to be like other girls?" Daniel said. "Besides, lots of them put up with worse from their male relatives."

"Oh, all right."

"Five minutes," Daniel says. "The clock is running."

He saunters out the kitchen door to where the Fiat sits gleaming in the sunshine. It's for Athena's own good. She needs to know how to do things for herself. It's all part of being an independent woman. It's the helpless girls, the ones who have to depend on men for everything, who end up in trouble. That's not going to happen to Athena. What kind of brother would he be if he didn't do everything in his power to prevent it?

Athena comes out of the house. She's wearing her gardening overalls over a t-shirt. Her hair is pulled back into a pony tail.

"As you can see," Daniel says, "the Fiat has a flat tire."

"No, it doesn't."

"Look harder," he says. "Look at the right rear."

"It might be a little low, but. . ."

"It's sitting on the rim. Must have picked up a nail. You can get it plugged down at De Gaetano's Shell. But you've got to get it off the car and down there first."

"Daniel, that'll take all morning."

"You don't actually have to get the tire fixed," he says. "Just changed and stowed in the trunk."

"Right."

She sets to work. He sits down on the kitchen step to watch. She doesn't hurry. She follows the sequence to the letter, like blocking for a play. Whether she can do the same in the dark in the high school parking lot after a rehearsal runs overtime, which he considers the most likely scenario, is another question. Or in the rain. But that's not really the point. The point is to give her enough confidence that she won't panic when the time comes and make some stupid mistake which could result in a serious injury or, his greatest fear, accept help from the wrong boy. Before he knows it, she's finished.

"How's that?"

"Very nice," he says. "Now for part two. You're driving home at night and the headlights go out. What do you do?"

He watches as she gets the flashlight, removes the lid from the fuse box, and locates the blown fuse he placed there while she was still in bed. She inspects it, chooses a replacement out of the carton of spares in the trunk, inserts it, and closes everything up.

"How did you know which replacement fuse to use?"

"Amp rating is stamped on the base. I matched the rating on the replacement with the one on the faulty fuse."

"What do you do whenever you install a replacement fuse?"

"Order a new one from the import parts house in Tucson. The very next day. Replenish the spares carton."

"Good girl. Now for part three. You've just come out of rehearsal and the car won't turn over. Show me how to hook up the jumper cables."

"You've seen me do that before."

"So it'll be easy."

"O.K."

She's got it done in no time. Daniel inspects and gives a thumbs up.

"Are we finished?"

"Not quite. It's time to check the oil."

She doesn't argue. She doesn't know he's drained a quart from the crankcase, but she must have suspected because there isn't a hint of surprise on her face when she sees the level on the dipstick. With no wasted effort or time she gets all the things from the garage. The right oil, he notices, not the stuff Dad uses in his GMC but the Castrol Daniel has shipped in. She inserts the funnel into the proper orifice, opens the can with the correct tool, and gets the oil into the car without spilling any. Then she cleans up and puts things away in their proper places. Perfect.

"Anything else?" she asks.

"Car looks a little dirty," he says, though he knows he's pushing it.

"So wash it," she says. "Did I pass? No, don't say anything. I know I passed."

"Yes, ma'am," Daniel smiles, "looks like you did."

Late afternoon Thursday. Daniel's last shift ever at the pool. From his lofty perch, he surveys the nearly empty deck, the all but deserted parking lot beyond the fences. The families have gone home. Athena has already closed the gates. A few loiterers are still there, waiting for her to throw them out.

"We're going to have to look out for young MacTavish here, Captain MacDonald," Jeremy says.

"Too right, MacAllister," Patrick says, "some of these Inuit women aren't to be trusted around our men."

"I think it must be our red tunics, sir. When they see us approaching, it's like waving a cape in front of a bull."

"Interesting hypothesis, MacAllister. Worth pursuing, I'd say. When I think of how they brutalized young MacKenzie, dragging him from his cot in the middle of the night without a stitch on his hockey player's physique, the glare from the aurora borealis dancing off his satiny boy skin. . ."

Daniel won't miss that.

Athena emerges from the shower hut and gives three long blasts from her whistle signaling closing time.

"Thar she blows," Christopher calls.

"I ought to throttle you with this," Athena rages, brandishing her lanyard.

"Don't bother," Jeremy calls. "He enjoys being tied up. Your threats only encourage him."

"Egad, mates," Patrick cries, "It's Aquarina, Queen of the Mermaids."

"Can it, gentlemen," Daniel says through his megaphone. "We're closed. Time for you to clear out."

"Egad, mates," Jeremy yells, "it's Poseidon, mighty and terrible Ruler of the Deep. Lock up your womenfolk, lest he take his lusty pleasure with them, spreading his seed hither and yon."

No. Daniel won't miss those idiots a bit.

For his sixteenth birthday, Daniel got his driver's license and a membership at the YMCA. "You've made about as much progress as you're going to with that little weight set of yours in the basement," Dad said at the time. The weight set, ordered from the Sears Roebuck catalogue, was Daniel's thirteenth birthday present, and it served him well. But Dad was right that he'd outgrown it. Daniel's been a regular at the Y ever since. The company has been very generous with the Y. The gym equipment is better than at the Y in Tucson where Daniel went once just to have a look.

It's mostly wasted, however. The miner statue in courthouse square notwithstanding, hardly any of Daniel's fellow citizens use the facility. He's never come here when more than five or six of the lockers have been in use. Today, only two others have locks set. He changes into his workout gear, clicks the lock closed, and twirls the combination wheel. As if he needs to bother. Friday afternoon is a particularly sleepy time. There's nobody around to steal anything. In the weight room there are only a couple of other guys present. He knows them by sight. They work evening shift at the mine, so they're free to come in during the afternoon. Benny Cortez is the older brother of a girl Daniel graduated with. She had twins a few weeks ago. Benny's dating one of the Montoya girls. Daniel's not sure which one. There are about a dozen of them, sisters and cousins, in that huge clan. Zack Cujowski got out of the service in May and drives an ore truck, but that's just temporary. He's studying for his exam to get into the police academy in Tucson. Daniel remembers watching him play football. Back when Daniel was in junior high, Zack Cujowski was the biggest deal around Red Dog. He can't imagine what it must feel like having that kind of history and now being just another twenty-two year old.

They're big guys, but not any bigger than he is. They're nice enough, but basically solitary types like him. They spot each other on exercises sometimes, but that's the extent of their interactions. He thinks they're interesting to watch as non-examples.

"Do not pass go," he mutters to himself. "Do not collect two hundred dollars. And whatever you do, do not end up back here in Red Dog in your twenties. Or ever."

It's the existential equivalent, he thinks, of being sent to Devil's Island. There was only one man who ever got away with coming back to Red Dog. He was man enough to do it and still get exactly the life he wanted. It's the one trick he wasn't ever able to teach Daniel—their only piece, really, of unfinished business. And it wasn't a failure on Tony's part that stood in the way.

It's Daniel's flaw: a taste of forbidden knowledge and, in consequence, flaming swords at the gates of Eden.

Daniel looks around the gym and remembers—too much. It all culminated in those last weeks back in April, preparing for the competition. He thinks of that night on the stage in Phoenix, performing his posing routine. Those moments under the lights sealed his relationship with Tony for all time. Tony had taken him there. The years. The workouts. The gruff voice giving instruction as quietly and in as few words—Tony never wasted a single one—as possible. Every rep and set. Every drop of sweat. Every cookie and candy bar not eaten. Every detail leading up to that success. Every step of that journey was one Tony had taken before him—in some cases many times. There could have been no surer guide. Even before the placings were announced and Daniel learned he'd won the teen division and taken second in the juniors, he sensed the culmination. That last pose: front lat spread with his chest up and out, abs pulled in tight, fists clenched at his waist and sweat and oil streaming off him. His posing music reaching its crescendo and the crowd screaming its encouragement and approval. That's when he'd expressed it all most transparently, and Tony must have understood.

Now he imagines the goodbye scene that won't be played. He knows he couldn't have gone through it. No matter what he'd have seen in Tony's eyes in that moment, too much feeling or not enough, a perfect match for his own feelings or no match at all, it would have meant disaster. Did Tony sense the danger he was fending off—for both of them—when he scheduled his family vacation for the very two weeks surrounding Daniel's departure? The danger that someone would say too much? Or too little? He must have. It's the only explanation that makes any sense. And that confirms for Daniel like nothing else could that Tony knows. Tony's last handshake, as they left the Y a week ago, was, in addition to everything else, his agreement to ignore the knowledge. To go on pretending he never understood. To leave things as they've always appeared. That's the gift Daniel will cherish, wherever the coming years take him, whatever comes his way—Tony's determined, carefully assembled ignorance. He can't imagine what it had cost Tony. For Daniel, it's truly priceless.

IV

"What do you mean, you're not going?"

"Not going is not going," Daniel says. "No mystery. Unless you don't speak English this week."

"But it's the Very Last Party of the Summer," Athena says. "You have to be there."

"No, I don't," Daniel says.

"Everyone is expecting you. It's your grand farewell."

"Who needs a grand farewell? Don't you remember the ninth commandment of life in the theatre?"

"Leave them wanting more?"

"That's the one."

"I can't believe you're really not going."

"Taking Dad to dinner at *Tia Elena's*. Boys' night out."

The Very Last Party of the Summer is a Red Dog High School tradition. Each year the incoming seniors organize it as a way of staking their claim to the top of the pyramid. Most years it's in Founders' Park, just a couple of blocks from the town square, but it's been held in other venues as well. One year the seniors got permission to hold it in the Opera House. One year they were able to rope off the parking lot behind the courthouse. Last year it was at the Kilpatrick Ranch, ten miles or so east and north of town. At the height of the evening, CeeCee Kilpatrick gave a demonstration of show jumping. She missed a barrier and took a pretty bad fall but insisted she was fine. A couple of days later she showed up at the emergency room. She had a miscarriage late that night. Nobody had known

43

she was pregnant. The meaner-spirited individuals on the cheerleading squad insisted that she staged the accident on purpose. To this day, nobody's sure who the father was.

Tonight the Very Last Party is taking place at the Baliches' house, the closest thing there is in Red Dog to a Beverly Hills style mansion.

"I hope this isn't an awful mistake," Dad says, looking down at his dinner. He's ordered the house specialty, a platter of three enchiladas, one *chile verde*, one sour cream, and one *chile colorado*. Red, white, and green—the colors of the Mexican flag. Hence its name. *La Bandera*. The Flag. Served with refried beans and Mexican style rice, it's a substantial meal.

"Have you ever had a bad meal here?" Daniel asks.

"Not talking about the food."

"Dad, please," Daniel says. "Not that again."

"I know," Dad says. "Your mind is made up. I'm sorry to be like this. I know I raised you to make your own decisions, but I can't help wishing you were leaving for college instead of boot camp."

"I'll go to college when I get out," Daniel says. "I promised, didn't I?"

"I don't care whether you go to college or not. There are plenty of other worthwhile things you could do with your life that don't require a degree. I just don't want anything happening to you over there."

"Nothing's going to happen to me," Daniel says.

"Son, you can't possibly know that," Dad says. "If it were as easy as saying so, none of those boys would be coming home in body bags."

"Do you think Athena would let anything happen to me?"

"It's not something to joke about," Dad says.

"Who's joking?"

"Honestly," Dad says. "You've taken it far enough. There's nothing for you to prove."

"What's that supposed to mean?"

"Anton would understand if you. . ."

"This has nothing to do with Tony."

"It has everything to do with Anton," Dad insists. "If you won't admit it to me, at least admit it to yourself."

This is Dad at his most serious. Daniel knows better than to argue.

"I'm not blind, you know. I've been watching this for years. And I'd be the first to say that if you're going to emulate anyone around here he's by far the best choice. But you don't have to do this for him. He'd never think less of you if you didn't go. When he was in the Corps there was no war. Anywhere. There was the threat of it, sure. But not real shooting. That doesn't make his service any less noble. I'm just reminding you that the situation is different now. And besides, he's a father himself. He'd never want to lose you unnecessarily any more than he'd want to lose one of his boys."

"It's not like that."

"Please, Daniel," Dad says. "Don't play it that way. I know what I know."

Daniel catches his breath. Exactly what is it that Dad knows? He's been so careful, but there are still a thousand ways he could have given it away.

"Hero worship is all well and good. You've practically turned yourself into him: fine. Like I said before—who better? But eventually you have to stop measuring yourself against him—or anyone, really—and live your own life."

Hero worship. Perfect. Daniel is woozy with gratitude at the ravishing simplicity of the explanation Dad holds out to him like a father offering a four year old a new toy.

"That's what I'm trying to do," Daniel says. "Tony never said a word. . ."

"I'm not accusing him of trying to influence you," Dad says, "but the only way I can face the risk you're taking is if I'm sure you're not doing it to satisfy anyone but yourself. Can you tell me that?"

Every Memorial Day weekend, Daniel hoists the chaise lounge onto the roof, runs extension cords, installs his portable TV, record player, and radio in their new home, and establishes *al fresco* summer headquarters. Summer is the rainy season in the region, which means tarps and other water- and wind-proofing measures must be employed, but the facility gets lots of use. Nights when there's no rehearsal to attend, he's in the open air from dinner until bedtime. Tonight is no exception. He's dismantled most of it, of course, with his departure imminent. The television and record player are back in his bedroom, but he's still got his radio. There was rain earlier, but as usual with the local monsoon thunderstorms, the clouds move on quickly after the rain ends, and the sky overhead is clear and nearly blinding with stars.

The local radio station only plays rock and roll for a few hours each night, and that of the most insipid variety. Only junior high girls bother listening to it. Everybody else in town between the ages of fourteen and twenty-one listens to the station in Oklahoma City that has a nighttime signal powerful enough, apparently, to reach Mars. Daniel, however, prefers the classical music station from Tucson. Reception isn't always good. Atmospheric conditions have to be just right. But tonight the signal is as clear as if the transmitter were just blocks away.

Daniel knows little or nothing about classical music. He's been listening to it for years but he's never bothered to learn anything. That would be easy enough, because Dad is a real buff—hundreds of records in his library and lots of books on the subject as well. But Daniel doesn't need the arcane knowledge, just the experience. He likes it because he likes melodies he can hum, but its main attraction is that he likes music without words. Song lyrics are other people's ideas forcing their way into his head, and most of the time they're not ideas he finds interesting. They're just another distraction, or worse, an annoyance. Tonight it's Brahms, the fourth symphony. It's great music for having your own thoughts to.

Why does everybody have to be the same? Everybody Daniel knows, at least everyone who lives outside this house, seems obsessed with fitting in. America is supposed to be the land of the free, but his fellow citizens apparently are all determined to enslave themselves to some ideal he thinks of as intolerably boring. They watch all the same shows on television. They listen to the same music. They wear the same clothes and hairstyles. The guys on his teams all play the same way. It's insane. It can't be the way people are meant to live.

The steep, rocky walls of the canyon are like a fortress guarding the town. Or like a prison, depending on your perspective. For every one of Daniel's neighbors that sees them as protection there's someone else who sees them as barriers to be escaped. People luxuriate in the sense of coziness and safety the canyon gives them or chafe at the restriction it represents. Daniel has spent his life trying to ignore those walls. They're real to him only in the most literal sense. They're just there. They don't mean anything. They don't provide security. They don't prevent entry or exit. They don't define the world. They don't keep people from following their dreams. They're just geological formations that some have decided to inhabit and others are determined to flee. Despite Daniel's determination to leave the town behind him, it's not mere topographical features that impel him.

As far as he's concerned he's not running away. He's running toward.

But what?

Anyway, before he can run very far, there's business to attend to. He's not going to live his new life with things left undone. He wants to enter that new existence free of regrets, capable of looking himself in the mirror and sleeping well at night. There's not going to be anything people can reproach him for. He's been seeing the signs for years, courtesy of his crypto-Trotskyite father, who seems to spend half his life arguing with the television news broadcasters. Southeast Asia is going to haunt Daniel's generation. He's sure of it. Twenty years from now, men are going to have to account for what they did or didn't do when their draft notices came. Their bosses, co-workers, wives, and children are going to judge them based on the choices they made as seventeen and eighteen year olds. It may be unfair to expect guys his age to make decisions that far-reaching and with that much potential to disrupt their futures, but that's the way life is. What seems to be perfectly reasonable now, when you're young and basically not accountable to anyone, may turn out to be tragic twenty years on and under completely different circumstances. The times they may be a-changin', but some things will always be the same. America will never be a country that takes pride in its cowards and shirkers. So though he expects the conformity of military life will feel like a prison, he won't be one of those. He'll face the risk. He'll give the country a few years of his life and after that he won't have to feel like he owes anyone anything.

That's freedom the only way he understands it, freedom that's been honestly earned, even if it comes only as a result of agreeing to be a slave for a time and with the risk of losing out on any kind of future at all.

He doesn't want to spend his life like Dad, alone and misunderstood by everyone he knows. Dad's career in the county attorney's office lasted only a few years. During that time, and as a result of discussions he took part in at the Y and in certain bars and social clubs, he came to identify so completely with Red Dog's miners that he ended up on retainer for the union local, having resigned from his government job. Soon, the smelter workers in Donaldson, thirty miles away, retained him to represent their local as well. The volume of additional business that resulted from that "ordination" made his private practice the largest in the county. To the local population he's a saint as much as any of the cherished local doctors, priests, or ministers. And meanwhile, he became a guru to all the young lifters at the Y. He didn't build the kind of trophy-winning physique some of them did but he had a gift for coaching anyone who came through the door of the gym toward his potential. So he was that kind of local legend as well. If he'd ever decided to run for city council— mayor, even—he'd have won in a walk. Yet nobody really knows him but his own children. Daniel's sorry as hell that Dad's life has turned out like it has, but his deep respect doesn't mean he has to follow Dad's example. That's why coming back here after his hitch in the Corps isn't an option. That's what makes going into the Corps a necessity in the first place. He may not think of the walls of the canyon as prison walls, but it's only because his choices make it possible to ignore them except as rock and soil.

Meanwhile, there has to be somewhere where everybody doesn't have to be alike. Someplace where a secret like his doesn't have to be such a life and death thing. And he's going to find it if it's the last thing he does. How long has this been his litany? He can't recall for sure. Back beyond high school. Beyond junior high. Beyond any kind of school. He must have awakened one morning, looked out the window at the world as he knew it and decided that there had to be an alternative.

The music ends, and in the lull before somebody at the station figures out that they're broadcasting silence—something that happens with surprising frequency—he can hear music and party sounds from way down the canyon. The Very Last Party of the Summer is in full swing. Despite Athena's protestations, he's not being missed. Talked about, certainly. Remembered. But not truly missed. Nobody really misses a pebble once it disappears below the surface of the pond.

* * *

"You're back already?" Daniel asks as Athena's head appears over the edge of the parapet.

"It's after midnight."

"Party's still going strong," Daniel says. "Listen."

Party sounds are indeed floating up the canyon through the night.

"Surprised nobody's called the cops."

"Oh, the cops are there," Athena laughs. "Drinking beer and ignoring the potheads."

"Huh?"

"Those Balich girls. Hostesses with the mostest."

"You're kidding."

"Where do you think you live?"

"Not for much longer."

"About that," Athena says.

"Don't start."

"I'm not starting anything. I just thought you'd like to know about tonight's party game."

"Do I want to hear this?"

"Jeremy has a betting pool going. It's called 'What's the last local attraction Daniel Kmetko plans to visit before he leaves town?' It's supposed to be a clue as to your true nature and intentions."

"You're kidding."

"You're going to sneak into the football stadium and sit in the stands. You're going to sneak into the opera house and stage a private pyrotechnics show. You're going to sneak onto the baseball field and stand on the pitcher's mound contemplating your existence. You're going to sneak into the courthouse, climb to the cupola on top of the dome and pee."

"With the wind, I hope," Daniel laughs. "That's lots of sneaking around."

"You're going to sit outside this girl's house or that one's or someone else's. You're going to watch the sun rise from Inspiration Peak."

"Betting pool, huh?"

"That's right," Athena nods.

"So how are they going to know who wins? Is Jeremy planning to put a tail on me?"

"I guess I'm the tail. I'm assigned to report on your movements."

"So what are you going to tell them?"

"Been working on that. A little story of my own concoction. Nobody's going to win that bet."

"I like the part about nobody winning the bet," Daniel said. "I'm not sure I'm crazy about that 'my own concoction' stuff."

"You're going to sneak out of the house tomorrow night and I'm going to be right behind you. You're going to follow the river down the canyon to that bridge where Annie Morgan jumped off and killed herself. You've been grieving her passing all this time. Ever since your freshman year."

"She was a senior," Daniel nodded.

"You worshipped her from afar. You haven't been able to look at another girl since. What do you think?"

"It's as good a story as any."

"It's better than that," she insists.

"You're right."

He has to hand it to Athena. It's actually the perfect final chapter to his days here. Perfect because it adds to his mystique, and perfect because it conceals the truth completely. Add "Queen of Misdirection" to her already exhaustive list of titles. If people really knew her. . .

Daniel checks the knot in his necktie and gives his hair a last touch up. The hair has to be perfect. More than any other physical characteristic he possesses, it's his symbol. If his friends and neighbors remember nothing else, let them remember him by that. So he stares at the mirror for a long time satisfying himself that he'll exceed expectations in terms of its perfection. Then it's time to go. On week-days Dad drives his trusty GMC to the office and on weekends it's his vehicle for errands, but whenever they go anywhere as a family he takes the dust cover off the Citroen and pulls it out of the garage. In France this model is nicknamed *le shark*, but to Daniel it resembles a UFO masquerading as a four door sedan. It's as out of place here in Red Dog as an ostrich would be on a ski lift. It should be cruising down the *Champs Elysees* by night, the lights of Paris gleaming off its glossy, midnight blue finish. Dad and Daniel perform all regular maintenance on the car, aided by a set of shop manuals rivaling the *Encyclopedia Britannica* in heft and Dad's almost equally comprehensive set of tools, special ones for this car only. They don't fit the GMC, for which there is another, simpler set. Once a year it goes to the dealer, a hundred miles away in Tucson, for a thorough going over. Meanwhile, in the eight years of its trouble free service with the Kmetkos, it has covered less than twenty thousand miles. The original Michelins, with plenty of tread left on them, were replaced eighteen months ago as a precaution against the desert climate. The replacement tires had to be special ordered from the west coast. There wasn't a tire store in the county that stocked the size.

Dad is widely considered a local "character". Utterly conventional in per-sonal appearance and outward behavior, his eccentricity is legendary. There's the house, for instance, which was a near ruin when he bought it. Restoration required nearly two years and the expenditure of far more money than anyone in town thought was sensible. It's a beautiful home now but it will always resemble a Conquistador fortress and it will always be inconveniently remote from any neighbors. If Dad were to sell it, almost every cent he spent on renovations would be lost. Most of the townsfolk find it incomprehensible. There are his politics, which put him at odds with his own class and profession. Then there's his status as a single man. The people of Red Dog understand widow- or wid-owerhood as an unfortunate fact of life. But it's not a condition to be prolonged any more than necessary. And the idea that a man as handsome and successful as Tad Kmetko hasn't remarried in all this time—well, it's hardly credible. Finally there's this bizarre excuse for an automobile, which, it's reliably reported, cost more than a Cadillac. The car embodies everything Dad's friends and neighbors don't get about him.

Dad was raised in the Moravian Church. In the small farming community where he grew up everyone had Moravian forebears and everyone who went to church went to that one. Needless to say, there's no Moravian congregation in this town. Some of the Croatian and Slovenian families are Protestant, however, and on their arrival in these parts a couple of generations ago, they decided to worship alongside the Scots at St. Mark's Presbyterian. It's a gothic revival gem, a close cousin architecturally of St. Matthew's Episcopal down the block. The Methodists recently moved into a huge new glass and concrete structure that looks like a Frank Lloyd Wright knockoff. The Serbian Orthodox church is St. Basil's, Moscow in miniature. The Catholic Church the Irish, Croats, and Slovenes attend is Romanesque, while the one the Mexicans go to is in California Mission style. The Baptists have a slump block barn of a place that hardly looks like a church at all. The Jews have a set of rooms on the upper stories of Drs. Vogelmann, Klein, and Steinberg's office building downtown. All that's visible from outside is their ornate bronze entry door decorated with castings of Stars of David and menorahs. The handful of Jehovah's witnesses have a trailer at the edge of town.

Daniel hasn't been to church since early July, but Athena and Dad attend almost every Sunday. The sermon board outside the sanctuary asks "God's Warriors?" Daniel finds the question mark amusing as they pull into the parking lot. Inside the sanctuary they take seats in Athena's preferred spot. The notice board to the right of the pulpit lists the hymns for the morning. "A Mighty Fortress is Our God," "Once to Every Man and Nation", which is one of Daniel's favorites, and "Eternal Father, Strong to Save," which Dad has loved since his days as a junior officer on a submarine during World War II. Daniel senses a theme here, not to mention Athena's string pulling. She's probably the only seventeen-year-old in the county who can orchestrate Sunday's order of worship.

Rev. MacLeod is about a hundred years old and legendary for his kindness. His thick Scottish accent requires concentration on the part of his hearers. His sermon for the morning stresses the unfortunate necessity, given the essentially violent and warlike character of the human race, for men to take up arms periodically in defense of their families and homelands, the nobility of those who assume that duty, voluntarily or involuntarily as the case may be, and the perpetual need for all Christians to pray for them. Not just for their physical safety, but that their characters not be distorted and corroded by the horrors they will certainly witness and the acts they might be forced to perform. As early as sixth grade, Daniel noticed that Rev. MacLeod's sermon points were often alliterative or arranged into acrostics. He finds this intriguing. Not content to depend merely on the clarity, logic, and sincerity of his sermons, Rev. MacLeod employs this simple device to strengthen the possibility that they will actually be remembered and perhaps even acted upon by his flock.

Though Athena and Daniel have been raised as agnostics, there is nothing outrageous about Rev. MacLeod's brand of theology, which tends strongly toward the pragmatic and mundane. Love your neighbor. Treat people ethically. Feed the hungry. Care for the sick. Work for justice. There's nothing a crypto-Trotskyite like Dad could possibly find objectionable in any of it. Daniel assumes this is what explains their membership in the congregation. The Jesus mumbo-jumbo is ever present, of course, but not oppressively so. It's almost as if it's just there for atmosphere.

After communion and just before the benediction, Rev. MacLeod calls Dad, Athena, and Daniel forward. Laying his scrawny old hands on Daniel's forearm, he signals the congregation to rise. In his slow, soft-spoken manner he exhorts them to keep Daniel always in their prayers, protecting him with their love and good wishes. Looking out at the people, Daniel sees church ladies dabbing at their eyes with hankies. Their menfolk's expressions are grave. In his usual place, Dr. Jeffrey Greene, who with his tall, lanky build, thick, floppy hair, and WASPy features could easily be one of Dad's brothers or cousins, puts an arm around his son. Dr. Greene usually attends church alone, his wife and son apparently being otherwise occupied. But Daniel remembers Athena mentioning that lately Christopher has been attending church with his father every week. Daniel assumes that this is just another aspect of Christopher's current offensive, which, he believes, shifted into high gear just about the time *Earnest* closed last April. He hopes Athena realizes how transparent this is and will maintain her vigilance.

Despite the efforts of the company for generations now, Red Dog is still a strong union town. Thus, the first Monday in September is one of its high holy days. Daniel remembers various strikes over the years. The union has always come out on top, but management never seems to learn the lesson. Dad has raised them to be staunch supporters of the working class, which he considers the backbone of America. Dad and Athena will attend all the festivities today. Daniel is glad they'll have something to take their minds off his departure. There will be a parade. There will be a city-wide picnic in Founders' Park, followed by a band concert and a dance. There will be day-long baseball games. There will be scores of backyard barbeques. But before any of that the whole town will sleep in. There will be no shift whistles from the mine to disturb the residents and they will slumber on, dreaming their dreams. They will all rise well after their usual time.

Daniel knows this, so he makes no effort to conceal his movements. There's no need, beyond borrowing Dad's GMC for the short drive and parking it in the lot behind the courthouse instead of in the square itself. His objective looms in the dim pre-dawn light. Some patriarch of long ago decreed that the perimeter of the square be lined with cast iron park benches. Daniel chooses the one with the best angle for viewing his objective. He sits.

He waits.

Since he was a small boy, this has been his icon, his totemic figure. Its presence here has been the pole of his existence. Twelve feet tall. The body of Superman surmounted by the head of an Art Deco angel, hair swept back in the manner of a hood ornament on some luxury automobile of decades ago; the upper body bare, the physique extravagantly sculpted, the muscles bulging like warm, living muscles have never bulged, the rest of the figure's body clad in the dungarees and boots of a miner. His shovel, pickaxe, and helmet lie at his feet.

This statue has been Daniel's inspiration. His aspiration and goal. Each waking hour carries with it some fragmentary awareness of this image. It is a promise he made himself back in the forgotten shadows of his boyhood and has never deviated from, still unfulfilled but drawing ever and always closer. Close enough now, after all his years of toil and dedication, to reach out and brush with the tips of his fingers if not actually, firmly grasp.

He sits. The light comes. Beams ooze into the square slowly, and their touch caresses the smooth surface, rousing it from its dark slumber, awakening the gleam lying inert in the cool, night-chilled metal.

This, Daniel sighs.

Yes, this.

Back at the house, they're all stirring. The smell of bacon hangs like incense in a cathedral. The table has been set with the good china. Candles blaze in his grandmother's heirloom holders. He sticks his head into the kitchen.

"Mrs. Robek, you shouldn't have gone to all this trouble."

"Nonsense, dear. Can't send you off without a decent breakfast in your stomach. Go call the others to come sit down before it all gets cold."

Athena kisses him goodbye. Dad shakes his hand. Their eyes brim with tears. Daniel swallows at the lump in his throat. He hands his single bag to the driver. He ascends the stairs. A handful of passengers are already on board the bus, which made its first stop of the morning in Donaldson. He's the only one getting on here.

Out the deeply tinted glass of the bus window, he watches Athena and Dad get into the Citroen. They don't look back. The alien-looking automobile glides out of the parking lot onto streets still nearly deserted this holiday morning.

Halfway down the mountain, the bus is passed by a dark blue convertible. It is Graciela Melendez-Greene's Alfa-Romeo. Not a Giulia, the four cylinder equivalent of a Triumph or MG, but the big six cylinder 2600 model, more like a Jaguar disguised as a Maserati. It's a very rare car. There probably aren't more than three of them in the entire state. If that. Daniel has promised himself one just like it someday. How many times has he imagined himself at the wheel of that car? He knows Italian sports cars are supposed to be red, but he loves that dark blue and the saddle colored leather of the interior.

The convertible top is down. Christopher's mother is in the passenger seat, her hair protected by a scarf, her eyes concealed by dark glasses. She looks like a glamorous actress in a movie with subtitles. Christopher is behind the wheel. His smooth hair is plastered to his head by the slipstream. A suitcase sits in the tiny back seat. There's probably another in the trunk. It must be an airport run. Christopher's mother travels a lot.

That's all Daniel gets—just that glimpse. The car accelerates past the bus and rounds the next curve. Soon it's out of sight.

LANCE GARRISON: 1968

I

All Lance knew about his new roomie was that he was from a small town in the general area of the university—which constituted a territory substantially larger than Lance's home state—and that his two best buddies from high school lived two doors down the hall. And, though this was hardly worth mentioning, that Christopher was far too good looking for it to be of any practical use, being male. Lance had perennially been accused of this infraction himself and knew first-hand how much suspicion was attached to it and how meaningless it was as a measure of anyone's character. Thus, it was something he couldn't help taking note of, albeit, he assumed, in a different way than most people did. Christopher and his friends were freshmen. Lance was a sophomore. Lance's roommate from the year before had quit school at the end of spring semester and moved to an ashram just off campus. Lance had been too lazy, or perhaps fatalistic, to make new arrangements on his own, leaving the job of finding a replacement roommate to the work-study elves slaving away in the student housing office. That's how he ended up with Christopher. These days the former roomie had a new name and hung out at the airport trying to give flowers to unsuspecting travelers in exchange for donations, a fairly harmless form of extortion but extortion nonetheless. Lance hoped Christopher would be an improvement on Dewey but had little real hope of it. Dorm life seemed to include as a given a disproportionate number of crazies. Christopher might even turn out to be worse than Dewey but least he showered regularly. Dewey had regarded personal hygiene as an irrelevance, so in this regard if no other, Christopher was an improvement. In fact, Lance's preliminary impression of him was that he seemed to shower obsessively.

Christopher, Patrick, and Jeremy were recognizably the sort of threesome that could have been observed prior to their graduation on any day of the week in the hallways of any high school in any one of the fifty states and ten provinces. The phenomenon might even be observed beyond the confines of the continent of North America for all Lance knew. Collectively they were a cliché. Lance had known of dozens of such trios in his own graduating class and still others in the classes before and behind. Though he'd never been part of one himself, being an exponent of another cliché altogether—the "lone wolf"—his older brother had led one and his younger brother still did. Patrick was the Eagle Scout, stalwart, not actually humorless but relentlessly literal-minded so that he often became the butt of Jeremy's jokes, and unconsciously bossy. Tall and lanky but with a tendency to slouch, he was one of those monochromatic types, tawny skin almost matching his sun bleached hair, and pale, watery eyes that provided no appreciable contrast to either. Those eyes had a strained expression. Too much squinting into the sun from his lifeguard tower, Lance supposed, or perhaps too much responsibility, either real or imagined. He seemed like the type that was a little masochistic about responsibility, suffering under its weight yet dependent on it to justify his existence in equal proportions. He'd be a good man to have as a professional associate, Lance sensed, but a pain in the ass as a friend. Jeremy was the raconteur and self-styled ladies' man. His chatter was unending and didn't require attention being paid so much as it assumed it. It consisted almost exclusively of the kind of wisecracks precocious guys generally mastered by eighth grade, references to popular culture including an extensive repertoire of quotations from movie and television dialogue, double entendres of a particularly obvious character, innuendo so hyperbolic as to lose its power to shock, and puns, the more juvenile the better. Apparently nothing was too trivial for him to remark on or have an opinion about. His role in life seemed to be to subvert anyone and anything but especially Patrick, who was perpetually deemed inexcusably serious and uptight. Lance could certainly see the point of this critique, though he considered that Jeremy made more than necessary of it. He reckoned that Jeremy was generally considered funny, but probably more so by himself than anyone who knew him. His humor was the kind that really depended on the ingestion of alcohol on the part of his audiences to achieve maximum impact. Patrick and Jeremy's room

down the hall was decorated to the point of visual overload with all the most current dormitory clichés. Their collection of black light posters attracted visitors
from all over campus. Their stereo, blasting from morning to night, featured
the most up to date collegiate play list. Their hair was fashionably shaggy—a
look which almost worked on Jeremy but was just sad on Patrick—their clothing
fashionably tattered, and their slang so *au courant* as to qualify them for work on
AM radio.

Christopher was the odd man out. His hair and clothing were unnervingly
neat, and his manners matched them. He was almost like a kid from the dark
ages before the Sixties really took off—one of Beaver and Wally's friends, for
instance. The one who never had any lines yet managed always to be first in
line when Barbara Billingsley handed out the fresh baked cookies. He seemed to
make no effort in the direction of conformity or otherwise. He was quiet without
actually coming off as shy. Unlike his friends, who appeared to go out of their
way to cultivate larger than life personae, he seemed oblivious to the possibility
of self-presentation. He simply was. Rather like a cat, Lance thought. He occasionally contributed some remark or other to the parallel monologues of the other
two which passed for conversation among the three of them. Occasionally the
monologues converged, and the result was generally an argument. Which band
was superior, the Rolling Stones or the Who? All three seemed to believe that the
Beatles were for girls, which any more wasn't as controversial a position as it had
been a couple of years earlier. Which novelist should you be seen reading or at
least carrying a copy of, Vonnegut or Roth? Which poet, Ginsburg or cummings,
should one claim inspiration from? Christopher, Lance noted, never took sides in
these debates. Once the dispute subsided, he generally spoke up for his own alternatives: the Moody Blues, Herman Hesse, and Edna St. Vincent Millay. By then
no one was invested, and Christopher's preferences were greeted as footnotes if
they were registered at all. Here was a guy, Lance thought, recalling the description of Gatsby, who didn't want trouble with anybody. It was almost enough to
make Christopher intriguing.

Lance gathered all of this intelligence by observation courtesy of the prevail-
ing campus etiquette which dictated that as Christopher's roommate he had to
be included in the threesome's activities at least to the extent of being invited to

join in. Patrick seemed particularly concerned at how far away from home Lance was. Jeremy never could remember the name of Lance's home town—or state, even—and Patrick found this so embarrassing that he pretended not to himself, so as, apparently, to make it less noticeable. The first time they invited Lance to go off campus with them for pizza, it was so much like a little old lady being offered a helping hand across the street he almost laughed at them. But he went. He didn't want them to think he thought he was too good to hang out with them. That night they took Patrick's car, Jeremy's battery being in need of replacement. Jeremy insisted, rather elaborately Lance thought, on relinquishing his apparently accustomed position at shotgun in deference to Lance's size, which he and Patrick had already remarked on to just the degree their lack of familiarity with him permitted, making a production of climbing instead into the back seat of Patrick's Austin Mini alongside Christopher.

Lance's size. Jeremy's reaction to it was exaggerated, of course. Everyone's was. Lance wasn't nearly as big, say, as a varsity football player might have been, nor was he in actuality as tall as Patrick or Jeremy either one. They both came in comfortably over six feet, while he just managed five-ten. Still, it was always like that. Lance knew what the glances and remarks signified, no matter how carefully couched. He was musclebound. He was grotesque. Even in clothing, this was unmistakable. Only in the wrestling ring was he judged as anything other than freakish. Only in the locker room was he safe from the critical glance, the skeptical quip. And by no means was he always safe from censure in those places. In his case, it wasn't a matter of overall bulk. Lots of wrestlers were his size or larger, but not many looked like him. Not any on the university squad he had joined on scholarship. Back east, his bodybuilder's physique was, if not exactly common, at least less unusual than it seemed to be around here. Patrick and Jeremy left him in no doubt that this made him questionable company. They were as nice about it as they could possibly be, but their opinion of what they saw when they looked at him was clear, and so, by association he assumed, was Christopher's, though there'd been no indication of it. Still, Lance was quite certain there had been some discussion among them as to his suitability as Christopher's roommate, perhaps already having gotten as far as questions about what might be done about the situation.

He didn't care. He never had. He had no intention of starting to. The feminists on campus ranted about their bodies being their own property and nobody else's business, and he found he could relate to the sentiment. And he suspected that at least some of the disapproval he experienced on account of his physique was poorly disguised jealousy.

Still, the second time they all went for pizza, riding in Jeremy's Nova this time, which was certainly roomier, he employed what had long since become his standard defense by way of explanation, the real one being too involved, too personal, and ultimately incomprehensible to anyone but another bodybuilder anyway. Without his wrestling scholarship, he told them, he couldn't afford to attend college full time. This was a lie, but Christopher and company didn't know that and didn't need to know it. The point was that if he wasn't in college or was attending only part time, there was no way he could avoid the draft. They were the type of guys for whom this was the Holy Grail, and any excess resorted to in quest of it was above reproach. The gambit worked. Over the pizza, he could see reassessment glimmering in their eyes. He was the way he was because he was a victim of the system. The Man forced him to be a freak. He was still grotesque, but now that they comprehended the motivation, his body wasn't quite as objectionable as it had initially appeared.

There was, inevitably, a girl attached to them. Lance met her almost immediately. Her name was Athena. She was tall, statuesque, golden haired, breathtaking. She couldn't have been named for anyone but a goddess. Otherwise, Lance mused, the universe would certainly have raised objections. She had graduated with the guys. She was Jeremy's ex. Patrick proclaimed undying love whenever her name came up in conversation, even when she was present, and from the look on his face Lance was convinced he wasn't exaggerating. Lance couldn't help but wonder if Christopher's apparent lack of interest in her was genuine or just a stratagem. Christopher's inscrutability threatened to make Lance paranoid if he dwelled on it.

Christopher and he had both enrolled in Abnormal Psychology. They scheduled themselves into the same section for the convenience of being able to skip
occasionally and cover each other's absences, and the first morning of class there
Athena was, saving a place for them—or for Christopher at least. She greeted
Lance with the requisite enthusiasm of the time and place. That wasn't unexpected. But on the way to the gym afterward, he realized that her expression
when Christopher introduced them was anything but what he was accustomed to
from girls. She didn't look at him like he was a freak at all. Rather, she seemed
to take his appearance for granted. He had no idea what to make of it. He ran
into her in front of the student union the next day, and once again her warm
greeting seemed unfazed, entirely sincere, and totally lacking in typical feminine
calculation.

"I'm starving," she said. "Let's get lunch."

He ordered two burgers. He pulled the patties out of their buns and ate them
bare. People were generally baffled by this, but though she clearly noticed it she
seemed to take it for granted. Lance offered Athena the fries that had come with
the burgers. She had a healthy appetite for a girl. She didn't once mention dietary
issues either with regard to her complexion or figure.

"I don't know why I don't do what Christopher's doing," she said, dipping a
fry in mayonnaise as Lance had seen people do in Montreal.

"What's that?"

"Majoring in pre-med."

"Seems like an awful lot of work," he pointed out, "unless you actually want
to be a doctor."

"Which I don't," she said. "At all. It just sounds so much more useful than
actress-slash-dancer."

"Depends on your perspective, I'd say," he told her. "So that's your major?
Acting-slash-dancing?"

"Theatre," she said in a fake British accent, "and modern dance."

"My mom was a dancer," he said.

"Really?"

"Rumanian state ballet school," he said. "Then when she moved to England
she ended up in the Royal Ballet."

"That's amazing."

"No," he laughed. "Her brownies—they're amazing. Her dancing defied any sort of verbal description, according to Dad. So what did your parents think when you told them about your major?"

"It's just my dad," Athena said. "And it was his idea."

"No kidding."

"I think he's using reverse psychology," she laughed. "Hoping I'll get it out of my system."

"Is it working?"

"Too early to tell," she said, "but probably about as well as it worked when my brother said he was planning to join the Marines. He's going to Viet Nam soon."

When the buzzer sounded, Lance was deep into the assigned chapter in his philosophy text and almost didn't register it. He had never gotten used to that sound. He didn't know if it would ever mean "telephone call" to him. He pulled on gym shorts over his jockstrap and headed down the hall to the phones.

He spoke his room number into the receiver and somebody on the desk downstairs connected him.

"Hello."

"Hi, it's Athena."

"Oh, hi, Athena. Christopher's not around,"

"I know. I just sent him off to the library."

Which meant she had actually called Lance. In Lance's experience, girls only called you on behalf of other girls. Since he hadn't yet met any of Athena's female friends, that couldn't be the explanation this time.

"Listen, I need a favor."

"Sure," he said. "What is it?"

"I'd feel stupid asking you this over the phone. Meet me."

"Where?"

"Let's say in front of South Hall. You know that bench?"

"Sure."

"Five minutes."

"O.K."

Back in the room, he put on jeans and a tank top and combed his hair. In observance of Murphy's Law, he brushed his teeth. He was on the appointed bench in exactly five minutes, and he waited. Somebody in the dorm across the street was playing "Whiter Shade of Pale" over and over. It drifted lugubriously out the window and over the tops of the palm trees. He had heard it faintly as he approached the spot. It disturbed him that something so profound could nevertheless have become disastrously clichéd through repetition. This had all kinds of implications he didn't like to consider, perhaps even about sex. Who knew? In twenty or thirty years. . .

"God, I am so sorry," Athena panted, appearing suddenly out of the darkness. "On my way out of the dorm I ran into Jeremy. I couldn't get away from him. The cross examination he puts you through. The explanations you have to come up with."

"You could always tell him the truth," Lance suggested.

"No," she said. "That's the one thing you don't dare do with Jeremy. Ever. Not even when it seems harmless. Once you do he starts expecting it. It's much better when he thinks you're lying to him. He not only wonders what the truth is, but why you're not telling him. It ties him in knots. But thinking up stories for him is exhausting. Especially because they have to be transparent. I told him I was in a hurry, which was a stupid mistake. He had to know where I was going, why, who I was meeting. You can't just say hi and bye with Jeremy, I'm afraid."

"I've seen him giving Patrick the third degree," Lance said. "Someday he's going to pull out a rubber hose."

"You get it," Athena said. "That was always the problem with Jeremy and me. He'd have absolutely smothered me."

"With a pillow in the library? Or are we talking metaphorically?"

"So you're not just a pretty face," she laughed.

Which was the point he'd been hoping to make. And of course it meant she'd noticed. The smart ones always did, eventually, but Lance didn't like to take it for granted.

"I thought I heard something about a girl needing a favor," he said, not interested in talking about Jeremy.

"Really?"

"I could swear I did," he said, miming scratching his head, though he wasn't sure it would read in the darkness.

"All right," she said, "be that way."

"What way?"

"Mr. Straight to the point. Mr. Forthright. Mr. Opposite of Jeremy, for all practical purposes."

Good. She'd noticed that, too.

"Got an Abnormal Psych chapter I should be annotating, is the thing," Lance said. "Very challenging class, Abnormal Psych."

"O.K.," she laughed, "yes. I need a favor."

"I know a certain former lifeguard who'd give a certain part of his anatomy for the opportunity of doing a certain girl a favor. Me, I'm just a guy she hardly knows."

"I don't dare encourage Patrick," Athena said.

"Why not?"

"Because I feel guilty enough about him already," Athena said.

"So that's how it is," Lance said. "How do you know you're not encouraging me?"

"Maybe I am encouraging you," she laughed.

"Or maybe it's reverse psychology," Lance said. "I hear that runs in your family."

"If those idiots could hear you," she said.

"What idiots would you be referring to?"

"The guys," she said. "You know they think you're a big dumb jock."

"No kidding," Lance said. "So this favor?"

"There's a party," she said.

"Happy to oblige, ma'am," he drawled like a television cowboy. "If you need a date for the ice cream social I'm ready to pitch in. Just don't want to rile up the tribe."

"The guys aren't invited," she said. "If I ask one of them they all want to come along. Besides, it's not that kind of party."

"What kind of party is it?"

"The kind you don't bring your old high school gang to," she said.

"Uh huh. Need a little more info than that."

"Theatre department mixer."

"So I should wear—what? A fake mustache, a beret, and a black turtleneck? Rent a set of bongo drums?"

"Don't you dare," Athena said. "Just look normal."

"I'll work on that," he said.

"Saturday night," she said.

"Fine," he said. "Saturday night, theatre department mixer, look normal. So what's the part?"

"I guess you could say pretending to be my boyfriend."

"It'll be a stretch, of course. But I think I can handle it, Mr. DeMille."

"There'll be all kinds of chicks there," Jeremy enthused. "The ratio of chicks to dudes will be four or five to one, minimum. That's the kind of movie *Doctor Zhivago* is. We'll make out like bandits. It'll be like taking candy from a baby."

"The novel is much more philosophical than the film," Patrick said, "and much more faithful to the socio-historical context. David Lean should be ashamed of himself. He must know better. I mean, didn't he read the book? Pasternak would be horrified. Omar Sharif, of all people, in the lead role. Does he even know where Russia is? Could he point to it on a map? I wonder."

"Pasternak wouldn't object to Jeremy getting laid," Lance said, just to be provocative. "Surely."

"He might," Christopher grinned.

"Just from sheer contrariness," Patrick agreed.

"Or in the spirit of socialist realism," Christopher suggested. "Or am I supposed to say social realist-ism? It's such a confusing term when you think about it."

"Not really," Jeremy said. "It means what it says. Realism from a socialist perspective."

"Or does it?" Patrick asked. "They're sneaky, those reds."

"My confusion was grammatical rather than conceptual," Christopher said.

"They do that kind of stuff on purpose," Patrick said. "It's the old 'confusion to our enemies' tactic."

"And what better way to bring America to its knees?" Christopher suggested, "than to keep red-blooded young Yanks too grammatically confused and sexually frustrated to maintain our vigilance against the Red Menace?"

"Who said anything about sexual frustration?" Lance asked, hoping to indicate that he was having trouble following the conversation. He occasionally did this just to make sure he seemed sufficiently obtuse.

"I'm telling you, amigos," Jeremy said, ignoring him, "hundreds of women, all of them worked up to a frenzy. We might cause a riot just by showing up. Saturday night, Temple of Music and Art downtown. We can't miss it."

"Going to have to pass on it, I'm afraid," Lance said.

"Really?" Patrick asked.

"Girl in my philosophy class," Lance explained. He'd prepared the story ahead of time. "Turns out she's from, like, the next town over from where I grew up. Her cousin actually dated my older brother. Small world, huh? Anyway, she's having a wine and pizza thing with other refugees from the old country. Probably be bored shitless hobnobbing with the huddled masses, but I promised I'd go."

There it was, just the slightest flicker in Christopher's eyes. Athena must have clued him in.

"We need to talk," Athena said, slipping on her panties.

Sarah, her roommate, spent every weekend at home trying to convince her Korean mother that Athena wasn't trying to influence her to take drugs or sell herself into white slavery. This was a never ending task, apparently, but it simplified the sleeping arrangements. It wasn't legal by any means for Lance to spend the night in Athena's dorm room, but the R.A. on the floor had a fiancé who had practically moved in, so who was going to enforce things?

"It's cool," Lance said. He'd been expecting things to peter out quickly. "Never thought you'd date me again after that theatre department thing. If this counts as dating."

"It counts as having sex, at least," Athena said. "I felt so guilty the first time. Raping you like that."

"You can't rape a willing partner," Lance said. "Thought everybody knew that."

"I didn't know you were willing. How was I supposed to know that?"

"Guys are always willing."

"You sound like my brother Daniel," Athena said, pulling her t-shirt on, "but it's not really that simple. The guys who are willing are the ones you want nothing to do with. And vice versa."

"I'll take that as a compliment," Lance growled.

"You, my dear, are in a class by yourself."

Somehow it didn't sound like he was being dumped. The alternative was not a development he'd anticipated.

"The thing is," she said, sitting on the bed and tousling his hair, "I don't like all this sneaking around. It's too much work. And I don't like it when things are disorganized."

"I'm organized," Lance protested.

"You certainly are," she agreed. "But this—whatever we're doing."

"You started it."

"I know," she said. "God, if you'd been able to read my mind that morning when Christopher introduced us."

"That far back, huh?"

"Don't get conceited," she laughed.

"Too late for that," Lance said. "Just ask Jeremy. He'll tell you what a narcissist I am."

"Rather not talk about him, if that's all right."

"Suits me," Lance said. "So?"

"I'm not complaining about anything that's happened so far," Athena said. "Honestly. I just need some structure."

"I've got a structure I can share with you."

"Don't I know it," she laughed. "You're fun to be around. You're sweet. The sex is great."

"You're welcome."

"The thing is I'm not looking for a boyfriend."

"That's easy," Lance said. "I promise not to be your boyfriend. Cross my heart."

"Well, that takes care of that," she said, "but if it's not too much trouble, I'd very much like you to continue pretending to be my boyfriend."

"Huh?"

"I find life much simpler when people think I have a boyfriend. Knowing my friends and associates as you do, I think you can understand."

"Fine," Lance said.

"So nothing changes, O.K? And above all, nobody falls in love with anybody. Oh, one more thing. We tell the guys, all right?"

"And how do we do that?" Lance asked. "Throw an engagement party?"

"Christopher will voice his suspicions. All I have to do is give him the signal."

"I was pretty sure he suspected something."

"That will force Jeremy to tell Christopher it's impossible and he's full of shit. Which will force Patrick to admit that he has suspicions, too."

"Patrick has suspicions? But we've been so careful."

"He doesn't, really," Athena said, "but he'll pretend he does to bait Jeremy."

"Got it."

"So then Jeremy will have to stage some kind of pizza parlor confrontation. Be ready."

"Aye, aye, ma'am."

"We'll pretty much have to improvise when the time comes. Just take my lead, O.K?"

"You play those guys like a violin, don't you?" Lance laughed.

"Damn right, I do."

"Thing is, got a condition or two of my own."

"I know," Athena winced. "Work on my blow jobs. I've heard that one before."

"Nothing wrong with those," Lance said. "Believe me, no complaints in that department. It's just I don't want to be poisoned in my sleep by my roommate."

"Christopher? He's been in on it for a while. You don't have to worry about Christopher."

"For how long has he been in on it? Roughly?"

"First time you and I slept together," Athena said. "That's when I got the idea this might work. Christopher and I have no secrets."

"So he knows this is just pretend, right?"

"Not quite," she said. "Actually, I may have given him the impression that I was head over heels."

"You two have no secrets, huh?"

"Well," she said, "that's the story for public consumption. Anyway, it isn't a problem for Christopher. Trust me."

"And what's our story?" Lance asked. "For public consumption. What's the motivation behind our torrid affair?"

"Oh, that," Athena grinned. "Opposites attract. What else?"

"I get that," Lance said, straight faced, "but which one of us is the opposite? You or me?"

II

———————————————————

"You go to the gym every day, don't you?" Jeremy asked.

"Sometimes twice," Lance said.

"I just don't get it," Jeremy said. He lost no opportunity to offer critical commentary on the phenomenon of Lance from a variety of perspectives—sociological, psychiatric, medical. And his efforts had only intensified in the weeks since Athena and Lance officially started dating. Lance didn't think there was much question about what it meant. In any case, he was used to being considered abnormal, to say the least. So far Jeremy hadn't said anything Lance hadn't heard before, and he wasn't holding his breath.

"Jeremy, please," Athena said. "You're always trying to start something."

"I'm not starting anything," Jeremy said. "I just want to understand our new friend here a little better."

"You want to start an argument," Athena said. "That's what you want. That's all you ever want these days. Now stop, or we're leaving."

Which wasn't on the cards, since Jeremy was their ride back to campus. And besides, there was still half a pizza left.

Christopher sauntered back from the jukebox as the intro to "Nights in White Satin" oozed into the room like a mournful benediction.

"Other thing I don't get," Jeremy said, turning to face him, "is why you let your *girlfriend* fight your battles for you."

"Because," Lance said, "she feels she has to defend me on account of I'm exactly the big old pussy you think I am."

"Easy there," Patrick murmured.

73

Christopher snickered. Whether it was at Lance's remark, at Lance's expense, or at some random notion unrelated to Lance he wasn't certain. Almost midterms, and Lance still couldn't read his roomie.

Jeremy's original objection to Lance's physique had been on aesthetic grounds. *"I just don't see why anybody would want to look like that."*

"Either you get it or you don't."

The awkward silence that followed Lance's response, during which someone at the table was obviously supposed to say something that employed words like "freakish," "grotesque," and/or "muscle bound" but no one actually spoke, was, Lance considered, intriguing. This lack of overt support was apparently what impelled Jeremy, a few days later, to move on to a more utilitarian critique.

"Think of the time and energy you put into it," Jeremy continued, "when you could be feeding the hungry or working for world peace."

"Like you do," was on the tip of Lance's tongue, but got no farther. He wasn't about to give Jeremy the fight he was so obviously spoiling for.

"It just seems so narcissistic," Jeremy completed his thought.

By this point, Patrick had, for his always indecipherable reasons, decided to play devil's advocate.

"I don't know about that," he said. "I mean, if a person has a natural ability in some area, is it narcissistic for him or her to develop it? For instance, Athena and Christopher are both extremely talented actors. Is it narcissistic for Athena to study and practice to perfect her craft? Do you really mean to say that she should give all that up and join the Peace Corps?"

"It's not the same thing at all," Jeremy said.

"Perhaps you'd like to explain how it's different," Athena said.

"Yes," Christopher said. "That certainly would be interesting."

"I wouldn't have thought it needed explaining," Jeremy said, "but O.K. See, in Athena's case what we're talking about is talent and art and culture. But Lance's chest muscles. . ."

"Pectorals," Christopher corrected him.

"Pectorals," Jeremy said, "are—well, what are they? Really?"

"You wouldn't be so blasé about them if they were Sophia Loren's pectorals," Patrick said.

"Sophia Loren is one of our finest living actresses," Jeremy said. "And if that's not art I don't know what is."

"I can't help wondering," Christopher said, "about the *Mona Lisa*'s pectorals. That's art."

Since he had nothing invested in Jeremy's opinion of him, these discussions affected Lance less than anyone else present. There was undoubtedly a great deal of entertainment for all of them in watching an asshole work so hard at his craft. Jeremy's ultimate aim, discrediting Lance in the eyes of his girlfriend, hardly mattered to him in the way Jeremy thought it did. It actually helped to legitimize their "relationship", since the guys seemed to take for granted that the more Jeremy criticized Lance, the more Athena would defend him. Other than that, the episodes served mostly to illuminate these people and their interactions. Lance wasn't sure exactly how that was significant, but it was at least interesting.

One morning, however, Jeremy finally went too far. He had tried out the exhibitionism argument the week before after Lance was seen riding his motor-cycle without a shirt, but that one hadn't worked any better than the others, and Jeremy was apparently getting desperate.

"There's something homosexual about it, seems to me," he said.

"Jeremy, stop," Athena pleaded. "Why do we have to go through this again? That horse is dead already. Just stop."

"I mean, don't you think?" Jeremy went on. "Such intense preoccupation with the male body? What else could it mean?"

Lance could feel everyone's eyes on him. This time, apparently, he had to respond. But that didn't mean it had to go the way at least some of them seemed to be expecting.

"All right," he said. "I've been hanging out with you guys for a while now, and you're all pretty cool I guess. But every time we're together I get to sit and listen while you, Jeremy, talk about how I'm a dumb jock and a narcissist and an exhibitionist and a queer, not to mention criticizing me for letting my girlfriend stand up for me when a real man would fight back. You bait me and insult me and what all, but the one thing you haven't been able to do is convince me that your opinion is something I have to care about. I guess you're not important enough to do that. You're just some guy with a nasty attitude. And if I broke up with Athena and moved out of Christopher's dorm room tomorrow and none of you ever saw me again, you, Jeremy, would still be just some guy with a nasty attitude."

"Bravo," Jeremy said, clapping his hands, "the big man speaks. Finally. With such eloquence. And employing so many polysyllables. Did everyone notice? I'm sure we're all very impressed."

"Some of us just might be," Patrick mused, very quietly.

"Well, dear," Athena said, "just so you know, you're absolutely right about Lance. Every time he sticks his penis in me all I can think of is what a big old homosexual he is. Big homosexual with a giant penis in fact. And boy does he know what to do with it. He makes me come and come and come. Dozens of orgasms—swear to God, dozens. Every single time we fuck. I'm practically enslaved to him. Because he's just such a big old homosexual."

"Steady, girl," Lance chuckled, squeezing her hand.

Across the table, Christopher's eyes were as big as saucers.

"You know," Patrick said, "I wonder what Daniel looks like these days. I bet the Marines have the finest gym equipment on the market. Wouldn't you say, Christopher?"

"Nothing but the best for our fighting men," Christopher said.

The next time they were all together, Patrick cut Jeremy off at the pass.

"I'd like to come to the gym with you sometime, Lance," he said. "Maybe you'd give me some pointers."

"Glad to," Lance said.

If anyone should have been showing signs of hostility, Lance thought, it was Patrick. Jeremy's irascibility was mostly a pose. Sure, Athena was his ex-girlfriend, but Lance didn't see a wounded heart's pulsations fueling the glint in Jeremy's eyes. He was, rather, a bully who refused to share his toys, even the broken ones and the ones he was tired of. They were his and always would be. Then, too, Jeremy was the guy for whom no argument was ever truly lost. Long after everyone else considered a matter settled, Jeremy would still be hammering away at it, holding to his contrary position like a solitary general doggedly manning a fortified position though long since outflanked by the advancing enemy army. His quest to regain Athena had little or nothing to do with love. He just didn't want anyone else to have her, and if he could make her mildly miserable in the process of fending off suitors, well, that was fine, too. It was a product of the force of his personality and nothing more.

Patrick, on the other hand, was pure of intent and quietly tenacious. He apparently thought of himself as, indeed styled himself after, the clear-eyed, cool-headed hero of a Victorian novel. Stiff-upper-lipped, soft-spoken, rapier-witted, he seemed to understand instinctively that to squabble over a girl like Athena would serve only to lose her respect and thus any possible interest in him he might be able to elicit. His presumption that she desired a gentleman rather than a hooligan was contrary to the spirit of the times in the same way that a mounted cavalry charge against the machine guns of the Western Front in 1917 had been a misguided notion, but that didn't mean it was incorrect. For Athena defied stereotypes and the pressure of her peers with equal determination. And she apparently did want a man who knew how to behave himself rather than a spoiled boy, however charismatic.

Christopher alone seemed to harbor no aspirations in her direction. Either Athena and he already had some explicit understanding or he instinctively recognized, like Lance did, that she wasn't the girl to attach herself to someone she'd known in high school. They were close, certainly. Uncannily so, it seemed to Lance. It was the easy camaraderie, natural and unforced, of a brother and sister—perhaps fraternal twins—from an unusually well-adjusted family. Lance knew that both Jeremy and Patrick envied Christopher this intimacy with her.

Lance understood Athena because in one important regard she reminded him of his mother. Growing up, he had heard the stories over and over. There had been legions of schoolboys back in Bucharest, there had been serious, proper young men in London and brash, socially adroit, only slightly older men in New York. All of them had wanted her. But it was the university professor, son and grandson of university professors in fact, recently widowed and with a young son—Lance's stepbrother, Martin—whom she had chosen, chosen with the calculation and certitude of an Amsterdam diamond buyer. Lance's experience with Athena confirmed the similarity. She knew her own mind and made her own selections. She would carry this *modus operandi* with her into her future. It was easy to imagine her years hence, her Broadway heyday behind her, raising children in some Connecticut enclave, her husband toiling away on Wall Street or in an operating room.

"You can't say anything to anybody," Athena said.

"About what?"

"Even Christopher. Especially Christopher."

"'Christopher and I have no secrets'," Lance said. "I'm quoting you, you realize."

"Christopher and I have no secrets," she said, "except when there's something I don't want him to know."

"How often would that be?"

"All right, I admit it," Athena said. "Pretty much all the time, really. It's what?—a convenient fiction. My whole relationship with Christopher is. We're both actors, so we never stop playing off each other. You'd think people would figure it out, but they don't. Even Patrick and Jeremy. Hell, especially Patrick and Jeremy. And the thing is, it helps me manage the three of them. They do take managing, you realize."

"So what is it you don't want them to know about now?"

"Promise you won't say anything."

"Fine, I get it," Lance said.

"Daniel's coming for a visit."

"I don't understand."

"You know, my brother Daniel. He's coming for a visit."

"I'm not deaf," Lance said, "just stupid. I thought everybody knew that. Why shouldn't I say anything about it? Why does your brother coming for a visit have to be a secret?"

"He doesn't like them. You know what an asshole Jeremy can be."

"Right."

"They were never mean to him to his face," she said. "They were too scared of him for that."

"He scared them?"

"You'll see when you meet him," she said. "They made sure they only talked about him behind his back. So of course he knew all about it. Without me saying anything. He used to quote them verbatim."

"I still don't get how this is supposed to work."

"It wasn't anything but jealousy, really. Everybody in the county was jealous of Daniel. He's that kind of guy."

"But Athena, how the hell are you planning to keep it a secret from them while he's here?"

"They'll all be back in Red Dog. It's Homecoming. And not by coincidence at all, it's also a three day weekend."

"You're not going to your Homecoming? Aren't you the reigning queen?"

"Not with Daniel coming to visit."

"So you'll tell them—what? About Homecoming, I mean."

"I won't tell them anything. They'll assume I'm going, but I won't be there."

"Won't they suspect something?"

"By then it'll be too late for them to spoil Daniel's visit. He'll have to stay with you. I'll bring you some clean sheets for Christopher's bed."

They were waiting in the dorm lobby when Lance came in from the gym. Daniel had Athena's eyes and a version of her face. The quarter-inch-long fuzz on his head was as blond as her luxuriant mane. In his uniform, he looked as out of place as a giraffe at an ice rink.

"I've got to get to rehearsal," Athena said after introducing them. "I'll be done about seven. We'll go get you some decent Mexican food."

"I'm in good hands," Daniel said, grinning at Lance as she kissed his cheek.

Upstairs, watching him change into civilian clothing, Lance saw that his first impression of Daniel had been correct. What he saw was unquestionably the body of a kindred spirit.

"Short hair for a college boy," Daniel said, flashing that grin again. Unlike Jeremy's, it was guileless. Unlike Christopher's, it didn't remind Lance of the Cheshire Cat.

"Got to keep coach happy."

"Knew you were a wrestler," Daniel said. "Thought you'd be a little shaggier, though. Shouldn't be surprised. Guess Athena prefers the clean cut type these days. More fallout from Jeremy, apparently."

"Sorry if this seems awkward," Lance said.

"Awkward? Why?"

"Meeting the kid sister's boyfriend."

"Maybe if I was trying to make up my mind about you," Daniel said, "but ever since Jeremy Pryce, she's turned into a pretty good judge of character. And she's written me all about you. Not like you're a stranger. She says there's a good gym here on campus, by the way."

"Pretty good," Lance said.

"We'll go tomorrow," Daniel said. "See you in action."

"Sure."

"Sis says you have a bike," Daniel said, staring at Lance's motorcycle helmet with a faraway look in his eye. Lance kept his spare at Athena's dorm these days. "Real fancy one. Except she can't remember any details about it when she sits down to write a letter."

"Triumph Trident," Lance said.

"No shit," Daniel said. "Saving up for one of those myself."

"You ride?"

"Been known to."

"Let's go."

Lance stood on the curb watching the Triumph accelerate into the distance. Daniel was reluctant to take the bike out solo, but Lance thought as long as he was sleeping with Daniel's sister, trusting him with it seemed like the least he could do.

"Never tried wrestling," Daniel said, watching Lance fold laundry.

"No?" Lance said. "You'd have been pretty good, I bet."

"Yeah," Daniel said. "Played football and baseball instead. That kept me busy. Plus I won state championships in shot put, discus, and javelin."

"Athena said."

"Even had a scholarship offer here."

"Why didn't you take it?"

"Got to get this out of the way first. Coaching staff here told me they'd look at me again when I get out. Won't be too old for track and field by then. Like to go to the Olympics someday."

"My goal, too," Lance nodded. His relationship with Athena was making more sense by the minute.

Athena insisted on squeezing into the back seat of the Fiat. Lance tried to relinquish shotgun to her, but she fended off his gallantry with a giggle.

"Somebody's been making sure she keeps it clean," Daniel said, climbing in behind the wheel.

"I've never said a thing to her about it," Lance said.

"Right."

"I know it's your pride and joy," Athena said. "I just don't know why."

"Best car anybody bought for thirty-five dollars since the end of World War II."

"I check the oil every week, too," Athena said.

"She does," Lance said. "She makes me verify her work. That engine looks smaller than what I have on my bike. Is it really just two cylinders?"

"Sure is," Daniel said. "Six hundred cc's. Your bike has about three times as much horsepower."

"The food here isn't quite as good as at *Tia Elena's*," Athena said, scooping up *salsa verde* with a tortilla chip, "but it's not bad."

"She hasn't taken you to Red Dog for a visit," Daniel said.

"I've heard all about it," Lance said. "The boys make it sound like it's crammed full of local color."

"Local, yes," Daniel frowned.

"The lady will have a double serving of flan and a double serving of *almendrado*," Daniel told the waiter. "My buddy and I will watch."

"Very good, senor."

"This guy's abs are as good as mine," Daniel told Athena. "Maybe better."

"I figured you'd notice," she grinned.

"Well, youngsters," Daniel said, locking the Fiat, "time for this old man to hit the rack."

"That's not necessary," Lance said. "You're here to visit your sister. Don't worry about me."

"Actually," Athena said, "rehearsal this evening nearly killed me. You two go and do whatever guys do when their sisters and girlfriends aren't looking."

"I can probably score us some beer," Lance suggested. "Not much of a drinker myself, but. . ."

"No, man," Daniel said. "I really am serious about my abs. Nothing ruins your definition as fast as alcohol. All those calories—God."

"You should see the looks I get from the guys when I mention that."

"They wouldn't understand," Daniel said. "If it's O.K. with you, I'd just like to walk around on campus. See what I'm missing."

"Pretty dead tonight, I'm afraid."

"Isn't somebody supposed to be rioting around here?"

"Probably."

"They're not bad guys, really," Daniel said. "They're just into that small town conformity thing. Oh, I know they talk big about what free spirits they are, but really. If you have to tell people about it—I mean, isn't that something people should just know about you? Anyway, how many guys are there on this campus just like them? Ten thousand or so?"

"About that."

"Their business, of course," Daniel said. "Free country and all that. But the way they work on Athena—girl needs to live her own life just as much as they do. That's what you understand and they don't. They can be doctors and lawyers and buy those houses in the suburbs with white picket fences all they want. Just leave Athena out of it."

"Sounds like you want left out of it, too."

"It's like this," Daniel said. "What kind of fool thinks we can possibly know what will make us happy for life when we're still in our teens? I mean, does that make any sense at all?"

In her diligence about not being fallen in love with, Athena had refused to share anything but the most rudimentary of biographical detail. The here and now, she seemed to believe, was the only safe place for an independent young woman, existentially speaking.

"Athena never talks about your mother," Lance said from the upper bunk.

"She was four months old when we lost Mom. I was just over a year and a half myself. Don't remember a thing from back then. So all we know about her is from what Dad says and some pictures. Every once in a while one of her movies will run on the late show. Terrible stuff. She would never have won an Oscar."

"How did she die?"

"Automobile accident. Guy had just bought a new Aston-Martin and didn't know how to drive it without getting somebody killed. Out near Palm Springs."

"Shit."

"Really bad thing, she was in the process of leaving Dad. She and that guy were running away together. He already had a wife and a mistress. Mom was— God knows who he thought Mom was. Woman of his dreams or what. After that, Dad couldn't get out of L.A. fast enough."

"Your dad never thought about marrying again?"

"There's a woman back home we both think he's been in love with for years. But he won't let himself break up her marriage like his own was. That's the life you sentence yourself to when you move to a place like Red Dog. In L.A. there would have been plenty of opportunities. We'd have had a stepmother and prob-ably some brothers and sisters. That's why I don't want the boys dragging Athena into their little dreams. Jeremy and Patrick are going to open a law firm together, you know."

"Yes, I've heard."

"Can you imagine her married to one of them while the other one is her hubby's business partner? Stuck in that drama for the next fifty years or so?"

"Hardly," Lance snorted.

"Be better off with Christopher, crazy as he is. At least he'd never try to drag her back there."

Sunday morning they went to church. Athena had never given any sign of religious inclinations, but when Daniel suggested it her enthusiasm seemed genuine. It was a sober little Protestant church of a denomination Lance was unfamiliar with, apparently a remnant of their father's Slavic upbringing. They sang out the hymns with a kind of enthusiastic tunefulness, and they knew all the prayers by heart.

"Don't want you getting the wrong idea," Daniel said once they were safely back in the Fiat afterward. "Neither of us believes a word of it. Do we, sis?"

"Opiate of the people," Athena nodded.

"You should have seen our grandmother's face when Athena said that at Christmas dinner one time. Wanted to know where she'd learned at thing like that. Had no idea Dad was such a commie."

"He's not a commie," Athena said. "He's a neo-crypto-Trotskyite. With pacifist undertones."

"Except for church," Daniel said. "Took us every week. Cultural thing, really."

"Hey," Lance said. "It's cool."

"Need you to do me a favor," Daniel said, handing Lance the keys to the Fiat.

"What's this for?"

"Drive me to the bus station in the morning."

"Wouldn't you rather have Athena take you?"

"Nah," Daniel said. "Two of us will just cry. She hates that emotional stuff."

"In that case, sure."

"Awfully early."

"I never sleep late anyway."

"Great," Daniel said. "Just add it to my tab, you know?"

"One more thing," Daniel murmured in the darkness just as Lance was about to drift off to sleep.

"What's that?"

"Sounds a little strange, I know. But I need you to look out for Christopher, too. Poor fuck doesn't have the least idea who he is. Those two put all sorts of crazy stuff in his head. Too easily influenced. That's his problem."

"Really."

"They're all in love with Athena, but he's got the worst case of it. Follow her anywhere. Used to sit all night under a tree across the road from our house, staring up at her window. Saw him out there don't know how many times. Tragic, really."

III

Lance and the guys had been told over and over how unusual it was for a freshman theatre student to be cast in a major university production. Laboratory shows, sure, but main stage? It wasn't completely unheard of, but it was close enough that the distinction was practically insignificant. Obviously, this wasn't the reason they all went to see her. But it was one more thing for them to marvel over: Athena's meteoric rise through the ranks of the spear carriers to near stardom in less than a year. In little over a semester, really, because auditions had been the week they all returned from Christmas vacation.

Athena told the boys not to attend a performance until closing night, claiming their presence would give her jitters. Lance doubted that. From what he'd observed, she had nerves of steel. But they took her at her word and stayed away. Lance, who had attended opening night "undercover" by virtue of having made up a story about an injured teammate, sat with them.

The part was a small one and couldn't remotely be described as pivotal. Athena had only one line to memorize, though she spoke it repeatedly during the first two acts of the play. After that she wasn't to be seen again until curtain calls. The effect of her role was comic, though it wasn't advisable—and arguably wasn't even possible—to play it for laughs. Nor did it offer her any opportunity to steal the show. A perfect performance would be free of either irony or nuance, it seemed. The subtext, and at least there was loads of that, was largely historical and sociological and only distinctive to the character to the tiniest degree. The character herself suggested an archetype without ever taking on the importance of one. She was merely a foil of her mother, one more of Oscar Wilde's gorgons, but only in the most passive ways. There was no confrontation, there was no attempted subversion, and the whole thing was without any Wildean wit whatever. Athena proclaimed the poor girl a virgin martyr while admitting that she was totally devoid of interest. The challenge was minimal, in other words, but she relished it. It could only lead to bigger, meatier roles. She threw herself into it with as much fervor as if it had been positively a vehicle, and the guys competed to see who could most lavishly predict a star turn.

All this was chewed over incessantly during the weeks of rehearsal. The guys had all acted with her in high school and community theatre productions and readily offered advice, insight, and encouragement. Lance, listening time after time to these discussions, marveled at the focus on detail and sheer commitment they indicated. He wondered if he and his teammates sounded equally obsessed and pretentious talking about their sport—when preparing for a big meet, for instance. Eventually he decided that wasn't possible.

Opening night threatened to be an anticlimax after all the analysis Lance had sat through but turned into an epiphany instead. It wasn't that Athena was either sublime or excruciating to watch on stage. It was that he believed her in the role. Unexpectedly, nothing seemed artificial about her performance, not even the British accent. She was as natural onstage in those ridiculous period costumes, repeating that single, absurd line, as air. It seemed as if every time he turned around she was surprising him in some new way.

Closing night the boys wriggled in their seats like piglets as they waited for the curtain to rise. Lance felt like a den mother with a bunch of misbehaving Cub Scouts. Just as the house lights went down, Christopher turned to Lance and murmured, in a British accent as convincing as Athena's, "you know, old chap, I'm positively Lady Windermere's biggest fan". Which Lance thought was pretty funny but at the same time inexcusably predictable.

Afterwards they all waited for her at the stage door. Lance noted that none of the other women in the cast rated such a good looking group of admirers and assumed that this would occasion gossip in the theatre department next week.

The cast party was like the department mixer he had escorted Athena to back in September except more so. The play's run might be over but the performances continued unabated. Only the casting had altered. The whole lot of them right down to the stage crew, apparently actors who hadn't made the cast, seemed to be playing roles. The only people present who were recognizably not in character were like him—dates.

At one point, emerging from a restroom, he overheard someone of indistinguishable gender saying, "no, my dear, not like Lord Darlington at all. Not in the least. He's apparently as straight an arrow as Lord Windermere himself. And so *stalwart*, don't you think? She's rather divine for a freshman girl, it has to be said, but he's *positively* one for the books. He looks like he could snap one like a twig. With one hand tied behind his *broad* back. I mean, what else can one say? Is this the scowl that sunk a thousand ships? Perhaps?"

Recognizing the reference and understanding that it was being applied to him, Lance didn't know whether to laugh or cry.

"Not a bad job, if I do say so myself," Athena said, flourishing her British accent for what Lance hoped would be the last time. At least for a while.

"You were great," he said.

"Oh, I don't mean the performance," she said, shifting back into American. "There wasn't much scope, really. No, I'm thinking about the politics of it. That director is definitely going to want to cast me again. I was a dream to work with. I was never late to rehearsals and I never missed a cue. Plus, I was free of any sign of artistic temperament. Directors hate that, you know. They all cater to it, but they wish it didn't exist. Directors think they're the only ones entitled to be prima donnas. They want actors to be like robots. Wind us up and aim us at the audience."

"Oh."

There wasn't an opportunity to discuss this fascinating topic further, because waiting on a bench just outside the front door to her dorm was her father. At two a.m. on a Sunday morning, that couldn't mean anything but bad news.

She took it amazingly well, Lance thought. He supposed she must still be acting.

"Of course you'll stay at our house," Athena said. "Daddy considers you part of the family. So does Daniel, for that matter."

Lance found it deeply unsettling that she spoke of Daniel as if he were still alive. They'd been over it and over it, and he understood that she didn't believe Daniel was dead. He even understood, in hypothetical terms at least, why she refused to believe it. But referring to him as if he wasn't seemed to be symptomatic of some mental disorder.

"The housekeeper has already gotten the guest room ready," she said. "You don't want to let Mrs. Robek down."

"All right," Lance said. "It just seems—I don't know—inappropriate somehow. I could probably stay at Patrick's house. He even suggested it."

"The whole thing's inappropriate when you get right down to it," she said. "Holding a funeral for someone who's—all right, I won't say it. You and Daddy know what I believe. And the boys, of course. Now that I spilled my guts. They think I'm nuts, but that's nothing new. Anyway, I promise not to make an issue of it. And I'll be suitably grief stricken at the graveside. Just watch."

At least she let him drive. It was his first trip to her home town, and as many times as it had been described to him, he was still astonished at its remoteness. Long before they left the desert floor and started into the mountains, it seemed that they must have left all civilization behind. Cactus and mesquite stretched as far as the eye could see. He floored the gas pedal and they roared along the highway in no danger of exceeding the speed limit. The car seemed as suited for such a journey as a dingy for an Atlantic crossing. And that was well before they got to the mountains.

They took the last stretch up the pass crawling along in second with the engine roaring like a pygmy dragon preparing to breathe fire. On the other side of the crest the canyon was narrower and deeper than he'd imagined it, with much steeper walls. These were terraced and the terraces contained houses, the tiny yard of one on a level with the rooftop of the next, on and on down to the canyon floor. That was where all the public buildings were, it seemed: the churches, the schools, the firehouses, something that might be a hospital.

"Jeez," he said. "I had no idea."

"The boys don't describe it well," Athena said. "I always think that if you squint just right, it's like southern Europe."

"I've got to have a hot bath," Athena said, disengaging herself from her father's teary embrace. "Every time I make that trip in that rattletrap of Daniel's, I have to have a hot bath just to get my wits back."

"Take your time, sweetie," Mr. Kmetko said, wiping his eyes. "You've got all the time in the world. Mrs. Robek left dinner in the oven. We'll eat whenever you're ready."

"Speaking of Mrs. Robek," Athena said, "don't you dare let her throw out any of Daniel's stuff. Not so much as a mismatched sock, you hear? When this is all cleared up and he finally comes home, he'll be furious."

"Sweetie," Mr. Kmetko said, shaking his head.

"I'm serious, Daddy," she said. "I'm not moving from this spot until you promise."

"All right."

"Say it."

"I promise, Athena."

"He didn't have his fingers crossed behind his back, did he?" she asked Lance.

"Not that I could see."

"All right, then," she said on her way out of the room.

"I could use a drink," Mr. Kmetko said. "Join me?"

"Not much of a drinker."

"Mrs. Robek makes tea in a big jar in the back yard. Fills it up with water, throws in half a dozen bags, screws on the lid and leaves it in the sun. I never get over how smooth it is."

"My mom makes it that way," Lance nodded.

"I think it's basically harmless," Mr. Kmetko said, leading Lance toward the kitchen. "I think it's how she's coping."

"You don't think she really believes it?"

"I know she thinks she does," Mr. Kmetko said. "Her grandmother has been claiming psychic powers since I was a boy. She got her predictions and insights right just often enough to keep her convinced she really did know things. Athena has heard those stories dozens of times. Maybe hundreds."

"So it doesn't worry you?"

"Of course it worries me. I just have to make myself believe that eventually she'll deal with the reality and figure out how to go on with her life."

"How about you?"

"I've been through it before."

The house grew quiet, but Lance's curiosity wouldn't let him sleep. He got out of bed and moved to the window. He pulled back the curtain. He was pretty sure he knew where to look. He'd spotted what seemed to be the likeliest place as they drove in earlier. He stared out into the moonlight. He couldn't be certain, but it looked like someone was out there staring at the house.

He pulled on sweatpants and sneakers, readying his excuse in case he encountered Athena or Mr. Kmetko on his way out of the house.

Lance took his time. The glare of moonlight showed him the way, and chorusing coyotes masked the sound of his movements. He made a broad circle downhill from the rear of the house, going around and coming up behind his quarry. The story Daniel had told, bizarre as it was, carried the ring of truth. When he first heard it, Lance had already known Christopher well enough that it sounded completely in character. Now he realized that it wasn't the story itself he had believed in so much as its narrator. There was something about all three Kmetkos that inspired confidence; that almost forced you to trust them. Thus, it wasn't a surprise but an affirmation to see Christopher there staring up at the darkened windows of the Kmetko's house. Christopher—so close Lance could reach out and touch him.

The Kmetkos might not look like the kind of people you'd characterize as deep, but neither did Lance himself. He wouldn't tell Athena about this. She had enough on her mind. For that matter, she might well know about it already. If Daniel hadn't told her, it would be because he judged that she didn't need to know. And Lance wouldn't go against Daniel's wishes.

When the gang referred to the Red Dog Opera House, Lance assumed they were being ironic or that it was an example of misguided small town pride. But the structure was, if anything, even more impressive than they'd intimated. It was the only possible venue, Athena explained, for the memorial service. There wasn't another building in town that could accommodate as large a gathering as had to be expected except for the high school football stadium.

The mayor read a proclamation. A county supervisor read a letter of condolence from Congressman Miller, who regretted his inability to attend due to press of business in Washington. The Red Dog High School choir, sixty voices strong, sang "For all the saints who from their labours rest," which Lance remembered from his Episcopalian boyhood. The pipe organ roared like an especially tuneful wild beast, and on the final stanza, when the audience joined in, twin trumpeters played a descant. Reverend Miller, great nephew of the congressman and pastor of the Methodist church, read a passage from I Corinthians. His wife had been Daniel's senior English teacher. She deputized her husband for this duty because she didn't trust her emotions. The Kmetko's own pastor was about a hundred years old and spoke English with a heavy Scottish accent. His remarks were barely intelligible but at least short.

The president of the Red Dog High School student body, who it turned out was Patrick's cousin, Jason, read a lengthy tribute. The vice president of Daniel's graduating class read the Houseman poem, "To an athlete dying young." She had traveled all the way from Arizona State, where she was majoring in elementary education. It was a ceremony fit for royalty, Lance thought. Because small town American royalty demanded ritual and solemnity as surely as any other brand.

That's what Athena was giving them. She was producer and director of this show. Lance had listened in on the phone calls and knew exactly who was in charge.

Everyone sat silently as "Nights in White Satin" poured out of the speakers. The singer mourned the passing of time—among other things. The strings shrieked, sobbed, soared, and then were silent. The flag-draped coffin was passed carefully from the stage onto the shoulders of the waiting pall bearers on the auditorium floor. The chief mourners were seated on stage. Now Athena rose. Icily regal in a simple black dress, her hair pulled back in the tightest of buns, she looked like a Scandinavian movie star. Her father and Lance stood to either side of her. Together they exited the stage through the wings, emerging a moment later onto the auditorium floor to follow the casket. This was the moment of maximum public exposure for Lance, and he squared his jaw and shoulders and straightened his back, a worthy companion, he hoped, for a princess. They took their place, and the pallbearers, Daniel's former teammates one and all, began their long trudge. Lance turned his head for an instant, brushed the smooth cheek, perfect as statuary, with his lips.

At the graveyard all was performed with the same subdued theatricality as at the opera house. At the last moment, Christopher approached the now undraped casket, the neatly folded flag nestled securely in Athena's arms, and placed a single white rose on the gleaming lid.

"'Good night, sweet prince,'" he quoted, "'and flights of angels sing thee to thy rest.'"

"I know Daniel would hate that," Athena muttered for Lance's ears only, "but I had to give Christopher something to do. Without lines and blocking, he doesn't know who he is."

A moment later, apparently cued by police radio, the great steam whistle sounded at the mine. For decades it had signaled noon, shift changes, imminent blasting, and sundry misfortunes. Today, its long, mournful note embodied the whole town's lament. The sound echoed off the steep canyon walls so that they, too, seemed to share the loss.

"Nowadays they use an electric siren at the mine," Athena said, as they walked back to the car. "The steam whistle is for occasions."

Mrs. Robek and her cohorts had set up the buffet in the courtyard of the hacienda. Heaps of finger sandwiches—deviled ham, tuna, roast beef—held pride of place among relish trays the diameter of truck tires and platters of deviled eggs. The house teemed with mournful young ladies in their Sunday dresses, young men awkwardly balancing their drinks and paper plates, grief stricken ladies of the town, somber looking former teachers.

"He's not the first local boy killed over there," Jeremy said, "just the first Anglo one."

"You can't blame Athena and her dad for this display," Patrick said.

"Of course not," Jeremy agreed. "These people would burn down the courthouse if they thought insufficient respect was being paid."

Christopher stood between them, silent and tragic.

Between trips to restock the buffet, Mrs. Robek and her acolytes chattered away in the kitchen in something that wasn't English or Spanish either one. As Lance and Athena entered, Mr. Kmetko was laughing at something one of them had said.

"Dad taught himself to speak Croatian after we moved here," Athena said. "Daniel says he did it so he could flirt with the church ladies. It's apparently a lot like Moravian. Grandma Kmetko tried to teach us Moravian nursery rhymes when we were little, but Daniel wouldn't have it. 'Moravia is communist. What are you trying to do? Brainwash Sissie and me?' She nearly had a stroke. What a blessing that grandpa is too sick to travel and can't be left unattended."

"What's wrong with him?"

"Inoperable tumor," Athena said. "Exact size and shape of a whiskey bottle."

"Oh."

"They say it's a slow death. Completely painless, too. Except for the onlookers."

"What about your other grandparents?"

"There aren't any, as far as we know. Mom grew up in an orphanage. Said so in her studio biography. God knows what the truth is."

"What kind of woman walks away from kids like those two?" Patrick asked.

"Sssh," Christopher said, "You know nobody ever talks about that."

"That was some parting shot," Lance murmured. "Stuff about what's right and what's an illusion."

"Daniel will laugh until he cries when I tell him about it," Athena grinned. "He doesn't really like the Moody Blues."

"Just hope and pray Cousin Kenny doesn't come back like that," Jeremy said, showing more sentiment than Lance had considered him capable of.

"Lance," Mr. Kmetko said, "I'd like you to meet Anton Stankovik."

"Call me Tony," the man said, offering his hand. He had greased back blond hair, the mustache of a film noir bad guy, and the eyes of a timber wolf.

"Heard about you from Athena," Lance said.

"He was Daniel's trainer," Mr. Kmetko said. "Took him all the way to the Teen Mr. Arizona title. Nearly won Mr. America himself last time he entered."

"Athena says you're taking another run at it this year."

"Daniel was the one with the potential," Tony said. "He could have gone all the way. Damned shame. You look like you know your way around a gym yourself. Ever compete?"

"Took a couple of minor competitions back in Rhode Island," Lance said. "Getting ready for the Mr. Tucson next month."

"See you there, then," Tony said.

"Organizers have invited him to be guest poser," Mr. Kmetko said.

"They're dedicating the competition to Daniel's memory," Tony said.

The class vice president sobbed uncontrollably, and Lance watched as Athena attempted to comfort her.

"Now that Nat Vukovich has finally passed, may he rest in peace, perhaps Vetti and Tad will. . ."

"Never in a million years," Athena said, making a face. "Stupid church lady busybodies."

"Easy, dragon lady," Lance laughed.

"I don't care what plans you made, Patrick," Athena said. "You will offer Nancy a ride home. Christopher and Jeremy can take care of themselves. You can all meet up later and go cow tipping or whatever you've got planned. But you've got to do this for Daniel."

"Thanks for being here, young man," Mr. Kmetko said, sitting in his easy chair in a cloud of pipe smoke.

"I just hope I wasn't underfoot," Lance said.

"Nonsense. She couldn't have gotten through it without you. I know my daughter. I read her like a book."

"Well, anything I can do, of course."

"Daniel said you were steady as a rock. We're pretty good judges of character in this family. Oh, I know what you're thinking. You've heard the story of Athena and Daniel's mother. The truth is I knew even before I married her that it would never work. I just had to let my heart rule my head one time. To see what it was like."

"And what was it like?"

"Sublime," Mr. Kmetko smiled. "For whole minutes at a time. And I ended up getting two indescribable children out of it. There's nothing I wouldn't have gone through for that. Even if I was going to lose my son like this."

"I can't tell you how sorry I am," Lance said.

"He spoke very highly of you," Mr. Kmetko said. "I never thought he'd approve of anybody interested in Athena. That makes you somewhat remarkable."

"He was a terrific guy," Lance said.

"Yes, he was," Mr. Kmetko said. "All fathers think their sons are extraordinary, of course. But I'd like to believe that in this case there's a germ of truth."

"More than a germ," Lance said. "And now it's time for me to turn in, I think."

"You'll stick with her, of course. She's going to need you more than ever, now that this business is over. The really hard part comes later."

"Don't forget what I told you, Daddy," Athena said, kissing him goodbye. "Not a stitch of his clothing, not a record, not a magazine, not a single item of sporting equipment."

"I hear and obey, revered one."

"Finally," Athena said. "Finally somebody around here gets it."

They crested the top of the pass. This time Athena was behind the wheel. Lance had offered to drive, but she said she preferred to. And if the Fiat was going to explode, as seemed all too likely from the sounds coming from the engine compartment, he'd just as soon she was at the controls when it happened. Ahead of them the mountains fell away and the desert floor stretched toward infinity.

"Thank God that's over with," Athena said. "It's all downhill from here."

Lance kept expecting her to crack. She had to crack. But she didn't. Back at her dorm that night, he held her all night long.

V

On the plane on the way back from Nationals, Lance couldn't help being a little smug. He'd placed fourth in his weight class, a full seven places up from last year. Coach was pleased. Actually, coach almost smiled.

The team bus dropped him in front of the dorm. Upstairs the room was dark. Patrick and Jeremy's room was quiet, too. The guys were at the movies or had gone out for late night pizza. There was just enough time to call Athena before the dormitory switchboards shut down for the night.

"Hello."

"It's Lance."

"Hi, Lance, it's Sarah. Athena's not here."

"Oh, hey, Sarah."

"Heard you did really well at Nationals."

"Yeah," he said. "Got a couple of lucky breaks with the opponents I drew."

"I'm sure it wasn't as simple as that," she giggled. "Listen, I'm supposed to tell you to go look for her at Student Health."

"Student Health? She sick?"

"It's Christopher. Some kind of accident. She said it wasn't serious, but you should head over there."

Those idiots were always daring Christopher to do stupid things. Lance fumed on his way across campus to the infirmary. He didn't know who he was angrier with—Patrick and Jeremy, or Christopher for never saying no to them. It was a miracle something hadn't gone wrong before this. When he got there, the main entrance was closed for the night. He had to go around to the emergency entrance and then wait for somebody to respond to the buzzer. He finally found the three of them in the waiting room.

"Thank God you're here." Athena said, collapsing into his arms. She was red- eyed and shaking. She hadn't been this bad then they heard Daniel was dead.

"So what happened?"

"Christopher was assaulted," Patrick said.

"He wasn't assaulted," Jeremy glowered.

"Technically it's an assault," Patrick said.

"Gang rape," Jeremy spat. "Call it what it was, why don't you? He was gang raped by a bunch of football players. He dragged himself home—God knows how—bleeding out the ass. Fuckers just dumped him."

He looked like he held Lance personally responsible.

"You're joking."

"'Fraid not," Patrick said.

"But he's going to be all right?"

"Sure," Patrick said.

"Probably," Athena said a split second later.

"They don't know," Jeremy said. "He lost a lot of blood and he was in shock by the time we got him here."

"Thank God you guys were around," Lance said.

"It was Athena," Patrick said. "He went to her dorm. She called us. He didn't want her to, but she was smart enough not to try and handle the situation without help."

"Oh my God," Lance said, as she started to sob. He held her tight. He didn't know if it comforted her or not, but it was something to do. If he didn't have that job, he just might punch the wall.

"There's the doctor," Jeremy said.

"You all might as well go home," the doctor said. "There's nothing you can do here tonight. We've contacted his father. He'll be coming in tomorrow."

"How is he?" Patrick asked.

"We got the bleeding stopped," the doctor said. "We treated him for shock. We transfused him. I don't think any of his injuries will require major surgery, but we'll know more tomorrow."

"Can we see him?" Athena asked.

"Absolutely not," the doctor said. "Sorry, but I can't allow it. Besides, we've got him heavily sedated. Attack like that, he's traumatized, and reliving the emotional trauma isn't good for him right now. He needs rest and quiet. So please, just go home. You're not doing him any good here."

"What about the authorities?" Patrick asked.

"What about them?" the doctor asked.

"He was attacked," Athena said. "Don't you have to report it?"

"Already done. Campus police will probably want to interview all of you. You saw him before we did, and they'll want to know what he said."

"Those fuckers might have killed him," Jeremy said.

"He doesn't want to see anyone," Athena complained at breakfast the next morning, "and the nurse says they have to enforce his wishes. At least until his father gets here."

"Did they tell you how he is?" Lance asked.

"Improving," she said. "Whatever that means."

"Jocks think they can get away with anything," Jeremy complained over the lunch table.

Athena was missing in action. Lance had convinced her to get some sleep. Sarah had given her some of her sleeping pills. Athena didn't want to take them, but they ganged up on her.

"Because they can," Patrick said. "Jocks always do. Nothing in their collective experience has ever told them they can't, so they behave accordingly."

They were looking at him, Lance noticed, as if they considered him some-how responsible. He decided to ignore it until they actually said something.

"It'll be the same this time," Patrick said. "Just wait and see."

Now, all the emotional display Lance had expected of Athena when Daniel died finally surfaced. She howled, she sobbed. She threw things. Not at him, but she threw them. Sometimes they broke. God only knew what the other girls living on her floor thought when they heard those crashes.

Lance held her until she wouldn't be held any more. He sat silently while she let out all the passion of her grief. Eventually, when she ran back down, he'd take her in his arms again. He lost count of how many times the cycle repeated itself.

He didn't try to argue her out of her feelings. He didn't tell her everything would be fine. He didn't talk at all.

But he didn't leave her alone.

She always managed to snap out of it when there was somewhere she had to be. She didn't miss any classes, for instance, which was more than Lance could say for Patrick and Jeremy. He heard through the grapevine that in rehearsals for her new show Athena was steady as a rock, never missing a cue and never flubbing a line. Lance chalked it up to that Kmetko stoicism. He wished her friends were half as tough as she was.

Sarah all but moved back home so Athena and Lance could have the room to themselves. She told her mother Athena had mononucleosis and then had to explain why she hadn't been quarantined at Student Health. She giggled sheep-ishly telling Lance about having to convince her mother not to call their congress-man and complain about the university's negligence.

If he had been anyone else, Lance wouldn't have worried about what to wear to his interview with the dean. But he was attending the university on a wrestling scholarship. Anything he did or said reflected on the team and on Coach Foster. So he put on a sober tie and his second best suit. Patrick and Jeremy considered him eccentric for even owning two suits. They had no idea. Athena pretended to swoon when she saw him dressed up. She walked with him over to the administration building. She'd already met with the dean and, the next day, gave her deposition to university counsel and the campus police. There was nothing to it, she insisted. But she had no idea, either.

It was a long room with no windows. There was a long table in the middle of it, surrounded by chairs. There were a dozen of them sitting there, middle aged men wearing suits. They all turned to look at Lance when he walked through the door. He had no idea which one was the dean and what the rest of them were doing there. There was one familiar face, however. Reg Murphy, ex-football coach, current athletic director, campus institution. He might have been a hundred years old, the way he looked in that rumpled windbreaker. And there was one face that didn't really go with the others. A middle aged man, like them, but handsome in a way that reminded Lance of a character from one of those soap operas his brothers' girlfriends were addicted to.

"This is Lance Garrison, Dean Wunderlich," the secretary ushering him into the room said, and the man at the head of the table stood.

"Welcome, Mr. Garrison. Please take a seat. We appreciate your being here."

The only empty chair was at the opposite end of the table from the dean. Lance sat. The dean introduced the other men. They were assistant deans and university counsel except for the handsome man. Lance didn't know why he was surprised when that individual was introduced as Christopher's father, Dr. Greene. He supposed he should have noticed the family resemblance. Dr. Greene had fair hair, however, and Christopher's was black. Apparently that had been enough to throw Lance off.

"Mr. Garrison, we're hoping you might be able to help us shed some light on this unfortunate business," Dean Wunderlich said.

"If I can," Lance said, "but I haven't seen or spoken to Christopher since it happened. Everything I know I heard from someone else. I wasn't even on campus at the time. I was traveling with the team."

"Yes, yes," the dead nodded. "Reggie here called that to our attention. Congratulations on your excellent placing at Nationals, by the way."

"Thank you."

"And in your sophomore year. It's a real credit to the university. Now, we've already spoken with the students who cared for Christopher immediately after the incident and got him to the infirmary. Mr. Jenkins and Mr. Pryce. And Miss Kmetko, of course. I believe you know them."

"Yes."

"They've given us full accounts of what Christopher told them and what they observed. The information we need from you is of a somewhat different nature."

"Oh?"

"You see, the other young men involved claim that the incident was not an attack at all and, further, that your roommate instigated what took place."

"I don't understand," Lance said, not liking the direction this was taking. "Why would anyone instigate something like that? I'm not sure I can even imagine how it would happen."

"It's hard to imagine, I agree," the dean said, "but their story is that Christopher initiated the original, well, activity let's call it. Being unfamiliar with such, um, practices, the young men didn't realize what was happening. His injuries were totally inadvertent. They feel terrible about it. They admit that they'd been drinking. They say it would never have happened otherwise. That's no excuse, of course. And it's completely against university regulations."

"Sure," Lance nodded.

"In any case, that's their story. But we didn't bring you here to determine the likelihood of it's being true. Because, as you say, you only know what others have told you about the events. Really, we have only one question for you."

"Yes?"

"If I may, Dean," one of the attorneys said.

"Certainly, Eugene," the dean smiled.

"Mr. Garrison, you've been young Mr. Greene's roommate all this academic year, correct?"

"His name's Melendez-Greene," Dr. Greene interrupted, looking annoyed.

"Of course," the attorney nodded. "Melendez-Greene. Sorry, Dr. Greene."

"Yes," Lance said, "all this year."

"Would you say that you know him well?"

"Pretty well," Lance said. "I mean we got along fine. We spent time together. More than just when we were both in the dorm, I mean. He introduced me to several of his friends."

"Yes," the attorney nodded. "We get the picture, I think. Now had he ever done or said anything that might indicate. . . ?"

"Indicate what?"

"I believe you know what I'm asking you."

"Yeah," Lance said. "I guess I do. Well, the answer to that is no. He never said or did anything like that."

"You're sure?" the dean asked. "He never said or did something that might have seemed insignificant at the time, but in retrospect. . ."

"No," Lance said. "Nothing."

"Take your time," the dean encouraged.

"Really," Lance said. "It's not the kind of thing that would slip your mind, is it?"

"I suppose not," the dean conceded. "Gentlemen? Any further questions for Mr. Garrison?"

"Thank you," Dr. Greene said.

On their way out of the Dean's office, Dr. Greene had invited Lance to lunch. Lance was reluctant to accept after that harrowing scene but couldn't figure out how to decline graciously. A short drive from campus in Dr. Greene's Mercedes-Benz, the same color and model Lance's mother drove, and here they were facing each other across the small table with only a large bowl of tortilla chips and a small one of salsa separating them.

"I mean it," Dr. Greene went on. "I appreciate your trying to protect Christopher that way."

"I wasn't. I. . ."

"Of course you were," Dr. Greene smiled. "Not all young men in your position would have, but you did. You're his roommate, but I'm his father. I'm sure I sound like one of *those* fathers, but I actually do know my son."

"Maybe," Lance admitted.

"The thing is, unless he's with his close friends or is preparing some role for the stage, I'm afraid Christopher isn't quite sure who he is. He's always been like that. No, scratch that. He's been like that since junior high. Before that he was just quiet. My theory is that it has something to do with the onset of puberty. Lots of psychological conditions seem to become apparent at that time. Not surprising really. In Christopher's case it's a question of identity. Surely you've noticed his personality is, well, indistinct."

"Maybe a little."

"You understate the case," Dr. Greene said. "For that matter, he always takes other people's lead, socially speaking. You must have noticed. It's not a matter of bowing to their influence. I don't mean that. It's more like listening for cues. He goes through life like an actor who wanders onto the wrong stage during a performance he hasn't rehearsed and has no script for. When my wife and I saw *Rosencrantz and Guildenstern are Dead* in London, I was struck by how it seemed to describe my son's predicament."

Lance had to admit that the man's grasp of Christopher's character seemed uncannily on the mark. He had recently had a conversation with Athena that covered more or less the same ground.

"*Pollo con mole,*" Dr. Greene told the waiter, who had just arrived at their table. "*Tortillas de mais.*"

"*Si, senor.*"

"Could I get a hamburger, please?"

"Is that all you want?" Dr. Greene asked.

"Sure."

"Bring him two hamburgers," Dr. Greene said. "*Dos hamburguesas.*"

"*Si, senor.*"

"No fries," Lance said.

The waiter nodded and left.

"Yes," Dr. Greene nodded. "Your body fat is quite low, isn't it?"

Lance shrugged.

"I'm sure your coach appreciates your self-discipline."

"He hasn't actually said so," Lance said.

"But I'm sure he's noticed," Dr. Greene said. "It's really quite obvious to someone who knows what he's looking at."

Lance shrugged.

"It's not the sexual aspect of it that worries me, you know," Dr. Greene said.

Lance held his breath.

"It really isn't. Certain individuals are inclined that way. For them, what seems abnormal to the rest of us isn't. That's all. I'm a doctor. I know this. Science is increasingly verifying it, but it'll probably take a generation or two for the culture to catch up. Christopher has an uncle like that—on his mother's side. Perhaps it's not surprising. It's entirely possible it runs in families. I recognized it in him, or at least thought I did, a long time ago. I knew the signs because of a good friend I had in college. Best man at my wedding, actually. It's not important. To his mother or me. I hope you understand that."

Lance nodded.

"What is important is that I don't want him mistreated for it. Ever."

"Of course."

"So you see that?"

"Yes."

"Not everybody does," Dr. Greene said, "in this supposedly civilized country."

"No."

"I'm not saying he's blameless in this incident. Those young men may well be telling the truth. But even if they are, the thing got out of hand and he was injured. That's what I can't tolerate. I have to tell you, I don't have much confidence in Dean Wunderlich. He only seems interested in sweeping the whole thing under the rug. I understand it completely. I'd probably do the same thing in his position. But still, Christopher is in the infirmary."

"You know," Lance said. "You don't have to worry about him coming back to the dorm. His friends—we'll look out for him."

"I know you mean that," Dr. Greene said. "I appreciate it more than I can tell you. It speaks very well of your character, under the circumstances. But there's no question of his coming back here. I couldn't possibly allow it. Facing down the rumors every time he leaves your dorm room. No, that's too big a strain for anyone. Other than Dean Wunderlich, the university officials are being remarkably cooperative. There's to be no notation of any kind in his records. He just suffered a sudden illness and was unable to finish the semester."

"You can't be talking about him dropping out of college."

"Of course not. He'll transfer. One of my forebears helped found a small college in the east. Christopher will go there next fall. I have an old friend from Choate who's Dean of Students there. It'll just take one phone call to arrange it."

"Oh."

"I should have sent him there in the first place. You know, it's quite a paradox. The larger the university, the greater the imperative to conformity. It takes a small institution to respect difference. To tolerate eccentricity."

"I never thought of it that way," Lance said. "So you'll take him home when he's ready to leave the infirmary."

"No," Dr. Greene said. "Red Dog's not safe for him now. Jeremy and Patrick will surely have said something to some of his friends back there. No matter how sympathetically they try to describe the matter, the story will take on a life of its own. It would be as bad as if he stayed here. Worse, actually. No, my wife will take him to stay with her brother in Paris. He'll come back to the States at the end of the summer. You know, I should have sent him to Hamilton-Greene in the first place. Completely away from everything familiar. Those friends of his. They're nice enough young people, but their influence hasn't been good for him. How could it be? He isn't like them at all, yet they make him feel that he needs to be. As if he even can be. No, I should have placed him in a situation that would force him to develop an identity of his own. Perhaps it's not too late."

"I'm sure he'll be fine," Lance said.

"You know, Lance," Dr. Greene said. "One can't help noticing it. You're remarkably attractive. In a completely masculine way, you understand."

Lance had heard this in one variation or another all this life. He didn't see it himself, but otherwise it seemed pretty unanimous.

"And yet Christopher never approached you," Dr. Greene said. "That wasn't a question, so no response is necessary. I know he didn't. And I'll tell you why. Too close to home. That's what it was. That's all it could have been."

It wasn't a lie if you were protecting a friend, who, in any case, was no more than fifty per cent to blame for what had happened. Dr. Greene certainly understood that. And as for the college officials, Lance didn't much care what impression they had of him. Either they believed in his truthfulness or they didn't. If they didn't, the remedy was simple. Keep his nose clean and let his wrestling and his academics take care of the rest. The football players? They were football players. That was the whole point. Their account would determine the outcome of the investigation. Lance's testimony called their story into question but only peripherally. It did so without contradicting the football players in any material way. His lie harmed no one.

So that wasn't what he blamed himself for.

But he had known. He had seen that one football player leaving their room more than once. Dozens of times, really, beginning back in the fall. He had even asked Christopher about him one afternoon, arriving back at the room just after the football player had left. Christopher said they'd been studying for their algebra midterm, but his bedding had been a mess and the room smelled of sex. So Lance had known. And he supposed Christopher knew that. Lance hadn't challenged Christopher's explanation. Christopher's oblique denial of that unspoken challenge had become their truth. Lance hadn't asked again. He hadn't mentioned the football player at all. Ever.

Lance didn't blame himself for that, either. Pretending not to know what he knew for all that time. What else was he going to do? Christopher and he had to go on living together. Either that or explain why they couldn't. Explain to the people in the office of student housing and to Patrick and Jeremy and Athena. Come up with a plausible story about why one or the other of them was moving out and stick to it. And who needed all that hassle? It had made perfect sense to just ignore it at the time and it still did.

But that wasn't all Lance knew. Because he'd seen that football player plenty of times and the resemblance was unmistakable, if superficial. So what he blamed himself for at first was not stopping it. He could have done that so easily. Just say, "hey, Christopher" and unzip his fly and let it happen. He'd had his cock sucked by a guy before. It wasn't the end of the world.

What could be safer or more discreet than your own dorm room, with your own roommate? It would have had nothing to do with Athena. Christopher and he could have kept the secret. They were both used to lying to the guys. Athena might have been more difficult to keep in the dark, but who knew? She might even have agreed to look the other way. After all, it would have been pretty much the same arrangement that she and Lance had. He almost wished he'd done it. He might have been able to save Christopher whatever ordeal he was going through now. But there had been no guarantee things wouldn't have turned out worse rather than better. Athena was apparently independent and determined enough not to fall in love with Lance, but he'd had no such assurance in Christopher's case. That, finally, was what had tipped the balance. Now, though he felt terrible about what had happened, he was actually relieved that he hadn't gone through with it. Because look how things had turned out.

Lance didn't want to believe the story the football players had told, but he had to admit it was probably true. He'd never say as much to anyone, but he knew what he knew. That's why the dean was even willing to listen to the guys who'd hurt Christopher. Their story made sense, given what every man in that room knew. What had happened wasn't the kind of thing guys sat around thinking about doing whether they were football players, cowboys, or astrophysicists. When normal men fantasized, they fantasized about girls. Who would even think up a thing like that? Lance knew who: Christopher must have suggested some kind of group activity to the guy he'd been seeing. Hell, Christopher might even have blackmailed him into organizing it. That scenario made a whole lot of sense, unfortunately.

If Christopher hadn't been hurt, there might have been a second episode and then a third. That was all too easy for Lance to imagine. And he could have ended up in that trap himself.

"Nice practice, Garrison."

"Thanks, coach."

"Got a minute to come talk to me? After your shower?"

"Sure coach."

Lance was expecting this. It had been a couple of days now since his meeting with the dean. He'd had lots of time to think. There had been no mistaking the expression on Reg Murphy's face. And an unhappy athletic director was a student athlete's worst nightmare. Obviously, what Lance should have done was corroborate the football players' story, instead of which he'd defended Christopher. His defense hadn't been explicit, but there wasn't much subtlety about a man like Reg. He'd see the thing in black and white.

Lance had been trapped. That was all there was to it. If he had given the dean and the lawyers what they so obviously wanted, the question would have then been why, knowing Christopher as he did, hadn't he gone to Student Housing and requested a move? That's what anyone else would have done, finding out that his roommate was that way. They didn't like such requests at Student Housing. Not in the middle of the semester like that. But Lance was a varsity athlete. Wrestling might not have the clout that football or basketball did, but student housing would have worked something out just to keep Reg Murphy off their backs.

Worse, Lance had let himself be trapped. He'd been trapped, really, since the very first time he saw that football player come out of their dorm room checking his zipper. Now there was nothing to be done but face the music. Coach was going to yank his scholarship and throw him off the team. Depending on how pissed off Coach and Reg were, they might or might not help him transfer to another program. Well, if he was going down, he was going down like a man. No begging, no apologies, no tears.

"Come in, Garrison, come in," Coach Foster said, seeing him in the doorway. "Take a load off."

"Thanks, Coach."

Coach didn't look like a man about to crush anybody. But then, he never did. Lance had seen it happen before, like a tornado arriving out of a clear blue sky. Guys had been cut from the team. Had lost their scholarships. One guy had attempted suicide because of it. Coach never backed down. He was a tough bastard.

"Had a visit from Reg Murphy. Said you handled yourself real well with Dean Wunderlich the other morning. Cool as ice, how Reg described you. Stood up to that crowd like a man. Not surprised. Always represent the program well, clean cut guy like you. Good manners but no pushover. Just the type I like on my squad. Much appreciated, young man, much appreciated. Had to be tough, finding out something like that about your roommate. Reg said you didn't bat an eye. Well, why would you? Since it didn't have anything to do with you, I mean. So—well, proud of you, son."

"Thanks, coach."

"Wouldn't want to be in Harry Sorenson's shoes. That's for damn sure. Even if you believe those boys' story that it was an accident, fact remains they had their cocks somewhere they never should have been. No way around that one. Now he's got guys on the squad who did a thing like that and all the other players know it. Bad for morale. Very worst thing. Can't cut them from the squad. Looks like you're admitting something. Have to bluff your way through it. Harry's stuck with them. At least for another season. Poor bastard. It's a coach's nightmare. Never happened to me, and it's never going to. I'm more careful about the men I recruit. Right, Garrison?"

"Right."

"Isn't like there aren't plenty of young ladies around. Guy has to put his cock somewhere. Everybody understands that. Might even have made sense to do what they did back when I was in school and this place wasn't coed. But you didn't hear me say that."

"No, coach."

"Reg says that young lady of yours—real knockout. Smart, too, apparently."

"Genius, pretty much," Lance said.

"You'll want to hang onto that one."

"Yes, sir."

"Now, about next year, Garrison. Think we need to do a little better by you than we've been doing. Proved yourself over the last two seasons. That placing at Nationals. Have to start considering you a serious Olympic prospect. Seems a long way off, I know, but Munich is really just around the corner. Think we can swing a single room for you in the dorm at least. Probably some additional cash for incidentals. Need to take care of a fine young athlete like you. This comes right from Reg's desk, understand? 'He's a great asset to the university's varsity athletics program'—what he said. 'Course I agree with him on that. Hundred percent."

VI

"Patrick's O.K.," Lance said. "At least he is when Jeremy's not around. Like when we're at the gym working out. But Jeremy doesn't want anything to do with me. When I run into him in the dorm, he looks right through me. Or pretends to."

"Being ignored by Jeremy isn't such a bad thing," Athena said, pulling her hair into a bun.

"Oh, it's not like I mind," Lance said, pulling on his jeans. "I stopped caring about Jeremy's opinion of me about five minutes after I met him. I just think their reactions are—not strange, exactly but, oh, hell, here I am talking nonsense."

"The circumstances are unusual," Athena said. "No getting around that."

"You spend more time with them than I do," Lance said. "Do they ever mention him at all?"

"They talked about him a lot at first."

"Now it's like the whole thing never happened, isn't it?" Lance said. "Or no—like he never existed."

"They've had time to think about it," Athena said. "They've been recalling things about him. Things he said and did that seemed insignificant at the time, but now. . ."

"They don't believe the football players," Lance said. "Not really."

"They'd never come right out and say it," Athena said. "Jeremy won't even admit it to himself. But Patrick's always been the one blessed with an open mind. Which in this case turns out to be a curse. He can't help imagining it from all possible perspectives. And no good can come of that. Let's just say they both believe enough of what the football players said that it's affected the way they think about him."

Lance thought it was interesting that Athena and he could have a conversation about Christopher without mentioning his name.

"Do you believe the football players?" Lance asked, poking at his scrambled eggs with a fork that had passed through the hands of God only knew how many students during its career.

"It's not that simple," Athena said, staring at her waffle.

"You either believe them or you don't, seems to me."

"I know you don't," Athena said.

This was what he had wanted to find out when he started the discussion. What she thought he believed. Somehow, that was important.

"Well," she went on, "I believe that truth and facts aren't the same thing. It's like that thing with the two circles that overlap. You know that thing—one circle is truth and the other circle is facts and the little thing in the middle. . ."

"Venn diagram," Lance said.

"That's it," Athena said. "I couldn't remember what it was called for the life of me. O.K., in this case, the overlappy part is very small. Because the truth and the facts have very little to do with each other."

"You do believe the football players. You think that he. . ."

"I think it isn't either/or," she said. "I think nobody knows what really happened that night or why, least of all the people who were present at the time."

"Fair enough, I guess. Do you ever hear from him?"

"No," she said, too quickly. Or maybe it was that she sounded too emphatic.

"Funny," Lance said, "I got the idea you did. Like once or twice."

"Maybe," she said.

"But not for public consumption."

"Athena, I'm so glad I found you."

"Sarah what's wrong?"

"You're supposed to call your father," Sarah panted. "I didn't know if I should give him the number at Lance's dorm. I was afraid it might confuse him. So I just took the message. But call him right away."

"It's O.K., Sarah," Lance said.

"Oh, God," Athena muttered, "What now?"

"Easy, girl," Lance said, reaching across the table for her hand.

"He didn't say anything was wrong," Sarah said, "but he was really insistent that you're to call immediately. At home, that is, not at his office."

"My dorm is closer," Lance said. "Unless you want me to leave you alone."

"Your dorm," Athena said, standing up. "Let's go."

"Didn't I tell you?" Athena shouted into the phone. "Didn't I, Daddy?"

Apparently, the military had made a terrible mistake.

"There was some mix up with dogtags or something," Athena said. "Those poor people from Iowa showed up at the hospital in Japan expecting to see their son, and lo and behold it was Daniel. It's taken the authorities all this time to figure out who he really is."

"How is he?"

"He's conscious and ambulatory," Athena said, "but he still doesn't remember a lot. When he first came to, his amnesia was pretty much total. After those poor people left, the authorities got to work trying to figure it out. When they finally tried out 'Daniel Kmetko' on him I guess it fit. Daddy's flying out tomorrow."

"You bastards didn't believe me," she grinned. There was a smudge of pizza sauce on her chin. Lance wiped it off with his thumb. "Poor Athena. Poor crazy girl, deranged with grief. Twentieth century Ophelia, no doubt about it. Watch her carefully so she doesn't do something desperate. But I knew he wasn't dead."

"So how is he?" Patrick asked. "When your dad called from Japan, what did he say?"

"Physically Daniel's right as rain," she said. "Other than the hairline fracture to his skull, he wasn't hurt. Now that Daddy's there and he has a familiar face to look at, the amnesia is clearing pretty fast. Looks like they'll be sending him home on leave soon."

"Leave?" Jeremy was aghast. "Shouldn't they be getting ready to discharge him?"

"Discharge Daniel?" Athena laughed. "Not until he's good and ready. Daddy will just be happy if he doesn't go back to Viet Nam right away. He's hoping they'll send Daniel to Camp Pendleton."

"Do you think she really knew?" Patrick asked.

They had dropped her at her dorm and were headed back across campus.

"Not a chance," Jeremy said. "It's just a weird coincidence."

"I'm not so sure," Patrick said.

"That's not the point," Lance said.

They looked at him like he was a Martian.

"What I mean is," he told them, "she truly believes she knew. That's what matters."

"You know," Patrick said, "you may be right."

"Bullshit," Jeremy snorted.

VII

"And now, ladies and gentlemen, to assist in the presentation of trophies, please welcome back to the stage our special guests: three time Mr. Arizona, two time Mr. Western America, and three time Mr. America finalist, Anton "Tony" Stankovik, and former Teen Mr. Arizona and Purple Heart and Bronze Star recipient, United States Marine Corps Lance Corporal, Daniel Kmetko."

"That's our cue," Tony said.

"Roger," Daniel nodded. He reached up to adjust his cap.

Lance thought he was ridiculously handsome in his dress uniform. A caricature, practically. Tony's black sweatshirt carried the legend, "United Mine Workers Local 1079. Red Dog Copper." Two species of male glamor, in other words. Military and Working Class.

"See you out there in a few minutes," Tony growled.

"You've got first place in the bag," Daniel grinned. "Don't you think so, Tone?"

"I've known judges to come in with amazingly bizarre results in these local contests," Tony said. "But yes, Lance was obviously the top man out there."

Lance listened as the teen class placings were called. He was woozy from a combination of heavy exertion and extreme hunger. He'd be lucky not to fall flat on his ass when the men's open class went onto the stage. Next came the novice class. The teen winner took first there, too. After that the junior men went out. Backstage suddenly seemed deserted.

"Men's Open finalists, please come onstage," the emcee said.

Lance followed the others in from the wings.

"In fifth place, from Davis Monthan Air Force Base, Airman First Class Leland Jackson."

Daniel handed off the trophy, Tony shook the hand. Leland waved to the audience and fell back into line.

"In fourth place, from South Tucson, Rodolfo 'Rudy' Estrada."

Lance watched the tableau repeat itself. He knew now he'd placed no lower than third, but he didn't dare think about it. He was about to come out of his skin as it was.

"In third place, from Avra Valley, Johnny Miller."

Lance closed his eyes and took deep breaths.

"In second place, from Sahuarita, Martin Turner, and our overall winner, representing the University of Arizona where he's on the varsity wrestling squad, Lance Garrison."

He couldn't believe it. There had been at least four men there he thought were better. He already had a long mental list of things he'd do differently preparing for his next contest.

"I know you're dying for pizza," Daniel said, shaking Lance's hand like he was pumping water from a well, "but Dad's got his camera equipment here. You'll be glad you've got some shots of yourself in peak condition."

"Tad really knows what he's doing," Tony nodded. "For all practical purposes he's a professional. And his equipment is the best available."

"Athena and the guys can go to Fiorito's and put our orders in," Daniel said. "Give them something to do."

"You're not worried about Jeremy?"

"She's got 'em both in check," Daniel grinned. "We'll catch up with them there."

"They only came tonight because she threatened them with I don't know what."

VIII

"Don't take this wrong," Athena said, slipping on her panties, "but I'm not sure if it's a good idea for us to continue this arrangement next fall."

"Something wrong with it?" Lance grunted, half asleep.

"Nothing," she said. "Not a thing."

"So?"

"Seriously," she said. "I can't explain it. You're nice, you're fun to be around, you're as trustworthy and faithful as a Labrador Retriever. Not to mention the sex is as great as ever. I'm probably an idiot. No, scratch the probably. I'm an idiot for sure. I don't know what it is."

"You're not an idiot," Lance said. It sounded like a girl thing. Nothing to worry about.

"Then why do I feel so stupid?"

"Because you spend too much time listening to Patrick. And don't get me started on that Jeremy."

"You're probably right."

"You know I am," he said. "If Christopher were here, he'd tell you."

This was his trump card lately. It hadn't failed yet. That was probably just a matter of time.

"But I can't make up my mind," she said. "I don't know what I want. I need time to think."

"You'll have all summer."

"Yes," she said. "I will."

"Good," he yawned, "be sure to let me know what you decide."

"You'll be the first, rest assured."

"Hey, there's no need to be all tragic about it."

"Sorry," she said. "The thing is I just can't help feeling I'm being unfair to you."

"You should really let me worry about that."

"But what if you wouldn't say anything about it? That would be just like you. And what if I was keeping you from being with some other girl? Who'd treat you better than I do?"

"You treat me fine."

"Don't interrupt—someone who'd fall in love with you."

"Not interested."

"You say that," Athena said, "but can I really believe it?"

"People tell me I'm as trustworthy as a Labrador Retriever."

IX

July 18

Dear Lance,

I meant to write much sooner, but Athena keeps forgetting to send me your address. I'm enclosing some 8x10's of you that Dad shot after the Mr. Tucson. Impressive, my friend!

Tony says you could go a long way in the sport, and he knows what he's talking about.

Things here at Camp Pendleton are pretty good. Much better than my last post! I'm learning to surf. I never had the chance to do that in 'Nam.

I just want to thank you again for everything you did for Athena. Especially while I was dead. She says she wouldn't have gotten through it without you. I know that's true and I'm really glad you were there. She's a smart girl and very strong but everybody needs a really solid guy (like you) beside them sometimes.

She's having a great time working at the Shakespeare Festival. Dad went to see her last week as Hermia in *A Midsummer Night's Dream*. He said she was great.

I went to a bodybuilding show in L.A. a couple of weekends ago. You would have liked it. I'm thinking about competing soon. What do you think? Daniel Kmetko, Mr. California?

Anyway, amigo, thanks for everything. I'm sure we'll cross paths again before too long!

Daniel

ELI DANZIGER: 1969

I

The new guy on the hall looked like trouble. Eli had seen the unfamiliar, hyphen-
ated name on the roster at the R.A. meeting the day before the dorms opened.
The new guy couldn't be a freshman. He'd never have rated a single room even if
he had the money for it. A transfer student then, presumably one with some sort
of clout. An uncle on the Board of Governors, for instance. Lots of Eli's fellow
students had connections like that. This one remained a name only until the day
before classes started. Catching sight of him for the first time, even in the dim
corridor, Eli could hardly go on breathing.

Eli's usual type was broad shouldered and big chested. Eli's usual type was,
or at least looked like he could be, on the football team. Or the wrestling squad.
Or spent most of his waking hours in the gym lifting weights. Eli's usual type
was perfectly exemplified by his best friend Denise's boyfriend, Cliff. Baby faced,
huge muscled Cliff. A ridiculous juxtaposition: that pretty boy mug perched atop
those monumental shoulders. Eli admitted its incongruousness even as the fervor
of his admiration raged. Could you talk yourself out of what attracted you? God
only knew Eli had tried. But Cliff's arms were monstrous and his chest muscles
seemed to get bigger by the week. That trumped everything. The new guy wasn't
that type at all. From the neck down there was nothing out of the ordinary about
him. But that face, that hair, that skin, those eyes. Eli couldn't keep himself from
staring. His mouth was probably hanging open.

Trouble—that was all there was to it.

The kind of threat the new guy represented was nothing new or unusual.
It went back to Eli's childhood and was for all practical purposes ubiquitous.

Because of it, school was hell. In fact, life generally was hell. There had never been a time or a place when Eli wasn't aware of all the great looking guys in the world and at the same time aware that the degree of his awareness, his avidity at the phenomenon of masculine beauty, was the deepest, darkest secret a boy could have. Back during the summer, Denise had gotten all excited about some riots she heard about in Greenwich Village. She even tried to get Eli to go down there with her one night for a look, but he pled stomach trouble and she wouldn't go on her own. Not that there was anything particularly noteworthy about riots lately. It seemed like people were constantly rioting about something. Eli had been in a riot himself back in high school. Some of his classmates decided that their school's dress code was such an egregious instance of fascist and/or bourgeois oppression that a radical response was imperative. Denise even went to the New York Public Library to research how to make Molotov Cocktails. On learning they weren't a mixed drink, she lost interest. The day was cold and rainy and the riot fizzled out. Nobody managed so much as to get suspended from school. The administration rewrote the dress code extensively but made the changes effective only after Eli's class graduated. Since all that, Eli had been a skeptic on the subject of riots. He hardly paid attention when Denise first started talking about these. But the riots she was talking about involved gay people rioting against police harassment. Denise insisted that made them unique in the whole history of rioting. In the whole history of human civilization, for that matter. Denise said those riots were the start of something that would change Eli's life. He doubted it. It was one of those times he wished he'd never told her about himself. There were lots of them.

Eli didn't mention the new guy on his floor to Denise. She'd want to know all about him. If Eli described him accurately, she'd make a federal case of it. If he tried minimizing Christopher's attractiveness she'd sense his evasion and make a federal case of that. She'd end up diagnosing Eli as suffering from sexual jealously—again. It really got old. Denise knew him too well. He could hide things from everyone else, but with her he didn't bother trying. It had been that way since their grade school days, long before he'd known he was homosexual. The best he could do with Denise was delay the inevitable. It was a small campus, and she was bound to encounter Christopher sooner or later. She was the kind of girl who'd get his full biography out of him within five minutes, and even sooner than that she'd realize the significance of his presence just down the hall from Eli in the dorm. He'd have to face the music then. But as long as he could keep Christopher a secret he wouldn't have to listen to her analysis of his own psycho-sexual state. That was never fun, particularly when he was sitting across from her and Cliff in the student union cafeteria. He understood that Cliff didn't know quite what to make of the fact that his girl's best friend was a homosexual. Or, for that matter, that homosexuals existed outside the pages of textbooks on abnormal psychology. Other than Denise, Cliff was the only person on campus who knew about him. At least Eli hoped that was still true. With Denise you could never tell how safe your secrets were.

Denise and Cliff had met on the first day of freshman orientation, two years ago now. Eli was there. He heard their first words to each other, which couldn't have been more inconsequential. He still wasn't sure it had been love at first sight. Indeed, he wasn't sure it was love at all by the usual criteria. But Denise and Cliff were so perfectly matched, at least on a visual level, they simply had to be a couple. It was the romantic equivalent of the law of gravity. Regardless of how they actually felt about each other on any given day, they symbolized so much and embodied the dreams and aspirations of their peers to such a degree that their couplehood was a campus imperative.

Eli didn't know what that made him exactly. If he had been Cliff's best friend rather than Denise's, the situation would have been much clearer. As it was, their fellow students found the threesome a little baffling. They would have accepted it had Eli found a girlfriend himself and made the triangle a square. But he never did that. Worse, he'd never shown any interest in doing so. He understood the impression it gave. If Denise and Cliff had been less iconic, their classmates' skepticism might have been expressed in ways that couldn't be ignored. That was the current situation: everyone agreeing to pretend that there wasn't anything to be concerned about. In other words, Eli was pretty sure his secret wasn't much of one. More like a secret of convenience, if there was such a thing. Still, he couldn't set foot outside the dorm without being reminded of the ambiguity of his position.

As always when they were alone together, Cliff and Eli didn't have much to talk about. And they were alone together more than you might have thought. More, really, than either of them would have preferred. The reason for it was simple. Denise wasn't particularly punctual. For instance, she would suggest they meet at the student union for lunch at such and such a time and they'd get there and commandeer a table and wait for her for twenty, thirty, sometimes forty-five minutes. Eli found it infuriating and he couldn't imagine Cliff liked it any better. Eli couldn't leave for fear of giving offense to Cliff. More than that, he couldn't leave because giving up an opportunity to be around Cliff, as uncomfortable as it made him, was unthinkable. Those shoulders, that hair, the gruff rumble of that voice even though Cliff's vocabulary was distressingly limited, made Eli tingle all over. Meanwhile, Cliff gave the impression that he didn't care how long he had to wait for Denise except that being stuck with Eli obviously wasn't his idea of a good way to spend his time. Eli couldn't imagine what Cliff's teammates thought, or perhaps even said, about the situation.

Today, however, Denise was almost early. They'd only been sitting there for about five minutes and hadn't yet run out of meteorological topics to discuss when she sauntered up, her grin somewhat more relentless than usual. She wasn't by herself.

"Boys, I'd like you to meet our new friend," she said. "This is Christopher."

"We've met," Eli said.

"Yes," Denise said. Her nod was exactly the accusation Eli had been expecting when the time eventually came, "and this, Christopher, is my boyfriend, Cliff."

"You weasel," Denise said, setting her books down on the table across from Eli's legal pad and stack of index cards.

"Not so loud," he told her. "This is a library, in case the significance of all those shelves full of books is lost on you."

"Who am I supposed to be disturbing? We're the only two people in the whole building."

"Surely not."

"The staffers don't count," Denise snorted. "But they can hear. They do throw loudmouths out."

"Don't try to change the subject," Denise said. "It'll just be worse for you later."

"All right."

"You never said anything about the handsomest guy in the world moving onto your floor."

"I thought Cliff was the handsomest guy in the world."

"There you go again," she complained.

"Huh?"

"I'm trying to talk to you about Christopher."

"Nobody's stopping you."

"It's just, how are you ever going to find a boyfriend if you don't even try?"

"Who wants a boyfriend?" Eli asked, pretending to stifle a yawn.

"Everybody wants a boyfriend," Denise said.

"Around here?" Eli asked. "What are you talking about? One false move and all hell would break loose. I could get arrested. I could have to go see the dean and explain myself. I could even get expelled, and after that my parents would have me committed. Except before any of that could happen, the football team would kill me. Cliff would have to help them regardless of my friendship with you. You know all this."

"Those are just excuses," Denise said. "Nobody's that paranoid. Not even you."

"Who says?"

"Well, at least you'd agree with me that hypothetically speaking, Christopher would be perfect for you."

"I don't think he's wired the same way I am," Eli said, "and even if he was, why would a guy like that have anything to do with somebody like me?"

"You always sell yourself short," Denise said.

"Could we not have this discussion?" Eli pleaded.

"All right," Denise said. "I see that once again I'm not going to get anywhere with you."

"That's right."

"But don't think you're getting off that easy," Denise said. "I just may have to take matters into my own hands."

She had made that threat before. Frequently. Eli wasn't worried. Besides, Christopher hardly knew he existed. That day at lunch, Christopher had paid him no attention whatever.

II

Eli was in the habit of showering at off hours. His explanation for this, though no one ever asked, would have been that he couldn't stand the noise, confusion, and waiting in line that marked peak times in the shower room, but the real reason was that he was reluctant to be seen naked by the other residents of the floor. There wasn't anything particularly wrong with his body, though he incorrectly considered himself abnormally hairy. But there wasn't anything particularly right with his body, either. And though to a normal young man this wouldn't matter because to a normal young man that distinction would have little or no significance, it bothered Eli. He wondered from time to time why he didn't go over to the gym and ask Cliff for some pointers aimed at building himself up. He couldn't imagine ever developing the kind of physique Cliff had, certainly. But he might be capable of achieving something just impressive enough that he wouldn't feel so mortified at the swimming pool or the beach. So far he hadn't acted on this impulse. He was pretty sure it would never attain any status beyond that of a pipe dream.

Meanwhile, he liked having the entire shower room to himself; liked not having to feel self-conscious. He could take as much time as he wanted without worrying about who was waiting for a turn. He could shave undisturbed, which made it far less likely that he'd nick himself. After he finished his regimen, the short trip back to his room through the darkened, silent hallway past the rooms of his neighbors posed no threats. In addition, there was something tremendously soothing about showering just before going to bed. The whole business left him contented and almost relaxed. He wished he had thought of this routine sooner. His freshman year could have been completely different. He had figured out quickly enough that if he applied for and got a position as R.A. his sophomore year, he'd be able to live in the blessed state of roommate-lessness without busting his budget, but this ablutionary solitude was the icing on the cake.

Several times recently, however, he'd been interrupted by Christopher. In fact, it was happening more often than not that as he stepped out of the shower Christopher would be at one of the washbasins or just coming out of one of the stalls or whatever. It looked suspiciously to Eli as if their meetings were turning into a routine. Denise and Christopher were thick as thieves lately, enough so that even usually oblivious Cliff had mentioned it. It took a lot to make him take notice, and he definitely had. Eli wondered if these late night encounters were the result of something Denise had said to Christopher. Since the very first night Christopher had shown up there, Eli had taken great care to be pleasant, to respond to Christopher's remarks with, he judged, just the right mixture of humor and disinterestedness. But he'd certainly done nothing to encourage Christopher. Or discourage him, either. Dealing with Denise, even by proxy this way, was always like walking on eggs. Tonight, Christopher was at one of the washbasins cleaning makeup off his face with cold cream and kleenex.

"How was rehearsal?" Eli asked.

"Just like always," Christopher frowned. "A disaster."

"Opening night is tomorrow," Eli pointed out.

"I'm not worried," Christopher said. "Whatever happens, I'll be fine."

"We'll all be there," Denise had said a few nights earlier when Christopher joined their table at the student union for dinner. "We wouldn't miss opening night for the world, would we, guys?"

"Miss what?" Cliff asked, rousing himself from post football practice torpor for just long enough to grunt the question.

"Of course not," Eli said. "Opening night, here we come."

"You see, Christopher," Denise smiled, "I told you they were excited about seeing you in the play."

"It's not a very exciting play," Christopher said.

"*Major Barbara?*" Eli chuckled. "By the world-renowned George Bernard Shaw? How can you say that?"

"Shaw isn't everybody's cup of tea," Christopher shrugged.

"He ought to be," Denise insisted. "For a liberal arts college, this place is awfully low brow, if you ask me."

"*Major Barbara* is the name of the play?" Cliff asked. "Doesn't make much sense."

"It's satire," Denise said.

"At least it's supposed to be," Christopher said. "Not sure how many of my castmates realize that. Hell, I'm not even sure the director gets it."

"Well, we three will be there opening night," Eli said, knowing Denise expected a show of enthusiasm and would find a way of making him pay if he didn't hit his mark.

"Cheering you on, sweetie," Denise smiled.

Denise, Cliff, and Eli went to Christopher's opening night. Due to the college's fairly isolated location in the Vermont countryside, the students were more or less always starved for entertainment. The nearest movie theater was twenty miles away, for instance. So it was a standing room only crowd. Christopher had arranged good seats for them. Though he was majoring in finance, Eli was an English minor and believed he had a certain literary sensitivity. His English professors certainly held that opinion, or at least pretended to very convincingly. Every few weeks one or the other of them remarked that he really should change his major. He believed they were principally motivated by a fear that the supply of English majors might dry up leaving them no one but business majors to teach Shakespeare to, and not many of those. Still, Eli took it as an affirmation. There were plenty of other students they never encouraged that way. He was familiar with *Major Barbara*, having reread it the week before, and he foresaw a less than scintillating evening of theatre. The play certainly was full of ideas. Shaw always was, whether they were his own or other people's. But the play featured lots of witty dialogue coupled with very little action. The major conflict seemed too abstract to engage a collegiate audience, and the romantic plot was pretty much an afterthought. Eli wasn't surprised to see Cliff nod off early in act one. He nearly did himself.

The performance was about as Eli had anticipated it would be, marked by slow pacing that made the dialogue seem ponderous, all of it delivered in discouragingly approximate British accents. The audience was appreciative enough, but Eli was pretty sure that was largely due to the same kind of half-desperate home court enthusiasm that would have kicked in had the basketball team fallen seriously behind in the second period. The whole thing simply wouldn't do, though it had to be judged a valiant effort. As for Christopher's performance, Eli couldn't tell whether he was any good or not. He was just so damned handsome onstage that nobody could take their eyes off him. That was pretty much Eli's total impression.

Christopher was so handsome on stage, in fact, that Eli went back for a second look. He could no more have helped himself than he could have walked on water. He didn't tell Denise he was going to another performance. He knew what she would say. The fact that it would prove her more or less right about his silent infatuation with Christopher would only make it worse. It was much safer staring at him when Eli could sit in the dark to do it. And of course, in a theatre you were supposed to be staring at the stage, making it the perfect camouflage. In *Major Barbara,* the character Christopher played was a vapid young Englishman of the upper class who spent most of the play with his foot in his mouth. Eli was familiar enough with Shaw to understand that this individual was meant to embody all the worst qualities of the English bourgeoisie: philistinism, materialism, smugness, vanity, etc. Viewed in that light, Christopher's portrayal seemed uncannily convincing, though after a second exposure to it Eli still couldn't form an opinion as to his talent. Perhaps that spoke for itself, but he realized that with his biases he couldn't be a reliable judge.

The Monday after closing night, Eli's curiosity was aroused by a chance remark made by a girl in his European History class. Apparently, Denise hadn't missed a single performance of *Major Barbara,* which had run for nine performances over three weekends. At first Eli was horrified at the thought that she might have seen him in the audience the second time he went. But he hadn't noticed her and she hadn't mentioned seeing him there, so he might have gotten away with it. Once he got past that and was able to think clearly about what he'd overheard, what concerned him more than Denise's attendance at performances was the news that she'd been seen visiting Christopher backstage each night after the performance. Farm boy Cliff always went to bed with the chickens, but up to now Denise had never taken advantage of that with anyone but Eli, which hardly counted. This news alarmed him. He'd never believed she was that serious about Cliff, but he didn't like the idea of her sneaking around behind his back. Cliff, for all his limitations as a boyfriend was a pretty decent sort, and it really didn't seem fair. In addition, it struck Eli as downright irreverent. Like peeing on a statue of President Taft, for instance, or making up obscene lyrics to substitute when singing the alma mater. What was also unfair, as he saw it, was Denise having two spectacular guys at her disposal when he had no prospects whatsoever. His resentment threatened to get the better of him one afternoon as they walked across the quad toward the library and Denise mentioned that Christopher had asked her to the cast party.

"You're not going," he gasped.

"Why the hell not?"

"Well, you're dating Cliff, for one thing."

"What does that have to do with it?" Denise demanded. "Anyway, he's on a road trip with the football team this weekend. Again. Honestly, every fall it's the same thing. Then in the spring it's wrestling season. After that, it's track. Does anybody really care about decathlon? Anybody still living? Any Americans, at least? In any case, Cliff's gone every other weekend. Am I just supposed to sit around bored while he's off doing God knows what with God knows who? They say boys will be boys, but why can't girls be girls?"

"Cliff would never. . ."

"You know that for a fact?"

Eli didn't, but at the same time he couldn't imagine it. Cliff didn't have the initiative to cheat. Socially speaking, he was the equivalent of a tree sloth. Of course a determined young woman could get around that. Girls took the bull by the horns more often than men realized. Eli's sisters and his girl cousins had left him in no doubt about it. But he still thought it awfully unlikely in Cliff's case.

"It's not a date, Eli," Denise said. "What ideas you get. It's just an invitation to the cast party. Pretty much everybody in the world will be there. I'm surprised nobody has invited you. As a matter of fact, I'll tell Christopher I'm bringing you along."

"Please don't."

"Why not?"

"Just leave me out of it, O.K?"

"Honestly, you'd think I was up to something underhanded."

"Aren't you?"

"Of course not."

But the next Monday morning when he met Denise for breakfast, he could see that she was agitated about something and at the same time that she wasn't in the mood to talk about it. He'd run into Christopher the night before in the showers, but nothing out of the ordinary passed between them. Perhaps Denise's mood didn't have anything to do with Christopher. Perhaps she'd met someone else at the cast party. Perhaps—well, Denise was one of the most beautiful girls in the whole college. So perhaps anything. But Eli was her oldest friend, and if past experiences were any guide she wouldn't be able to keep a secret from him for long.

"I can't believe you slept with him," Eli said when she finally confessed. Unfortunately, he could. But he'd never have admitted to it.

"Don't look at me like I'm some scarlet woman, Eli. It was just sex. Pretty darn good sex, I must say."

"I'm not," Eli protested, though that's exactly what he was thinking.

"Listen," she said, "a girl has to keep her options open."

"What's that supposed to mean?"

"What do you think? Cliff has had nearly five semesters to show me that he's really serious about us, and he hasn't. And for that matter, I'm not so sure I'm serious about him. So I don't feel one bit guilty about what I did with Christopher."

"Jeez, girl."

"Eli, darling, I don't blame you for being a little jealous."

"Is that what I am?"

"Don't worry. I know things seem hopeless right now. But just you wait. Once you graduate and head off to New York to make your fortune on Wall Street and become the next literary sensation. . ."

She was referring to the cryptic little short stories he'd published in the campus literary magazine the previous spring. She correctly suspected them of having greater significance than Eli had admitted to.

"Spectacular men are going to beat down your door. Just see if they don't. Now please, can we talk about this like girlfriends?"

It wasn't disapproval she was sensing, though he was actually glad she interpreted his reaction that way. It was disbelief, but disbelief of a very specific kind. Denise had always had a mind of her own. He'd long since recognized that there was nothing she wouldn't do under the right circumstances. He wasn't surprised on her account. It was a more cosmic form of surprise. Simply put, Cliff was so spectacular that it was hard to imagine anyone cheating on him. Over and over during the next several days Eli found himself thinking that if he were the one with a boyfriend like Cliff he'd never have done such a thing. Those shoulders. That chest. That perennially sandpapery chin. That throaty roar that was a laugh. Who would risk losing out on all that? No, it was impossible. She simply couldn't have.

But she had. Well, women were fickle. Shakespeare had written about it. And just about everyone else worth reading. But life wasn't literature, and Eli was going to have a hard time getting over what Denise had done. And he wasn't even the guy she'd cheated on. Irony of ironies. It wasn't anything to be alarmed about, really. It couldn't be. She'd just been blowing off steam. Of course she had to be frustrated at the amount of time Cliff's athletic activities kept them apart or otherwise out of action. Any girl would be. Each and every one of them seemed hell-bent on being treated like she was the center of the universe. But Denise wasn't just any girl. She'd feel it more strongly, just as she did everything else, and with her temperament she'd be more likely to do something about her frustration than other girls. Sure, Cliff wasn't especially charming. He wasn't a sparkling conversationalist and he had a very short attention span, socially speaking. He wasn't a good listener, either, though he at least knew how to pretend he was. He wasn't very attentive to her and had never pampered her in the way Eli knew she thought she deserved. But he was considerate enough, after his clumsy, somnambulistic fashion. And he had no bad habits to speak of unless you counted taking his girlfriend for granted. Girls had broken up with boys over less. Eli knew that well enough. His sisters had made an art form of breaking up with boyfriends for no reason at all. But not a boy like Cliff. Girls were smarter than that. Girls were obsessed with value. Breaking up with a guy meant putting him back on the market. And what girl in her right mind would do that with a guy like Cliff until she had his replacement absolutely nailed down? Christopher was anything but nailed down. Christopher, Eli considered, was like mercury bouncing loose on the floor of the chem. lab. And could anyone really think, spectacularly handsome as he was, that he was a viable replacement for a varsity athlete?

Girls really ran the whole thing, from what Eli had observed. So Denise had gone off and played hooky. And she apparently appreciated the experience. Still, he was sure she'd think better of it in a day or so. Cliff would get back from his trip and she'd take a good hard look at who she'd just cheated on and that would be that. For that matter, Eli couldn't believe that the encounter had mattered much to Christopher. It was hard to believe that anything mattered to him. He was beautiful, but all the signs were that he was even shallower than he was attractive. And he probably wasn't any better than Cliff at paying attention to anyone other than himself. It was just sex. Denise had said as much. The less Eli thought about Denise and Christopher together, the better.

After that, Eli began to see Cliff and Christopher in terms of contrasting pairs. The difference between them was never as simple as black and white or good versus evil. Life didn't work that way, and in this case the casting would have been questionable any way you looked at it. Still, Eli's imagination came up with analogy after analogy. For instance, Cliff was a massive sheepdog guarding his herd while Christopher was a sleek jungle cat lurking in the undergrowth and waiting for prey to amble into range. In other words, the two weren't really opposites, just profoundly different from each other. Cliff was the stalwart knight galloping off on glorious quests, Christopher the wizard, cryptic and brilliant in his cave. Cliff was the decorated war hero, Christopher the cunning agent behind enemy lines. Cliff was the intrepid explorer scaling remote peaks, Christopher the inventor tinkering in his workshop. Cliff was the captain of the fire brigade, Christopher the international jewel thief sneaking into the hotel rooms of fabulously wealthy jet setters. Cliff was. . .

Still, Eli didn't see them as opponents. He saw them as two lobes of a Venn diagram. A weird Venn diagram where the circles didn't intersect. Except they had intersected.

Denise.

III

"What's gotten into you lately?" Denise snapped.

They were on their way to philosophy class. The day was bitterly cold and as bleak as New England could be. Eli wondered if going to college in Siberia would actually be this uncomfortable.

"Huh?"

"Jesus, Eli, it's like you're, I don't know. . ."

"Actually," Eli said, weary of biting his tongue, "if anybody's been a little off recently. . ."

"Don't try to push this off on me," Denise fumed. "I'm perfectly fine."

"Do you hear yourself?" Eli asked. "The last few days it's like I've become nanny to a junior psychopath."

"Psychopath?"

"Or," Eli said, finally getting it, "a young woman with a problem."

"I don't know what you're talking about."

"But I bet the folks at the Student Health Center do," Eli said. It was a shot in the dark, but the look in her eyes the instant he said it told him it had been right on target.

"Bastard."

"Your trouble," Eli said, "as opposed to your current problem, is that you think you're smarter than I am. And you're not. Now, as to your problem. . ."

"I thought it was just a false alarm at first," Denise said, frowning.

"You've had those before," Eli nodded.

"But the test results. . ."

"Oh, my God." Eli gasped.

"Not so fast," Denise said. "They were inconclusive. That's all."

"What? I've never heard of that happening."

"It does, apparently. So now I'm waiting for more results."

"And going out of your mind," Eli said. "Poor Denise. You should have said something to me."

"Say something? Hell, Eli, I can hardly even think it."

"It wouldn't be the end of the world," Eli suggested on their way to the library later. He was imagining what Cliff's baby would grow up to look like. Cliff himself, only more so. If that was even possible. "It's not as if Cliff isn't a great guy. I'm sure he'll want to do the right thing if it comes down to it."

"Yes," Denise said, "you would say that."

"Why shouldn't I say what I think?"

"Because you don't know what you're talking about."

"Oh, come on, Denise," Eli protested, "I know it's your body and your life and all that, but still. I am your oldest friend."

"Take it easy," she said. "No criticism intended. You simply don't have all the facts, so you can't possibly talk intelligently about this."

"I don't understand."

"Cliff's not the father, you dope."

"What?"

"At least probably not. This late in the season he's almost always too tired for sex. That's his excuse, anyway. But Christopher never makes excuses. Christopher never has to."

"I thought you only slept with him the one time."

"You thought," Denise snorted.

"You never said."

"Sometimes I don't think you understand me at all," Denise said, starting to cry.

"She won't tell me what's wrong," Cliff said, "And I thought, well, you two are so. . ."

He seemed to take up all the available space in Eli's dorm room. Eli couldn't imagine how Cliff and his roommate, a defensive lineman from Connecticut, managed to shoehorn themselves into their place on the fifth floor.

"I really don't know any more than you do," Eli said, mortified to be lying to someone like Cliff, who had always been nicer to him than he had any right to expect and who hadn't for a moment stopped being the handsomest guy in the world.

"I thought you two talked about everything," Cliff said, shaking his head.

"Usually we do," Eli nodded, "but when she gets into one of her moods it's hard to get her to make sense."

"No shit."

"Believe me, man," Eli said, "if I figure it out, you'll be the first one I call."

"Thanks, guy," Cliff said, stifling a yawn. "Just really hate to see her all moody like this."

Meanwhile, there was Christopher. Eli assumed Christopher knew that Eli knew he'd been sleeping with Denise. But that smooth face and those cerulean eyes might as well have belonged to a stranger. There was no indication that his awareness of Eli's knowledge had any effect on him at all. When they met in the hallway, Christopher looked through him. When they spoke to each other, Christopher's voice produced the smooth, uninflected tones of a television anchorman. When their eyes met, Christopher's revealed no more than that he was alive and conscious. Eli wondered if Denise had said anything to Christopher about her scare. It didn't seem possible. But he had decided that when it came to Christopher, you could never be sure of anything.

"How did the second round of tests turn out?" Eli asked. He knew Denise had been back to the Student Health Center two days earlier. It was strange that she hadn't said anything.

"Oh, didn't I tell you? I got the all clear. First test was screwed up."

"No," Eli said. "You didn't mention it."

"Must have slipped my mind."

Once again, she was making the mistake of thinking she was smarter than he was. And that he couldn't tell when she was lying.

"I'm worried about Pauline," Denise said on their way to the cafeteria later that morning. "Last time I talked to her she sounded really down."

Pauline was Denise's older sister. When her husband, Eugene (pronounced not you-JEAN but oo-ZHEN because he came from Montreal) was assigned to a post at the Canadian embassy in Paris, Pauline had stayed in Ottawa to continue work on her Ph.D.

"It's got to be hard for her," Eli nodded.

"Think I'd better head up there for a few days," Denise said. "Soon as I take my last exam."

"She'll be glad to have some company."

Eli didn't see Denise again until Christmas Eve when he ran into her at a party back home in Manhattan.

"Greetings, earthman," she said. "I come in peace."

"You look awful," Eli said. "Bad trip?"

"Just a touch of the flu," she shrugged. "Be right as rain in a couple of days."

So she'd done it. The procedure was legal north of the border.

"Flu or not," he told her, "I insist on a Christmas hug."

"Won't Pauline be lonely over the holidays?" Eli asked, trying to steer the conversation in a certain direction.

"She's visiting her in-laws. Who knows? Eugene might even be able to get away for a few days."

"Really."

"Hell, Eli, you know Pauline and me. We can hardly stand to be around each other. Four days—five tops—and we're ready to shed each other's blood."

"If you say so," Eli sighed.

"Have to say, she was very nice to me this visit."

Under the circumstances she'd have to be, Eli thought.

"Three Christmases and not a sign of an engagement ring," Denise said later in the evening. "I could strangle Cliff."

"I thought you weren't sure you loved him," Eli said.

"What's that got to do with it?"

"Everything," Eli said. "I mean, doesn't it?"

"Poor Eli. I guess it's not your fault you don't understand it."

"Come on. Don't be like that."

"Sorry," she said. "O.K. It's like this. A girl wants to be asked. Whether she has any intention of actually marrying the guy doesn't matter. It's about being wanted. And I swear to God, sometimes I'm not sure Cliff knows I'm alive."

"That's silly."

"It is not. Sometimes I think he's only aware of my existence when we're having sex."

"Christopher's not like that, I guess."

"No, he's not."

"Then break up with Cliff. Be with Christopher."

"Not on your life," Denise said. "Sure, Christopher makes me feel like a woman while Cliff only makes me feel invisible. But Christopher's really only good for two things. Looking at and fucking."

"And Cliff's good for what?"

"Maybe someday he'll wake up and I'll find out."

IV

"Need to ask you something," Cliff said.

"What's that?"

Classes were due to start up again on Monday, and Cliff had shown up at the Eli's door earlier that evening looking uncharacteristically glum. He was between seasons, and Eli understood that that was partially responsible. But in general he only looked like this when he'd been fighting with Denise. Or, to be more accurate, when Denise had been fighting with him, because Eli knew that it was always Denise who started their fights. Cliff had gone through three of the beers he'd brought with him and now slouched in Eli's beanbag chair looking somewhat more contented. He'd slipped out of his rugby shirt. The white a-shirt he had on underneath taunted Eli with its thin straps and flimsy fabric. If only.

"Just been wondering," Cliff said, "what it's like to suck cock. Or take it up the ass."

Eli could hardly have been more astonished if the building had caved in around them. He was speechless.

"You heard me," Cliff said, blushing faintly. "What does all that stuff guys like you get up to feel like?"

"I, uh. . ."

"Come on, Eli," Cliff said. "Talk to me."

"Not much to tell," Eli said. "I haven't ever really done any of that stuff."

"Huh?"

"Really."

"Like, not any of it?"

"I'm a total virgin," Eli said. "I haven't even been kissed. By a guy, I mean."

"You're not just holding out on me because you're afraid to talk about it? Because I wouldn't have brought it up if all I wanted to do was start trouble."

"No," Eli said. "It's the honest to God truth."

It wasn't something he was proud of. He was sure that if it were possible for Cliff to think any less of him than he already had, this admission would do the trick.

"Huh," Cliff said, nodding slowly. "I guess it makes sense. You are pretty shy. And there's probably not much going on in a place like this."

Pretty shy, yes. Eli could accept that. Better than what Cliff was probably thinking, which was that Eli wasn't particularly attractive. Girls generally didn't look twice at him. Why would a man?

"But if that's true," Cliff said, "how do you know you're that way? I mean if you haven't actually done anything?"

Eli thought for a moment before resorting to the answer he'd given Denise once upon a time. Cliff might find it offensive, but it was the best Eli had.

"How did you know you liked girls before you'd done anything with one?"

"Kind of question is that?" Cliff guffawed.

Eli didn't answer.

"You mean you're serious?" Cliff asked after a long moment.

"Um, yes," Eli said. "That's how I know. Same way you always knew you liked girls."

"Jeez." Cliff said, reaching up and running a hand through his gorgeous hair.

Eli decided to let him think about it a little longer. Cliff took his time processing things.

"Yeah," Cliff nodded. "I guess I get that. Just never thought of it that way before."

"Why would you?" Eli asked.

"You're right," Cliff said. "No reason. No reason at all."

"See," Eli said. "No mystery."

"Except why?" Cliff said. "I still don't understand why anybody would be that way. Denise says that's a stupid question. Like asking why there's air. That's what she said. Sometimes I think she's too smart for me. Other times I think she's too smart for her own good. Probably both, come to think of it."

"You talked about this with Denise?"

"Long time ago," Cliff said. "When she first told me about you."

"I see."

Which didn't explain tonight's discussion, as far as Eli was concerned. But he wasn't about to ask. They sat like that for a long time. Then Cliff reached for the sixpack sitting on the floor beside him and pulled loose another can.

"See," Cliff said, "kind of went and did something. I don't know. Wouldn't call it stupid, exactly. Just, well, not something I ever thought I'd do. Not really. Now I can't stop thinking about it. Trying to understand it, you know?"

He couldn't possibly mean what Eli thought he was hearing. Eli sat nearly afraid to breathe while Cliff swigged more beer and wiped his mouth with the back of his hand.

"I mean, if it had just been the one time I probably wouldn't have thought a thing about it," Cliff continued. "Guy gets a little drunk, no telling what he might do. But the second time it happened I'd only had one beer. And since then I've been cold sober every time. Christopher says it's better that way. Oh, shit. I wasn't supposed to mention his name."

"Wait a minute," Eli said. "Do you mean to tell me you and Christopher had sex? Like Denise's buddy, Christopher? Like down the hall from this room Christopher?"

"Five or six times now," Cliff nodded.

Which probably meant nine or ten. Or a dozen and a half. Numbers, except the kind printed on athletic uniforms, weren't Cliff's forte.

"You can't tell him I told you," Cliff said. "It's supposed to be a secret. It's just I can't help wondering what all that stuff I'm doing to him feels like. My cock in his butthole, you know? Can't imagine it feels good, but he sure gets off. You can't fake that. And anyway, why would you?"

"I can't believe it," Eli said.

"Probably shouldn't say anything to Denise about it, either," Cliff said.

It didn't mean that Cliff was gay. That was the one thing Eli was sure of. He had been on the point of saying as much. He stopped himself just in time. Cliff didn't need any reassurance on that point. There hadn't been a cock in his mouth. Or in the other place. Once upon a time he'd gotten a little drunk and let himself be taken advantage of. And he'd appreciated the results enough that he let it happen again and eventually it had become a kind of habit. That was all. Saying "it doesn't mean you're gay" would have been worse than pointless. Cliff might well have taken it as an insult. At the very least Eli would have looked even stupider than usual. Cliff hadn't needed reassurance and he hadn't needed to confess. If he needed anything from Eli, it was insurance. Telling Eli was far better than having Eli find out accidentally. Eli taken by surprise might blurt anything out to anybody. This way Cliff could depend on Eli's discretion. Because Cliff had been sure that his simple request would be enough for that.

What it meant about Christopher was impossible for Eli to fathom. A guy who'd had Cliff's cock in his mouth and in the other place half a dozen times or more could only be one thing. But when the same guy had been sleeping with Denise for upward of six months to her fervently expressed satisfaction and had even made her pregnant, things got confusing. Eli didn't like confusion. He avoided it as much as possible. But when the confusion centered on his best friend, his best friend's boyfriend—whom he was secretly in love with—and someone they were both sleeping with, Eli knew the confusion threatened to turn into something he wasn't sure he could control.

The more he thought about it the more he realized that it didn't really matter which way Christopher truly swung. Eli's first impression of him had been correct. Straight or otherwise, he was undoubtedly trouble. A second realization was more interesting to Eli. He had always thought of Denise as the brains and Cliff as the brawn in their relationship. It seemed obvious that whatever intellect Cliff might have was devoted completely to his athletic efforts and that real life pretty much escaped him. Cliff certainly did nothing to refute this notion. Denise continually made a monkey of him without half trying. And Denise's adventures with Christopher appeared to prove this. What kind of guy didn't realize that his girlfriend was cheating on him? Or even just thinking about it? Sure, Eli's understanding of relationships between men and women was limited, but it seemed impossible that a man of normal intelligence wouldn't figure it out. Certainly after this long Cliff should have put the pieces together. Now he had to reconsider this assumption. Because Cliff had been cheating, too. And if Denise had the least suspicion of it she'd have gone to any lengths necessary to find out everything. Who? What? How? How many times? She'd have been as implacable as the KGB going after counterrevolutionary elements. Instead, she went around with a silly grin on her face. There was no getting around it. She was as clueless as Cliff was. Not that Eli thought she should have suspected what was actually going on between Cliff and Christopher. What girl would suspect something like that? But she certainly should have suspected something. In the past she'd had the surest of instincts about Cliff, even when he'd gone no further than inadvertently flirting with another girl. But now she seemed to have lost whatever brain cells she'd ever had when it came to keeping track of her boyfriend.

V

"I suppose you have plans with your friends for spring break," Mom said, her anticipatory disappointment flooding out of the telephone like a storm tide moving up a beach, "but it would really be nice if you would at least show up for your grandparents' sixtieth wedding anniversary celebration. It's on Palm Sunday. Your Aunt Layne got a discount because all the goyim at her club will be busy. Maybe you could get Denise and her boyfriend to wait until Monday to take off on your adventure. Whatever it is."

Mom didn't think highly of Denise, whom she described as "unladylike". This was accurate enough as far as it went. But it wasn't Mom's real objection, which was twofold and paradoxical. She disapproved of Denise because she wasn't and hadn't ever been Eli's girlfriend, and at the same time she disapproved of Denise because she wasn't Jewish. Which meant, of course, that if Denise had been dating Eli, Mom would have disapproved even more strenuously. None of it was up for negotiation, so as always Eli found himself in a no win situation.

"Who's doing the Seders this year?" Eli asked.

"Your aunts," Mom said, "but I know better than to hope. . ."

He hadn't encouraged her over the phone, but the more Eli thought about it the more it seemed like the perfect excuse. Last year, it had just been the three of them, Denise, Cliff, and him, camped out on the beach in Florida. It was a glorious week of sunshine and sand. Cliff had hardly worn a shirt at all and much of the time not even pants. But this year Christopher was on the passenger list.

There hadn't been any discussion. Denise simply said "the four of us will have a fabulous time" and that was that. Since hearing it, Eli had been hoping for some sort of reprieve. So far the spring semester had been like being tied up and locked in a dark room next to a ticking time bomb. Even worse, in other words, than the prospect of spending spring break at home being badgered by the female members of his family.

And really, how could anyone object to him wanting to attend Grandpa and Nanna Neumann's celebration? How could anyone suspect his motives?

"Oh, Eli," Denise protested. "How could you have forgotten a thing like that?"

Eli shrugged. She knew him well enough that ordinarily he couldn't get away with playing dumb, but he seemed to have hit a home run this time.

"Hey," Cliff grunted, "guys aren't like chicks. We don't keep up with that family stuff."

"Or much of anything else," Denise complained. "Still, I guess there's no way around it. Cliff and I will spend the weekend with my folks and then we'll hit the road on Monday. I hate making Mom happy, but it can't be helped. I don't suppose Christopher could bunk at your place?"

"Actually," Eli said, treading lightly, "maybe the three of you should go without me. I missed Passover last year and Mom still hasn't forgiven me. If I miss again this year I'll never hear the end of it."

"We couldn't," Denise said, "possibly."

"Sure you could," Eli said. "And if it's just the three of you, there'll be enough room in Cliff's Camaro. You won't have to take the Peugeot like we were planning to. Remember how great it was last year cruising around the beach with the top down?"

By the time Cliff got through chewing over this, Eli would have won the argument.

"I don't see why you won't take the Peugeot," Denise said, grinding the gears as she pulled up in front of the bus station. "The bus is horrible. And that's just for starters. The train on into the city is worse. It makes the trip seem like a visit to the dentist that never ends."

"It's not that bad," Eli said. "I'll get lots of reading done."

He couldn't imagine having to deal with parking Denise's car for a whole week in Manhattan. Talk about going to the dentist.

"As long as it's not because you think I don't trust you with her," Denise said. "I know you're as responsible as the day is long. It's one of your worst qualities."

The Peugeot was ten years old, leprous with rust, and saggy of springs. Eli couldn't imagine anyone trying to steal it. Or why anyone had ever considered driving it to Florida and back over spring break. He had, he decided, done Denise *et al* a favor taking that particular card off the table.

Emerging into Grand Central late that evening, Eli finally felt released from all that turbulence back at school. He never really felt safe beyond the shores of Manhattan, but this homecoming was the best ever. Let those three get up to whatever mischief and depravity they chose under the insinuating Florida moon. It had nothing to do with him. Now that he'd made his escape, there was no reason to spend another second worrying about what might happen. Who might slip and give something away with dire repercussions. What grisly scenes he might have been called on to referee. No, he was free of them, his role cut from the script. Perhaps on their way south there would be a terrible accident and he wouldn't ever see them again. He'd be devastated, of course, but he'd be able to stop obsessing about consequences. And not even consequences of his own actions. How neurotic did you have to be to worry so much about people who couldn't bother to worry about themselves?

No question about it he thought, standing on the subway platform waiting for his uptown train. In Vermont he would always be a foreigner. Here he was at home. His freshman year, an earnest girl in his psychology class had said "Danziger—that's a German name, isn't it?" He nearly laughed at her. He finally muttered something about Danzig being a historic German seaport that was currently located in Polish territory, but he stopped himself before explaining that its name in Polish was Gdansk. In Manhattan, when he was introduced to people there was no such confusion. Either they weren't Jewish but knew every Jewish surname in the book and were totally blasé about such matters or they were Jewish and the stares meant they were pondering the best opportunity to ask him who had done his rhinoplasty. He hadn't had a rhino-plasty, but his nose was so perfectly goyish it looked like he must have. It was the evidence his sisters had always employed in support of their contention that he was adopted.

"We really should have gone out and bought you a new suit when you were home for the holidays," Mom said.

The big anniversary party was being held at the country club out in Westchester where his Uncle Marty and Aunt Layne had a membership. This meant a long ride in the back seat of his father's new Mercedes. It was the first time Dr. Danziger hadn't bought American.

"Mercedes—that's a German car, isn't it?" Eli muttered under his breath.

"What dear?" Mom asked.

"Leave him alone, Ma," his sister Alannah said. "His suit looks fine."

Alannah was a senior at NYU. She'd already been accepted by multiple medi-cal schools. Eli hadn't decided whether this put more or less pressure on him to change his major from finance. Their sister Judith was a second year medical student. Her boyfriend, Bobby DeLaCruz, was a Puerto Rican actor who played an improbably young looking, ridiculously dashing surgeon on a soap opera. Mom had been a nurse when she met Dad. Then there were his two grandfathers— surgeons both. Even his great-grandfather, the Eli he was named after, had been a doctor. The deck seemed stacked.

"I can't help thinking that all the other young men tonight will be wearing nicer looking ones," Mom said, "and I don't see why you couldn't have gone out this afternoon and gotten a haircut."

"Ma," Alannah said, "his hair is already shorter than ninety per cent of the male population his age."

"He's just so handsome when he's got a fresh haircut," Mom said.

"Please, Joyce," Dad said, turning up the radio and flooding the car with Mahler. "Enough."

"Mahler," Eli muttered. "Austrian composer, right?"

"What, dear?"

"Nothing, Mom."

When Aunt Layne was in charge of a party, she spared no effort or expense. As far as Eli could tell, everyone he was related to was in the room. The Landaus had all flown in from Chicago. Four generations of Neumanns—his mother's family—were represented, not to mention the Kleinbaums, the Richters, the Spektors, and the Rubinsteins. And of course all the Danzigers. Then there was everyone else. Friends, professional associates of Papa Neumann, three generations of rabbis and their wives. There must be three hundred people there at least.

Eli's cousin, Brook Kleinbaum, was wearing the suit Mom had probably been imagining in the car. A junior at Princeton, he was assumed by most of the family to be Eli's nemesis due partly to his good looks and partly to his gregariousness. Eli had never viewed them as rivals, however. Some people were so far out of your league that competing with them was too ridiculous to contemplate. Brook and his fiancée, Giselle Waterman, were all over each other, as usual, like an explorer wrestling a python, and simultaneously deep in apparently hilarious conversation with what looked like a pair of twins, tall, lanky guys with matching mops of golden curls and, Eli noticed as he drew closer, mischievous eyes. They had somehow managed not to wear ties, or had taken them off after arriving, which made them almost unspeakably daring.

"Little Cousin Eli," Brook called, pulling him into to the group by the elbow. "I bet you haven't met Jake and Josh. They're Ike's brothers."

Ike Luxemberg was engaged to Brook and Eli's cousin, Cherie Landau. He didn't look at all like these two beauties. Though as tall as they were, he was pretty much the stereotypical Jewish nerd. The twins' looks must make for a pretty interesting family dynamic. Especially with Ike set to graduate with honors from MIT in a few weeks.

"Pleased to meet you," Eli managed to mutter, awkward as always when faced with anyone this stunning. Since there were two of them, he supposed the effect was exponential.

"Eli, dear," Aunt Janet said. "I'm surprised to see you here without a date."

Her rampant impulse to match her nieces and nephews up with partners, however unsuitable they might be, was family legend. At her side, her second husband, Louis Adler, puffed away on a cigar Eli presumed had been smuggled from Cuba. Louis was an executive at one of New York's most prestigious banks. The presumption was that in the event Eli managed to avoid medical school Louis would help him get started in the city, so Eli was always careful to portray a suitably responsible persona around him. Aunt Janet's son, Stewart, was living in a hippie commune in Arizona, or so went the gossip.

"Go easy on him," Louis grunted through his pall of smoke. "Young man likes to play the field, you know."

"Don't be silly dear," Aunt Janet said.

"Brook, dear, how handsome you look tonight," Nanna Neumann thrilled. "Is that a new suit?"

"I'm Eli, Nana."

"Nonsense, Brook. I know my grandchildren. And it's not nice to try and pull the wool over the eyes of an old woman. You should know better."

Late in the evening, Eli saw Aunt Ella Landau talking with a woman who looked uncannily like Elizabeth Taylor, though she was much taller. Eli sidled closer to see what he could overhear. Aunt Ella was the most vicious gossip in the whole tribe. He often traded her snippets for favors from his sisters. Just as Eli arrived within earshot, the guy he had been unable to take his eyes off of all night approached them, leaned in, and kissed Liz on the cheek. Luxuriant raven hair, confrontational cheekbones, glinting eyes, and unbelievably broad shoulders. He'd taken Eli's mind off possible developments en route to Florida, and that was saying something.

"Cooper, darling," Aunt Ella cooed. "Your mother and I were just talking about you."

"I hope you weren't saying anything nice," the guy growled.

"Darling, you looked so handsome dancing with DeeDee Shapiro tonight," Mom said boozily from the front seat. "Why don't you ask her out while you're home?"

"Joyce," Dad grunted. "Enough."

By breakfast time, Eli was frantic with curiosity. He knew from long experience that he had to be as indirect as possible with Alannah, who even hung over was astute enough to be dangerous. He didn't want the whole family hearing that he'd been asking questions about that guy named Cooper. So it wasn't until Alannah and he had made critical commentary on various party guests that he trotted out what he hoped was a sufficiently innocuous question.

"Who was that woman last night who looked like Elizabeth Taylor?"

"You noticed her," Alannah nodded.

"Everybody noticed her," Eli said.

"That's Ike's mom. And consequently Cousin Cherie's mother-in-law to be, Shoshonnah Luxemberg."

"Really," Eli said. "I wouldn't have thought Ike would have a mom who looked like that."

"Maybe not," Alannah said, "but I know you met the twins. They certainly look like they could be the fruit of those loins."

"Jesus, Al," Eli said, starting to blush.

"You'll get a chance to look her over again Wednesday night. Auntie Layne has invited them to her Seder. God, I hope those twins will show up. What I wouldn't give for a shot at one of them. Or both, for that matter."

"Easy girl," Eli laughed uneasily. "Who are they anyway?"

"The Luxembergs? Well, for starters, they own a very exclusive jewelry store in Manhattan."

"They're those Luxembergs?" Eli marveled. "I had no idea."

"You're kidding, right?" Alannah rolled her eyes. "You have seen Cherie's engagement ring, haven't you?"

"It didn't occur to me there might be a connection."

"Sheesh. Talk about your babes in the woods. It's a good thing you're at school off in the wilds of Vermont. Not much goes on up there. In Manhattan you wouldn't be safe on your own."

"Well," Eli said, "it certainly explains why the aunts are all so crazy about Mrs. Luxemberg. It's the potential for discounts. You know how bloodthirsty that gang usually is on the subject of beautiful women."

By the time Wednesday night rolled around, Eli was practically beside himself. What if something happened to Aunt Layne and the Seder had to be called off? What if the Luxembergs didn't show? What if Cooper was otherwise engaged?

"Cooper's the youngest one here, I expect," Uncle Arnie said, handing the leaflets around the table.

"You know, Shoshonnah, I can't get over how grown up the boy looks," Aunt Layne said.

Just like Aunt Layne to talk about someone five feet away as if he wasn't in the room.

"He's what you'd call an early bloomer," Mrs. Luxemberg laughed. She might look like Elizabeth Taylor, but her cackle was right out of Phyllis Diller's playbook. "People can hardly believe he's not in college yet, much less that he doesn't have a driver's license."

Eli's blood ran cold. Staring at him across the table, he'd figured Cooper for nineteen at least. Those shoulders. That five o'clock shadow. How could he possibly be fifteen? And that New York truck driver's growl, Eli cringed, as Cooper asked the first question.

"Why is tonight different from all other nights?"

VI

"Wouldn't you like to know?" Denise smirked, sitting down next to Eli in their sociology class.

"I don't remember asking," Eli said.

"You can't wait to hear all the dirt."

But Eli already knew everything he wanted to know. Still discombobulated by his ridiculous crush on a fifteen year old, the follies of his associates didn't hold much interest. He'd seen everything in Christopher's eyes last night just after midnight when they hit the showers simultaneously. Simultaneously, yet anything but together. They barely spoke to each other. A little while earlier he had heard the Camaro rumble up in front of the dorm and saw Christopher climb out. Eli had been watching out the window of his dorm room in spite of himself. From doing everything he could to ignore Christopher last fall, he had been transformed by circumstances into the closest of observers. So he knew. The eyes said it all. Denise was still having sex with Christopher, who was still having sex with Cliff.

It was tempting to say something and blow it all sky high. But Eli wouldn't. They all knew he wouldn't. That was the single thing all three of them knew, and Eli didn't like what it seemed to say about him that they could depend on his silence.

"Spare me the gory details," he told Denise, pretending to stifle a yawn.

"Don't play coy with me," she snorted. "I know you're about to jump out of your skin."

He opened his text book and pretended to review the assigned chapter.

169

All that close observation Eli had been doing and he still managed to miss a crucial detail. The only explanation was that the change had taken place so gradually he simply hadn't noticed it. But after ten days away from Christopher, Eli's first glimpse of him brought it into focus. Somebody had been going to the gym. When he first showed up on campus last fall, Christopher had been built pretty much like Eli—like ninety percent of guys their age, in other words. But since then their physiques had diverged noticeably. Or, to be more accurate, Christopher's diverged from Eli's, because Eli was the same as he'd ever been physically. Eli remembered musing from time to time about the possibility of joining Cliff at the gym, learning the ropes from him and transforming himself to some degree. Christopher had gone and done it. Because Eli didn't believe for a minute that Christopher had made himself over without assistance. In other words, while Eli had been mooning around and pining for Cliff, Christopher had taken the bull by the horns. He hadn't gotten big by any means. But he'd made himself into something Eli could easily imagine himself aspiring to. There was additional bulk in all the right places. There was what Eli thought he recalled Cliff referring to as definition. The change, as he observed Christopher stepping into the shower that night immediately after his return from Florida, was striking. It all too obviously wasn't the result of two or three weeks of hard work. Months had been required. The association with Cliff, which Eli mentally dated as having begun sometime after Christopher's liaison with Denise, must have started much earlier and might even have predated it. It wasn't just his sexual shenanigans with Cliff that had gone on right under Eli's nose. It was this, too. Eli didn't know whether to laugh or cry, though he was clearly inclined in the latter direction.

It wasn't just that renovated body that struck Eli that Sunday night in the shower. Courtesy of that week in Florida, the new Christopher sported a deep satiny tan. Try as he might, Eli couldn't banish his imagined images of Cliff rubbing tanning oil onto Christopher's back. Last spring, Denise had been very particular about performing that service for Eli, as if asking Cliff to do it would somehow be unseemly. And to be truthful about it, Eli would have died of mortification having Cliff touch him even for such an innocuous purpose. Just thinking about it made him cringe. Of course that wasn't all it made him do. But though he hadn't been in Florida to see it, Eli was pretty certain how things had happened.

Christopher would have made sure of it. Cliff's huge hands and powerful fore-arms. Christopher's smooth back. It was enough to drive Eli crazy.

He was part way there already. The Christopher and Cliff drama was only the half of it. Eli couldn't get Cooper Luxemberg out of his mind. He might only be fifteen and a tenth grader, but he looked nineteen at least. An extremely mature nineteen. It was all too easy to imagine him as one of Cliff's teammates. According to the testimony of his mother Shoshonnah, Cooper was fifteen going on twenty-seven, and Eli knew he couldn't be the only one who was fascinated. He couldn't help himself. At odd times during the day, instead of thinking about his next exam or how he should call his mother that evening he'd find himself pondering how much more attractive Cooper would be in another year or two. Better yet three years from now, when Eli would have graduated and be living in Manhattan and Cooper would be attending NYU or Columbia. Of course none of Cooper's brothers had stayed in New York for college, but Eli's imagination didn't let such information deter it. Cooper *would* stay in Manhattan. He'd refuse to budge from that enchanted isle. He and Eli would become pals, then best friends. Then the inevitable would happen. True love. Moving in together. All of the things Eli had dreamed about over the years. It had been too much to hope that Cliff would wake up one morning, take a look at Eli, say to himself "shit, I've had it completely wrong all this time", and make Eli's dreams come true. But now there was another candidate for the position of love of Eli's life.

Ridiculous, of course. Nothing in Eli's daydreams ever turned out. Because Eli's daydreams were the daydreams of a fourteen year old girl with an overdevel-oped romantic sensibility. Besides, Cooper probably wasn't even gay. Even if you believed that ten per cent statistic, there seemed very little chance of it. And even if he was, what were the odds of the kind of happy ending Eli was obsessing about? Best to put it out of his mind.

He'd be seeing Cooper again at Cousin Cherie's wedding in June. Maybe by then he'd have turned into a troll.

VII

"It's the most ridiculous thing I've ever heard of," Denise said. "A beauty pageant for men."

Eli had just about given up on ever getting her to behave in the library. Sooner or later they were going to get banned from the place permanently, and he wasn't sure how he'd finish his degree.

"You heard Christopher," Eli said. "A bodybuilding competition is nothing like a beauty pageant."

"Please explain the difference to me," she said.

"I'm not the expert," Eli said. "Christopher is."

These days, Christopher seemed to be the expert on everything. Even if he wasn't, Denise and Cliff both deferred to him at all times.

"Why don't you like him?" Denise asked.

"Who said I don't like him?"

"Well, you certainly give that impression."

"Do I? I don't mean to."

Eli was lying to her more than he ever had in the past. If Christopher could get away with lying to Denise, maybe Eli could, too. It seemed like it was worth a try.

"You have to admit," Denise said, "this thing is absurd."

"It sounds serious enough, though," Eli said. "The All New England Teen and Collegiate Bodybuilding Championships. Rather grand, really."

"I suppose we have to go," Denise said.

"I think it would be mistake not to," Eli said. Actually, wild horses wouldn't have kept him away from an opportunity to see Cliff oiled up and mostly naked, posing onstage. But he'd die rather than admit it.

"Cliff's gotten so fierce about everything lately," Denise said. "He used to be easy going all the time."

"Practically to the point of catatonia," Eli nodded.

"So that's settled," Denise said. "We'll drive to Providence with them."

"Christopher made it sound like an all-day affair," Eli said.

"Yes," Denise said. "It'll spoil the whole weekend, I suppose. But I don't see any way out of it."

Not if you want to keep your boyfriend, Eli thought. Whichever of them that was.

He knew he was supposed to convince Denise not to go. Once he'd done that, he was supposed to stay away himself. He sensed that the whole adventure was Christopher's idea, a way of getting Cliff to himself and ensuring the kind of privacy that was difficult to arrange here on campus. Christopher couldn't come out and say all that, obviously. Christopher might consider Eli stupid, but nobody could be that stupid. That reality, and Denise's perennial refusal to have her plans made for her, would get him off the hook. Christopher's frustration at their presence, subtly as it might be expressed, would provide Eli with plenty of entertainment, though that was far from being his primary motivation. He had enough bodybuilding magazines stashed in his closet to know what to expect. He'd have been wild to attend even if Cliff wasn't involved. But he'd never have considered going to such an event by himself. Or suggesting it to anyone else. Christopher's machinations had provided Eli with just the excuse he needed. If Christopher was as smart as he thought, he'd understand how contradictory his expectations of Eli were.

When the negotiations finally concluded, nobody got what they wanted—with the possible exception of Cliff. Eli had no idea what his intentions or motivations were beyond the obvious: participating in the competition. Cliff and Christopher drove to Providence after school on Friday afternoon and got a motel room, since check-in for the preliminary rounds of the event was far too early on Saturday for them to make the trip comfortably then. Even if they left early enough on Saturday morning to arrive on time, Cliff's physical condition would suffer and his placing in the contest might be jeopardized. Outlining this plan, Christopher sounded like a father explaining gravity to a four year old. Denise and Eli followed in the Peugeot Saturday morning. So instead of having Cliff to himself for the entire weekend, Christopher would have him only for one night. That wasn't much better than he would probably have managed on campus, and given Cliff's moody, half-starved condition, was probably a distant second to that alternative. Meanwhile, Denise drew the short straw because she didn't want anything to do with the whole thing but was devoting her entire Saturday to it. Eli lost out because as her passenger, Denise took her displeasure out on him and also because Christopher had experienced at least partial victory.

Denise and Eli arrived at the motel late Saturday afternoon, having gotten lost on the way. Christopher and Cliff were about to leave for the venue. There was just enough time to watch them get into Cliff's car—Christopher at the wheel—and drive away. This only added to Denise's frustration, though Eli couldn't tell if it was on Cliff's account or Christopher's. Christopher took barely long enough to inform them that the preliminary rounds had gone well for Cliff and he was scheduled to appear in the finals. Denise had been hoping he'd be so disappointed with his initial placing that he'd agree to skip the evening show, eat an early dinner, and head home.

They found a bar near the auditorium and had drinks. At least Denise did. Eli felt it was crucial to remain sober. No matter what happened, he wanted to observe it in complete clarity. He tried to limit Denise's consumption because in her current mood she could turn into a really ugly drunk, but had little success.

"I can't believe the three of you talked me into this," she said as they circled the blocks around the auditorium looking for parking. "What an idiotic waste of time."

The evening program began with the teenage class. They had found seats closer to the front than Denise preferred but not as close as Eli would have liked. Once again, nobody won. Eli had no idea where Christopher was. Presumably he was lurking backstage. Eli would have expected to see him in the front row, the better to cheer Cliff on.

"Can you believe it?" Denise muttered as the teen class finalists were announced and the crowd applauded. "These people are actually enjoying this ridiculous spectacle. A sociologist would have a field day."

Next came a presentation by a guest poser, a man who'd placed fourth in the Mr. America the year before. Eli was surprised at how short he was. Finally the collegiate men came onto the stage. The thrill Eli had been anticipating since first hearing of Cliff's plan to compete finally made itself known. He squirmed in his seat, certain Denise was reading his mind and was revolted by it. Even with his untrained eye, Eli could tell that Cliff wasn't the best built man on the stage. But he was the handsomest. There was no question about it. Eli assumed that the judges weren't supposed to let themselves be influenced by something like that, but who could help being moved by such beauty? The figure posing in front of them was Cliff but at the same time something more. Glorified by the stage lights, he was everything Eli had ever wanted.

Eli had no idea what to expect in terms of Cliff's reaction to the results. He was pretty sure nobody entered a contest like this intending to come in fifth. But when Cliff emerged from the locker room, he seemed happy enough, if a little dazed. He wasn't interested in discussing the contest. All he seemed to care about was what toppings to order on his pizza.

"Eli, you ride with me," Cliff said. "Christopher, make sure Denise gets home in one piece. I'm holding you responsible if she doesn't."

While the other two stood gaping at these instructions, Eli moved toward the passenger door of the Camaro.

"I don't understand," Denise said.

"No, Eli," Cliff said. "Get in on the other side."

"You want me to drive?"

"What did I just say?"

"Cliff, what's going on?" Denise insisted.

"Am I the only one here who speaks English?" Cliff asked. He didn't sound angry or exasperated, just tired. "Must be. Will everybody please just do as I say?"

Since none of them were particularly used to this, it took a minute to make the requested adjustments.

"And Christopher, wear your God damned seatbelt," Cliff growled. "Just this once."

"Those two," Cliff muttered. "Doesn't matter which one I'm with. All they want to do is talk. Sometimes I think I'd give anything to be in bed with somebody who doesn't have anything to say."

Eli figured the best thing to do at that point was keep his mouth shut. He watched as the taillights of the Peugeot faded into a single point and that point became just another tiny source of light in the cityscape around them.

"You can start the car now," Cliff said. "They've got enough of a head start. I'm going to take a nap. Don't wake me up unless we burst into flames. And please don't drive off any bridges."

"Roger," Eli said.

They finally reached the countryside. Eli drove on through moonlight that was almost blinding. The body slumbering beside him was uncharted territory, an Eldorado waiting to be explored, to have its splendors discovered. Denise and Christopher took turn after turn with it. When would it be Eli's? Christopher had shown that was possible. Maybe Eli could follow his lead. And hadn't he earned his place? He had been discreet. He had listened silently, never speaking. He had kept everyone's secrets. He had been faithful to Cliff and to his own dreams. He had been loyal beyond any reasonable expectation. His devotion had been purer than anyone's. In another mile—around the next curve—in the shelter of the next grove of trees, blanketed by darkness and made magical by moonlight. . .

"What's wrong?"

"What?"

"We're stopped," Cliff grunted. "Why are we stopped?"

One simple question, and Eli's intention was blown to smithereens. There was no way. Christopher could brazen his way through a scene like that, but Eli wasn't Christopher. Not even close.

"Just needed to clear my head for a minute," he said.

"Good idea," Cliff said. "Let's get out and stretch our legs. I could use a pee. Where are we, anyway?"

"About forty miles out."

"Way Denise drives, they're back already."

"I'm sorry."

"Nothing to apologize for," Cliff said. "She's going to kill herself someday."

VIII

"I was sorry to hear about your father," Eli said.

"Thanks," Christopher grunted.

He had just returned from the funeral. Semester exams were due to start in two more days. Eli couldn't imagine how you coped with a situation like that, especially after hearing that Dr. Greene's death had been completely unexpected, a massive heart attack with no warning whatever.

"Seriously," he said, "I can't imagine what you're going through."

Eli had devoted a good deal of time to imagining what it would be like to lose his father. His father was ridiculously healthy and counted several ancestors who had lived past the century mark. Thus, when Eli contemplated bereavement he thought not of mortality but of unpalatable truths being accidentally revealed and profound paternal disapproval being expressed, resulting in a deathlike variety of estrangement. That, he now realized, had been no more than emotional masturbation.

"Things happen," Christopher said. "Oh, by the way, thanks for the other thing."

"I didn't do anything," Eli squirmed.

"That's the whole point," Christopher said. "You kept your mouth shut. You could have blown the whistle at any time. But you didn't."

"I didn't do it for you," Eli said.

"I know," Christopher said. "You did it because the situation overwhelmed you. You did it because you felt trapped. You did it because you were afraid you'd do more harm than good if you said anything. And because whistle blowers always lose out. All those things. Still, you kept quiet."

It was the first time Eli had ever been in Christopher's room. It reminded him strangely of his own. It was spotless for one thing. And the sparseness of the décor was the same as well.

"I just didn't want to see anyone get hurt," Eli finally said.

"Yes," Christopher nodded, continuing to unpack, "that would have been your motivation."

"What other motivation could I have?"

"All kinds," Christopher said.

Eli was glad that Christopher chose not to suggest what those might be. He really didn't want to know what Christopher imagined him capable of doing or thinking.

"I suppose you want to know why I did it."

"Do I?"

"Of course you do," Christopher said. "They're your friends. And that's the kind of guy you are."

"Right."

"Seriously," Christopher said. "There are two things you want to know. And one of them is why."

"All right," Eli said. "Why did you do it?"

"Why not?" Christopher shrugged.

"Is that all?"

"Isn't it enough?"

"No."

"Well then," Christopher said, "let's say I did it because I wanted to see if I could. I mean, the two best looking people on campus. Who wouldn't love a challenge like that? If they were really honest about it?"

Eli wanted to say he wouldn't. But he'd sound ridiculous. And he wasn't even sure it was true. That was the worst thing.

"Anyway," Christopher went on, "you're off the hook now. I'm not coming back here next fall. Those two will have to get their jollies some other way. Maybe even with each other now that I've taught them both some new tricks."

"You're not quitting school."

"I'm moving to France," Christopher said. "I'll finish school over there."

"Why France?"

"Mom's going. Her brother lives in Paris."

"But why?" Eli pressed. "I mean, I thought your mother. . ."

"She says France is the only place she was ever happy."

"And that means you have to move there?"

"I have to be somewhere. And I'm not crazy about here. I've managed to keep myself entertained, but other than that the place seems pretty pointless."

"You said I want to know two things," Eli said, "so what's the second one?"

"You won't thank me for saying it," Christopher grinned.

"Why'd you bring it up in the first place?"

"It's a night for telling the truth, isn't it?"

"If you say so."

"I do," Christopher said. "And I say this. The second thing you want to know is what it feels like to have sex with Cliff."

"What?" Eli squeaked. "No."

"Truth, Eli," Christopher said. "You want to know what it's like to have his cock in your ass. Lick his nipples. Bury your face in his armpits. All of it."

"No," Eli insisted.

"You mean yes," Christopher said. "You know I know all that stuff, and it drives you crazy that I do and you don't."

Eli couldn't think of a thing to say that wasn't embarrassing. Or just stupid.

"I know, Eli. I know what his asshole tastes like. I know the sounds he makes when he's about to come. I know how to make him come even when he thinks he doesn't want to yet. And how to make him come when he's already come twice and doesn't think he can shoot again."

"Please stop," Eli said.

"It's just, don't go getting any ideas about him," Christopher said. "He's not really into guys. It was all I could do to reel him in. Much more difficult than with Denise. With her it was like taking candy from a baby."

"But you did reel him in," Eli stammered.

"I did," Christopher nodded, "and I kept him coming back all this time. We fucked as recently as the day before my father died. Cliff hates the idea of being with a guy. He even thinks he hates me. But he can't stay away. Nobody can do the things I do to him. Nobody can make him feel what I make him feel. And every time we get together I make sure to have some new little treat ready. So he can never be sure what's coming next. Just that something is. I'm the Scheherazade of sex. A thousand and one nights, right? Each one hotter than the last. And he's Pavlov's dog. All I have to do is grin at him, and he starts drooling. That stupid Denise doesn't even try to make it hot for him. Girls don't. They just lie there and expect the guy to do all the work. Far as they're concerned they're doing us all a favor just spreading their legs. Even with a guy like Cliff. How hard is it for her to understand that he can get anyone he wants? It's unbelievable that any girl would take chances on letting a guy like that slip through her fingers. They know they're in competition with other girls. They don't forget that for a second. But they think it's all about hair and makeup and tits and that shit. It's not. It's about making sure the guy gets off. As often and as hot and hard as possible. Because if you don't someone else will. I tried to show Denise how to do it. Over and over. But she just isn't interested. Appreciative as hell of the good times I gave her, sure. 'Oh, Christopher, I wish Cliff knew half of the stuff you do.' But does she even think about returning the favor?"

It was even worse than Eli had been imagining. He'd have given anything not to hear all that.

"But just because I was able to get Cliff doesn't mean you can," Christopher said. "He really isn't available. He's going to miss me like hell, but it won't do you any good that I'm not around. You don't have what it takes. Now that he knows what it's like with another man, he might do it with any guy who encourages him, but not you."

"I wasn't," Eli insisted. "I had no intention. . ."

"Honestly?"

"Honestly."

"Maybe," Christopher shrugged. "I mean, I guess I could be wrong about it, but I think you're lying to yourself. I'm pretty sure you'd do just about anything for one night with him. But don't go getting any ideas."

JULES DE CROTEAU: 1972

Jules could have flown down from Paris, but he hated flying, even in private airplanes, and didn't for a moment consider it. He had forgotten how bad holiday traffic could be. He supposed that came of spending so many summers away from France. He didn't remember scheduling location shooting overseas that time of year purposely to avoid the chaos he could see outside with windows of the Maserati, but his subconscious must have insisted on it. Jules believed fervently in the power of the subconscious. He had never studied Freud, but he'd been told all about Freud's theories by his psychic. She was particularly adamant when it came to the role of the subconscious. Jules really had to listen more carefully to his psychic, who spoke such bad French that one was forced to believe in her whether or not one comprehended her utterances. If he had paid more attention to his subconscious, perhaps he would have made other plans this summer. Perhaps he wouldn't be sitting in the back seat of the Maserati with sweat pouring off him, listening to his driver mutter under his breath about the traffic. If he had listened to his subconscious, perhaps he would have hired a driver who possessed the expertise to repair the Maserati's air conditioning when it refused to continue supplying cold air just outside some nameless village where of course all the garages were closed because the proprietors were on vacation. Ah, the French Republic. . .

It was well after dark by the time they arrived, and Jules was nearly insane with the nervous exhaustion that only prolonged and extreme discomfort could cause. If it hadn't seemed like too much effort, he'd have strangled his driver and burned down the villa. But he started to settle down as soon as he walked inside. He assumed this was at the urging of his subconscious, which he had continued to contemplate all through the hot, dusty, non-air conditioned afternoon. He might be too addled from his journey to appreciate it, but his subconscious obviously recognized the villa as his sanctuary, his refuge, his scented pavilion of cool serenity, and reacted accordingly. And his subconscious must indeed be very influential, because by the time he had bathed and changed into the fresh clothing laid out for him by the housekeeper and eaten the delicious cold dinner she had prepared and drunk half a bottle of a very adequate Beaujolais he'd forgotten was in his cellar he was very nearly inclined to apologize to his driver for his boorishness during their journey and to withdraw his suggestion that the

Maserati be pushed over a cliff as soon as possible. The car was exquisitely beautiful, after all. Not to mention fast and temperamental, making it a wheeled analogue to any one of a dozen or more actors and actresses Jules had worked with in the past or hoped to in the future. And Volk possessed certain qualifications beyond those required of a driver which were of such a rarity and value to Jules that they must be judged as outweighing any deficiencies he might exhibit as a repairman of automotive air conditioning systems. That was assuming Volk had truly been unable, as opposed to unwilling to do so in this instance. As he considered this question of motivation as opposed to competence, Jules found that he had some fairly substantial suspicions on that point. It was not beyond the realm of possibility for Volk simply to have refused to look under the hood of the Maserati that afternoon. There were any number of reasons Volk might have desired to thwart him in that way, Jules knew. He suspected Volk of living to subvert him. A man of such unprecedented beauty and physique as Volk was a law unto himself. No one understood this better than Jules, who was a connoisseur of the type.

The housekeeper truly was a miracle worker, he decided, luxuriating between crisp clean sheets. She thought of everything. She anticipated his wishes before he was aware of them himself. She had even gone to the trouble of playing his favorite Chopin preludes on the phonograph to lull him to sleep.

Jules didn't get out of bed until sunset the next day. The night had been miserable. An hour or two of blissful rest, and then, like an artillery barrage the events of his last few days in Paris obtruded themselves into his dreams so emphatically that he was wakeful in spite of his exhaustion. There had been the meeting with the bankers, which made him long to smash furniture, though the furniture in that particular conference room was of too poor a quality for its destruction to assuage him. There had been difficult sessions with his editor—disputes over the final cut of *La Reine Dirigeable*—which made him long to sacrifice virgins in the bloodiest possible of rituals, though the only available one was inexcusably plain and thus her death was unlikely to placate and deity concerned. There had been a meeting with executives from the studio, which made him long to take up a flame thrower and discharge it in their direction. In that instance, he was still not certain what had caused him to refrain. Perhaps nothing more than the unavailability of a flame thrower at the crucial moment. He reminded himself to speak to Volk about acquiring half a dozen. He could hardly believe they hadn't already done so. The oversight was inexcusable, really.

Worst of all had been the unexpected confrontation with his arch-enemy and nemesis, Benny Rosenberg, in that dive in Montmartre. No one on the entire globe infuriated Jules as much as Benny. Benny did exactly what Jules did, only not nearly as well. Or on occasion, perhaps, much better. At least that's what people claimed, critics mostly. Benny went about his work differently enough, at least, for the differences to be remarked on, applauded even, by people who mattered in their world. Benny produced things—Jules refused to call them films—which made the critics sit up and take notice. Made their misshapen little penises stand up and squirt. Benny's "works" had even induced the judges at Cannes to shit a *Palme d'Or* or two out their tight little orifices, which Jules found utterly intolerable, having been a winner there on more than one occasion. The idea that odious, ugly, unkempt, uncouth Benny Rosenberg could be his equal—no. Truly, it was an obscenity that people even mentioned them in the same breath. He'd burn down all of Paris if that was what preventing Benny's further ascendancy required. Just see if he didn't. Volk would know exactly how it might be accomplished.

Jules tossed and turned in a kind of distracted horror at all of this, and principally at the way people perennially mistreated him, until Volk, sensing trouble or perhaps summoned by the housekeeper, arrived in Jules's bedroom to administer one of his treatments. This was a prolonged and intensive process, not to mention excruciating. But despite Jules's strenuous protests—the housekeeper was under strict orders not to summon the gendarmes no matter what she believed she was hearing—Volk persisted in his nearly superhuman efforts until they had reached completion. The result for Jules was a profound slumber graced by indistinct but extremely soothing dreams—the most soothing imaginable.

Upon awakening, Jules left his bed just long enough to bathe, which he certainly needed after his treatment, and take an omelet and salad while the housekeeper changed his bedding. The soothing music she selected for him that night was the *Etudes-Tableaux* by Rachmaninoff, whom Jules loved almost as much as Chopin.

His sleep that second night at the villa was the sleep of death, deep and completely free of disturbance. It so reminded him of coma that on rising he checked his arms for needle marks. Volk was under certain standing orders from Doctors Dreyfus and Berenger as to the administration of certain medications. He didn't find any, however. That was not conclusive. Volk's technique was so exquisite as to make it possible for him to conceal his work. But it was at least possible that Jules hadn't had to be drugged in order to sleep. As he ate his breakfast, he recalled the music from the last two nights.

"I see the phonograph has been successfully repaired," he said to the housekeeper as she served him coffee and croissants.

"*Mais non, monsieur*," she said. "The machine has not yet been brought back from the town."

"But I distinctly heard music in the house," he said. "The last two nights."

"I heard it too, *monsieur*," she said. "And very lovely it was. It came from next door."

"Next door?"

"*Oui, monsieur*. The people who have rented the Bergeron villa. A married couple, I believe. And their son. Down from Paris. Like you, *monsieur*."

Serge, his secretary, had come down from Paris on the train and was staying at a hotel in the town. By the time he arrived at the villa, Jules was seriously considering decapitation.

"See here," he said, jerking a thumb in the direction of next door, "didn't I give you strict orders about that house?"

"And I followed them," Serge smiled, "to the letter. I swear to all the saints both Christian and Socialist, I did. It's that treacherous landlord. Cashed the check and then never bothered to enter the reservation in his book, I'll just bet."

"But that house must be empty," Jules roared. "It is imperative. I must have solitude. I must have quiet. I demand these things. Demand—you understand?"

"Yes, Jules, I understand," Serge said. "However, what's done is done. And I believe you'll find it's not so bad, having Rene Melendez next door."

"Rene Melendez, you say?"

"*Oui, c'est vrai.*"

"You are quite certain? Because if you are not, if this is just a rumor or some provocation, I can guarantee you. . ."

"I'm absolutely certain of it. I've just seen him having breakfast in the town. I spoke to him."

Rene Melendez. With a wife and a son. That was certainly a surprising development.

There was several hours' worth of work for Jules and Serge to get through. The bankers had called and approved financing after all—on certain conditions. The studio executives had called as well, to green light the new project—on certain conditions. Not surprisingly, the bankers' conditions and the studio's conditions were contradictory. Jules could have predicted it. In fact, he had predicted it. He told Volk this was certain to happen as they sat steaming in the Maserati on their way down from Paris. Reconciling the differences between the requirements of the bankers and the requirements of the studio executives would require further negotiations and almost certainly delay the start of filming for several more months. This might well result in complications with regard to casting. But at least it was a beginning. And there was only one explanation for what little progress that constituted. Their departure from Paris had been noticed. Well, it should have been. Volk had practically set off distress rockets. Among Volk's skills was the ability to make their comings as goings as conspicuous or stealthy as circumstances required. Jules would not have been surprised to learn that the failure of the Maserati's air conditioning unit had been contrived in order that his tantrum in the middle of that nondescript village might be observed and reported on to certain parties back in Paris. Volk was capable of it. His previous career had left him with a particular flair for that level of verisimilitude.

Jules and Serge drafted responses to bankers and studio executives alike, but not without a great deal of strategizing. This had to be done correctly. Too much was at stake. Jules had the concept but was hopeless with the wording. That's what he had Serge for. Serge had been a starving poet when they first met, but he possessed the heart of a corporate attorney and the soul of a corrupt Jesuit. In other words, he was very nearly as perverse as Jules himself. By the time they completed their labors, the housekeeper was ready to serve lunch. It was one of Jules's favorites—*Salad Nicoise*. By the time Serge left to return to his hotel, Jules was in a remarkably fine mood.

Rene Melendez. Jules remembered the first time they met. It was late '59. Jules's first film, *Hors de Combat*, had just premiered. The critics swooned, and, on being revived, sung his praises far and wide. One morning he woke up to find that he was the toast of Paris. His name was in all the papers. People stood in line at the theatres where the film was playing. He was invited everywhere. Everyone wanted to know him. Women asked him on dates. They gave themselves to him with an abandon he would have thought impossible outside the pages of a pornographic novel. It was a dream come true for a young man of the provincial lower bourgeoisie with bad teeth, unfortunate hair texture, and a tendency to stutter. His success made it possible for him to forget all those imperfections. For a few euphoric weeks that autumn, he was a silver tongued Adonis.

That all changed one evening in early December. The disaster occurred at a gallery opening in Montmartre. Picasso was in attendance. And Cocteau. Ionesco was expected but never showed up. Late in the evening, Jules was engaged in conversation by the daughter of a *vicomte*, a young woman who had modeled for Chanel and Dior, gone on archaeological digs in central Africa, and was taking an advanced degree in economics at the Sorbonne in hopes of a posting at the United Nations in New York. She was divine—a perfect vision. And she appeared truly fascinated by Jules's explanation of his influences and inspirations. That's what she had asked him about, and she seemed to hang on his every word, nodding, smiling gently, eyes intent. Her replies, when she made them, indicated that she was that rarest of beauties, one possessed of true intellect and artistic sensivity. It was a heady moment. Jules knew, as their conversation extended itself through one, two, three drinks, that he had finally arrived. This was what he had endured the privations of his childhood and the frustrations of his early adulthood to achieve. All the suffering had been worth it. Before his eyes it was being transfigured by these exquisite moments of validation. And then the cruel stroke. He remembered it as if it had been yesterday. Suddenly, literally in mid-sentence, the young woman stopped speaking and shifted her eyes away from his, and in that instant he ceased to exist. She was lost to him forever. Rene Melendez had entered her line of vision.

That's the kind of young man Rene was that year. Paris in those days had been teeming with beautiful young men. You couldn't go anywhere without encountering half a dozen adonises at least. They rode around the city on their snorting motorcycles, cruised the streets in their sleek sports cars, infested the cafes and nightclubs like a plague of the most ravishing sort. Rene was one of them. But Rene was more. That season, he transcended them all. He was a veritable archetype. And that night he obliterated Jules completely. Without effort. Without even knowing what it was he did simply by stepping through the door of that gallery. The *vicomte's* daughter never addressed another word to Jules, directed so much as a single glance in his direction. His star, rising and brilliant as it might be, was totally eclipsed. By this young man with nothing to recommend him but his supernatural beauty and disproportionately broad shoulders. When he left the gallery, Jules seriously considered not returning to his flat but leaving the city altogether, abandoning his career and going back to his home in deepest darkest Brittany to take up vegetable growing. Perhaps a herd of goats might be acquired. Some rabbits, as well. That was how profoundly Rene had destroyed him, and without even knowing who he was.

The next few weeks were the darkest Jules could remember. No matter what he did or where he went—and he was still being invited everywhere in the city—he was incapable of shaking off his malaise. He recognized early in childhood that physical beauty trumped nearly everything, but he had convinced himself that this was because he lived in a provincial town among philistines. His belief that things were different in the greater world was what drove him to do well enough in school to convince his father that he wasn't meant to follow the family trade. His first years in Paris didn't reward his faith in the city and its people, but he never stopped believing that at a certain level of society matters would be different, and that at a certain level of success things would balance themselves out. But now—well, one could accept things when one was a nonentity that were intolerable once one became a person of note. Were he a mere nobody, that young woman's dismissal at the gallery might have been accepted philosophically, but here he was, his name on everyone's lips, and an invitation to tea with Chanel sitting on his mantel. No. He couldn't abide it.

Finally one evening, one of his friends simply wouldn't take no for an answer. They went to a party, Jules complaining all the way. When they arrived, Rene was there. Jules nearly turned around and left. The friend threatened never to speak to him again if he did and he was a good enough friend that Jules couldn't imagine purposely offending him, so he stayed. Jules tried his best to ignore Rene, who, it seemed, he could see out of the corner of his eye no matter where he went in the small flat. He managed to have a good enough time that he didn't notice it when his friend left. And finally, as the party started to wind down, he found himself, without warning, face to face with Rene.

"You think you know all about me," Rene said, which sounded to Jules like such a non-sequitur it could only be explained in one way. Rene must have mistaken him for someone else. "But really you don't."

"I'm not sure what you mean."

"You don't really know me at all," Rene said, "but it's time you did. Past time, to be totally accurate."

His experiences with women hadn't afforded Jules as much physical satisfaction as he had expected. He didn't know if the problem lay with the women themselves or had been occasioned by something lacking in him. He was aware that certain men found other men attractive but had never been able to imagine just what it was they did. As he left the party with Rene he had no inkling that he was about to learn. He was expecting that they'd walk along the Seine for a time or adjourn to an out of the way bistro for drinks and conversation. Even when Rene expressed an interest in seeing where he lived, Jules remained oblivious. Afterward he wondered what had made Rene so certain he would succeed in this seduction. Surely one couldn't simply walk up to men at random expecting them to agree to such a thing.

It was the most horrifying and unpleasant experience of Jules' life up to that point, yet the eventual result was a kind of ecstasy he'd never suspected the possibility of. He couldn't imagine desiring another encounter with those preliminary sensations, but he neither could he imagine living the rest of his life without renewing his acquaintance with that ultimate bliss. The process itself was so physically intolerable, as it occurred, that he found himself literally hoping to die just so the discomfort would end, and he tried desperately to fight Rene off. This was laughable, because Rene in those days was a consummate athlete. He easily overmastered Jules and went right on doing those inexcusable things, inflicting all that degradation and horror on his unwilling victim. He seemed to believe that Jules' frantic resistance was some sort of game or play acting. All it did was force Rene to redouble his efforts and prolong Jules's agony.

There was no rematch. At least not for a long time. Even if Jules had desired it, Rene was in such great demand as to make it impossible. Everyone wanted him. Men, women, men and women in concert. Presumably he did the same things with them that he had done with Jules. This was almost more than Jules could comprehend—people wanting that. But it had to be true. There was no other explanation for it. There was simply something about other people that Jules couldn't grasp.

Perhaps the most important result of the encounter was that they had been seen leaving the party together. People had seen it, people talked of it, people drew certain conclusions as to its meaning. When he realized this, Jules was humiliated beyond words. He found it almost impossible at first to leave his flat. Every time he walked the streets he imagined people recognizing him and talking about what they had heard. But before long it proved to have had an effect opposite to what he anticipated. Somehow it made him more desirable, more approachable. He viewed this as a triumph. It was, but only in the shallowest of senses. He experienced no more pleasure from sex than he had in the past. It was the bitterest disappointment imaginable.

The next time he saw Rene, they made no mention of it. Rene greeted him like an old friend. Jules's relief was indescribable. There must be hundreds of Rene's former conquests walking the streets of Paris. There was nothing, apparently, to distinguish Jules from any of the others. In time the sheer volume of Rene's conquests might make Jules' dishonor insignificant.

It was that relief which made possible what passed between them next. Jules was casting for his new film, *Une Reve de les Cometes,* and Rene casually expressed an interest in reading for a role. Jules had no conception of Rene as anything but a beautiful creature and couldn't imagine him as an actor, a believable presence on the screen. But somehow he couldn't help himself. So a small part—very small—was inserted into the screenplay for Rene. When the film opened, those few moments of film caused a sensation. All Paris spoke of it. A star had been born. Jules was the only dissenter to this opinion. Rene looked spectacular on the screen. There was no disputing that. But he had no discernable talent as an actor, and he spoke French with such a heavy accent that it hurt Jules's ears to listen to it. In actual conversation it wasn't so obtrusive. But on film—no, it just wouldn't do. Still, he cast Rene in two more films. After that first sensation, people expected it. Rene seemed to expect it himself. The studio executives certainly did. Everyone seemed to think of Jules as Rene's patron. And Rene expressed his gratitude in the way which came naturally to him. Jules tried his best to be appreciative of this, but each time they were together the experience was as horrendous yet profoundly satisfying as the first. It was like entering Nirvana by way of the most harrowing passage through the gates of hell. If this was the only way he could experience ecstasy, and he was beginning to suspect that such was the case, he might as well take holy orders and subject himself to a life of celibacy.

So finally he decided that he had had enough. He offered Rene a role in a fourth film, but only half-heartedly. Rene must have heard the reluctance in his voice. He declined. Jules didn't yet know it, but Benny Rosenberg had recently discovered Rene, and Benny had none of Jules's qualms, artistic or otherwise.

When Jules saw the young man stride out of the surf he thought he was dreaming. After his siesta he had come out onto the veranda, pulled the chaise lounge into position looking toward the water, and stretched out in the late afternoon sun. Time, which passed in the most frenetic of tarantellas in Paris, stood still when Jules looked at the sea, and his mind drifted with the moving waters. The sun sank lower, the shadows lengthened, the horizon, such a clear line earlier in the day, lost definition and became blurred and indistinct. All this, he knew, denoted the passage of time, but he didn't feel it. He floated. He hardly seemed to breathe. And when the young man appeared, as if from nowhere, tossing his head and sending diamonds of spray flying from his hair, his wet body gleaming in the dying sunlight like a young god—well, what else could it be but a dream? It was too perfect a vision for anything else. The young man himself seemed scarcely human. His beauty was more than the mind could conceive, or indeed absorb the reality of. Jules stared, drinking it in. He knew he would wake soon and the vision would disappear, but he bent his entire consciousness on prolonging the moment to the fullest extent possible, his only wish to go on slumbering with that exquisite creature dancing like a faun in his dreaming eyes.

"*Monsieur,*" the housekeeper's voice shrilled from the house, "*Monsieur*—it is the telephone. From Paris."

But as Jules silently cursed her for waking him, he became aware that the young man still capered on the sands. His heart pounded with this comprehension of the sublime made flesh.

Curiosity quickly got the better of Jules. It was not possible, he realized, to ignore the presence—even reputed—of Rene Melendez just next door. But he refused to betray his eagerness, or even his awareness that it was Rene he was addressing the invitation to. He simply wrote it out on a piece of note paper and folded his card inside: "dear neighbors, please do me the honor of coming to luncheon. . ."

But, as on that long ago night when he'd left that party with Rene, he got more than he bargained for. The next day at the appointed time, his guests arrived. Rene, no longer youthful but still spectacularly attractive, was accompanied by an elegant woman who must have been exquisite twenty years or so ago. Rene introduced her as his sister, Madame Greene. Jules recalled her as one of the most glamorous women of her time. A decade before he ever met Rene, she had modeled for Chanel and Dior. And this was far from her only claim to fame, it seemed. She was a very fine pianist. The music Jules had been hearing in the evenings hadn't come from a phonograph. On their arrival from Paris, Rene rented a Bechstein and had it delivered to their villa so his sister could entertain them.

Madame Greene and Rene were accompanied her son, Rene's nephew, Christopher.

The young god from the beach. It was like a message from heaven.

"You used to hate sex," Rene smirked, slapping his chest hard enough to make it sting.

"I didn't," Jules insisted.

"Yes, you did," Rene insisted. "It wasn't just me. Everyone spoke of it. All Paris was struck by the irony of Jules de Croteau, the most sensuous of all film directors, having no taste at all for sensuality in life. Surely you must have realized."

"I assure you, I wasn't aware."

"I used to make you do certain things just because I knew how much they distressed you. I loved testing you to see how much you were willing to endure for the sake of my beauty. What a delicious game that was. You have no idea how my friends and I laughed about it when I told them my stories. But times change. Now you actually seem to enjoy it. A small bit."

"Experience is a great teacher," Jules said. "Everyone knows that."

This might even have been true, had they been speaking of anything else. This afternoon's sport with Rene had called on all Jules's skills at dissimulation. It was nearly more than he could bear, even in such a sacred cause as he had embarked upon. He was relieved to have been found convincing, at least.

"Funny old Jules."

Rene had spent the last decade or so building up his body. Always beautifully proportioned, he was now as opulently muscled as a wrestler or gymnast. His face, now more mature, had become at the same time more manly. Jules had always thought of him as one of those men whose looks wouldn't peak until he reached the cusp of middle age, and this expectation proved correct. Rene's technique, too, had improved. He was as selfish and demanding as ever but had mastered certain nuances. Jules couldn't help regretting his inability to appreciate them.

None of this mattered, however. He'd have invited Rene into his bed even if he'd weighed two hundred kilos and lost all his hair. The gods had shown Jules his new path and were waiting impatiently for him to follow it.

Luncheon two days ago had demonstrated beyond argument that the young man from the beach was a living creature, not a dream, not a demigod. Rene's sister had married an American, a doctor. Christopher was their only child. The marriage had been happy enough, but Graciella never really adapted to small town life. She still spoke very little English. And when Dr. Greene died a year and a half previously, she had come to France to live. Christopher preceded her. Due to unspecified "incidents" in American colleges, it was considered better all around for him to finish his studies at the Sorbonne. He had achieved some success there. He would be starting medical school in a few weeks.

This left Jules very little time to achieve his objective. But he was not worried. He had, as a British friend of his was in the habit of saying, an ace in the hole. Jules had no idea what this idiom had originally referred to. He understood it from context only. On a literal level it was as inscrutable as a moonless night sky.

But he did like the sound of it. Someday, obviously, he had to give serious attention to learning English, if only to deplore the British all the more trenchantly in their own tongue.

A few years after his first big success, Jules found himself being courted by several Eastern European governments. Encouraging him—rather agressively, he thought at the time—to film in their capital cities, or rural villages for that matter, they offered a dizzying array of inducements. It was all fairly incomprehensible, even in light of his films' enormous popularity with communist audiences. This in itself was baffling. Why were his films even shown in Warsaw? Prague? Budapest? Why hadn't the authorities proscribed him? Wasn't he the epitome of the bourgeois artist? Didn't his work celebrate the most decadent excesses of capitalist society? "Ah, but *monsieur*," the dapper little gentleman from the Czech embassy said when he raised this objection, "you fail to take into account the irony inherent in your vision. That irony transforms all, making you a prophet of the world revolution." Well, Jules knew he was ironic, of course. It was his stock in trade. But he had never viewed this penchant as a political statement. It seemed he'd been incorrect in this, or at least insufficiently conscious, politically speaking.

He and his assistants visited several cities scouting locations. Budapest was gorgeous but too much like Paris. Prague was visually enticing, but somehow insufficiently exotic—there was something strangely Germanic about it. Like Switzerland only not as hygienic or as mountainous. And he had always hated the Swiss. So smug. So unimaginative. So puritanical. In that last respect they were even worse than the British, and that was saying a great deal. So he scratched Prague. But he didn't scratch the idea of shooting in Eastern Europe. Given the incentives involved, he'd have been a fool to.

So the next spring found him in Romania, along with his entire company of actors, technicians, assistants, liaison people from the studio and the banks—the whole gaudy circus parade of a film production going on location. On arrival in the capital they were wined and dined by the officialdom. Three whole floors of the city's finest hotel were cleared for them. A fleet of sinister looking black limousines was placed at their disposal. All doors were open to them. At least that's what they were repeatedly told, though Jules took this with a grain of salt. A commissar was attached to their company for the purpose of "expediting" their every requirement, and they were provided with what seemed to be a whole regiment of security personnel. Serge joked that he had no idea whether the function of these menacing looking men was to protect them from the locals or vice versa, but it made Jules feel like a dignitary, noteworthy for his international reputation and important to the state.

The security detail was headed by a Captain Volk. The commissar assured Jules that Volk was one of the finest officers in the state security service. Jules assumed this meant that to at least some extent he and his group were being spied on. But he decided he didn't much care. He couldn't imagine that any of their activities would be found objectionable by even the most hard-nosed of officials, and besides, Captain Volk was such a spectacularly imposing individual that Jules didn't think he'd particularly mind being denounced and possibly even interrogated at his hands. Volk was nearly two meters tall, but even at that height his shoulders were disproportionately broad. He was massively constructed from what one could tell beneath his almost cinematic uniforms, and handsome as a film star. But in this instance, the director would almost certainly have been Leni Riefenstahl. Golden haired and blue eyed, Volk seemed the archetype of the Aryan ideal. A few adjustments to his costume and he wouldn't have looked out of place carrying a flaming torch at Nuremberg. Picturesque as Volk was, however, Rene recognized that he wasn't the sort of man one thought of as typifying the Romanian people. The commissar, apparently sensing his curiosity, informed Jules that the country's populace included a large Hungarian minority. Serge assured Jules that this was indeed the case, and given that information Volk's appearance almost made sense. His remaining skepticism on the subject rapidly dissipated. Volk's spectacular good looks all but guaranteed it.

After a few days in Bucharest, the company traveled to their location in the mountains, where a castle and several small villages were to provide the settings for the new de Croteau production. Under the yapping of the commissar and the chilling glances of Volk—who seemed to communicate almost exclusively by scowling—their move proceeded without incident. The castle, in addition to providing settings, served as accommodation for Jules and the cast. They were joined there by the commissar and Captain Volk. Their presence under the same roof as Jules was obviously considered desirable by some bureaucrat somewhere. Jules had no objection, really. His hosts had been remarkably accommodating so far, and he had no desire to seem unappreciative. Every centime the studio didn't have to spend on the shooting widened the film's profit margin and at the same time impoverished the despised bankers who would have charged exorbitant interest, and Jules was still enough of a capitalist to value that. The commissar was annoying enough to be a distraction, to be sure, with his obsequiousness and his incessant talk, but the monumental Volk was enough of an aesthetic treat to make up for it. It was like agreeing to consume a somewhat unpleasant main course in order to be served a particularly exquisite dessert.

Shooting was the usual fiasco. They fell behind schedule immediately. The reasons were as varied as they were predictable. Nothing happened to delay them that hadn't happened during the shooting of at least one of Jules' previous films. Bad weather, unreliable electrical service to the site, minor illnesses among the cast perhaps occasioned by the local cuisine, perhaps psychosomatic. These things were all too foreseeable but by no means preventable. The situation was no worse and no better than at any time during Jules's career. He was confident that in the long run nothing would prevent him from completing the film. None of these minor annoyances posed the least threat to the eventual success of the project, and he accepted them all with perfect equanimity. But that didn't mean that his reactions to the delays were outwardly calm. A certain theatricality was required in order to demonstrate to everyone else the gravity of their predicament. Jules took care to compose these tantrums as precisely as he did the shooting script itself. They must convey in no uncertain terms that it wasn't just the movie that was at risk. It was his reputation as a director. Time was money. Delays meant additional costs. They meant anxious telephone calls from the studio and the bankers, who at this point hadn't realized the extent of the support Jules was receiving from the Romanian officials due to Serge's expertise at cooking the accounts. They meant the threat of having the production shut down. They meant the very real possibility that this production might be his last. Jules scripted his part in all the relevant histrionics painstakingly. At all costs he must maintain the upper hand in his struggles with the philistines. Otherwise, he might as well abandon the whole thing. Then, too, there was the cast to consider. His leading lady hadn't been his first choice or even his second. Those two had been vetoed by the studio and the bank, respectively. This one had been approved by both groups, which made her immediately suspect. She turned out to be a shrew, and a lazy one at that. Lazy, stupid, and ten pounds overweight. The leading man was as amiable as she was difficult, but was a drunk. The actor playing the villain was a drug addict and pedophile. All this required managing. Lots of managing each day—before a single frame of film could be shot. The Romanian crews were cooperative enough, but communism had liberated them from taking directions, it seemed. He constantly had to call on the commissar to translate his orders into suggestions which they would then confer about at length prior to agreeing to follow—at least approximately. It was all tremendously exhausting. Eventually Jules became incapable of bottling up the resulting frustrations. As he had always done in the past when that stage was reached, he took them out on Serge.

Ordinarily, Serge was rather prickly in such instances. He was at least as mercurial as Jules, and his tongue was just as sharp. He had quit his job over questions of Jules's temperament more times than Jules could count, and he was not above throwing things. Or, indeed, smashing things too heavy to throw. By all rights they should have been at each other's throats at least once a day after the first couple weeks of shooting. That was their usual pattern. But for some obscure cause Serge chose, just this once, to take any and all abuse hurled at him with the serenest of smiles. This went on for several weeks. Jules couldn't recall Serge ever remaining so extraordinarily agreeable for such an extended period. It unnerved him more than any other response he could imagine. So much so that eventually he was forced to remark on it.

"But you see," Jules said, a cryptic grin on his face. "I've found something to occupy my time. To help me blow off steam."

"I don't know what you're talking about," Jules said. "You have no time to occupy. You work as many hours as I do."

"Time in an existential sense, I meant," Serge said, making, Jules considered, no sense whatsoever.

"I ask you a question," Jules said, "and you insist on talking gibberish."

"Gibberish, is it?" Serge laughed. "Come to my room tonight at eight o'clock. I'll show you some gibberish."

It would serve Serge right if Jules ignored him. Jules was sorely tempted. But if Serge had discovered some way of dealing with the stresses which Jules was finding so overwhelming, he had to know about it.

"Ah," Serge grinned, answering his door. "I wondered if you'd bother to come."

"Look here, Serge," Jules said. "I have no time for nonsense."

"You never do."

"So?"

"In the bathroom," Serge said, cocking his head in that direction.

"Oh, no, Serge," Jules said. "Not drugs."

"Certainly not. Follow me."

Jules did. There was nothing to see in the small room except what one would expect.

"Serge."

"Pull back that shower curtain."

Jules did. And was amazed. The whole back wall of the shower enclosure was like a picture window giving a view of the bathroom next door. He supposed it was some sort of one way mirror. This was surprising enough, but these old castles were full of bizarre and unexpected features. What truly astonished Jules was the scene taking place on the other side of the glass. Captain Volk, naked as God made him, was shaving his monumentally muscled chest with a straight razor. His physical development was beyond any Jules had ever seen. Indeed, it seemed to exceed the potentialities of any actual human being. He didn't merely appear godlike, he must actually be some species of superhuman creature. That was the only possible explanation. Yet, of course, it was no explanation at all.

In front of him, a young woman knelt worshiping his organ of manhood with her mouth. That part of Volk's anatomy was noticeably out of proportion with the rest of him. Due to Volk's extreme size, Jules would have expected it to appear small. He had observed this phenomenon in athletes of various kinds and always found it sad, from a visual perspective, that their perfectly normal parts looked miniscule in proportion to their sturdy bodies. But in this instance, the disproportionality was in the opposite direction. Despite being attached to a giant, this member appeared grotesquely outsized. It wasn't a penis at all in any conventional sense, Jules thought. It was, instead, a sort of platonic ideal. It was the penis of all penises. It appeared capable of fathering whole nations. Indeed, it appeared equal to the task of populating entire planets.

Volk continued shaving his monstrously inflated chest, exquisitely sculpted belly, and heroic arms, and the young woman continued her efforts. Her task was not an easy one. Only the head of the organ actually fit into her mouth and that just barely. The shaft defied all her attempts. Her jaws simply wouldn't open wide enough to allow it admission. What kind of sex life must this man have, Jules thought, possessing a part so immense that it couldn't actually be inserted anywhere? Eventually, Volk finished with the razor and cleaned himself thoroughly with a cloth. All the while, the young woman never ceased her labors. Volk, totally erect, nevertheless seemed oblivious to her presence or her exertions. He began oiling his body. The deep bronze of his skin—Jules must find out about the Romanian seaside resorts—gleamed like burnished metal as he massaged the oil into it.

This ritual finished, Volk reached down with his massive hands and pulled the young woman to her feet. At this point Jules was astonished to realize that she wasn't a woman at all, but a young man with fine features and long, luxuriant hair. Volk grabbed him by the buttocks, hoisted him into the air, and impaled him in one smooth motion. Jules expected screams of agony at the very least. Or perhaps the pain of this assault would render the young man immediately unconsciousness. But the unbelievable occurred. Somehow the young man took the entirety of the appendage into himself, at the same time sucking at Volk's grotesquely large nipples in alternation. The resulting frenzy went on for an unusually long time. Jules almost forgot to breathe. When it was over, he was horrified to realize that he had fouled his clothing.

"Every evening," Serge said. "You could set a clock by it."

Jules had forgotten Serge was even present.

"Not that same thing every time, of course," Serge continued, "but every evening there in his bathroom. Sometimes with a man, sometimes with a woman. Sometimes with two women or a man and a woman. He's worked his way through most of your cast, though I probably shouldn't tell you that. In any case, there's plenty of him to go around. He's astonishing. Indefatigable."

Jules found it impossible to speak. He fled to his room for a bath and change of clothing.

Eventually, they completed shooting. A delegation came from Bucharest to help them celebrate. The officials had received nothing but glowing reports from the commissar. They begged Jules to accept honorary citizenship in the Peoples' Republic as a reward from a grateful nation, which he found an easy enough request to agree to. It seemed no less than he deserved. As a citizen and an invaluable asset to the state, the delegation said, they would like to suggest in the strongest possible terms that he also accept the Romanian government's perpetual protection. Now that he had accepted the friendship of the Romanian people, the capitalists were undoubtedly already plotting against him. They might well have agents concealed among his retinue. He must, they insisted, find room for Captain Volk on his permanent staff.

It took Jules several years to come to the realization that all those nights in front of the one way mirror had been no random occurrence. They had been orchestrated for the purpose of rendering him favorably disposed to the Romanian representatives' overtures. By then he had become so totally dependent on Volk that he regarded that manipulation as the instrument of his salvation.

Volk was no run of the mill security officer. Jules recognized that more or less immediately on being introduced to the giant. Jules had assumed he was some sort of intelligence operative, but he was no ordinary spy, either. His work for the intelligence service of Romania had been of a highly specialized nature. It was so specialized, in fact, and the level of his expertise so totally unmatched, that he was often loaned to the other intelligence services of the Eastern Bloc. He was Einstein, and the use of extreme sexual sensation as a form of coercion and torture was his Relativity. There wasn't a relevant technique he hadn't mastered. There wasn't an implement, no matter how obscure or terrifying, with which he wasn't conversant. He was said to have brought a *grande dame* of the pre-revolutionary aristocracy to repeated orgasms simply by massaging her little finger and staring deep into her eyes. Later that night she died. Her doctors called it heart failure, but Jules, hearing the story, believed it had been nothing less than complete sexual exhaustion. Volk was by no means always as subtle as in that case. His massive strength meant that he was capable of exerting tremendous force if that was what the situation required. And he had stamina, too. Women had gone permanently mad after a few hours in his hands. Men had committed suicide at the thought of having succumbed so totally to the sexual energy of another male. Members of both sexes did away with themselves rather than face the prospect of experiencing such unspeakable sensations, horrifying yet enthralling, only once in an entire lifetime. Millionaires threw away fortunes vainly attempting to duplicate the singular experiences he had forced on them. Story after story told of his astonishing prowess. Volk never spoke of any of these things. Jules only learned the truth over the course of several years, collecting one unbelievable rumor, one shocking anecdote, at a time. None of what he heard surprised him. He had long since experienced Volk's skills first hand. On their return to Paris, with Volk newly installed as his factotum, Jules had made the initial discoveries, recalling the tremendous satisfaction he had experienced over and over during those nights in Romania. It hadn't gone well at first. He literally had to be tied down. He honestly thought he was dying. The long ago escapades with Rene, which had so revolted and terrified him, now seemed like the play of small children. He learned two things his first night with Volk. First, that he was exactly the kind of man that made a career like Volk's necessary, and second, that he could experience ninety-eight percent of the satisfaction he was capable of from watching Volk exercise his gifts on someone else. After that, his path was clear. Making legitimate films became merely the means to an end. Somehow his unholy obsession had to be paid for.

Now the stakes had shifted, subtly but profoundly. For the first time he had found a partner for Volk who was his equal in transcendent beauty. Jules knew he could never hope for satisfaction again until Rene's nephew had been sacrificed and enslaved. Bringing the two men together would be a delicate operation. Rene and Madame Melendez-Greene would have to be managed. The young man himself would be no problem. Volk's involvement insured it. Jules had never yet encountered an individual with sufficient powers of resistance to fend the giant off.

What Jules envisioned was a scenario from a revisionist mythology of his own conception. The young god Apollo, overpowered, brutally raped, and permanently subjugated by that matchless mortal, Hercules. The preternaturally beautiful youth, so thoroughly corrupted and debased by the mature warrior that he was stripped of all his innate nobility; so enthralled by the incomparable prowess of his new master that he willingly cast away his divine powers for the sake of a sexual fulfillment inaccessible to him through any other avenue. That was the story Jules wove for himself each afternoon as he watched Rene's nephew cavorting in the surf and sunning himself on the beach. Serge, sensing that something extraordinary was afoot, flew into action. The cameras concealed around the property had to be checked, cleaned, and loaded with film. Courier services had to be arranged for the transportation of each day's footage to Paris for processing and its subsequent return to them at the villa for viewing and critique. The cinematographer and his legion of assistants had to be summoned and accommodations and daily transportation from the town arranged for all of them. Jules would not have them staying at the villa. Their mere presence disturbed his ruminations. There were a million additional details for Serge to see to, and he went at his tasks like a dervish. Volk knew, too, through some sixth sense of his own, that his services would soon be called for and began his own preparations. He instituted a regimen of abstinence so as to marshal his powers, lifted weights with religious fervor, shaved his body repeatedly until its satiny surface shone like metal, had his hair cut by a man in the village who was a retired military barber, and maintained his tan with precisely timed sessions in the sun and the application of exotic unguents.

Jules kept his own counsel. His acolytes, he knew, could be relied on absolutely. He had trained them to perfection. When the time came, his instructions would be minimal, yet their execution of them would be as precise and perfect as if they had been conceived, formulated and communicated to them by a deity. The scenes of domination, torture, and debasement would play themselves out spontaneously. With one glimpse of the boy, Volk would comprehend instinctively what was required of him in every exquisite detail and proceed accordingly, like Degas staring at a blank canvas. At the same time, not a moment of the proceedings would be missed by the cameras. The crews knew *cinema verite* like fish knew water and would clearly understand the technical imperatives implicit in the action unfolding in front of them.

Yet as Jules sat observing the young man and imagining each scene at it was to play out, he came gradually to the understanding that what was to be captured on his film was not the sole and entire reality of the case. There was another layer of reality that must be confronted in a way he had never forced himself to confront such a thing in the past. There were those apotheosic images teeming in his brain that, though totally incorporeal were to his mind as real as anything could be. There were the acts themselves which would realize them. There were the hundreds of feet of film that would preserve those acts. But finally—and this was the reality to which he had remained oblivious in the past—there was the living, breathing young man himself, whose perfection made everything else not only possible but necessary. Jules was suddenly struck by the impossibility of allowing that exquisite creature simply to be employed as a kind of living puppet and then allowed to pass from the scene as completely as though he had never existed. The young man himself, as much as his beauty and his experiences in Volk's hands, must be made permanent. He must be fixed and mounted, as a scientific specimen is prepared in order to place it on display in a museum. The initial vision being so celebrated must itself be realized not merely on film but in physical form. Christopher must literally be made the slave of Volk's mythic yet at the same time all too corporeal masculinity. His previous existence meant nothing. His anticipated future was equally insignificant. He must become someone entirely new, a figure embodying Jules's own conception of him as Volk's adjunct being. In order for this to happen he must be broken. Broken but not destroyed. Broken and refashioned, rather. Let the powers of the mighty Captain Volk work on him like the blazing heat of the forge and the implacable weight of the great sledgehammer ruled and directed by the enormous strength of the blacksmith's arms and his ruthless intent, transforming the softened metal into something nearly as sublime, nearly as perfect as its creator.

The youth must be remade in a new form. In the form of the one absolutely perfect recipient of all of Volk's manly energies. Medical school was all well and good. Let him be a doctor if he wished. A doctor by profession. But let his true and enduring vocation be his transformation into the ultimate and permanent receptacle of and monument to all that was Volk. Let that be his purpose and let him understand it not merely with his brain but in and with every fiber of his being. After the filming was complete, Volk might elect never to expend his energies on the youth again, but let the youth pass the rest of his life in the anticipation of Volk's return, over and over, to be exalted and worshipped. Let the youth forsake all other manifestations of the masculine principle, however and whenever he might encounter them. Let him be dedicated as exclusively and purely as the chastest vestal of ancient times had been dedicated to the worship and adoration of the one true and mighty deity reigning over the world of men. Let him be enslaved, totally enslaved, with the slavery not merely of the body and its myriad sensations but with the slavery of heart and mind and spirit, the slavery that cannot and will not conceive of the possibility of its liberation.

Yes. Let him attend medical school and begin his career. At the same time, let him take up residence in Jules' compound in Paris so that daily Jules could witness and be enthralled by the purity of his devotion. But first let him be broken as he must be broken. Let him be broken through suffering the most intense agonies Volk was capable of inflicting on his perfect young, beautiful young body, rising through those fleshly horrors and depredations to the unimaginable, stupefying ecstasies only such sufferings at such hands could grant him access to.

Yes, let it be.

It all went wrong more quickly than Jules could have imagined. And, inexplicably, the catastrophe did not result from any of the hundreds of possibilities he had lain awake frantically anticipating and making mental preparations to forestall. The failure was more fundamental than that, and there was no one else to blame for it. It was his failure and his alone. He had completely misunderstood the young man. He had seen, but he hadn't comprehended. His preconceptions had prevented that and the result was that his grandiose design fell flaming from the dark firmament of his phantasmagoric imaginings, shattering on the stones of a new and barely credible reality. His imagination had not merely been mistaken. It had been, apparently, too small and weak.

Everything appeared to proceed according to plan at first. That morning dawned with exceptional clarity. It was the most exquisite of days. Sunny, warm, and breezy enough to prevent the heat from becoming oppressive as the day wore on. All had been checked, rechecked, and re-rechecked and was in readiness. After lunch and his siesta, Jules lounged on the terrace and waited for Christopher to appear. His observations had taught him that the young man's habits were so regular that it was possible to set one's watch by them. Concealed at their duty stations, his minions waited. The drowsy air bore a slight tinge of electricity, as if their collective anticipation seeped into it like a static charge just beginning to propagate through storm clouds.

The young man entered the scene as the late afternoon light was beginning to turn golden. As was his habit he ran into the surf and capered there, the water spangling his alabaster skin like thousands of jewels. Over his own shoulder, Jules could just hear the muted whirring of the multiple cameras trained on Christopher. Then, while the young man's delighted play was at its height, Volk appeared. He had timed his entry to the scene to perfection. The boy noted his arrival with some surprise. He was a stranger, of course, but no mere stranger. Jules, holding his breath, saw clearly that the youth could scarcely credit the reality of the vision. Volk's gargantuan scale and godlike handsomeness were almost too much for anyone to take in. Then, too, nude sunbathers were perfectly customary on that beach, but the sheer magnitude of Volk's nakedness couldn't be ignored. And indeed, the young man appeared fascinated with that particular aspect of Volk's appearance, as a man encountering a fabulous but previously unknown species is fascinated.

Jules watched as the two greeted each other, as they played together tentatively on the fringes of the surf, the boy like a pup and Volk like a mature wolf, the leader of their pack. They moved gradually up the sand toward the grounds of the villa. Volk didn't rush the progress of the scene, yet every move, every gesture, every word addressed to the boy was an indispensable part of the seduction. Jules found himself enthralled by the perfection of everything he was witnessing. Its exquisiteness transcended his original conception. It actually seemed to validate all his previous works. And when Volk finally took the young man by the hand and led him through the entrance to the hidden courtyard at the side of the villa, Jules sensed that his ultimate success was about to unfold before his eyes. His heart raced at the thought of what he would be witnessing during the next few moments.

It took scarcely an instant for him to reach his new vantage point, and settling himself there he was barely on time to witness the moment when the youth first realized with certainty what Volk had brought them there for. Volk leaned down to kiss him, and as Jules had expected, Christopher flinched. But there was something unexpected in this reaction, because what should have been an expression of revulsion and terror was neither of those things. Certainly, there was momentary disbelief on that beautiful face, but there was not the least hint that the young man's intention was to resist. His expression passed quickly from surprised comprehension of the situation to a subtle but unmistakable delight, as if this, indeed, had been what he'd silently hoped for on first seeing the titan approach him across the sand.

Even the sight of Volk's enormous manhood, rampantly engorged by this point, the foreskin completely retracted and Volk's trademark "pearl of greeting" glimmering at the slit, which should surely have terrified the young man, seemed merely to confirm for him that these moments would prove to be the culmination of a lifetime's anticipation. Jules could hardly credit it, but it was as if, in the absence of any knowledge that Volk actually existed, the boy's imagination had long ago conceived him. And Volk's triumphant entry a scant few moments later, which should have been greeted with shrieks of the purest agony, proved to be no assault at all. What Jules was witnessing, he recognized suddenly, was not desperate struggle followed by conquest and subjugation, but fusion. It was as if the young man was not Volk's victim but in some heretofore unanticipated manner his collaborator.

As Jules viewed the raw footage of the first day's shooting in a state of profound bewilderment, he took comfort in one thing at least. Visually, the man and the youth made a perfect pair. The young man's pale skin contrasted exquisitely with Volk's oaken tan. The young man's thick mop of black hair, exactly the shade and sheen of a raven's wing, was the perfect counterpoint to Volk's precisely barbered, immaculately groomed, spun gold. The two men's faces were equally flawless. Their physiques were ideal complements. The youth's fleet and sinewy as a messenger to the gods, the man's that of the destroyer of worlds. And finally, there was the youth's manhood, which was only average in size but breathtakingly proportioned and detailed, its foreskin barely concealing the head when in repose, while Volk's, far larger, was nothing less than the weapon of a barbarian warrior, the long foreskin tapering to a point and closing into that tight aperture almost as if secured in place by a length of rawhide, as had been the practice of the ancient Greeks in preparation for their sports.

Each day man and youth met upon the warm sands of the dying afternoon. Each day their encounters grew more intense, in the manner of two titans colliding ever more forcefully. The scenes of domination and torture were enacted with terrifying and almost ritualistic fervor, as if Christopher were daring Volk to inflict the utmost indignities of which he was capable upon his perfect, insatiable young body. Their ferocity in these acts stunned Jules, who sometimes feared that the forces being unleashed might literally prove permanently damaging to the young man. It was as astonishing a spectacle as he had hoped, but totally altered by the addition of that one unanticipated component—Christopher's willing assent, yes, to be sure, his complete insistence on his own horrifying abuse. The monumental struggle between Volk and Christopher was not, then, conflict on an almost cosmic scale but a bizarre collaboration, as if only through the most stringent exertions together could they ascend to some transcendent state beyond any sensual possibility previously imagined by living, breathing men.

Volk had been worshipped with willing and enthusiastic acquiescence in the past. This, indeed, was nothing new. But his previous capitulators had been women, of whom it was only to be expected and which rendered the phenomenon meaningless since it was in their nature, or men already so hideously deficient and debased that their ready surrender was equally trivial. This sacrificial victim was to all intents and purposes as perfect as those had been flawed. He was as perfect as the young Apollo who had been Jules' original inspiration. His avid acceptance of his subjugation, his conscious and willful insistence on it, marked him as a remarkable new species of man. He was a man who himself could easily insist on worship, demanding and requiring unimaginable acts of devotion, yet who gave himself up wholly to the veneration of his own master, whatever cost that veneration inflicted on him body and soul.

It was not at all what Jules had imagined. He was not certain he approved of the way in which the young man demanded all that was meted out to him. Instant, passionate acquiescence where prolonged, almost mortal resistance would have been expected seemed nothing less than obscene. But the aesthetic perfection of the footage spoke for itself so eloquently that Jules' disapproval of its psychosexual subtext was insufficient disqualification. It was merely the most ravishing footage he had ever seen. That alone meant it had to be preserved and the filming continued until it reached whatever conclusion the two actors brought forth out of their prodigious collaboration.

What he might do with the film after that was more than Jules could bring himself to consider as he sat, night after night, recalling the afternoon's visions and reviewing the footage returned from the laboratory in Paris by the couriers.

He had forgotten how complete was Rene's familiarity with the villa. It had been over a decade since the days when Rene enjoyed free run of the place. Surely such an obscure fact as the location of Jules' private editing booth should have been lost to Rene's memory, if, indeed he had ever known of its existence. And so it was with considerable shock when that deep, velvety voice shattered his reverie late one night several weeks into the process.

"You old goat," Rene said, "so this is what you've been up to."

"What do you mean?'

"I knew something was going on. You've been far too intent on keeping me distracted. There is no way you've come to love the act that much, not even as I perform it. It's simply not in your nature. Yet for days on end you've pretended to be insatiable. And now I see the reason why. Corrupting my nephew behind my back. And by delivering him into the hands of that glorious monster of yours. I have heard of Captain Volk's talents, of course. Everyone knows of him. But this—this is certainly a surprise."

"Rene."

"Don't you dare try and tell me I don't know what it is I'm seeing."

"Very well," Jules admitted. "It is exactly as you say."

"Indeed."

"I must beg of you, Rene, the project is not finished. If you could find it in your heart to forget what you have seen for just a short while longer, I will give you anything you ask. Anything that is in my power to give, you shall have."

"How much longer?"

"A few days," Jules aid. "No more than that."

"A few days? What does that mean?"

"No more than a week," Jules said. "Please, Rene, it is exactly as you describe. I admit it. But you of all people understand the nature of my art. And surely the boy cannot be harmed any more than he already has been by your agreement to ignore this matter for such a short time."

"My objections to whatever my nephew may have involved himself in are hardly the point, my dear Jules," Rene said with a smile Jules found both inexplicable and alarming, "and I understand quite well what you are offering me. I'm sure we could eventually come to some satisfactory arrangement. But the time you are asking for—there is the problem. In four days we shall be gone."

"Gone?"

"Yes."

"Well, no matter," Jules said. "We can film whatever else we may find we lack back in Paris, at the boy's leisure."

"Paris?" Rene exclaimed. "Why, we shall be nowhere near Paris. You will have to go much farther than that to film any more scenes of Christopher and Volk."

"What do you mean?"

"When we leave here in four days' time, we leave for America. Christopher is to attend medical school in San Francisco, and I go there with him. He will spend the few weeks before the beginning of classes reacquainting himself with American life and the English language, and I will find housing for us. You have just made that task much easier for me, my friend."

"How so?"

"You have corrupted my nephew, Jules. Surely you don't think you can do such a thing without paying a steep price."

Jules had never been able to tolerate having his hand forced and thus was compelled to formulate a rationale to support such a radical change of circumstances. The boy must not be allowed to escape his grasp before Jules could arrive at some new plan for exploiting him. And Rene, especially armed with his new knowledge, could be a formidable opponent. There was, for instance, his association with that odious Benny Rosenberg. The threat posed by the two of them in collusion against him was too dire to be contemplated. Such an eventuality could not be permitted.

There was no time to waste. The filming would continue. It must be completed in the time frame Rene had outlined, and it could be, just. And in addition, during those same scant hours a way had to be found to transport Jules' entire enterprise six thousand miles or more, to the shores of the Pacific.

He was beginning to sense the possibility that the boy, whom he had originally imagined as Volk's ultimate victim and subject yet who had so unexpectedly proven impregnable to being cast in such a role, might prove instead to be Volk's counterpart. The ultimate recipient of masculinity would, hypothetically at least, possess a power equal to yet at the same time totally different from that possessed by Volk. And the men of America, with their aggressive and pugnacious forms of masculinity, might prove to be more vulnerable to the apparently passive approach of the ultimate orifice than the overt assault of the ultimate appendage. What Volk would struggle to destroy by direct attack the boy might destroy with equal success through the appearance of surrender. What Volk would batter out of those athlete-warriors of the New World through his sheer power, the boy would absorb from them silently, draining them to husks before they were any the wiser.

It would by no means be merely a matter of unleashing Christopher, of turning him loose on the male population of that fabled city to exercise his powers however he might. He was too unpredictable. There was no telling what catastrophe might ensue. Most probably he would flash across the skies like a meteor and burn out just as quickly with a white hot flame. Jules had no intention of permitting that kind of denouement. Christopher's energies must be channeled. Nurtured and preserved. Focused, not expended mindlessly. He must be kept under the most rigorous control. It would undoubtedly require several sessions with Volk every week to ensure it. It would probably be best for Christopher actually to be housed in Volk's own quarters, where, despite whatever other activities the titan was engaged in, the youth would at least absorb his aura. That in itself would have a salutary effect, Jules was convinced. But more than anything, Jules' satisfaction demanded torture. The destruction of men Christopher might prove capable of effecting by his own particular means could prove nearly as absolute as that achieved by Volk, but it could not possibly create a spectacle which would afford Jules genuine satisfaction. It was impossible to film emptiness. A dark screen signified nothing. What Christopher must do for Jules instead would be to lure those defiantly virile American men into the trap with his almost feminine seductions, have his way with them until they believed themselves completely satiated, and then bring them, exhausted and depleted, to Volk for their ultimate debasement and destruction as men, helpless sacrifices on his altar of fire, steel, and masculinity. In his mind, Jules saw it all, the manhood of an entire continent shrieking and groaning in agony, its magnificence and potency utterly obliterated, the scene of its destruction illuminated by the fires of Volk's forge and the gleam of betrayal in Christopher's bottomless eyes.

It was an experiment worth attempting. And at the very worst, it would, Jules was certain, make for exquisite footage.

ASHBY SAINTE-CLAIRE: 1972

I

When Eleanor Rousseau Duckworth McKinney initially married her third husband, the wedding took place in Las Vegas. There were only three of them present, Eleanor, her groom, Stormy Davis, and her first husband, Matthew Duckworth—known to everyone acquainted with him as the Captain—who served as a combination of best man and father of the bride. It was all she believed she wanted at the time. But before long she thought better of it. She didn't have reservations about her marriage to Stormy. Not by any means. This new marriage brought her batting average back up to .667 after that disappointing dive to .500. Poor dear Hobart McKinney. The biggest mistake of her life, but at least a short-lived one. No, she wouldn't breathe, or listen to, a word of criticism about her new marriage or her resplendent new husband. But the thought of how Stormy would have looked at center stage of a "society" wedding with his gleaming hair and brilliant grin and looming shoulders on display for the crème de la crème of Newport Beach—that was more than she could pass up once she gave proper consideration to it. She imagined the wedding album with all Stormy's extravagant qualities in perfect focus and began immediately to plan the ceremony. It wouldn't matter a bit that the date on the marriage license was two years old and that she'd been going around calling herself Mrs. Davis since returning from their honeymoon. All that mattered was giving Stormy the big day her perversity had originally cheated him out of. And getting to witness it herself.

The Captain and Ashby didn't attend Eleanor and Stormy's second wedding. Nate had threatened a boycott if the Captain didn't come unaccompanied, and the Captain refused to submit to emotional blackmail from anyone, especially his oldest son. At the same time, neither the Captain nor Ashby was willing to keep Eleanor from seeing her only grandchild, Nate's boy Osgood, on the big day. She wasn't sure what made her more furious, Nate's intransigence or his attempted manipulation, but the three men, her husband, her ex-husband, and her ex-husband's lover, convinced her of the truth of that old saying about living well being the best revenge. As a consolation prize, she booked herself and Stormy into the Fairmount for a second honeymoon. This would provide her an opportunity for a pleasant, extended visit in San Francisco with the Captain and Ashby while at the same time thumbing her nose at the recalcitrant, judgmental Nate in exquisite surroundings.

On the second morning after the wedding, they all met for brunch at Top of the Mark. Ashby found the symmetry of the foursome fascinating in a particularly cryptic way. The ex-spouses had both allied themselves with young men the age of their eldest son. There was something almost karmic in this arrangement, he felt, though as a medical student he was a man of science and should consequently be immune to such a speculation.

After brunch, Eleanor insisted on seeing the apartment the Captain and Ashby had just moved into. It was a pleasant, if slow, drive in Stormy's convertible through the ravishing streets of a surprisingly sunny Sunday. The sunshine gleamed off Stormy's perfectly combed hair, and not for the first time Ashby compared himself unfavorably with his lover's ex-wife's husband. As if he was reading Ashby's mind, the Captain squeezed his hand. That made him feel better, though it didn't solve the underlying conundrum.

"It's just too perfect," Eleanor exclaimed, looking around the living room, "this lovely old building, those gorgeous views, and it's in walking distance of the medical school."

"Ned Westerleigh found it for us," the Captain nodded. "He's a genius."

"Dear Ned," Eleanor nodded. "Such a charming man. Don't you find him charming, Ash?"

"He makes me feel like a little kid who's been sent to the principal," Ashby said. "But the Captain says it's all in my head."

"There's too much in that head of yours," the Captain said. "That's your problem."

"All I can say is, it makes me feel fucking useless," Stormy grinned, tossing his own magnificent head, on which not a single hair stirred.

Ashby couldn't imagine what possible set of circumstances would be required to render a man like Stormy superfluous.

"What does, darling?" Eleanor asked.

"Ash here starting med school tomorrow."

Stormy made his living, a very good one actually, selling Ferraris and Lamborghinis in Newport Beach. He was to all intents and purposes the male human equivalent of one of those automobiles. Ashby imagined customers buying those expensive cars solely for the pleasure of getting to shake Stormy's hand at the end of the transaction.

"Darling," Eleanor laughed, "we can't all do noble, selfless things like healing the sick and suffering."

"That's right," Stormy nodded, "what would those noble, selfless doctors drive to the hospital in if not for guys like me?"

"Good point," Ashby laughed. "Make sure to give me your business card. I'll probably be in the market in about fifteen more years."

"Are you excited, Ash, dear?" Eleanor asked.

"If he tells you the truth, he's going to say he's terrified," the Captain said. "God knows why."

"Rooming with Nate in college," Stormy suggested, "would have been enough to terrify me right out of school forever, pretty much."

"But you're fearless," Ashby said. "You're practically Batman. At least according to Quinn."

Quinn was the fourth of Eleanor and the Captain's sons and Stormy's biggest fan among them.

"Quinn exaggerates," Stormy smiled, "but he's a great little guy."

"Answer the question, dear," Eleanor persisted. "Aren't you excited? I know I would be. I'm sure you're going to meet the most fascinating people."

"Are these seats taken?"

"Help yourself," Ashby said.

"I'm Yolanda,"

"Ashby."

Ashby recognized Yolanda Ibarra from several of his classes. He figured that a Hispanic female who could get into medical school had to be a pretty tough cookie. More than one of their professors had been openly skeptical of her presence among the first year students. She maintained her cool in the face of this, which Ashby admired, having faced withering skepticism from the world in general in his earlier life.

"How's the chicken a la king?" she asked.

"Not especially royal," Ashby said. "Not even upper-middle-class, come to think of it."

"Lesser of two evils, I thought," she said, looking dubiously at her Salisbury steak.

It seemed paradoxical that a medical school cafeteria would serve such unhealthy looking food.

"Hello, fellow martyrs."

"There you are," Yolanda said, "finally."

"Delicate negotiations with the girl at the register," the handsome guy grinned.

"I'll bet," Yolanda said.

"Hi," the handsome guy said, turning to Ashby. "I'm Christopher."

Ashby knew who Christopher was. Everyone knew who Christopher was. Hands down, though Ashby was certain he'd heard one female second year student say "pants down", the hottest guy in the first year class. Perhaps the hottest guy in the whole medical school, though Ashby wasn't yet assimilated enough to know that for certain. Looks shouldn't matter here of all places, but they unquestionably did. Pondering the phenomenon, Ashby didn't know whether to laugh or cry.

"Ashby," he said, offering his hand.

"Oh," Christopher said, "we know who you are. Don't we Yolie?"

"If you say so."

"And I say we do," Christopher continued, "and furthermore and moreover, I say the three of us should go out for drinks this afternoon to celebrate surviving our first week of medical school. They said it couldn't be done, yet here we are. Undefeated. Undaunted, even."

Ashby tried and failed to imagine what it would take to "daunt" a guy like Christopher. He had encountered the type before. He didn't much like them. But they sure were pleasant to look at.

The Captain had told Ashby to make some friends. He was very insistent on the point. And the Captain didn't give advice idly. Ashby knew that the Captain suspected him of pathological shyness, against which rigorous and constant exertions were required. Still, he wasn't sure the Captain would have been quite so insistent if he had known who it was Ashby was supposed to be meeting for drinks. Yolanda wasn't the problem. The Captain would surely approve of a young woman that smart. He had a real weakness for brains. But Christopher was too damned attractive. Nobody should be that good looking and smart enough to be a doctor. It had to violate one of the laws of thermodynamics or something. Despite being married to one of the handsomest men on the planet, Ashby couldn't help himself. At least once a day he caught himself staring at Christopher when he should be paying attention in class. The Captain was one of the most self-confident men anywhere, but Ashby didn't believe he could possibly approve of that degree of interest. But it wouldn't be polite of Ashby not to show up. He didn't care that much in Christopher's case, but he didn't want to treat Yolanda that way. She seemed very nice, actually. Ashby took a deep breath and pulled open the door to the bar.

"Who's ready for another round?" Christopher asked.

"Me," Yolanda said.

The bar was a riot of every Haight-Ashbury cliché imaginable. Ashby could only imagine what Eleanor would say if he brought her here.

"*Et vous, Monsieur Sainte-Claire?*"

"Yes, thanks," Ashby said. He was having fun in spite of himself. Christopher spoke French with what sounded like a genuine Paris accent. Ashby added that to the list of things about him to both admire and disapprove of.

"Club soda again?" Christopher asked. "You sure you don't want anything stronger?"

"I told you," Ashby said. "I'm picking someone up at the airport later."

"Right."

"Yolanda was disappointed that you didn't go on to dinner with us Friday night," Christopher said, sitting down next to Ashby in the lecture hall on Monday morning. "Just between you and me, I think she has a crush on you."

"What is this?" Ashby asked. "Seventh grade?"

He had seen how Yolanda was looking at Christopher Friday night at the bar. If she had a crush on anybody, Ashby knew who it was. He couldn't blame her. He nearly had a crush on Christopher himself.

"Seriously, Ash," Christopher said, "I think you're in there."

This was so ridiculous that it couldn't be a misunderstanding on Christopher's part. Ashby assumed he was being untruthful about it. Or at the very least provocative. He wondered what Christopher thought the point of that was.

"She seems really nice," Ashby said, "but I'm already seeing somebody."

"Really?"

"Yes."

"Seeing somebody?" Christopher asked. "Or seeing somebody?"

"Huh?"

"Well, you might just be making an excuse," Christopher said, "or you might really have something going on."

"Oh," Ashby said. "Well in that case, it's actually pretty serious."

"Whatever that means."

"Is living together serious enough for you?"

"If you're telling the truth about it," Christopher said. "Then again, it's not serious enough that you're wearing a wedding ring."

"Maybe somebody will clue Yolanda in," Ashby said, "before she gets too interested."

"Tell me something," Yolanda said, sitting down next to Ashby in the anatomy lab.

"What's that?"

"Do you think a guy like Christopher could ever be interested in someone like me?"

"What is this?" Ashby asked. "Seventh grade?"

He was glad to have his suspicion confirmed. It was important to know what kind of people you were dealing with.

"I'm sorry Christopher," Ashby said, "but already I told you and Yolie I would be busy all weekend. I'll see you on Monday."

He hung up. When he got back to the bedroom, the Captain was out of bed and running his electric razor over his stubbly chest. For best results the Captain preferred hot lather and his trusty straight razor, but there wasn't always time for that ritual. Ashby was still tingling all over from the stubble. His first two weeks of medical school had been almost overwhelming with the Captain away from home the whole time on flights between New York and Frankfurt. Knowing the Captain had returned, Ashby nearly ripped off his clothing on the elevator earlier he was in such a hurry to get up to the apartment.

"Let's grab a quick shower," the Captain said, "then we'll go somewhere for dinner."

"Who was that on the telephone earlier?" the Captain asked, cutting into his Chateaubriand.

"Guy from school," Ashby said. "Christopher."

"What's he like?"

Ashby took a deep breath. He might as well get the visuals out of the way.

"A lot like Stormy as a matter of fact," he said.

"Really?"

"If Stormy dropped twenty pounds or so but didn't lose any definition."

"A gymnast, in other words."

"Right," Ashby nodded, "though I'm just guessing about the definition part. We all wear our clothes full time at medical school. So I'm going by the arms, pretty much."

"Glad to hear it," the Captain grunted.

"Oh, and if Stormy didn't use all that stuff in his hair."

"Stormy and I," the Captain grinned, "both feel naked without it."

The Captain always appreciated an opportunity to identify with his ex-wife's new husband, whom he considered a kindred spirit and spiritual heir. Ashby thought it was an extremely healthy, if bizarre, dynamic.

"Is Christopher nice?" the Captain asked.

"No," Ashby said. "I don't believe you would actually say that unless you were drunk or stoned."

"Why? What did he do?"

"Nothing," Ashby said. "Yet."

II

"Thank you for coming by to see me, Mr. Sainte-Claire."

"Of course, Professor Isaacs," Ashby said. Professor Isaacs was one of the most feared members of the medical school faculty. Legend asserted that he thought himself a failure if at least two members of the first year class hadn't dropped out by Halloween. That was just two weeks away, and Ashby figured this summons indicated he had been placed on the short list. He didn't know what he'd expected the professor's office to look like. He was surprised at how nondescript it was. Didn't someone as distinguished as a professor of medicine deserve to work in grander surroundings?

"I wanted to speak to you about the results of your mid-term exam."

"I know, Professor," Ashby said, "an eighty-one per cent. I'm really disappointed in myself. I'll do better next time. I promise."

"Actually," Professor Isaacs said, "that's not what I meant. An eighty-one is a perfectly respectable result at this point in the course."

"I don't understand."

"Well, you see," Professor Isaacs said, "it's just that your good friend, Mr. Melendez-Greene, scored eighty-one percent as well."

"I know," Ashby said.

"And by a strange coincidence," Professor Isaacs continued, staring at what Ashby had by then realized were his and Christopher's test papers in the file folder open in front of him, "he got exactly the same questions correct and incorrect that you did."

"I didn't realize."

"Didn't you? Are you sure about that, Mr. Sainte-Claire?"

"Of course, Professor."

"I have to say, I find it very interesting," Professor Isaacs said. "I'm sure some would call it a coincidence. But I'm a scientist. And in science, as you know, we generally disallow coincidence as an explanation for unexpected correspondences such as this until we've ruled out all other possibilities."

Ashby wondered if strict scientific principles could really apply to human behavior and interactions, but this was no time for metaphysics.

"Christopher and I studied for the exam together," Ashby said. "I suppose that must explain it."

"Yes," Professor Isaacs said. "That's one possible explanation, certainly."

"We studied with Yolanda Ibarra as well," Ashby said.

"Did you?" Professor Isaacs asked. "Then I assume you know she scored an eighty-nine."

"Yes," Ashby said.

"I want you to know that I've already spoken to Mr. Melendez-Greene about this."

"I see," Ashby said. This was not the best possible news. Over the past weeks, he'd observed a certain willingness on Christopher's part to shift blame for things onto others that to be absolutely accurate were his own fault. The incidents so far had been inconsequential, and Ashby chose to give him a pass. When he raised the issue privately with Yolanda, she looked at him like he was a lunatic, so he didn't pursue it.

"He suggested another possible explanation for the unusual similarity between your exams."

"What?" Ashby asked.

"I think you know what I'm implying," Professor Isaacs said, riveting Ashby with a gaze which, even blurred slightly by the professor's bifocals, was terrifying. "I'm extremely reluctant to accuse you—either of you, you understand—of cheating in my class. Such a thing would necessitate your expulsion. You realize that, I hope."

"Professor," Ashby said, "I would never cheat."

"Yet Mr. Melendez-Greene seems to be of the opinion that you might have."

"If he said that, he's mistaken," Ashby said. "That's all."

"Then you must think he cheated."

"I didn't say that," Ashby insisted. "I'd never accuse him of it. There simply must be another explanation. I'm not sure what it might be, but please believe me."

"What I may or may not believe isn't the issue," Professor Isaacs said. "This is an extremely serious matter. It's not merely a question of a student or perhaps two of them making a serious error in judgment. The lives of patients could be put at risk by doctors who have taken that kind of shortcut in their preparation. I'd be derelict in my professional responsibilities if I let it pass."

"I understand that, Professor," Ashby said.

"What I have to say to you is this," Professor Isaacs said. "I'm a very busy doctor and teacher. I don't have time to give this matter any further attention. I've drafted a letter outlining my concerns, and I intend to forward it to the dean. You should expect to hear from him."

Ashby's immediate reaction was to run away. It had always been like that. Whenever Grandpa threatened him with a beating, Grandma got crazy drunk and started throwing things, or Mama held him down and encouraged the boyfriend of the week to tickle him until he peed in his pants, escape was his only thought. Beyond them it was schoolyard bullies, smug know-it-all church ladies, and school teachers of irascible and unpredictable temperaments. All these he eventually learned to subvert but never to face down. His urge to flee never abated. In adulthood, he avoided confrontation at all costs. The last time he had been faced with such a threatening situation was the day of Nate's wedding when the whole Duckworth clan found out the truth about him and the Captain. Ashby had learned an important lesson then. When someone else's happiness and welfare were involved as well as your own, running away wasn't an option. Sometimes you had no choice but to stand your ground. Whether you thought you had the strength for it or not, you had to pretend to be a man and hope for the best. Quitting medical school because some professor suspected him of cheating would merely put an end to his professional aspirations. Disappointing the Captain was what Ashby really couldn't face. It would be worse than anything else he could possibly do. Still, he wished he had gone with his instincts in the first place. He should never have had anything to do with Christopher. He had known it more or less at first sight. He should have trusted his gut. That had been the time to run away. Now it was too late. He couldn't believe he'd allowed himself to get into a position like this.

"Calm down," Christopher said.

They were walking toward Christopher's bus stop. The breeze was frigid, but that wasn't why Ashby was shaking.

"I'm calm," Ashby insisted. "Nerves of steel."

"Next you're going to try and sell me a bridge," Christopher laughed. "They can't prove anything, you know. It's practically impossible to prove cheating on a multiple choice exam. Unless you get caught in the act, they have absolutely nothing but their own suspicions to go on."

Ashby thought it was extremely interesting that Christopher chose this line of defense rather than an outright denial. It was exactly what he'd expected, not that this made him feel any better.

"I mean, you don't seriously think they'll require us to take a polygraph or anything like that," Christopher said. "There's no way they want to go to all that trouble. Besides, they'd have to have probable cause."

"This isn't a criminal case," Ashby said. "Nobody's talking about prosecuting anybody, so that rule doesn't apply."

"They don't know we know that," Christopher said. "They think we're a couple of scared lightweights who don't know how things work. That's why we have to call their bluff."

Ashby had always been a terrible poker player. Certainly worse than Christopher was. But in this case deficient card playing technique was the least of his worries. The real problem was that Ashby couldn't make himself see what was happening as just a game. Apparently Christopher could. It put Ashby at a disadvantage, but maybe Christopher didn't have to know that.

"They're waiting for one or the other of us to crack," Christopher said. "I hope you realize that."

"It won't be me," Ashby said, thinking that if he got through this without having his ambitions and his marriage shot to smithereens, he'd seriously consider going back to church.

"All we have to do is keep our cool," Christopher said. "It will all blow over. You'll see."

The thought that Christopher was willing to end Ashby's medical education and destroy his dreams in order to save himself would have been devastating if Ashby hadn't experienced similar treatment so often in the past. That people were as rotten as they could get away with wasn't news to him. That someone who'd befriended him could be so treacherous was merely par for the course. It hurt, of course. That kind of thing never stopped hurting. But Ashby had survived it before and he'd survive it this time. The emotional component of the whole thing was, he knew, the least of his worries. He couldn't afford to indulge his feelings. He had to set them aside. He couldn't allow himself that kind of distraction. He had to be practical. He had to be smart. He had to stay cool, not just with the professor and the dean, but with Christopher in addition. Christopher might be his enemy now, but Ashby couldn't let Christopher know that he considered it possible. He had to be tough. Everything was at stake, his marriage included. There was no telling how the Captain would react if he was thrown out of medical school. Even if the Captain supported him through the crisis, the humiliation would probably be too much for Ashby to face. It would poison everything. He wouldn't be the person the Captain had fallen in love with. He wouldn't be the person he wanted to believe he was. This might be a game to Christopher, but in reality it was life and death.

There was no way for Ashby to prove that he hadn't cheated for the simple reason that a negative couldn't be proven. Ashby shouldn't waste his time worrying about that. Any effort he made in that direction would just make him look guilty. And it wasn't just the faculty who were in on it. It was the hottest rumor of all among the other students. If it was a game in any respect, it was a game of impressions. Ashby had to convince his professors that he wasn't the type to cheat. And the best way to demonstrate that was to show he didn't need to cheat. It was like that old saying about the best defense being a good offense. He had to work harder. He had to get good enough marks in his classes that there wouldn't be any questions about his integrity. That's where he had to put all his energy.

And, of course, he had to do it in such a way that Christopher couldn't cheat off him. He hadn't even considered the possibility before, but now it seemed certain that's what had happened. It wasn't the original "coincidence" that made him uneasy. It was Christopher's behavior since. It would do Ashby no good to excel in his classes if Christopher turned that success against him. He'd have to defend against that. And, he supposed, he'd have to defend himself without appearing to. If Christopher caught on to his gambit, he might find a way to become even more dangerous.

"It's a really cheap trick, Ashby," Yolanda fumed, slamming her books down on the library table, "going to Isaacs and accusing Christopher of cheating off you on the mid-term. When it was nothing more than a coincidence, I mean. Cheap and cowardly. I didn't think you'd do a thing like that. And yes, I have calculated the mathematical probability of a coincidence like that. Which is more than you were willing to do to support a friend. Numbers don't prove anything, you know."

This, he thought, was a remarkable thing for her to say—a medical student and woman of science. Numbers did prove things, or at least give strong indications about them. Numbers were used every day to verify all kinds of things that doctors had to know about beyond mere hunches. That was how the whole thing worked. He couldn't believe she'd say something that stupid. She had to know better. Of course when a hot guy was involved, reason flew out the window. But Ashby couldn't blame her for that. He'd exhibited the behavior himself in the past. More than once. He'd probably do it again sometime, somewhere. But never again for this particular hot guy.

Yolanda was acting like every girl who had ever looked down on him when he was a kid. He had never won an argument with one of those girls, and eventually he had figured out he should stop trying. He had never expected medical school to be so much like junior high. In some ways, that was the biggest surprise involved in the whole sorry affair.

"Sorry, Yolie," he said, "can't talk now. Don't want to be late for anatomy lab."

"So I have to go see the dean," Ashby said, mortified at having to tell the Captain the whole miserable story. The long distance charges alone were enough to make him nauseous. The apartment felt like a prison cell.

"Ash, listen to me," the Captain said. "You know you didn't do anything wrong. And these are very smart people you're dealing with. They'll get to the bottom of it and you'll come out smelling like a rose."

"God, I hope so."

"Now repeat after me, 'it's going to be fine'."

"It's going to be fine."

"Good boy. I wish I could be there with you. But you can handle this. I know you can."

Ashby made that his mantra. He repeated it to himself all the way to classes each day. He muttered it under his breath at moments of particular stress. He went about his business like nothing was wrong. He tried to treat Yolanda and Christopher the same as he had before the whole thing started. He suspected that no one was fooled.

"So you see, Mr. Sainte-Claire," Dean Maxwell said, "while I understand Professor Isaacs' concerns and agree with him that there is a clear appearance of academic dishonestly here, all we really have is one man's word against that of another. And that being the case, I'm not prepared to take things any further at this point. I simply can't see any other way of coming to a fair resolution. I would be remiss in my duties, however, if I didn't issue you the sternest possible warning. The entire faculty has been alerted to this matter. You and Mr. Melendez-Greene are going to be under the most rigorous scrutiny in all of your classes as from now. Guilty or innocent in this instance, you should assume that next time, if there is a next time, you won't be given any benefit of the doubt. Whatever."

"I understand, sir."

Within a minute, Ashby was vomiting in the men's room down the corridor.

"What did I tell you?" Christopher gloated into his empty beer glass. "They folded. I knew they would. That's how you have to handle these dinosaurs. Show them that you've got bigger balls than they had back when they still had balls."

"You told me," Ashby said. Somehow he couldn't believe that justice had triumphed. The other thing he couldn't believe was that it was actually over.

"Now you can stop going around like an inmate on death row."

"I hope you learned your lesson," Yolanda said. She was staring at something or someone over his left shoulder. Ashby assumed that any conversation he had these days was being overheard.

"I did, all right," Ashby told her. He knew they weren't talking about the same thing.

"Good," she said. "I'm sorry I was a little hard on you about the way you stabbed Christopher in the back. I apologize. I guess you just panicked. I suppose it could happen to anybody. That Isaacs is such an ogre. It must have been terrible having him trying to get you. But you can't panic like that when you're a doctor, you know. Patients' lives depend on your ability to keep a cool head."

"I know," Ashby said. "It won't happen again."

"It better not. People around here take loyalty very seriously. They won't let you off this easy more than once."

"Right."

"So I guess we'll just chalk this one up to experience," she said.

She was certainly right about that.

When Ashby got a note to meet with Professor Isaacs again, he knew he'd been right to suspect that the matter wasn't really closed. The dean hadn't done anything official, and Isaacs obviously wasn't satisfied. It was like a nightmare Ashby couldn't wake up from. He had thought that such a thing couldn't happen at medical school, among people dedicated to the ideals of curing disease and easing suffering. People like that should be above pettiness and dishonestly. Obviously he'd been wrong to believe it. What price he'd have to pay for his miscalculation was the only question still unanswered. It didn't look like he'd have to wait much longer to find out. When he got there, Christopher was waiting in the corridor.

"What do you suppose he wants?"

"What do you think?" Christopher snorted. "Some people are never satisfied."

"I guess not."

"All I know is, you'd better not blow this, Ash."

"Gentlemen," Professor Isaacs said, ushering them into his office and motioning them to take seats, "I appreciate your making yourselves available to meet with me this afternoon. As you're both aware, the dean has elected to take no official action in this matter. In fact, he has encouraged me to consider it closed. Which is what I propose to do."

"Thanks, Professor," Christopher said. "That's great news. Right Ash?"

"Not so fast," Professor Isaacs said, with a quiet smile. "I have agreed with him not to pursue this situation any further from an official perspective. But I still have my own curiosity to satisfy. And as a scientist, I won't be able to rest until I've done so. That's the kind of people we are. So I've devised a small experiment of my own."

"What's that?" Christopher asked.

"You may well ask," Professor Isaacs smiled. "I'm sure you're curious as well, Mr. Sainte-Claire?"

"Yes, Professor."

"It's simply this. In my files I have several alternate forms of the midterm examination. I administer them in rotation so that my students cannot receive inappropriate help from students in previous years' classes. I have two different forms of the exam right here, as a matter of fact. What I'm proposing is that you each retake the exam right now. Mr. Melendez-Greene, you will sit here with me. Mr. Sainte-Claire will go into the outer office and my secretary will proctor him. I believe the scores you earn this afternoon will be most instructive. Do the two of you feel agreeable to this? Well, that hardly matters, actually."

For the first time since the whole fiasco began, Ashby began to feel hopeful. He knew the material the exam covered. He'd reviewed it again the night before on a sudden impulse, though he wasn't supposed to believe in them. If he couldn't make this opportunity work out for him there was no explanation but that he was cursed. He sat down at the small table the Professor had conducted him to and opened the test packet.

"I, of course, do not feel free to share Mr. Melendez-Greene's score with you," Professor Isaacs said.

By this point, Ashby almost felt he knew the people in the photographs on the professor's office wall personally.

"He may do so if chooses, certainly. Assuming that the two of you remain on speaking terms."

"You'd have to ask him about that, sir," Ashby said.

"I see. Well, let's just say that for your score to have improved by three points was not particularly surprising, since I believed from the first that you were the one who had actually gone to the trouble of preparing for the exam. Then too, since you had already taken it once, some improvement in your score was to be expected. Your refusal shift the blame onto Mr. Melendez-Greene even after you knew he had accused you of cheating was extremely revealing, I thought. The dean agreed with me on that point, I'm happy to say. The dean is a good man, but he doesn't always comprehend matters as quickly as he might. And at the same time, a fall of over twenty points in Mr. Melendez-Greene's score didn't particularly surprise me, either. That, too, was exactly as I'd been expecting. It was as close to catching him red-handed as I'll be able to get. Such slippery fish are extremely difficult to deal with, but now I'm satisfied that I know the truth. I'm only sorry to have put you through what I'm sure was a very distressing experience."

"You didn't do anything to me, Professor," Ashby said.

"No," Professor Isaacs grinned, "I don't suppose I did, did I?"

"What will you do now?"

"Nothing," Professor Isaacs said. "I supported the dean's original decision. This doesn't change that. Given his wait and see attitude, the crucial thing was to establish your innocence. That was my one and only motivation in continuing my investigation. I hope you understand I had no agenda beyond that. By now, Mr. Melendez-Greene has either learned his lesson from this experience or he hasn't. Only time will tell. But the whole faculty has been put on notice that he's a potential cheater, so they'll keep him on a very short leash. He'll either clean up his act or adopt much more sophisticated techniques in the future. As I said, time will tell. I do worry about Miss Ibarra, though. I know she and Mr. Melendez-Greene are very close. I'd hate to think he was an unsuitable influence, but under the circumstances I can't help being suspicious. And God knows he's a charming devil. I don't suppose you could have a word with her? Just as a gentle warning?"

"I'll try, sir."

"You seem dubious."

"I don't suppose I should say this, but she's not a good listener when the subject is a certain fellow student."

"That's too bad," Professor Isaacs said. "A doctor needs to be an objective listener despite his or her preconceptions. Sometimes it can be a question of life or death."

"Ah, Sainte-Claire, come in, come in," Dean Maxwell smiled. "Sit down, please."

Ashby seemed to spend as much time in faculty offices these days as in lecture halls and laboratories.

"Thank you."

"I've had a talk with Professor Isaacs. He tells me that he's satisfied himself with regard to a certain matter."

"Yes," Ashby said. "He spoke with me yesterday afternoon."

"Took him long enough."

"Sir."

"Isaacs seems rather hard-nosed, I realize. But the entire faculty depends on him to help maintain a certain standard of academic integrity here. It's one of those unspoken things that in their own way are more important than all the official policies and procedures."

"I think I see that," Ashby said.

"I wanted to let you know that I've communicated to the faculty— unofficially, you understand—that the professor and I both consider you completely blameless in this matter."

"I appreciate that, sir. Truly."

"And just let me say that both he and I consider your behavior throughout to have been exemplary. You're going to be a credit to our profession, Sainte-Claire. I'm certain of it."

"Thank you, sir."

"These things crop up from time to time. There's an individual like that in almost every entering class here. I wish I could tell you that we're always able to weed out the dishonest ones, but it would be dishonest on my part to say so. Of course there are unethical doctors in practice, and they didn't get that way overnight. Many of them showed signs of it during their medical school days, I suspect. We're teachers here, not police detectives or priests. Overall, however, I think we do a fairly good job. Generally in the case of a first year student, it's a one-time thing. They almost always realize they don't want to go down that road, and there's no more trouble."

"You know, Ash," Christopher smiled across the library table. "Someday we'll look back at this and laugh."

"I'm sure that's true," Ashby said.

"What matters is that you learned a valuable lesson. You can't let these professors push you around. You have to show them that you have backbone. That's what they look for in young doctors. They want to know who can stand up to everything the job throws at us and who can't. If you can't, you lose their respect. And once you've done that, it's very hard to get it back. It was a close call, but you'll know better next time."

"I certainly will," Ashby said.

"Don't worry about Yolie. She'll come around. She knows how much I respect you. That carries a lot of weight with her."

"Sure," Ashby said. "Well, I'd better head out. I'm picking someone up at the airport."

"Oh, right, Dr. Sainte-Claire, man of mystery," Christopher laughed. "Eventually you're going to have to tell all. I hope you realize that."

"See you Monday."

"You see, Ash," the Captain said, sponging him off with a washcloth, "I told you everything would turn out fine. And you know why I knew it would? Because I know what kind of man you are. Now, let's grab a quick shower and then we'll go somewhere and have a late dinner."

"You must be starving," Ashby said.

"That place in North Beach, I think," the Captain said. "With the pasta carbonara you're so crazy about. I love to watch you eating it."

TRISTAN BENTLEY: 1973

I

When Big Steve suggested a threeway, Tristan didn't know what to say. Or even what to think. It was a real curve ball. They hadn't been together very long, about a year actually, and Tristan still wasn't completely clear about who Big Steve was—or, more to the point, who he was himself. And as always he was preoccupied with subtext. It couldn't just be about sex. Nothing ever was. There had to be more to it than that. So what was Big Steve really trying to say? Not that Tristan had ever known him to be oblique. That wasn't Big Steve's style, much to the regret of individuals who ended up on the receiving end of his critiques. Long-time local oracle and arbiter Ned Westerleigh once observed that Big Steve only had to open his mouth for stone tablets to fly out of it, and no one who heard him disagreed. Still, Big Steve hadn't expressed any interest in extra-curricular activities before, and Tristan wasn't prepared to consider it.

Truth to tell, he didn't find the idea of sex with an additional partner appealing. It wasn't that it was shocking. He knew that lots of couples were in open relationships. It seemed to be more common than not. You couldn't go anywhere without hearing talk on the subject. You'd be chatting with a nice young guy at a cocktail party, for instance and the next thing you knew you'd been invited to post coital breakfast with him and his husband. Or you'd be standing next to a pleasant gentleman in a buffet line and he and the man tending one of the chafing dishes would start a discussion of the potential of a young man across the room as a guest top for a couple of their acquaintance who. . . Hell, you could hardly go to the supermarket without being confronted with the phenomenon. The participants Tristan knew personally took inordinate pride not just in the practice but in

243

being blasé about it. Indeed, part of the attraction to being in an open relationship seemed to be sharing the details. And people did. Incessantly, it seemed. They insisted the whole thing was no big deal and proclaimed themselves completely satisfied with every aspect of the experience. But Tristan's observation was that their claims generally weren't truthful. It always seemed that one member of the pair was a happy participant and the other one wasn't. When the time for Big Steve and him came, Tristan was pretty sure he knew who would be who. And even though he lived to make Big Steve happy, he couldn't make himself to look forward to this.

As he observed most of the couples he knew of, Tristan liked to think, or rather wanted desperately to believe, that Big Steve and he were different. But he couldn't have told you what that was supposed to mean. That they could have a threeway or even a succession of them and not go haywire over it like everyone else who tried it eventually did? Or that they shouldn't need that kind of adventure to validate their relationship? If Big Steve and he weren't different, if they were really just like all those other couples with their dogs and houses and furniture and vacation trips and boyfriends on the side, Tristan didn't think he wanted to know it. And Big Steve's suggestion threatened to answer that question definitively. Tristan reckoned that he had already lost enough illusions for a lifetime, and he was pretty determined to hold onto that one. Still, he could no more have said no to Big Steve than he could have walked on water. He knew that much and he suspected that Big Steve did, too.

The sole reason Tristan could abide Big Steve's understanding of this was that he trusted his husband. He had trusted Big Steve more or less instinctively since the beginning. The very beginning. Long before there had ever been a question of love between them, there had been trust. He had been in country for less than twenty-four hours when that rattletrap jeep deposited him and his stuff in that clearing and creaked and rattled back away. He stood there, his duffle at his feet, staring disoriented into the late afternoon gloom. He saw there the biggest, most powerfully built man he had ever encountered, dwarfing even his football playing uncles. There was no question about it. It was a giant standing there nearly naked and squinting into a small mirror hung from the branch of a tree while shaving with a straight razor.

"You the new medic?" Without a stitch of uniform in evidence, the giant's voice was unmistakable indication of rank.

"Yes, sir. Bentley, sir."

"Bentley, huh?"

The behemoth focused on Tristan with eyes so brilliant and blue that everything else in the clearing seemed to inhabit a universe limited to black and white. The man's stare said that he was weighing Tristan's chances, calculating the likelihood of his exceeding the average life expectancy of an inexperienced combat medic there at an advanced infantry camp with God only knew how many Charlie lurking behind any given tree or entrenched in the shelter of any given rock.

"All right," he finally grunted, turning back to his mirror. "Stick with me, Bentley. Right by my side at all times, you hear? And do exactly as I say the second I say it. Got that?"

"Yes, sir."

"Hesitate for as long as a heartbeat and you'll be dead. Or wish you were."

"Sir."

"You do what I tell you. That's your job. I'll keep you alive. That's mine."

Big Steve kept that promise. Tristan couldn't count the number of times Big Steve had saved his bacon. And those were just the instances he had been aware of at the time or identified retrospectively. He was certain there were other situations Big Steve knew of but had never mentioned. Big Steve believed that life was too short to go around bragging. And also that you were only as good as whatever it was you were going to do next. So when the time came to return the favor, Tristan was prepared to die trying and nearly did. He saved Big Steve's life under heavy fire and managed to survive the experience. Back here, back home, in what everybody referred to as peacetime—as nonsensical as that obviously was—Tristan quickly realized that as far as Big Steve was concerned the rules hadn't changed just because they were stateside. There were boonies here, too. So he still stuck close. He still did exactly as he was told the second the words came out of Big Steve's mouth. He still trusted Big Steve with his life. Experiencing what he had, he believed he'd be a fool not to. Seeing what he saw around him, he sensed there was no reason to change.

The Southern Baptist schoolboy yet lurking inside him—unlikely as that seemed after all this time—crossed his fingers and hoped that this story called "Big Steve Plans a Threeway" would turn out like the one in the Old Testament where God told Abraham to sacrifice Isaac only to change the instructions at the last minute. The whole thing might reverse itself just like that, and he'd have endured all this anxiety for nothing.

So Tristan didn't protest when Big Steve said what he did about having a three way. He didn't say anything at all, which was always the appropriate initial response when dealing with Big Steve. He just stood there at Big Steve's side, feeling his warmth and smelling his smell but thinking of the serpent in the garden in spite of himself. He sipped his drink and tried to follow Big Steve's gaze as he surveyed the murky interior of the bar. Who was Big Steve referring to? Try as he might, Tristan couldn't see anyone present as a likely candidate. Eventually it dawned on him that Big Steve hadn't meant right that minute, tonight, that guy over there ready or not, but only some eventual time, some yet to be determined where, some theoretical guy. A possibility, in other words. No more for the moment than a hypothesis. And that calmed Tristan right down. But only briefly, because in addition to knowing he could trust Big Steve he also knew that Big Steve always did what he said he was going to do. He was the king of follow-through. Thus, this was no whim. It was a quest.

Realizing this, Tristan understood that Big Steve's working title, however unspoken, was "The Search." Because if it was truly a project and not a momentary caprice, finding exactly the right guy was essential. It couldn't be just anyone. For Big Steve, it wouldn't be the act that mattered but the actors. This implied something rather remarkable in a partner. It wasn't just face and physique that were at issue. The concept of worthiness always featured prominently in Big Steve's worldview. He drove Maseratis, the piano in the living room was a Steinway even though Big Steve knew no one who played, and his Labradors had pedigrees longer than Tristan's. Tristan didn't know whether all this portended tragedy or something altogether sublime, but knowing Big Steve it had to be one or the other. Operatic at the very least. So the casting had to be perfect, no matter how long it required. Big Steve eschewed approximations and was nothing if not patient. For all the heat of his Italian blood, he was astonishingly methodical.

Tristan imagined someone blond and blue eyed like himself—because it was already apparent that this was a particular fetish of Big Steve's—but rugged looking rather than boyish: like Big Steve himself in that regard. He would be several years older than Tristan but at least as much younger than Big Steve. He would stand taller than Tristan's five feet nine and a half but shorter than Big Steve's six feet six, weigh more than Tristan's current two hundred but less than Big Steve's three twenty-five. A kind of hybrid of the two of them, in other words, but at the same time an archetype in his own right. And you couldn't simply order that from a catalogue. When this individual materialized several months later, Tristan recognized him instantly though there had been no intervening discussion of specifications. If nothing else, Tristan thought this demonstrated that he knew Big Steve as well as he believed he did. A moment later, however, he admitted to himself that it might not be evidence of understanding at all. It might be no more than instinct. Then again, it might just be his own unconscious motivations he was projecting onto his husband. He didn't like to think of himself having such things, but acknowledged, silently and with extreme chagrin, that he must.

But if he comprehended Big Steve, it turned out it was still incompletely. Because as he had clearly understood, physical specifications weren't the half of it. If they had been, the quest might have ended, for better or worse, later that week. But it didn't. It was the rest of the package that remained inscrutable. The two of them stood around in bars night after night for weeks that seemed endless while Big Steve did nothing more than observe his quarry. And even after their acquaintanceship began, there had to be a thorough background check before Big Steve would proceed as far as a dinner invitation.

"You see how he's built," Big Steve pointed out, the eighth or ninth time they encountered the prospect in some bar or other, well before they had exchanged a single word with him.

Tristan saw all right. The man was nothing less than a walking fantasy. He was all the relevant clichés in one amazing package—nearly as monumental as Big Steve himself though on a noticeably smaller scale—and already well on his way to establishing himself in the local pantheon.

"Built," Big Steve repeated, nodding slowly. This was a word he seldom used to describe anyone. Applying it indicated Big Steve's recognition that some degree or other of attainment of his physical ideal had been achieved, and that standard was so high that such a phenomenon was extremely rare, even among hard core gym rats.

"Everyone notices him," Big Steve continued. "They watch. They stare."

Yes, Tristan saw. They did. They were. Everybody in the bar that night, more or less. And by extrapolation, everybody in gay San Francisco. That's what a spectacle the man was.

"But he never takes off his shirt, you notice," Big Steve said, finally completing his thought. This was the point he'd been on the trajectory of for at least a week, Tristan realized. And it was a crucial one. Big Steve never took off his shirt in that or any other bar, or in the park, or on the street. And just barely, for that matter, at the gym. Except in the showers. And, it went without saying, neither did Tristan himself. This was not due to modesty. It was Big Steve's own particular, deeply perverse, form of exhibitionism: *watch closely, everyone, in case this once, just for an instant, you glimpse something more than you've seen previously.* That was how Big Steve presented himself and commanded the attention of other men, and he recognized the same impulse in this stranger.

Like everyone else in the bar that night, Big Steve stared. Exactly the same way, Tristan realized, as he was accustomed to being stared at by Big Steve himself. It was the gaze of a lover or a husband. There was no question about that, and thus it was terrifying to contemplate. But increasingly, Tristan was recognizing it also as the stare of a connoisseur or even a collector. This he could almost accept. But if looks—even looks that spectacular—weren't enough to spur them into action, what else was Big Steve searching for? What was it that required such intense observation prior to moving on to the objective? Tristan had frequently heard Big Steve express the belief that you could tell almost everything about a guy simply from careful analysis of the men he picked up, and apparently this was the motivation for Big Steve's continued patience. In this case, the answer was almost nobody. In all those weeks, Tristan saw the man score only three times. And it most emphatically wasn't for lack of opportunity. He was approached almost constantly. An embarrassment of riches all but threw itself at him, yet he remained abstemious for the most part. He was obviously very particular. He too, it seemed, was a connoisseur. That's exactly what Big Steve wanted to know about him. That was the criterion Tristan hadn't suspected. And when the question was settled. Big Steve approved. This was exactly the quality he had ruthlessly cultivated in himself over many years, so it was no surprise that he valued it so highly in others. Tristan couldn't believe he hadn't figured it out. And what of the young men who left the bar with the man those three times? Boyishly handsome but unmistakably sturdy, athletic specimens. In other words, Big Steve's own preferred type.

The remainder of Big Steve's requirements? That was no mystery. Tristan had apprehended this almost before the search began. As police officers, both their livelihoods depended on discretion. Nearly everyone's did, so it was a little surprising, really, how little it could be depended on. They heard horror stories at every brunch they attended. Their kind had absolutely no rights. Nothing protected them from the straight world's ubiquitous, comprehensive malice but their own caution and diligence. So the question was crucial—was this person discreet?

More important than that, was he solid? Meaning, in Big Steve's lexicon, dependable? But not merely in the sense of being honest and reliable. What Big Steve most wanted to know about was the man's internal compass. Was he emotionally stable? Was he courageous? Was he immune to trivial distractions? Did he choose his battles wisely? How big a man was he, gauged by how much pettiness in others he was prepared to ignore? If he had the right combination of all these qualities, he could perhaps be cultivated. Finally, was he smart? By this Big Steve meant educated and street smart in roughly equal proportions. Big Steve couldn't get it up for idiots no matter how physically dazzling they might be. With his own eighth grade education and later G.E.D. he seemed the unlikeliest of intellectual snobs, but in this, as in everything else, his standards were high and he resolutely maintained them.

You would have thought, so stratospheric were his expectations, that what Big Steve was looking for was a husband. When Tristan—only half joking—shared this observation one evening on their way home, Big Steve said he already had one of those, thank you very much. Next, he stuck his tongue so far down Tristan's throat he might have been attempting to force open the esophageal sphincter. This act set Tristan's mind at rest, but only momentarily. What Big

Steve was doing, he realized, was applying the same criteria he advocated in shopping for a husband—had been employing apparently, that gloomy afternoon of Tristan's arrival in camp—to the present search. This epiphany did nothing to dispel Tristan's ongoing confusion, however. What part did all this play in the quest to vary their sex life?

"The only sex worth having," Big Steve said a few nights later, "is with a guy you might marry under the right circumstances. Because only a guy like that is worth the effort and the risk. And only a guy like that is worth having as your best friend." This notion gave Tristan food for thought for several months. Meanwhile, the present was unfolding like an action sequence from an epic. Big Steve set his glass down, flashed just the hint of a grin and a look that said "wait here", and headed off across the bar to initiate contact. Tristan didn't take his eyes off Big Steve for a second. He was a bundle of disparate impressions: anxiety, curiosity, skepticism, and, almost as an afterthought, lust. This last surprised him. He had thought the whole adventure was predicated on Big Steve's lust. He had convinced himself that he had no such investment of his own. He realized suddenly that Big Steve must have made his selection as much to elicit a larger than life response from Tristan as to satisfy any hunger of his own. This, he realized, made him culpable in whatever eventually resulted in a way he hadn't recognized until that instant. He'd thought of himself all this time as a mere spectator, someone just along for the ride. But Big Steve had silently decreed that he be a full partner in the enterprise and had ensured it with this selection. Tristan stared at the two of them, eyes frantic for some telling detail, but from that distance their meeting couldn't have appeared less consequential. There was no Wagnerian soundtrack screeching with portent in the background. No lightning bolts shredded the skies overhead. No temblors cavorted underfoot. It wasn't like a movie at all. It seemed, if anything, smaller than life. In that respect, Tristan recognized, it resembled ninety-five per cent of the time Big Steve and he had spent together in Viet Nam. This seemed more than appropriate. A low-key meeting, he realized, was as imperative as any other part of the plan. Big Steve led his new friend back across to where Tristan was standing, rooted. They exchanged names, shook hands.

Nikolai Sergeyevich Romanovsky, Esquire. That honorific wasn't the deal breaker you might have expected, because Nick was the one variety of attorney Big Steve tolerated at the time—a prosecutor. And that exotic name, unadulterated by any effort at assimilation, hinted at an extreme species of authenticity that was particularly attractive to Big Steve. Tristan listened avidly as Big Steve conducted his interrogation. By the time Tristan left them to go get the next round of drinks, it was obvious that Nick was more than just a potential sex partner. Like electric light and indoor plumbing, he had become indispensable more or less the moment he materialized. He was indispensable because he existed, that rarest of commodities, the embodiment of all of Big Steve's ideas about what constituted a real man. If you managed to meet that standard, Big Steve wanted to have you around.

Over time, he became indispensable to Tristan for many other, and far more complex, reasons. For starters, while Big Steve was elemental, a veritable force of nature, to a large extent unknowable, and most of all the embodiment of destiny, Nick, for all his ostentatious and intimidating masculinity, was nevertheless someone Tristan could readily enough imagine having attended high school or college with. Easily spooked as Tristan was by a man of such physical attributes, Nick was easy to be around, comfortable, a convincing facsimile of your oldest, dearest buddy yet untainted by all the risk and drama associated with coming out to said individual. As weeks and months passed, Tristan found more and more in Nick to appreciate and depend on. Indeed, for Tristan, that semblance of familiarity at the very beginning was the crucial ingredient that made the whole thing possible.

That night when Big Steve approached Nick in the bar was the last time he would ever approach a man in a bar for sex, although that night, as it turned out, the sex was still several weeks away. Big Steve had fallen hard for Nick, not in love but in like, and his previously unexpressed but suddenly comprehended determination to make this man his best friend for the long haul forced him to go slowly and carefully. The sex would be whatever it was and would last however long it lasted. But with Nick there was the potential at least for something else. Something bigger and more lasting. This was all to the good. It helped ease Tristan into the new state of things in a way that made it possible for an abiding friendship among the three of them to evolve. After that night, Tristan and Big Steve would never again be an island entire to themselves. The pronoun "we" came more and more to denote the three of them as surely as it still did the original two of them, the proper connotation dependent solely on the context. They were becoming something Tristan was never quite certain what to call. Some gays designated such a relationship "family", but Tristan balked at that label. Families were essentially biological associations—this, whatever it was, bore no resemblance to those multigenerational networks of blood-related individuals because it depended totally on their collective will for both its genesis and its continued maintenance, yet at the same time it seemed equally as inevitable as biological kinship did, albeit as a result of a completely different set of influences. Tristan never came up with an alternative term for it which satisfied him. It continued to resist both label and definition. It was the most totally existential phenomenon he had ever encountered. There are, of course, as many varieties of this as there are gays, but everyone gets the concept. It's almost universally taken for granted in the community. Big Steve once ventured the opinion that more than anything else it resembled the camaraderie of wartime. Men who cared so passionately and selflessly for their brothers that they were literally willing to lay down their lives. At this, certain people present at the brunch table began to look nervous and make disapproving noises as if someone had let an extremely loud, extremely smelly fart, one that actually seemed willful and provocative and thus couldn't possibly be ignored. Military metaphors were not *de rigueur* that season. Gays—with the possible exception of drag queens—preferred to think of themselves as essentially peace loving people: *all you need is love*, etc. Realizing his error, which was not of mistaken content but of expressing it in an irremediably hostile context, Big Steve fell immediately silent and never again addressed the topic in public. Though he remained firm in his belief he didn't press the point, not from embarrassment but because he recognized that some battles aren't worth fighting, just as, presumably, some people aren't worth knowing. One of Big Steve's fundamental mantras was *all gay men are NOT my brothers*. But in the sudden, dense silence that had descended on that brunch table Tristan recalled those early days with Nick, and having been in combat himself he thought, of course, that's it, that's exactly who they were—three comrades in arms, facing the fire together. And that would be how they remained.

The sex? Well the whole point, Tristan realized long before the sex actually took place, was that what was happening wasn't really about sex at all. Or rather, it was about a whole lot more than just sex. Understanding this, he didn't know whether to laugh or cry. The prospect of sex with a third party had been alarming enough. The all too certain approach of the actual event was far worse. Still, it was just like Big Steve, elemental though he was, to leave no stone unturned or nuance unexplored and in the process to have discovered something previously unsuspected.

But still: the sex.

Nick undressed was everything you'd have anticipated from observing him at the bar. No disappointments in that department. If anything, you'd have had to say he exceeded expectations. And that was saying a great deal, though perhaps it wasn't surprising. Nobody ever had a better eye for the type than Big Steve, after all, and his standards were stratospheric. So yes, Nick was mythic, with some intriguing details thrown in. Because it turned out that his looks weren't the half of his appeal. To say he was *at least* Tristan's intellectual equal was saying a great deal.

What did he do in bed? More or less everything, though he claimed never to have bottomed for anyone before Big Steve, and Tristan never had any reason to question the assertion. His inventiveness and expertise were breathtaking. He could top Tristan as virtuosically as Big Steve or bottom for Big Steve as enthusiastically as Tristan did. He could perform both these tasks simultaneously. He could role play with absolutely conviction where others might have succumbed to self-consciousness or resorted to absurd posturing or at the very least been reduced to nervous giggles. And he never seemed to care what he was doing sexually as long as he was doing something. Compared to Big Steve, he was perhaps a tiny bit less proficient technically, but he was also less, well, clinical and calculated. He followed directions, no matter how arcane, as if they were orders, with alacrity and exactitude, but he was capable of issuing them convincingly as well.

Was he any good? Tristan was the wrong person to ask. He'd been extremely inexperienced when he met Big Steve. So if he said—though he never discussed it with anyone except in the most general of terms—that was dumbstruck, transported—that might or might not mean anything. If you asked Big Steve he wouldn't say anything, but the look in his eyes would tell you the answer. Nick was as good as it was possible to be, and Big Steve had more than enough basis for comparison. But you didn't even have to depend on that, really. Even in those days the city was crawling with Nick's satisfied customers.

How did it feel, knowing that your husband was having the best sex of his life with your best friend? That was a question Tristan refused to dwell on. He'd been there, too. Each and every time. Present and accounted for. That was the fundamental rule. Tristan and Big Steve could pair off because they were a couple. But any other potential pairings were taboo. Tristan's feelings about what went on between Big Steve and Nick might have been different otherwise. Or if he'd been less resolute at slamming the door on any such speculation. On just such decisions are long and happy marriages made. At least involving gay men. Tristan had no idea, beyond "the children", what kept most straights together. Except for isolated examples, the straight couples he knew were miserable most of the time.

As extravagantly qualified was Nick was in every respect, it was perfectly natural to wonder why he and Big Steve weren't the couple and Tristan the adjunct. Tristan pondered that question obsessively night after night as the two titans finished each other's sentences, laughed at jokes he somehow wasn't privy to, and conversed in an increasingly arcane argot clotted with esoteric references. Observing this, his blood ran cold. Not that either of them ever gave him specific, unambiguous cause for alarm. It was an impression, nothing more, but it seemed glaringly obvious that the two of them enjoyed amazing chemistry. They couldn't have been more attentive to Tristan, more solicitous and protective, but this attention made him feel more like a mascot than the equal of either of them. He'd have died before admitting to his insecurities, but he was certain he'd be abandoned by both of them before the summer was over. It seemed as inevitable as gravity.

Then, one night not long before Labor Day, when Big Steve pointed out a certain constantly gossiped-about newlywed couple who had just entered the bar, Nick laughed and suggested that it would never last.

"How can you say that?" Tristan protested, hypersensitive by that point on the topic of potential marital breakups. "Look at them. They're perfect together."

Big Steve and Nick shared another of their private glances, and Tristan felt like his heart was about to stop. The moment seemed full of portent. He sensed that he was about to learn something critical with regard to their thinking about what made relationships work, or why they didn't, or why Tristan's and Big Steve's was about to vanish as if it had never existed.

"Because," Nick said, turning his grin away from Big Steve and focusing its laser beam on Tristan, "you can't have two alpha dogs in one pack."

"That's right," Big Steve agreed.

Tristan stared at the couple in question as they laughed at some private joke and sauntered over to the pool table. He couldn't for the life of him perceive either of them as the submissive party, though even by then he knew you couldn't tell by looking. Still, the absurdity of the match was suddenly obvious to him. And he finally comprehended what he was doing there, why he would always be there, just as he was—Tristan the born sidekick, the quintessential wingman. He had understood this aspect of his nature far back in boyhood. He had always considered it the worst of his many flaws. He was an American male, after all. How else could he have apprehended such knowledge? Now, ironically, it was the one quality that made him an ideal match for Big Steve while simultaneously disqualifying Nick from the position. Though Tristan was ecstatic at that realization, he wasn't a bit happy about its other implications. It seemed, in fact, particularly bitter knowledge. He assumed that most people were like him and preferred to believe that their lovers treasured them for the qualities—real or imagined— they most prized in themselves. But in his case at least, that belief had been demonstrated to be an illusion. He'd never be able to take comfort in it again. Moreover, now that this aspect of his nature had been cast into the spotlight, not only by Big Steve but by Nick as well, it would be even harder for him to pretend to himself, or anyone else for that matter, that it didn't exist. He had long since despaired of becoming reconciled to it, but life with Big Steve had allowed him to shove it into one of the more obscure corners of his consciousness. Now it was unmistakably in the forefront, and he regretted the renewal of the inner conflict that promised.

Still, their sudden, unexpected affirmation of Tristan's position in Big Steve's life, whether he appreciated its basis or not, filled him, for those few delirious moments at least, with profound and giddy relief. The fear and confusion he'd been struggling with since their earliest weeks with Nick, and especially since the sex began, evaporated. He started to laugh, laugh like he couldn't remember having laughed in years—perhaps ever. Nick joined him, reaching over and tousling his hair. Big Steve pulled him in tight. Their combined aromas and heat engulfed him.

"You worry too much," Big Steve whispered.

And so it was that the ultimate configuration of their relationship was acknowledged by the three of them. But that left one matter unattended to. The reality was, they soon learned, that Nick's aspirations exactly matched Big Steve's. In every respect. Big Steve had Tristan, and Nick had—yes, that was the issue. There was no one to fill in that particular blank. It turned out that the whole time they'd known him, Nick had been shopping. Assiduously. Almost, though not quite, desperately. And uninterruptedly, it could be acknowledged once it was admitted as a topic of conversation. Nick's tenacity in pursuing the quest was another quality which Big Steve lauded highly, though only to selected listeners, in the process of asserting that domesticity was the ultimate expression of their essence as men who loved—as opposed to men who merely had sex with—men. This was, of course, such a radical position for the time as to threaten to relegate Big Steve to membership in a minority of one and make him a pariah into the bargain. But at least Nick and Tristan made it a group of three. And Big Steve was gratified almost beyond words to learn that Nick's relationship with Tristan and him hadn't deflected him from his search. In fact, Nick insisted that their friendship helped him maintain necessary perspective.

"Without you two," he once explained, "I'd be tempted to settle for less than the best."

"I know how that works," Big Steve nodded. "It's easy to get discouraged. Don't forget, it took me the best part of fifteen years to find this one."

"Nobody else would have you," Tristan snorted, as Big Steve's arms engulfed him. He was nearly peeing himself at the implied compliment. He wished that Big Steve didn't have to have Nick for an audience before he could say a thing like that, but at least it had been said.

"Don't ever sell yourself short, T.," Nick said. "You were worth waiting for. I get that. If I could just find myself a guy like you I'd marry him so fast it would give you whiplash."

"You're a chump if he's not twice the guy I am," Tristan grumbled.

"Stop talking yourself down," Big Steve muttered into his ear. "It's your least attractive habit."

"He's afraid people will think he's arrogant," Nick said.

"He needs to be arrogant," Big Steve said. "A little bit, at least. Look at him. He's got plenty more to be arrogant about than most guys. He doesn't get that. I just happen to think he deserves to know how it feels."

"You won't get any argument from me," Nick said. "I know him about as well as anybody. Except you of course, Big Steve. And I think he. . ."

"Would prefer not to be spoken about as if he weren't present," Tristan said.

"He needs to stop being so flip," Big Steve said, "in the face of sincere appreciation. He needs to learn how to accept a compliment when it's given."

"But I'm not the point," Tristan insisted. "Nick wants a husband."

Months passed. Nick searched on. From what Tristan could see, it was a search as arduous as Big Steve's search for Nick had been. But Nick's approach to it was altogether more hands on, as was only to be expected. Big Steve and Tristan never caught sight of most of the men Nick auditioned. Only the most promising candidates merited an introduction to them. They only heard of all those Dereks,

Seans, Gavins, Brents, etc., in passing. When Tristan tried to visualize them he couldn't. But every now and then Nick would usher a Glenn or Michael or Tad over to their corner of the bar, or their regular Friday night table at the Italian restaurant in North Beach Big Steve had christened "Auntie Violetta's Cucina West" in a tribute to the culinary skills of the relative who had raised him, or the weight bench where Big Steve was spotting Tristan on his presses and snarling out encouragement like the drill instructor he had never really stopped being. This was possible because by that time Nick had switched over to the gym where Big Steve and Tristan were members, which in its own way represented a commit-ment as profound as a religious conversion. Guys who reached the milestone of a third date with Nick Big Steve and Tristan hosted for a dinner at their house. Most of them must have found that intimidating at best. But regardless of how those evenings went, Big Steve and Tristan refused all commentary afterward, even if Nick begged for it.

"No one's opinion matters," Big Steve would insist, "but your own."

"When you finally meet the right guy," Tristan opined, "we're bound to be crazy about him."

If Nick grew discouraged as month succeeded month, Tristan never detected the least flicker of it. Nor did Big Steve and Tristan's interest flag. They watched every move, avid as parents in the grandstands at Junior's big game.

The first time Nick mentioned Christopher Melendez-Greene it seemed to be in passing. Nick mentioned lots of people. His conversation was practically a direc-tory of gay San Francisco between the ages of seventeen and thirty-nine, with thirty-nine being an age that seemed almost infinitely elastic. Tristan attached no more significance to that name than any of the others Nick spoke at brunch that day. But his curiosity was piqued. He was certain he had heard the name in some connection or other which now escaped him. His memory for names was usually very good, but this once it seemed to have failed him. Another week or so passed before Nick spoke the name again, and once again Tristan experienced that tantalizing response. Unable to recall what he had heard of Christopher in the past, he was all the more curious. But while he was pondering that, Big Steve was registering some note in Nick's voice—or perhaps just some random vibration hovering in the smoke and cologne clotted atmosphere of the bar that night— and before Nick finished his sentence, Tristan found Big Steve giving him really significant eye contact. That shocked him into the present and drove everything else out of his head. It was a very long time until their friend Matt clarified the connection which seemed so elusive. If Tristan had solved the riddle in a timelier manner, things might have been different.

Christopher was a hard fish to land, it appeared. Because although his name found its way into their conversations with increasing frequency, accompanied by descriptions, anecdotes, and quotations, it had to have been another two months at least before Tristan and Big Steve met him. By then, Nick's commentary left them in no doubt. This was the guy. Everything Nick reported about him rein-forced that initial fleeting impression Big Steve had fished so astutely out of the ether. At the same time, everything they heard about him made Tristan intensely skeptical. How could Christopher live up to all that hype? How could anyone?

The young beauty Nick finally introduced to them, though undoubtedly stun-ning and certainly charming enough, was ultimately just a guy, flesh and blood like anyone else. Friendly but a little reserved, articulate but not an initiator of conversation, Christopher seemed perfectly happy to let his looks do the talk-ing for him, but they didn't talk so much as proclaim. His father had been to Andover and then to Harvard and had rowed on the American team in two suc-cessive Olympics. A few weeks later, Tristan saw a photo of Geoffrey Greene in which he looked like Grace Kelly's brother—or cousin at least. Looking at Christopher, you could see unmistakably that quintessential up east preppie. But you could see something else, too, in the background as it were, that hinted strongly but at the same time subtly of other ingredients. Since Nick had already alerted them to the more exotic aspects of Christopher's lineage and Tristan and Big Steve knew what they were supposed to be seeing, they did. The mother who had modeled for Chanel and Dior; the grandfather, pure Castilian, a minor diplomat in the service of the Mexican government and typically posted in some European capital or other; the grandmother an heiress to a farming and ranching fortune, descended from Moravian immigrants to the northern plains of Mexico;

and finally, his mother's younger brother who attracted prominent patronage of a certain sort and eventually had a brief but sensational acting career in French film. These spoke of aspects of Christopher's physiognomy and coloring that were visible in the pale, perfect skin, the raven hair, the clear, light eyes which could be described as blue or gray with equal accuracy, the faintly exotic cheekbones and sharply modeled chin.

"Swimmer's body" was an idiom ubiquitous in the argot of gay San Francisco, but it was so wide ranging in its application as to be almost totally devoid of meaning or usefulness as a description. Casually disregarding the broad shoulders and deep ribcages of true competitive swimmers, it denoted nothing more specific than a youthful, smooth skinned, faintly athletic physique distinguished most notably by what it was not, lacking as it did both any visible flabbiness and at the same time any mass even remotely resembling that of the bodybuilder. Still, that's how Christopher was generally described around the city, as casually and thoughtlessly as one would assert that an eggplant was purple. A more considered assessment would have had to take into account his noteworthy degree of lean, highly defined muscle.

And what was Big Steve, after all, if not the ultimate connoisseur of the male physique in its various highly cultivated manifestations? Big Steve's description, "captain of the Ukrainian men's Olympic gymnastics team", apprehended Christopher totally. Tristan had previously proposed "captain of the Czech men's water polo team", but Big Steve and Nick both objected on the grounds of Christopher's height, which was within a hair of Tristan's own five nine and a half and inadequate for that sport.

In addition to speaking fluent Spanish, which wasn't particularly surprising given his parentage, Christopher had a degree in French Literature, which was. He'd earned it at the Sorbonne, which impressed Big Steve no end. He was a second year medical student and lived in a guest cottage in Pacific Heights. When Tristan mentioned how convenient he must find this to the medical center, he shrugged in what seemed an excessively blasé fashion. This was the first time Tristan focused clearly on Christopher's evasiveness, which struck him at first glance as being calculated, rather paradoxically, to increase people's curiosity about him rather than elude or suppress it.

Once Nick finally reeled him in, there was no discernable period of transition. They became virtually joined at the hip. Tristan and Big Steve saw Nick less than usual after that, even at the gym. Their socializing with him almost always included Christopher. Over candlelight dinners, drinks at their regular bar, lazy Sunday brunches, picnics in Golden Gate Park or at the Palace of Fine Art, and gossipy intermissions at the opera or symphony, they learned surprisingly little about Christopher. He insisted just firmly enough that there was nothing particularly interesting about him to discourage questions. And this insistence was perfectly calibrated to avoid raising suspicions, except that in the case of Big Steve and Tristan it didn't take into account the nature of his audience. Tristan found his mastery of such a tactic intriguing in a man so young. It struck him as typical instead of someone older and perhaps female. Gradually Tristan concluded that Christopher's inscrutability was no gambit but a true preference for privacy. This was astonishingly contrary to the spirit of the times, which called for self-promotion and emotional exhibitionism, but seemed like a harmless enough eccentricity. He chalked it up to the European influences in Christopher's upbringing. Eventually, however, Christopher did let slip a crucially important detail. The guest house he lived in was located on the grounds of a Pacific Heights mansion owned by a noted but reclusive French film director, and Christopher's Uncle Rene reigned there as prince consort. To Tristan, that seemed to put a completely different complexion on, well, just about everything about Christopher. He didn't share his misgivings. Even with Big Steve, he kept them to himself. Surprisingly, Big Steve, with his usually unerring sense about such evasions, completely overlooked Tristan's lack of forthrightness just this once.

Time passed, and increasingly Christopher and Nick gave every impression of being the perfect couple. Even Big Steve was convinced.

Alain Delon's better looking brother. The uncanny resemblance struck Tristan the first time he met Christopher's uncle, at one of those elaborate parties he and his lover, the filmmaker Jules de Croteau, frequently hosted at their Pacific Heights mansion. Tristan and Big Steve had known Christopher for about six months by then, and Nick had recently begun speaking—somewhat plaintively, Tristan thought—of the possibility that Christopher might soon move in with him. Apparently this was without any encouragement from Christopher. This concerned Tristan a great deal, but in deference to Big Steve he never mentioned it when Nick was around. Meanwhile, the four of them had settled into a comfortable pattern of socializing as two couples.

When the invitation to the party arrived, Tristan didn't connect the hosts with Christopher, addressing Big Steve with a question something on the lines of, "who are these people anyway? And why did they bother inviting us?" They had heard about those parties, and they weren't very interested. Parties of that kind represented a brand of gay Big Steve disputed the legitimacy of, and Tristan found any gathering boasting that level of opulence unacceptable on socio-economic grounds. Big Steve brought him up short by referring to the hosts as Nick's in-laws, and Tristan RSVP'd in the affirmative more or less immediately.

Tristan couldn't have said how many such parties he and Big Steve had attended even in their fairly short time as a couple, as if there was a Jay Gatsby lurking inside every gay man who ever struck it rich. Had there been dozens of them? Or scores? Tristan couldn't remember for certain. Sometimes, however, it seemed as though there had really only been one party which dragged on interminably, so similar were they all with their elaborate catering and astonishing decorations and naked waiters and exquisite boys present there for no discernable purpose other than their availability. Such gatherings always featured drugs laid out like *hors d'oeuvres* and unspeakable acts being performed for the edification of the shocked but titillated onlookers in the apparently obligatory dungeons those houses were equipped with. Jules and Rene's party differed from the others in no significant detail whatever. It was just a matter of date, time, and address.

Rene and Jules, the story went, had moved to San Francisco for the sole purpose of providing a home for Christopher while he attended medical school. As Nick's in-laws, the hosts required no other recommendation to justify Big Steve's initial interest in them. Their house, which due to its mammoth scale Tristan couldn't manage to think of as a home, gave the impression of a movie set. Sonny Dallas had found it for them and pocketed a commission that ran to five figures. Tristan and Big Steve arrived, ate, and drank. They danced and mingled. It was, they later learned, one of the tamest soirees their hosts ever presided over, which Tristan found all but impossible to believe considering what he'd witnessed that night. At one point, Christopher introduced them to Rene and Jules. When they left, long after midnight, all Tristan could think was that from his perspective at least it had been a case of all foreplay and no insertion. That kind of party, that kind of people.

Something had happened, however. Tristan and Big Steve had been seen there. Nick was already a familiar face to their hosts, but with his friends suddenly identified, the whole was much more than the sum of its parts.

The significance of this became apparent a week or so later, when Tristan and Big Steve received an invitation to brunch. Tristan was reluctant to accept. The date fell on one of those rare weekends when Big Steve and he were both off work and he was reluctant to share a minute of it with anyone. When Tristan had met them at the party, Jules and Rene turned out to be boring in the most objectionable of ways. But Big Steve insisted. They needed to support Nick in his new relationship. It was their duty. And when Big Steve trotted out the "d" word, all argument invariably screeched to a halt. In Big Steve's worldview, duty trumped pretty much everything. So Tristan got a haircut—he was due for one anyway— and they went. The occasion was austere, sedate, as refined as the previous party had been phantasmagoric. They were greeted at the front door of the mansion by a retainer with the gravitas of a bishop and an accent that wouldn't have been out of place at Buckingham Palace.

At the table there were just six of them present: Jules and Rene, Christopher and Nick, and Big Steve and Tristan. There wasn't much in the way of conversation. Jules didn't speak any English. His monologue, in what didn't even sound to Tristan like very good French, was translated for them by Rene with assistance from Christopher when Rene's English failed to serve, which was frequently. It was a disorganized rumination on his variable fortunes as a filmmaker: his vision, his choices, his art, and the juxtaposition of those with the profound yet nevertheless insufficient respect he received from his peers, the almost complete lack of comprehension displayed by the critics, the superficial fanaticism of his adherents which was itself an indictment, and the duplicity of everyone who had anything to do with the fiscal aspects of his calling. All this was delivered in fits and starts, with much coaching by Rene and occasional editorializing by Christopher.

It made for a compelling enough diatribe, had anyone present been inclined to take it seriously, but Tristan found himself increasingly skeptical as it wore on, cliché following cliché *ad nauseum*. Jules was, Tristan decided, more than anything else a caricature, and an egotist besides. All he could think of as each succeeding course was served and cleared was that he wanted to go home and salvage as much of the day as he and Big Steve could. His growing frustration at what they were being subjected to distracted him so that he lost the thread of the director's musings at what was apparently a crucial juncture, because the next thing he knew Big Steve was speaking and Nick looked extremely tense.

"If I didn't know better," Big Steve said, "I'd think you were suggesting that we team up with you to make pornography."

"No, no," Rene insisted, "not at all."

"I guess I misunderstood," Big Steve said, in a tone that indicated his certainty he hadn't.

"No, my friend," Rene said, "you must not think that what Jules has suggested has anything to do with pornography. What he's proposing is, well, I believe the term in English is documentaire."

"Documentary," Christopher corrected him.

Looking at his serious young face, Tristan was shocked to realize that Christopher wasn't the least surprised at the suggestion. He seemed to be advocating for it as strongly as the other two.

"Exactly," Rene nodded as Jules remained inscrutable. "The three of you in your accustomed sport."

The idea was so outrageous that all Tristan could do was laugh about it as Big Steve and he made their way home. It didn't occur to him that either Big Steve or Nick might have taken it any more seriously than he had. How absurd. And with Nick's current boyfriend sitting right there. How must the suggestion have made Christopher feel, despite his apparent support? That gesture, Tristan supposed, had been occasioned by Christopher's relationship with his uncle but couldn't be taken at face value. So when a few evenings later Big Steve suggested that they attend a showing of Jules' most recent film at an art theater in Berkeley, Tristan sensed no agenda at work, merely curiosity. And when Big Steve remarked, as they walked out of the theater, that whatever else you might think of Jules as a man you had to admit that as a film maker he was a genius, Tristan still got no sense of the direction in which things were moving. But things undoubtedly were. Big Steve and Nick had already met more than once with Jules and Rene. Terms had been discussed, a tentative contract had been drafted, a scenario had been sketched. And all of a sudden one evening no more than ten days later Tristan was sitting at his own kitchen table being briefed by Big Steve and Nick as if the whole thing were a *fait accompli*.

"Seriously?" he asked. "Both of you?"

"It makes sense," Nick said, "as a social document. The world at large knows nothing about what men like us really do. Or, for that matter, what we're capable of together. To them we're just a bunch of limp-wristed, lisping fairies traipsing around in caftans and looking for straight men to service. We'll blow that stereotype to smithereens."

"Social document?" Tristan said. "You've got to be kidding. Next thing I know somebody's going to tell me the film's going to end up being screened in a dedicated theater at the Smithsonian."

"He's not kidding," Big Steve said.

"Have both of you lost your minds?" Tristan asked. "Simultaneously?"

"I know it sounds crazy," Nick said.

"You're right," Tristan said. "That's exactly the word that comes to mind."

"So did relativity," Big Steve said, "before people got used to the idea. Look at it now. Even little kids know Einstein's formula."

"The formula, yes," Tristan said, "but who even comprehends the speed of light? Really? What solid citizen staring at the high end of his speedometer has any comprehension at all?"

"There you go," Nick said, "being philosophical."

"Is it philosophical?" Big Steve mused, "or metaphysical?"

And Tristan knew that for whatever unfathomable reason the decision had been made for him.

II

They spent several weeks shooting the film on weekends and at other off hours. The Pacific Heights mansion had a fully equipped soundstage in its basement, and Jules called on his regular cinematographer and camera operators for the production. All that was lacking was equipment and personnel for sound recording. The reason for this omission was simple enough. The film was to be silent. A musical soundtrack would be added later, but Tristan had no idea where that would take place or who would be involved. More than once during the filming, it occurred to Tristan that Jules was investing a great deal more in the project than he would have expected. That seemed surprising given the terms of the contract, but he didn't voice his misgivings. After shooting concluded several more weeks passed while Jules toiled away in his editing studio. Finally the three of them went back to the mansion to view the finished product. By that time, the whole thing seemed more like a bizarre dream than something that had actually taken place. All Tristan could think was that it was a relief to finally put it all behind them. He wanted to forget the whole thing. He had a souvenir, of course—the nipple piercing that would always remind him of that penultimate scene. In addition to that, their contract with Jules and Rene specified that each of them receive two prints of the film. When these were delivered, Big Steve took his and Tristan's to their safe deposit box. But this seemed pointless. Tristan couldn't imagine ever wanting to see the film.

Whatever else it may be—art, work of the devil, political statement, or incitement to sexual crime—pornography is the sum total of a collection of choices made by a team of people with a view to eliciting certain responses from its ultimate consumers, the audience. It is the anticipated audience and that audience's needs and desires which drive every aspect of production. In this essential regard pornography is like all the other types of performance from ballet to the circus, and so are its performers like all other performers. Whatever they're doing they're doing not to please themselves but their viewers. We accept this easily enough when we're contemplating the work of actors or violinists. However much they may seem to be committed to what they're doing, we understand that ultimately it's a job. Even if they're amateurs and the pleasure of the act itself is their only compensation beyond applause, the fact that they're engaged in a public performance makes the audience the ultimate consumer in the same way as if they were highly paid and internationally renowned and tickets cost three hundred dollars a throw. And if somehow on any given day a performer's work seems uninspired, the members of the audience may feel shortchanged but they don't take it as a personal betrayal. More likely they understand it as somebody having a bad day at the office.

But in pornography the performers don't fiddle or walk tightropes. Or if by some weird chance they do, those activities are peripheral. What they do is have sex. And generally it's sex of an athletic, extravagant, extroverted type. Whatever variety it may assume, whatever specific actions are portrayed, the presentation is not subtle. But unlike the sex members of the audience have in real life, the sex the performers are having is not for their own pleasure. It's for the audience's titillation. Even so, it's still sex they're having, so presumably they're enjoying themselves to some extent even if the specific acts they're performing may not be part of their repertoires in real life. The "gay for pay" guys, for instance, are getting their rocks off whether they'd admit it or not because a come shot can't be faked. And since the members of the audience may be incapable of compartmentalizing the way the performers do, it's difficult for them to think of having sex as just doing a job. For prostitutes, certainly, but who actually expects a prostitute to get off on what she does? And besides, her audience is generally an audience of one. Show anyone pornography where the dicks are limp and nobody ever comes, and what they're seeing is an audience about to ask for its money back.

And that was the paradox of most gay porn. At least the gay porn Tristan had seen up to that point. That wasn't much, but enough that he understood the basic principles. Watching porn was not an activity engaged in based on the assumption that audiences would afterward engage in philosophical or aesthetic analysis. Its true purpose couldn't be clearer, really. And it's difficult if not impossible to get off on guys only pretending to get off. Their painstakingly calculated moves and workmanlike detachment could only result in a product that wasn't hot enough to make a lasting impression except on the most impressionable. Perhaps impressionable audiences were all porn could hope for. But if that were true, there would be no way to account for its ubiquity or its lucrativeness as an enterprise. Some porn, even if only a tiny fraction of what was produced and distributed, had to be titillating enough to justify the entire phenomenon or the phenomenon would disappear. Some porn had to give the audiences what they truly wished for—at least temporarily. As Tristan sat in the basement screening room of Jules and Rene's mansion pondering all this, it occurred to him that their director's original claim had been valid after all. The results spoke for themselves. Nick, Big Steve, and he hadn't made pornography at all. What they were viewing truly was documentary instead. They hadn't given any thought at all to what some hypothetical audience somewhere might want to see because they had been assured during contract negotiations that there would be no audience of that kind. They hadn't calculated any effects. They hadn't concerned themselves with what Jules might want them to do or want them to look like while they were doing it. They hadn't choreographed anything beyond what was necessary to facilitate the work of the cinematographer. They had done nothing more or less than please themselves individually and as partners. And their complete disregard for the considerations or sensibilities or conventions of some hypothetical aesthetic appeared to have resulted in something completely unfit for commercial exploitation. So all that legal finessing and massaging Nick had performed on the contract appeared superfluous. Tristan couldn't imagine anyone wanting to watch this—whatever it was. Paradoxically, this made what they had filmed far more objectionable than actual porn. Those performers were acting. Tristan and his partners had done nothing less than reveal themselves. That person on the screen was not Tristan performing, but Tristan behaving in accordance with his most profound impulses. Sitting in the darkness of that screening room, he'd never been more mortified. Indeed, he'd never imagined it was possible to be as mortified as he was right then.

Not long after the screening, Big Steve and Tristan became aware that all was not well between Nick and Christopher. Nick refused to discuss matters beyond giving a transparently false explanation involving Christopher's refusal to move in with him. Tristan found Nick's uncharacteristic evasiveness incomprehensible. Even more unusual, Big Steve refused to pursue the matter. And Christopher, the few times they actually saw him, was more cryptic than ever.

Finally, one Sunday a few weeks later, Nick arrived unaccompanied to brunch. Tristan couldn't remember ever seeing him so upset. He assumed there'd been a fight with Christopher.

"That bastard Jules," Nick fumed, draining his initial mimosa like it was kool aid. "He lied to us."

"What do you mean?" Tristan asked.

"Christopher and I went to a party at Cutter Wolfson's new place last night. It was Pierce Bohannon's birthday. God, I still can't believe it."

"What?" Big Steve asked.

"They were screening it there. Sonny Dallas told me he'd rented it from Jules for the occasion."

"It?" Tristan asked.

"Our. . .documentary," Nick exploded. "Christopher claimed he didn't know anything about it, but I think he's lying. In fact, I know he is. We ended up having a pretty bad fight."

It took no more than half a dozen phone calls that afternoon for Big Steve and Nick to ascertain that multiple prints of the film were available for rental and that it had been screened as far away as New York. Nick steamed off to start paper-work for the lawsuit he planned to file, but Big Steve was more philosophical.

"I never trusted Jules and Rene in the first place," he told Tristan. "I knew this would happen. All that bullshit about how they're connoisseurs and it was just going to be for their private use."

"But the contract," Tristan protested. "Nick's a very good attorney, and he says the contract's air tight."

"Sure," Big Steve said. "The contract. I read it. Nick's right. It's air tight. He's a great attorney but he's a lousy chess player. Which is inexcusable for a Russian."

"I don't understand."

"Do you really want to go to court over something like this?" Big Steve asked.

"They've given us no choice."

"Think about that for a minute," Big Steve said. "Think about what filing suit will mean. Whether we win it or lose it, we'll both lose our jobs. Two police officers appearing in a gay porn film? The department will have shit fits. And Nick's in pretty much the same situation."

"Fuck," Tristan said. "We're screwed even if we don't sue. Once the brass find out about the film."

"Nah," Big Steve said. "As long as they don't find out about it. And even if they do, they can ignore it as along as we don't acknowledge that it's us. Believe me, I've seen it before."

"Other cops have done gay porn?"

"I mean that's the way the department deals with extra-curricular misconduct in general. But going to court over it is a whole different story. Jules knew that from the beginning. He's had us trapped since the minute the cameras started rolling."

"But. . ."

"No," Big Steve said, "I knew all along they were figuring we'd never hold them to the contract. That's why they were willing to sign it in the first place. They knew it was unenforceable for all practical purposes. They knew how all this would play out. Sure, we could take them to court. We'd almost certainly win. But what would we win? Nothing worth having. Once you lose your virginity there's no getting it back."

"Then why did you agree to go along with it?"

"Didn't want my buddy to lose face with his boyfriend's family."

"Right."

"You'd have done differently."

"I guess not," Tristan admitted.

"No."

"But how can we just let them get away with this?"

"Oh, don't worry," Big Steve said. "They won't get away with anything in the long run. Guys like that never do. Always outsmarting everyone, but they eventually outsmart themselves."

"What's that supposed to mean?"

"Watch and wait, *tesoro*. Watch and wait."

"So you really don't intend to take them to court," Tristan said.

"No."

"What if Nick decides to take them on by himself?"

"He won't," Big Steve said.

"Sure sounded like he was planning to when he left here."

"He just needed to blow off steam. You'll see."

Big Steve was right. Tristan never heard another word about litigation. And because they didn't make an issue of it, the immediate sensation died away more quickly than he would have credited. Big Steve had been correct when he insisted that it wasn't the end of the world. And Tristan learned that nobody gets away with anything unless somebody agrees to be a victim. Big Steve prohibited any communication with Jules and Rene, any admission at all that he and Tristan knew what they had done. The closest they got to any real drama was Nick's continuing plaint over the next few weeks: "How can I break up with that little shit if he won't return my calls?"

"Christopher Melendez-Greene?" Matt Duckworth exploded, twirling the dial of his combination lock. "That bastard?"

"You know him?" Tristan asked, pulling up his sweats.

Matt's flight schedule had been erratic of late. He'd managed to be almost totally absent from the gym during the most crucial weeks of the action, so he was baffled by Nick's current moodiness. It fell to Tristan to fill him in that morning by the lockers.

"Damn right, I do," Matt nodded.

"How so?"

"Got caught cheating on an exam his first year of medical school and tried to shift the blame onto Ashby."

"That was Christopher?" Tristan was thunderstruck.

"Sure as hell," Matt said. "Surprised none of you geniuses remembered the story. You were horrified enough about it at the time."

That's where Tristan had heard of Christopher before. Now he felt even stupider.

Their reactions continued to be varied. Tristan felt violated. He had revealed himself far beyond any reasonable extent, trusting in a promise of privacy that had been nothing of the kind. He was humiliated not only at what he'd seen on film, but at what he knew Big Steve and Nick saw every time they looked at him. He took a long time getting over that. At the other side of the tunnel was a deeper intimacy with his husband than he'd comprehended the possibility of before, and that was his ultimate consolation.

Nick's sense of fair play had been deeply offended, and as an attorney his frustration at forgoing legal redress tortured him. He stopped looking for a husband and generally went around living up to the reputation as sex god that the film would have given him if he hadn't already established it so definitively in real life. Big Steve told Tristan not to worry, that this was just a phase, but it went on for a distressingly long time. Tristan wondered if it would ever end.

But gradually Tristan realized that Big Steve was the most disappointed of all. He'd had to witness the betrayal of a close friend in the name of love. Because the conclusion the three of them inevitably, but silently, drew was that Nick had never meant to Christopher what Christopher had meant to him. Christopher, they had to acknowledge, had been acting from the first as a talent scout and not a prospective husband.

Big Steve and Tristan got over the fiasco fairly quickly. They had each other. Eventually Nick decided against the confrontation Tristan knew he'd been intent on, thereby rising even higher in Big Steve's estimation—as if that were possible. Real men, it seems, don't have to get even. Real men are too tough to be hurt by the likes of a Christopher Melendez-Greene. Or at least to admit to it. Real men hold their fire and allow others to pay the natural consequences of their acts, even if those consequences take a very long time to materialize.

The epilogue took place several months later in Big Steve and Tristan's bed. It was a Saturday night and they had just hosted Nick and his date for dinner. They left early, the date apparently unhappy about something. It had been, Tristan thought, like watching a rerun of a television show that wasn't very good on initial viewing. He didn't expect they'd ever see that young man again and he couldn't manage to feel bad about it.

They lay cuddling after sex. Big Steve had never been one to roll over and go to sleep. That night he was more than usually wakeful. So much so that for a moment Tristan thought he wanted thirds.

"I wish you'd get rid of that nipple ring," Big Steve finally growled.

So that was the reason for his agitation.

"Oh? I thought you liked it."

"It is hot," Big Steve admitted after a moment.

"I was thinking of having the other one done."

"Don't."

"All right."

"Just get rid of it, please," Big Steve said.

"Why?"

"I don't like to think about all that."

"It wasn't that horrible," Tristan said. "You said yourself that it wasn't the end of the world. And you were right. It's all blown over."

"It's all blown over for us," Big Steve said, "not for Nick."

"Getting rid of my nipple ring won't do anything to help Nick," Tristan said.

"I know."

"So why should I do it? I know I'm supposed to just because you say you want me to. I get that, and I'm not telling you no. I'm not arguing the point at all. I just want to understand why."

"I live with the memory of my mistakes every day, Tristan."

"What's that supposed to mean?"

"I know I'm fallible," Big Steve said. "I don't need that thing reminding me of it."

"Maybe I do," Tristan said.

GREGORY YATES: 1975

I

"You're awfully jumpy tonight," Stone said, staring at the ceiling.

"I don't know what you're talking about," Greg said, faking a yawn.

"You can't bullshit a bullshitter," Stone laughed. "Particularly a professional one. Not even after multiple orgasms. You shouldn't try. Something's eating you worse than usual. Get your explanation ready while I'm taking a piss."

"Are you spending the night?" Greg asked.

"Don't I always? You're great sex, Greg. Almost as good as Cooper. How many times do I have to tell you that?"

This didn't sting like it might. Coming in second to Cooper Luxemberg in bed, or anywhere else for that matter, was like coming in second to the Eiffel Tower or Michelangelo's *David*. It was like winning silver at the Olympics. It was like. . .

"But you're the undisputed champion of one thing," Stone continued.

"What's that?" Greg asked, dreading the answer.

"Cuddling afterward," Stone said. "Nobody else comes close."

At five-ten and a ripped two hundred fifteen pounds, Stone was as close an approximation of the guys Greg had worshipped since junior high as he'd ever wound up in bed with. The luxuriant blond hair, strong but boyish features, and clear, pale blue eyes were the icing on the cake, aesthetically speaking. He was funny and charming and as considerate as any reasonable person could hope for, and Greg wouldn't have hesitated for a moment to embark on long term domesticity with him but for one disqualifying factor. Stone was a hustler. He made his living having sex for money. Usually it was with men, but occasionally he did scenes with women. Greg wasn't sure how the logistics worked out, but Stone was in serious demand. This wasn't something Stone boasted of. Greg knew it the way everybody else did. The same way they knew the local landmarks and where to get good pizza. Nevertheless, Stone found his way into Greg's arms and bed with surprising regularity considering that Greg never offered any of the usual remuneration and Stone never asked for it. At first, the phenomenon was a mystery. Cooper had explained it. There was one item Stone absolutely refused to include on the menu he presented to clients. Paradoxically, it was an item Stone was ferociously devoted to. He relished the act the way some people relished exotic desserts: an absolute essential but at the same time not something for every day. It was something he withheld from his clients because he didn't want it on his resume, his desirability apparently depending on a certain painstakingly cultivated mystique. Every week or so Greg would find himself looking unexpectedly into those eyes. Sometimes he'd be nursing a drink at his favorite bar, sometimes he'd be leaving his gym just as Stone was arriving, sometimes they'd run into each other on campus even though Stone wasn't a student there. Somehow, uncannily—though Cooper insisted it was simply that Greg was such a creature of habit that his movements were ridiculously predictable—Stone always knew where to find him when that particular itch needed to be scratched. It was great sex, invariably, though it wasn't what Greg would have liked most. Eventually, he worked up the nerve to ask if they might take turns in the active role. To his relief, Stone had no objection to such an arrangement. Indeed, Stone seemed not to have objections to anything—with that one exception.

Things were easier with Cooper. Cooper didn't bother claiming he was an exclusive top. He simply never bottomed for anyone and eventually the world got the message. Greg wasn't sure the request had ever been made. In any case, with Cooper Greg could be sexually authentic one hundred per cent of the time instead of fifty. That should have tilted the balance in Cooper's favor, because physically and aesthetically Cooper and Stone were equals. Cooper was slightly more imposing physically and, though not a professional, boasted equivalent stamina and technique. As for looks, Greg couldn't choose one over the other. Some days Stone's Nordic magnificence seemed indispensable. Some days

Cooper's raven hair and exotic features held sway. Some days it was the thought of Stone's long, uncut cock that distracted him during his graduate seminars or nodding over his dissertation research in the library, while at other moments it was Cooper's not-quite-as-long-but-noticeably-thicker, circumcised one that intruded on his thoughts. The first time the three of them had sex together, Greg thought he'd died and gone to heaven. But even that close a comparison hadn't pushed Greg off dead center. At least Stone had one thing going for him that Cooper didn't, and it compensated for the disparity in their levels of sexual compatibility: Cooper cuddled with the best of them, but Cooper almost never stayed the night. If you wanted to eat breakfast with Cooper, you had to arrange to meet him at some restaurant or convince him to come over so you could cook for him. Thus, a tossup. Because Cooper, not a hustler but available to the general public on a similar basis as socialized medicine in Canada, was no more the marrying type than Stone was.

"You found the chocolate," Greg said, as naked Stone sauntered back into the bedroom.

"Not like you actually hide it," Stone grinned, "and it's always easier to get you to talk when you've had a couple of kisses."

"Really."

"Scoot over," Stone said, "and prepare to tell Stonie all about it. What's bothering you?"

"Unwrap one of those for me," Greg said.

"Sorry, no," Stone said. "Not now. Talk first."

"I've got a friend coming in from out of town," Greg said.

"Is he cute?"

"Her name is Maria."

"Is she cute?"

"I don't know that cute is really the best word for what Maria is."

"Describe," Stone said, popping a kiss into his mouth.

"Audrey Hepburn playing Peter Pan," Greg said.

"Interesting," Stone said. "Cooper would call that an intriguing juxtaposition."

"He would," Greg agreed.

"And you know her from. . ."

"High school," Greg said. "She graduated a year ahead of me."

"Did you date her?" Stone asked. "It's nothing to be ashamed of, you know. Many of us flirted with heterosexuality in our younger years. Some of us still do."

"Yes," Greg said, "I remember you with Jennifer my first year of grad school."

"That doesn't count," Stone said. "It was for pay, and there was no sex involved. Now, you and Maria."

"We did not date," Greg said. "I already had a girlfriend."

"The whole four years?" Stone asked. "Sorry—three. You said Maria graduated ahead of you. See, I was paying attention."

Another kiss made its way between his pouty lips.

"Actually," Greg said, "Rosalie and I started dating—if you can call it that—in fifth grade. Her idea. Kept the jocks and assorted riffraff at bay. She was real big on that. We went on like that right through graduation."

"I get it," Stone said. "You were a boyfriend of convenience."

"Exactly."

"Now, Maria is arriving when?"

"Day after tomorrow."

"Visiting for how long?"

"A week. She'll want to meet my friends, of course."

"Pretty booked up this weekend," Stone said. "Any time after Monday should work."

"I don't want you turning down jobs," Greg said.

"Of course you do," Stone laughed. "You want me all to yourself. When you're not pining for Cooper, that is. Staying with you, is she?"

"I'll take the couch."

"Where's she visiting from?"

"New York. Can I have chocolate now?"

"Not so fast, mister," Stone said. "We've just scratched the surface. We're nowhere near identifying the source of your angst."

"Damn."

"What does Maria do in New York?"

"Various things. Theatrical stuff."

"Oh, no," Stone said, ingesting yet more chocolate. Given the volume of his intake during a typical overnight with Greg, the state of his abdominal muscles was inexplicable. "Not one of those actress-slash-waitress types."

"Her interests lie in a somewhat different direction," Greg said. "For instance, she works as a rehearsal pianist much of the time. She's also a vocal coach. Prepares people for their auditions—that sort of thing."

"She any good at it?"

"She's building a serious reputation in theatrical circles, from what I hear," Greg said. "This is New York we're talking about, you realize. Off-Broadway mostly, but still. . ."

"She's good then," Stone nodded. "New York's the toughest city on the planet if you don't have talent. Even if you do, it's no picnic. The two of you get along?"

"Like houses on fire."

"She know about you?" Stone asked. "The sucking cock and assfucking part?"

"Absolutely."

"So she's not coming with unrealistic or unsuitable intentions," Stone said. "Good."

"No," Greg said. "Not that."

"Then why are you bothered about seeing her?"

"It's not her," Greg said. "Not really. It's a friend of ours from high school. Thespian Society, right? He's living out here. She wants me to organize a get-together."

"What's the problem?"

"He and I don't really get along," Greg said.

"So? Surely you can all go out for dinner one evening without bloodshed resulting."

"Not so sure of that," Greg muttered.

"Come on, Greg. What kind of monster can he be?"

There it was. The crucial question. Suddenly, unburdening himself, at least to the degree that would satisfy Stone's curiosity, proscribed though it might be, almost seemed like a good idea.

"It's someone you know," Greg said, understanding that he was taking an irrevocable step but unable to stop himself. "And if I told you who he is, you'd see the point immediately. But the last time the two of us met, he more or less swore me to secrecy. For life."

"Wait just a goddamned minute," Stone said. "The Greg Yates I let fuck me silly earlier this evening doesn't deal in melodrama. So if I'm going to swallow this story of yours, you're going to have to come up with a more thorough explanation."

"You can't tell anyone," Greg said.

"Sure," Stone said.

"Especially Cooper," Greg said.

"Why not Cooper?"

"Please," Greg said, "just promise me you won't. . ."

"Oh, my God," Stone said. "It's Christopher Melendez-Greene, isn't it?"

Among other things, Stone was almost supernaturally intuitive. Greg had known it, but he went down this road anyway.

"I didn't say so."

"Wait a minute," Stone said. "I thought. . ."

"Sorry," Greg said. "Question time is over for tonight."

"This is a nice cologne," Stone said, spritzing some into the steamy bathroom air and sniffing. "Mind if I try it on?"

"Take the whole bottle," Greg said, determined not to cut himself shaving.

"What?"

"I don't like it on me," Greg said.

"You never like any fragrance you try," Stone said. "God knows, Cooper and I have made suggestions."

"Some people just aren't meant to wear scent," Greg said.

"You know what Cooper says on the subject," Stone laughed.

"What does Cooper say?"

"For unfathomable reasons, probably having to do with your experiences in earliest childhood, you're basically incapable of thinking of yourself as sexually attractive, hence. . ."

"*Hence?*"

"Mankato State College," Stone grinned. "Freshman comp. B minus—the second time I took the course. That was the semester before I ran away to join the circus."

"Hence," Greg nodded. Even if only half the stories Stone told about himself were true, he'd lived a remarkably eclectic existence up to this point. And he was what? Twenty-two?

"*Hence,*" Stone continued, "any overt act aimed at calling that sort of attention to yourself—well, you think of it as pretentious. Or absurd, at any rate. A little boy walking around in his father's shoes. *Hence,* your neat but nondescript clothing. *Hence,* your neat but nondescript haircut—every two weeks with Mr. Chang, right? *Hence,* all those other efforts to make yourself more or less invisible."

"Oh, come on," Greg protested.

"Because God knows, invisible is preferable to unattractive."

"Jesus," Greg said, "Cooper said all that?"

"You don't think I came up with a theory like that on my own," Stone laughed, crossing his eyes.

"But where does he get it from?"

"Well," Stone said, "he is a university student. You attend the same school, actually."

"He's a sophomore business major, not a professor of clinical psychology."

"He's eventually going to rule the world," Stone said. "You've said it yourself. Listen, thanks for offer of the cologne, but you know I don't wear it. People's tastes are so specific. It's better for business if I don't smell like anything."

"Except sweat, presumably," Greg said.

"Right. You know, I wouldn't worry about the thing with Maria and Christopher if I were you."

"Oh?"

"Worst comes to worst, you just tell her you tried to arrange something but he had to leave town suddenly. If she knows him at all, she won't question it."

"I considered that strategy," Greg nodded, "but don't Cooper and you always insist that I'm the worst liar in the Western Hemisphere?"

It was a ridiculous thing to complain of, Greg admitted to himself as the MUNI car squealed and rumbled into West Portal Station. Bleary eyed students on their way to early classes slumped in the seats. Greg recognized many of them from other mornings. Yes, ridiculous. Most guys would kill to have a fuck buddy like Stone. Or like Cooper. Greg had both of them. He ought to feel like the luckiest twenty-four year old doctoral candidate in the universe. But befriended by demigods as he was and sexually satiated as they managed to keep him month after month, what he really wanted was a husband. Even more than his unease at trying to negotiate a dinner date with Christopher, this was the reason for his dread of Maria's arrival. Her first glimpse into his eyes would tell the tale. She'd sympathize. She'd empathize. She'd break multiple vertebrae in her efforts at being supportive. But she'd know. She'd return to New York with this insight, and inevitably Athena would come to share it. Sooner or later they'd tell Patrick. Then Jeremy would get in on the dish. Eventually, the vibrations would make their way as far as Los Angeles, and Rosalie, Mick, and Trent would join the throng of the initiated: Greg Yates, miserable in his spinsterhood. A veritable cautionary tale. Friend would tell friend, and eventually the known world would be informed. Everywhere he went, people would recognize him as a loser. On a day as foggy as today, and as gloomy as his mood, Greg could almost understand why people jumped off the bridge.

As for his broken promise to Christopher, Greg had no regrets. Apprehensions, yes. Those were obligatory, given Christopher's character. But really, he wasn't a Mafioso. Yet. At least, not that Greg knew of. *Hence*, Greg was unlikely to end up in the bay wearing bricks for shoes. Christopher could make things unpleasant enough if he chose, but Greg no longer feared fatal consequences. For that matter, Stone could hardly think less of Christopher than he already did at this point, and the same was true for Cooper. Because as discreet as Greg knew Stone would be with his new information, there was no way Cooper wouldn't find out.

II

"You can bamboozle Stone," Cooper growled, "but you can't bamboozle me."

"Hey," Greg complained, "go easy with that loofah, will you? I'd like to have some skin left back there."

Stone craved post coital chocolate followed by overnight cuddling. Cooper's analogous obsessions focused on hygiene—of an advanced degree. Sex was inevitably followed by a shower. Sometimes the shower involved additional sex, as tonight. But eventually the quest for an empyrean level of sanitation asserted itself.

"You're deflecting," Cooper complained, but at least he lessened the intensity of his scrubbing.

"No," Greg said, "I'm just trying to survive until lights out."

"The only reason you got away with it," Cooper said, reaching around Greg to adjust the temperature of the spray, "is that he has the attention span of a gnat."

Here it came. Greg had been anticipating this third degree ever since Cooper fell into step with him in the corridor outside his graduate assistant's office-cum-detention cell that afternoon. It loomed all through dinner and hovered over the bed during round one.

"The problem is this," Cooper said. "Until yesterday morning, Stone and I were both under the impression that when I introduced you to Christopher last fall, I was actually introducing the two of you. As in *meeting him for the first time,* yes?"

"Yes," Greg said.

"Now you're claiming him as a boyhood friend—however alienated by time and circumstance. So we're a little confused. Understandably so, I believe."

"Yes," Greg repeated.

"Have you got anything more than that to say on the subject?" Cooper asked. "This isn't a game we're playing, you realize."

"It's true," Greg said. "And I'll tell you the whole story if you like."

"Damn straight, you will," Cooper said.

"But can we at least get out of this shower? The hot water's about to run out."

✶ ✶ ✶

"I told you you should buy your fruit from that little guy down in the Mission, didn't I?" Cooper asked, munching on a pear. He was sprawled naked on Greg's couch, on the opposite side of the tiny living room.

"You were right," Greg said.

"And you're always the perfect host, aren't you?" Cooper smiled. "Hershey's Kisses for Stone—it's a very unsophisticated taste, but that's Stone, right? Fruit for me. If I rummaged around in your kitchen, I wonder what else I would find."

"Be my guest," Greg shrugged.

"Not necessary," Cooper said. "You see whoever you want to see. You stock their preferred treats just like you do ours. You live your life as you choose. You don't need our permission. For anything."

"What if I'm not seeing anyone else?" Greg asked.

"That would be a shame considering what an unbelievably eligible bachelor you are," Cooper said, "but it wouldn't be any of my business. Or Stone's."

"But Christopher is your business," Greg said.

"That's not what I'm saying," Cooper said. "And nobody's going to be bent out of shape because you kept a secret. But I am curious. Stone is, too, now that I explained to him why he ought to be."

"Christopher is your business because he still won't leave you alone," Greg said. "He'd take you back in a second. Or Stone. Presumably, he'd like to keep both of you on retainer."

"But we know him too well to agree to that, don't we?"

"So you say," Greg nodded.

"Yet at the same time not as well as we thought," Cooper smiled. "Apparently."

"I know the kind of things he's going around telling people about himself," Greg said, "and I'm in a better position to know they're not true than just about anyone in the city. But honestly, it makes no difference to me. I'm not interested in spoiling his little game."

"It's hardly a game."

"Sorry," Greg said.

"He's a charlatan," Cooper said. "A charlatan on training wheels, at least. And potentially a very dangerous man. And no, I'm not exaggerating."

"I know that," Greg said, remembering the dead look in Christopher's eyes the last time they met. On his way home from that meeting, he'd described them to himself as the eyes of a psychopath. And then he ridiculed himself for being overly imaginative. Paranoid, even.

"So?"

"So he's not from France originally. He's not the bastard son of a reclusive nobleman and a movie star. There are no Nobel Prizes, Oscars, Emmys, Pulitzers, or Olympic medals on display in any of the residences of his alleged family members. His penis is only average size—that's according to you, actually, since I have no firsthand knowledge. He's not any of the things he tells people he is. Or that people decide he must be based on cryptic little hints he drops. He's just Christopher Melendez-Greene from a tiny little mining town in the middle of nowhere. A statistically average middle class American kid who had all his vaccinations on schedule, was never a Cub or Boy Scout, didn't play a single sport, and graduated from high school with straight B's. Other than his looks, there wasn't anything special about him back then. Anything else is just smoke and mirrors."

"Got it," Cooper said.

"When he showed up at the bar with you last fall and you introduced him as your boyfriend, I hardly knew what to think," Greg said. "I didn't even know he was living in San Francisco at the time. Between high school graduation and that night he'd managed to do a pretty thorough disappearing act."

"Best poker playing I've ever seen," Cooper laughed. "Now that I think back on it."

"Him or me?"

"You," Cooper said. "Really. I didn't notice a thing. Neither did Stone. Just your usual cool."

"The second he looked at me, I knew I had to keep my mouth shut."

"Why?" Cooper asked. "What would it have hurt to say you knew him? He could have figured out some kind of back story to give us. It would have been fun to watch him doing it."

"You introduced him as your boyfriend," Greg said.

"So?"

"You know what they say about stoning the messenger," Greg said. "It wouldn't have been Christopher I was putting in an awkward position, it would have been your boyfriend I was doing it to. You might not have appreciated it. You might have considered it unforgivable. And in front of Stone like that. I couldn't risk it. I mean, you guys are. . ."

There he was, about to reveal an additional layer of emotional vulnerability, something he knew—or at least suspected, based on gossip—Cooper despised in his bedmates.

"It's O.K."

Greg took a deep breath.

"And then there are those eyes of his. I remembered those better than anything else about him. Windows to the soul, right? He came to see me at my office a few days later. Those eyes again. Informed me that we had no prior history and bad things might happen if I said, or even implied, otherwise."

"That's pretty much how I figured it when Stone told me what you'd told him," Cooper said. "You had to have a reason to give Christopher cover like that. And the Greg Yates I know will never be a likely target for blackmail by any stretch of the imagination. What does that leave but intimidation? And even after I quit dating the bastard, that fear was enough."

"You're going to blow it sky high, aren't you?"

"Me? Certainly not. I didn't hear a word you just said. And Stone didn't either. You realize I have to tell him the story now that he figured out he's supposed to be wondering what the hell is wrong with the picture. But Stone carries the code of the courtesan in his DNA. He'll never talk. And I won't, either."

"Why not?"

"What would be the point?" Cooper asked. "Why not let him go on as he is? It'll be great watching him put on his show. And watching people fall for it."

"People are likely to get hurt," Greg said.

"Not my fault," Cooper said. "Not yours. Anybody who isn't smart enough to figure out he's nothing but a big old fake deserves whatever they get."

Greg wasn't the kind of gay who lived and died by the rumor mill. As a graduate student who spent relatively little time in the bars and clubs, most of its material bypassed him. That explained his ignorance of Christopher's presence in the city until the night Cooper "introduced" them. After that, he made more effort to keep current, but he still didn't give much credence to what he heard. Rumors weren't a particularly reliable source of information, for one thing. But mainly he didn't want to know. It seemed pointless. His past association with Christopher was an embarrassment he couldn't allow himself to acknowledge during the short period when Christopher and Cooper were calling themselves a couple. Once they broke up, Cooper refused to discuss Christopher on the basis that doing so was a waste of valuable time, and from Greg's perspective that was a relief. Stone was more forthcoming. He described Christopher as the biggest sleazebag of their generation. He offered no evidence or commentary in support of this, and Greg didn't ask for it. Coming from a hustler, that sort of assessment seemed definitive. Nothing in Greg's memory of his childhood and high school years was sufficient to support or refute it. And he was perfectly content allowing his fuck buddies to do his thinking on the matter for him. Whoever or whatever Christopher had turned into—or might actually have been since grade school—held no relevance for him once Cooper cut himself loose.

III

All over San Francisco, Greg encountered women who seemed unaware that Halloween was only one day out of the year. He understood that the Sixties had passed the death sentence on prior notions about fashion and that the Seventies had ratified it, apparently without any hope of appeal, but the result was anything but pretty. Maria De Gaetano, however, demonstrated clearly that the new aesthetic—if you could even use that word—didn't mean a girl couldn't have style. Her unconventionality of dress actually worked. She was the exception that legitimized the rule. That's what he was thinking as he watched her toil up the jetway amid a mob of zombie like fellow pilgrims. Greg had spent enough time in New York to understand that there was rarely a truly sufficient reason to exit the city even temporarily. But as a proud resident of San Francisco, he thought of his new home as America's analogue to the Vatican. Even more than visiting the nation's capital, a trip to San Francisco was the essential American experience. Washington told you what the country was made of and why, but San Francisco's hills and streets orated about what America could become given enough imagination and effort. Disneyland was merely a dream, and a pretty insipid one at that. San Francisco was a dream realized, a dream that originated in the hearts of true visionaries and eventually came to pass through the sweat and tears of countless inhabitants. As long as New York anchored the Atlantic shores of the nation and San Francisco the Pacific, America would flourish.

Then his eyes met Maria's and he realized that yet again he was being a fool.

"Gregory Yates," she chuckled, wriggling into his arms like an open ocean swimmer making love to her towel after several hours in chilly water, "thank God."

"What?" Greg asked, wondering about inflight turbulence, surly seatmates, or squalling infants.

"Still tall. Still going with that Mormon-Missionary-playing-hooky shtick. Still keeping those hidden depths hidden. Oh, it does a young woman's heart good to see that you still march to the beat of your own drum."

"Oxygen deprivation," Greg laughed. "That's what it must be. Sudden cabin depressurization, and you couldn't be bothered with your mask."

"What's life without taking a few risks?" she said, pulling back to look him full in the face.

"Survivable?" he suggested.

"Bullshit, my friend. Bullshit. Now this is from Athena."

A kiss on his left cheek.

"And this one is from Penny."

A kiss on his right. He should be giddy, being kissed by a woman this attention- grabbing in front of so many witnesses.

"Those two getting along?"

"It's a bona fide love feast," Maria said, grasping his hand. "They start rehearsals in three weeks."

"And Penny's surviving?"

"Athena and I are the only two women in the entire Tri-State Area who don't hate her, I believe," Maria said. "Tall, slim, beautiful—and that's just for starters. Smart and talented. All Manhattan knows she's on her way to the top. And then those boys of hers—little angels. The hottest ex-husband under the sun. A nineteen year old Adonis for a boyfriend. Women have been slaughtered for less cause."

"She leads a charmed life, all right," Greg said, recalling how Dash had left her—eight months pregnant with the first of their sons—for her younger brother.

"It's all right for you to be a cynic," Maria said. "Somebody has to keep our riotous perceptions of the cosmos under control. Now, which way is baggage claim?"

"I have to apologize," he said, biting the bullet as he turned the key and the VW rattled awake. "I haven't been able to contact Christopher. I left several messages, but he never got back to me."

"Oh, that's all handled," Maria said. "Athena talked to him last weekend. We're set for dinner Thursday evening. A place called Tonio's in North Beach."

"I know it," Greg said.

"Is it good?"

This was more than a casual inquiry. Restauranteurs dangled from more than one branch of the extensive DeGaetano family tree.

"You'll be right at home," he said. Trust Athena to succeed where he'd failed. Those Kmetkos were a stalwart bunch. They'd even been known to rise from the dead on occasion. Athena was probably the one person on the planet Christopher would still take direction from.

"It'll be good to see him," Maria said.

"Will it?"

"Athena says," Maria nodded, "so it's true. Though her definition of 'good' is sometimes extremely cryptic. Now, I know you're in school for a few weeks yet. I don't want you to worry about keeping me entertained. I've got a bunch of people to see while I'm here and a very long list of errands Athena sent with me."

"Such as?"

"Never you mind," Maria said. "More than enough to keep a girl occupied, let's just say."

"Anything I can help with?"

"We'll see," Maria said.

"Will I see you at all?"

"Don't worry about that," she laughed.

IV

Patrick, Jeremy, Christopher, and Greg. All the way back to grade school, they moved as a unit. When one itched, the other three scratched. When one chopped an onion, all their eyes watered. Their schoolmates—and even some teachers—referred to them as The Four Musketeers. As the youngest, always one grade behind, Greg was the obvious D'Artagnan. When Patrick, Jeremy, and Christopher graduated and left for university, certain girls (though not Rosalie) wept at the poignancy of Greg's "abandonment" by his brothers-in-arms, but what could you do? Life didn't rearrange itself to accommodate such minor tragedies. And through all those years, if any of them questioned the impregnable solidarity of their "ganghood", Greg was never aware of it. Circumstances were always changing, of course. Junior high followed elementary school. Previously undreamed of extra-curricular opportunities presented themselves, and it turned out that girls weren't an alien species after all. Ironically—at least it seemed ironic to Greg, but that was based on secret familiarity with his deepest feelings—he was the first of them to become "seriously" attached to one. It was like when Patrick, Jeremy, and Christopher had originally inducted him. Rosalie simply walked up to him one day at recess and announced that if he knew what was good for him, they were, from that point onward and 'til graduation did them part, girl- and boyfriend. He immediately recognized this as the promise of camouflage he increasingly sensed the need of, and God bless her, Rosalie seemed instinctively to understand and accept this, or at the very least to possess secret self-knowledge of her own that made the arrangement imperative.

It must have been when Greg and Rosalie were in tenth grade—and at least partially under the influence of her clear-eyed analyses of the foursome—that Greg began to realize that though his gang had attained the status of Red Dog High School legend, it was smaller than the sum of its parts. It was as if Athos, Porthos, and D'Artagnan were accompanied on their quest for significance if not outright glory not by Aramis but by the Cheshire Cat. Increasingly, everyone seemed to sense something out of the ordinary about Christopher, though Patrick and Jeremy feigned obliviousness. He was no longer "that quiet guy". He had evolved silently and almost unnoticed into "that strange guy". Not that this was ever described or discussed in psycho-sexual terms. Nobody at Red Dog High School seemed aware of such potentialities. He was simply "strange". Stranger, indeed, than could be accounted for by his membership in the Thespian Society, that perennial refuge of individuals who deviated from the well-established and universally understood norms of American high school culture.

Strange, perhaps, but inoffensively so. The inoffensive nature of Christopher's deviance—whatever it amounted to in concrete terms—was what made it possible for the rest of them to persist in their oblivion. Then that fiasco during his freshman year at the university. Greg still didn't know for certain what had happened. He didn't believe anyone but Christopher could say, but Christopher had never been available for comment. Total comprehension wasn't required, however. Only the merest detail was enough. Overnight, Christopher came to be understood as one of "those." As far as anyone had previously known—anyone except Greg, that was—such creatures were practically mythical. Like unicorns. Or the Sphinx itself. They inhabited some realm far from the one the rest of the world's population did. Suddenly that comfortable illusion had been exploded. They were right here. "One of the gang" could be "one of those". That realization about Christopher changed everything. At the very least, there was no Four Musketeers any more. There weren't even three. In the confused aftermath of Christopher's misadventure, Greg extricated himself without encountering any resistance. He'd been feeling increasingly oppressed by the implicit imperative to conformity which membership in the gang entailed, and this was his opportunity to declare independence. His girlfriend of convenience almost beat him out the door. She already had plans for her escape from orbit. Until then, Greg had known Athena as the school's universal object of desire as well as fellow thespian, and Maria as her sidekick. In his new existence, they were the first ones to fill the vacuum resulting from his newly accomplished liberation. They were beautiful, they were smart, they accepted no external limits on their behavior, and they required no explanations.

The gay San Francisco that Greg inhabited was a land of refugees. Everyone was from somewhere else. You rarely met a native of the Bay Area, and even those few were running away from something. Guys Greg knew insisted that being gay necessitated geographical adjustments as well as psychological and emotional ones. Coming out was just a start. Some sort of subsequent relocation was more or less obligatory, even if it only amounted to a change of neighborhood. Upon that ground zero you assembled a completely new existence, one that offered a supportive environment for your renovated identity. The bottom line: you didn't have to be that guy any more. The one cowering in the closet, dating women for cover, sneaking and skulking, concealing your authentic self from friends and loved ones. Yet as the community's experts generalized, Greg questioned. They might be right as far as they went, but it seemed to him that the process was infinitely variable, different for everyone who underwent it. People were as individual as their fingerprints, and so were their experiences. He'd instinctively understood how it had to work long before he ever heard anyone pontificate on the topic from the head of some brunch table. He'd sensed it as far back as grade school. There were three kinds of people in his home town. And by that, he wasn't thinking of its white, brown, and black residents. There were the people who never left, the people who left for schooling or military service only to return later—his parents fell into that category—and the people who left and never came back except for weddings, funerals, family reunions, and the like. Long before sex entered his consciousness in any meaningful way, he assigned himself to the final group. It wasn't adolescent trauma or gaudy ambition that made him a refugee. It was simply an awareness that there wasn't enough going on within the walls of that canyon to fulfill him. This awareness was probably the glue in his relationship with Rosalie. She possessed the same impulses, and while she had no intention of navigating the shoals and rapids of adolescence as a single woman, neither was a boyfriend who might attempt to control or deflect or obstruct her an acceptable proposition. They left Red Dog the same day, less than a week after graduation. Everybody Greg was really close to, except his family, left, too. Patrick, Jeremy, and Christopher had already been gone for a year. Athena was at the university with them. Maria had already ranged as far as New York.

But it wasn't just geography. It wasn't as simple as leaving the small town isolation, the desert, the familiar details of his existence behind. He thought of himself as some sort of creature leaving its previous developmental phase behind. He didn't have to be that guy any more. He could be someone else. He wasn't sure who the new guy was. Finding out was the quest that lay ahead. Presumably, Christopher shared a parallel experience. By rights, they might have met up in San Francisco and renewed their friendship. But by the time Greg collected his high school diploma and went home to finish packing, he wasn't sure Christopher and he had ever been friends. The answer to that question hadn't seemed particularly significant. There were many others of far greater moment. Mostly, Greg didn't ponder it.

Years passed. He went to college, fell in love, fell in love again, lost out both times, finished his degree, started graduate school, moved west. He kept uncovering aspects of the guy he was becoming and letting go of pieces of the guy he didn't have to be any more. Life unfolded bit by bit each day. Those friendships from high school, all but a handful of them, faded, diminished in intensity, appeared increasingly quaint. Any remaining unresolved issues and questions became irrelevant. Still, he wondered sometimes. Was Rosalie really happy with her husband and new baby? Would Patrick and Jeremy ever open that law practice together back in Red Dog or would they kill each other—probably over some girl—first? Would Athena hit it big on Broadway? Would people ever appreciate Maria's genius like she deserved? What became of all those guys he'd fallen for over the years? And, almost a footnote, who was Christopher, really, and what would pass between them if they ever met again? The look in Christopher's eyes the night Cooper "introduced" them was all the answer he needed. But by then the question seemed pointless. And when Christopher visited his office and hinted at dire consequences if Greg insisted on, well, broadcasting certain biographical truths, it didn't seem important at all. He was annoyed, but not at Christopher's mandate, which struck him as trivial. It was Christopher's manner that upset him. *That's who he was all along,* he remembered saying to himself on his way home later that afternoon. *He wasn't quiet or eccentric or a dreamer or possessed by an artistic temperament. He was just an arrogant, narcissistic prick who never let us know him.* Greg didn't even feel bad for Cooper, saddling himself with a boyfriend like that. Cooper could take care of himself.

V

"It's not a very impressive campus," Greg said, staring down the tunnel for the arrival of the train. "But then, it's a second tier university. Perhaps only third tier, really."

"Cut the crap, boy," Maria growled. "You know all that prestige university stuff is a load of bollocks."

"*Bollocks?* What? Are you preparing Athena to audition for *Masterpiece Theatre?*"

"Brit roomie we just took on," Maria shrugged. "That transatlantic slang is mighty infectious. *Bollocks* just feels so good bouncing around in your mouth."

"Don't take a header on that Freudian slip," Greg chortled. "Is this another of your strays?"

"He followed Athena home," Maria said.

Guys frequently did that, Greg knew, but they weren't usually allowed to take up residence.

"As someone who never attended college," Maria said, "I have a certain perspective on higher education. I've shared it with Athena and Penny and they agree with me in general terms."

"Uh huh," Greg said.

"When someone we know complains of the education they received—at the University of East Nowhere or The College of Marie Antoinette, for instance—I pose a few questions. Did they ever figure out where the library was located, for instance? Did they notice any smart people in their classes, faculty included? Bother to interact with them, assuming they did? See, as far as I'm concerned, nothing's more important in terms of getting an education than what you're willing to put into it yourself. You went to that nothing little school in Pennsylvania and came out a Renaissance Man because you ruthlessly exploited everything the place had to offer. Your old classmate, Scott Morgan, failed out of Notre Dame in less than a semester because he couldn't be bothered to make an effort—him with his sky high SAT's."

"It wasn't that simple," Greg said. "He was saying 'fuck you' to his father. And his grandfather."

"Granted," Maria said. "But who willfully decides not to make a go of a school like that? Anybody with the opportunity for it who fails to get a good education simply didn't try."

"Turning into a fascist, are we?"

"Call it what you like," Maria said. "I can't believe how clean the subway stations are here."

Even in the brightest sunshine the Bay Area could muster, the campus seemed more drab and characterless than usual. So much for Maria's pep talk.

"I know you're dying to show me sights like your graduate assistant office and your carrel in the main library and the washroom where you received your first blow job west of the Mississippi, but first things first. Which way is the music building?"

"Why?" Greg asked, though he knew the answer.

"We're going to hijack a practice cubicle and you're going to sing for me," Maria said. "I can't possibly die a happy woman unless I hear you in some selections from *Pirates of Penzance* and *The Desert Song* one more time."

"Who said anything about dying?" Greg asked, making a face.

"We are all dying," Maria intoned in an imitation of Vincent Price Greg recalled from junior high, "with every breath we take."

"Very funny."

"Come on, Yates," she insisted. "Lead the way. You're not getting out of it, you know. I'll never be able to face Athena."

Greg wasn't a music student in college, but he'd known a few of them. The one thing you could depend on was that they never practiced until the last minute. And that morning apparently wasn't even close to qualifying for the description. They had their choice of practice cubicles, and they didn't have to sneak.

"All right," Maria said, "you say you haven't sung since *The Desert Song.* Two years, give or take."

"Right."

"So we'll take a nice, Maria DeGaetano style warmup first. Give you a taste of how I work with my little clients."

"I don't know how you expect me to perform for you," Greg said. "We don't have anything resembling a score between the two of us."

"There's a red herring if I ever saw one," Maria laughed. "Your photographic memory is almost as good as mine. Here. . ." she played a C major scale, "sing that.

Start at the bottom and end up on middle C. Nice and slow, and don't forget how mama taught you to breathe."

"Gorgeous, young Gregory Yates. Absolutely heart-melting. And now auntie can check that one off her list."

"Huh?"

"Athena believes you're wasting your life out here," Maria said. "You do realize that. And this crazy scheme of yours about a career in academia? You're under some kind of delusion. So it's Maria to the rescue, charged with bringing our wandering boy home, by which she means to Manhattan, once more to tread the boards and submit to the will of the gods of comedy and tragedy. Perhaps even learn to dance, as well."

"Sounds like the plot of a bad Thirties backstager," Greg said. "Script by Henry James in collaboration with the Marx Brothers."

"Scoff all you like," Maria said. "The girl is in deadly earnest."

"Film noir," Greg said. "1943, with Peter Lorre in a silent but pivotal role and score by Erich Wolfgang Korngold. You really shouldn't egg her on, you know."

"I don't," Maria insisted. "Cross my heart. But now that she and Penny are thick as thieves—well, Ms. Fuller-Pakkunen, in addition to being a rising star directorially speaking, is still one of your biggest fans."

"Please don't let's fight about this," Greg said.

"Fight? Nobody said anything about fighting. *Just deliver the message, Maria.* And I have. So lead on, Macduff. Show me your kingdom and subjects."

"Not so fast," Greg said.

"What?"

"It's your turn," Greg said. "Sit back down and accompany yourself."

"Oh, that."

"That."

"You know I don't perform any more."

"Neither do I."

"Fair enough," Maria said. "What would you like to hear?"

"Surprise me."

"Lovely," Greg said. "Thanks so much. I didn't recognize that, but it's very nice."

"It is, isn't it?"

"Kind of like an aria and a torch song got together and made a baby."

"Athena will love that you described it that way. She's working on it for her cabaret act."

"What is it? Who's it by?"

"Guess."

"Seriously."

"Seriously, boy."

"I'd have to hear it again."

She began to play that simple introduction.

"All right," Maria said. "Talk."

"I still can't place it," Greg said, "but it has to be Sondheim, right?"

"Based on what?"

"Based on if 'Send in the Clowns' wasn't so disastrously overexposed, there'd be a better chance people would take it seriously as good music," Greg said.

"And you hear the same quality in this number?"

"What I hear," Greg said. "Well, I guess, the deep polish of the lyrics. Not a badly chosen word. Or even a badly placed one. And the extreme care with which the lyrics have been set. Sondheim, definitely."

"And you win the prize," Maria laughed. "That's 'Losing My Mind.' It's from *Follies*."

"I thought that bombed," Greg said.

"522 performances isn't a bomb," Maria said. "Most bombs don't win several Tonys. On the other hand, it lost most if not all of its investment. But who says even the doggiest of shows couldn't include one good number? Even a great one?"

"Point taken," Greg said.

"You're right, though," Maria said. "It should have done better."

"You saw it?"

"Eight times," Maria nodded.

"What went wrong? Bad production?"

"Production was great. Cast was super. Sondheim and company only made one mistake."

"Which was?"

"They got out too far ahead of their public," Maria said. "Mark my words, thirty years from now, that show will be a classic. And there's a perfect role for Athena. She'll be old enough for it when the revival rolls around, and Penny will direct."

"Is that her big number?"

"No," Maria said. "She'll play the other girl."

"Who's this pretty lady, Yates?"

"Oh, hi, Steve," Greg said.

The main English Department office was its usual late Thursday morning snoozefest. Greg wasn't sure how the secretaries stayed awake until time to take their lunch breaks.

"No," Steve said, "don't tell me. Didn't you say you have a sister?"

"Two of them," Greg said, "but Maria isn't. . ."

"We get that all the time," Maria laughed. "We're both tall and slender. We have the same haircut and the same coloring. Maria DeGaetano—and you are?"

"Steve Mannheim," Steve smiled.

"That's Steve Mannheim, Esquire," Greg said.

"Oh?"

"That's right," Steve smiled. "Failed the California Bar Exam five times running. Took it as a sign that I was on the wrong track. Road to Damascus kind of thing. So, you're not Greg's sister, and I know you're not his girlfriend. . ."

"Old friend from high school. Visiting from New York for a few days."

"New York? That's cool. Wait a minute. I'm getting a vibe. Publishing, right? Because I've got this novel I'm about ready to shop."

"I'm a theatrical producer, actually," Maria said.

"Wow," Steve said. "How cool is that? I've always wanted to do a book about theatre types living in Manhattan. Kind of a *La Boheme* set in contemporary New York. Maybe you and I could. . ."

"I'm awfully booked up this visit, I'm afraid," Maria said, "but if you're ever in the City. . ."

"Sure," Steve smiled. "Yates can give me your particulars."

"Jesus," Maria laughed once they were on the elevator. "What ruthless charisma that one's putting out. Or maybe it's a curse. It's like I never left Manhattan."

"He's not a bad guy, really," Greg said. "He's the first straight male I came out to around here."

"And he obviously took it just fine," Maria laughed. "He seems to think of you as a fellow lothario."

"Can't imagine where he got that idea," Greg shrugged.

"Thing is," Maria said, "I've gotten a lot less particular than I was when I first moved to New York. If I wasn't here visiting you, I'd do a looker like that at the drop of a hat. I always was a sucker for those clean-cut, ex-jock types. Even though they are all fascists."

"Steve isn't," Greg said. "Particularly."

"I almost asked you for directions to the nearest broom closet."

"You're going to make me blush," Greg said.

"You always did blush too easily."

"Should I tell him what you said about him?"

"Only after I've left town," Maria said. "Can't make it too easy for a guy like that. He might not appreciate it. Of course, I don't have to explain it to you. You've made an art form of playing hard to get, I imagine."

"I don't believe that's how anyone around here would describe me," Greg said.

"No?"

"But let's talk about you, madame *theatrical producer*."

"I'll have you know that in the playbill for *Entertaining Mr. Sloane*, I'm billed as Associate Producer."

"Hence your delay in making this trip," Greg said. "Athena says opening night was a smash."

"The thing with that show," Maria said, "is either you have a leading man with the presence to carry the whole production or you don't. And if you don't, you shouldn't bother opening."

"You apparently do," Greg said.

"You'll judge for yourself," Maria said. "I'll get you a seat. You are coming east for Patrick's wedding in June, aren't you? I mean, he didn't *forget* to invite you?"

"No," Greg said. "I got a really nice letter from him. I'll be there."

"Thank God," Maria said. "Another thing to scratch off Athena's list."

"You know," Maria said, looking around the station platform, "people here are prettier than in New York."

"You think so?"

"No question," she nodded. "Not as pretty as people in L.A., however. Remember that year Athena was working on her M.F.A. at U.C.L.A? I stayed with her for a month and I couldn't believe how photogenic everyone was."

"I haven't spent enough time down there to have that impression," Greg said.

"You haven't shown me pictures of Rosalie's baby yet."

He'd been dreading this topic. Talk of Rosalie and David would lead inevitably to mention of Mick. Greg should never have agreed to share a hotel room with Rosalie's brother the weekend of the Brit. Even with David paying, it was a mistake. The real mistake had been sleeping with Mick. It confirmed the feelings Greg had been nursing since twelfth grade, and that was the last thing he needed. Being in love with unavailable guys was a weakness of his that revealed itself long before the advent of Cooper and Stone. Or Dash and Luke. Or Paul. So the less said on the topic of Rosalie's family, the better. But he couldn't stay completely silent. That would be as revealing as an emergency flare in a night sky.

"Maybe I'll bring them to dinner so Christopher can see them, too."

"There's a thought," Maria laughed.

"O.K." Greg said. "Here's your train coming in. You've got my spare key to the apartment?"

"Check."

"And your transit map?"

"Yes, grannie," Maria laughed. "I practically live on public transportation, you know."

"All right," Greg said. "I'll come home right after the gym."

"I'm not sure when I'll get back," Maria said. "I'm dropping in on Maya's rehearsal. You remember her. She was in that gang I brought to see you in *Pirates of Penzance*."

"Yes," Greg said. He remembered the name if not the actual girl.

"She's understudying a role in *The Trojan Women* at American Conservatory Theatre. Then I'm supposed to go see my—I don't know what she is. My great-grandmother's second cousin. In Chinatown, of all places. She married outside."

In nearly six years of regular gym attendance—*attendance* because the guys who originally initiated him thought of working out like devout souls thought of going to church—Greg hadn't accomplished much in terms of building lean muscle mass. Nobody worked out harder than he did. And he followed his mentors' diet instructions as if they were holy writ. "You're an ectomorph," Cooper would explain whenever the subject arose. "Some guys don't have the genetics to get really big," Stone would agree. "But look at your definition," Cooper would continue. "And your overall conditioning." "You could teach a lot of guys around here a thing or two about work ethic," Stone would say, completing the pep talk. But how Greg wished for something more impressive than what he saw when he looked at himself in the bathroom mirror. It came so naturally to some guys. They showed up at the gym, and six months later they were transformed. Yet he was pretty sure that another year or another six wouldn't make an appreciable difference in his case. Still, he wouldn't have dreamed of giving it up. At the very least, it kept him on the periphery of Cooper's gang of muscleheads, and they were the hottest guys in the city. They represented a kind of ideal Greg would always hold in reverence. And someday, if he was lucky, one of them would look at him and decide it was time to get engaged.

"How's the visit going?" Stone asked. He had materialized a moment earlier under the shower head next to Greg's. Greg hadn't noticed him during his workout. Sometimes Stone showed up at the gym just to shower, either getting back from or on his way to "work", Greg assumed, though it might be more serious than that. Greg wasn't sure he actually had a permanent residence. Maybe this shower room and the locker out there were all he had. There might be an opportunity in it, but Greg couldn't imagine what kind of angle he might be required to play in order to pull it off. He certainly spent enough time pondering it, but he never came up with a plan that seemed viable rather than pathetic.

"Great," Greg said.

"Did you ever get in touch with You Know Who?"

"Didn't have to," Greg said. "Maria and her roommate made the arrangements last weekend. We're meeting him for dinner tonight. Tonio's in North Beach."

"Interesting," Stone said.

"Yes," Greg said. "As in that ancient curse: *may you live in interesting times.*"

"Exactly," Stone laughed.

"I really don't care what happens," Greg said, "as long as he's nice to Maria."

VI

Maria wanted to use public transportation, but Greg didn't trust the weather. He made Maria take one of his extra jackets, and he went down the block to fetch the VW.

"Ah, good old Vasco," Maria said, climbing into the passenger seat.

At Red Dog High School, it had become a fashion—after strenuous and prolonged promotion by Jeremy and Patrick—to christen vehicles. Rosalie considered this a sign of feeble-mindedness, so Greg didn't participate until Athena and Maria intervened. "He either has to be named after Prince Henry the Navigator," Athena said, "or Vasco da Gama. Because you have much exploration in store for you." "Some of it may even take place from behind his steering wheel," Maria laughed, "rather than in his back seat." "I thought it was traditional for all conveyances to be named for women," Greg said. "You mean, like 'The Spirit of St. Louis?'" Maria asked, "or Apollo 12?" "Go ahead," Rosalie said. "Follow the crowd." "Someday you'll thank us," Maria promised, and that was that. The innocent little putty colored Beetle that never aspired to anything beyond regular fillings of its tank and occasional washes and oil changes took on a rather grand identity. Once Greg departed on his migration eastward for college, he never again thought of the car as having a name.

"I seem to recall that you and Athena never got around to naming your cars."

"Neither of them actually belonged to us," Maria said. "So how could we? It would have been a presumption. Like naming someone else's puppy. The Fiat was Daniel's, and the Falcon got passed down to my brother Joe."

"And from him to Marty and Paolo," Greg said. "Anyway, it was just your graduating class that went in for it."

"Yes," Maria said, "but the gold medal class of Sixty-eight was the *ne plus ultra* of graduating classes. A veritable pinnacle. One might actually call it a Platonic Ideal. Everybody recognized the fact at the time, and I'm sure the locals still speak of it with reverence. You're lucky you were a member by association."

"Rather than officially," Greg said. "Sort of like the Communist Party of the United States in an earlier era."

"Something like that," Maria agreed. She went on to narrate the adventures of her day. Rehearsals for *The Trojan Women* were like every rehearsal you'd ever witnessed or suffered through, her ancient relative in Chinatown still spoke perfect, if strangely accented, Italian, the bus drivers of the city were remarkably stoic compared to their Manhattan counterparts while the streetcorner markets were more sanitary looking, and the cable cars constituted the unquestioned Platonic Ideal of public transportation.

"I wonder," she finally said, "if we shouldn't have invited your buddy Steve Mannheim along with us."

"Why would we do that?"

"Aside from the obvious, by which I refer to those shoulders and that hair," she said, "safety in numbers, right?"

"You don't feel safe meeting Christopher for dinner?"

"You don't," Maria said. "That's the point. And don't try to deny it. I know your signs."

Here it was. He could try and argue her out of her impression, but he knew such an attempt was doomed to failure. It was bad enough that she'd never lost her skill at seeing through him.

"We didn't part on the best of terms last time I saw him," Greg said, groping toward an explanation she'd accept. "That's all."

"I have no idea what that means," Maria said. "Nobody's ever on the best of terms with Christopher. There's not enough of him present and accounted for to make such a thing possible."

"Then you understand," Greg said. "It wasn't much of a reunion."

"How could it have been?" Maria asked. "One or the other of you had no idea how the script went. It probably stumped both of you. He never could improvise, and you never could lead the waltz. Tell me this much. What does he look like these days? Has he changed much? Did he ever grow into his looks?"

"I'm not sure exactly what you mean by growing into his looks," Greg said.

"He was always a little too pretty," Maria said. "And my God, was he soft. He needed some additional maturity, or perhaps just toughness, to achieve his full impact. If he has, people better watch out."

"I see," Greg said. "Well, when I saw him last fall, he gave the impression that he'd spent a great deal of his time since high school hanging out in gyms."

"Like Penny's ex?"

"No," Greg said. "Not like Dash. Christopher didn't get nearly that big. If I had to describe him in one sentence, I'd say something like *captain of the Hungarian National men's gymnastics team.*"

"Interesting," Maria said. "Like your old nemesis, Penny's younger brother."

Why hadn't he realized it before? Ever since seeing Christopher last fall, he'd kept those two in their own boxes—not consciously, but presumably out of some instinct for self-preservation.

"Yes," Greg admitted. "Like Luke."

"Athena and I had a bet," Maria mused, looking out the side window at the thronging sidewalks of North Beach.

"Oh?"

"How long would it take you to ask me about him."

"I don't remember saying a word about Luke."

"You haven't," Maria said. "And God knows I've brought up Penny and Dash enough times since I got here, and that kind of makes him inevitable, but you never took the bait. Which means I win another bet with Athena. I'm batting a thousand so far. Girl's too romantic in her outlook. That's her trouble. You used to be able to rely on her cynicism."

"We're supposed to be meeting a friend," Greg said to the hostess, who resembled a Barbie doll or perhaps Brunnhilde's prettier cousin.

"Ah," she nodded. "One moment while I check."

She consulted her reservations book for a moment, a look of serene concentration on her face. Greg thought of Madame Curie contemplating the unearthly glow of radium in a darkened room. Leni Riefensthal in her editing booth came to mind next.

"Are you Miss DeGaetano?" she asked, smiling brilliantly at Maria.

"What if I say I'm not?"

"Then I'm not sure which reservation is yours," the girl said, suddenly concerned.

"Well, as it happens, I am Miss DeGaetano. Maria DeGaetano, theatrical producer. Just here for a few days from Manhattan."

"Manhattan?" the girl exclaimed.

"It's part of New York."

"Oh, I know," the girl nodded. "I have your table ready, if you'll follow me."

"I know, I know," Maria said, sipping her *pinot grigio*. "I'm going to hell for behaving that way. But girls like that. . ."

"She didn't remind you of Athena?" Greg laughed. "Even a little?"

"Get this straight," Maria said, "if you'll pardon the term, that is. Athena is nothing like that young woman. Not a single iota. Athena has a brain."

"I'll bear that in mind," Greg said.

Fifteen minutes didn't constitute disastrous tardiness. Especially not with parking conditions in North Beach being what they were and the light rain that had started to fall since they were seated. But now that they'd reached twenty-three minutes and counting, Greg couldn't prevent himself from being concerned. He stared at his menu and pretended nothing was wrong.

"You know," Maria said, "I can't get over how much this place reminds me of Uncle Sal's restaurant back in Red Dog."

Which, Greg was sure, was why Christopher had chosen it.

"Here they are, gentlemen," Barbie giggled.

Greg looked up.

"Sorry we're late," Stone announced.

Greg wasn't used to seeing him so dressed. Cooper wasn't quite such a surprise.

"You know this one is never on time for a social engagement," Cooper smiled, "so I don't know if that means his apology is redundant or needs to be ignored. You must be Maria."

"Yes," Greg said, finding his tongue. "This is Maria. And these are my friends, Stone and Cooper."

"Nice to meet you gentlemen," Maria said.

Greg heard the curiosity in her tone. He was curious himself.

"Christopher's detained," Stone said, sitting down. "We're his replacements. And I do mean replacements, not deputies. He doesn't know we're here, of course."

"Detained?" Greg asked.

"Yes," Cooper nodded, taking the chair opposite Stone. "There's been an emergency."

"I hope it isn't serious," Maria said.

"I wish it was," Cooper grunted.

"His doctor told him he couldn't meet you two for dinner because if he didn't throw a party at his place *this very night*, he'd turn into a pillar of salt," Stone explained, "and though he's a great connoisseur of phallic objects generally, he drew the line at becoming that particular kind."

"Are you sure you dropped out of college after three semesters?" Greg asked.

"Two and a half," Stone said, "but while I was there, I paid attention."

"Stone's right in general terms," Cooper said. "And Christopher always follows doctor's orders. Since he's about to be one himself."

"Now, when I say party, I mean *party*," Stone explained. "Caterers. Musicians. Bartenders. Sword swallowers. Gypsy fortune tellers. Psychics. Professors of Esperanto. An accordion player with a monkey. Drag queens, go-go boys, leather daddies, hustlers. The usual menagerie. Greg can verify the scale Christopher entertains on, what with his nearly unlimited budget and rolodex the size of a bus tire."

"Anyway," Cooper said, "we hope you're not too disappointed that he didn't invite you."

"He invited us, of course," Stone said, "but we're boycotting."

"Oh?" Maria raised one eyebrow. Greg recognized it as her characteristic expression of amusement as much as inquiry.

"Greg's probably been too delicate to talk to you about some of Christopher's less desirable character traits," Cooper said, "not to mention our history with your former classmate. But Stone and I will be glad to fill you in if you have any questions."

"Guys, please," Greg protested.

"Greg, it's O.K." Maria said.

"But. . ."

"I knew he wouldn't show," Maria smiled. "Or maybe it would be more accurate to say I hoped he wouldn't."

"What?"

"We'll discuss it later, sweetie. And once again I win a bet with Athena. I never imagined he'd go to such lengths, however."

"Well, it's no surprise to us, is it, Greg?" Stone laughed. "Exactly like him, really. He couldn't just stand you up. He had to make a production of it."

"He started making calls to organize everything and issue invitations on Monday morning," Cooper explained.

"Athena spoke to him on Sunday night," Maria nodded. "He didn't waste any time."

"His parties aren't usually so impromptu," Stone explained. "And yes, even on a Thursday night and with practically no advance notice he can draw a note-worthy crowd."

"Gossip worthy, at least," Cooper nodded.

"You both knew what he was up to," Greg said. "But you never said anything?"

"Why worry your pretty head over something no one had any control over?" Stone asked. "And besides, Cooper and I had the situation well in hand. Wouldn't you rather be dining with the two of us than with that would-be Benito Mussolini?"

"I can't speak for dear Gregory," Maria laughed, "but as far as I'm concerned, things worked out perfectly."

"Ah, here's our waiter," Cooper said. "Evening, Franco."

"Cooper. And Stone. What a pleasant surprise. Who are your friends?"

"This is Maria. And her handsome escort is Gregory."

"Pleased to meet you folks," Franco said.

"Quiet in here this evening," Stone observed.

"Yes," Franco said. "Probably the rain."

"Lucky for you, though," Cooper said.

"How so?"

"They'll probably send you home early," Stone said, "and you'll still be able to make it to Christopher's party."

"You know about that? I wasn't sure if he invited you."

"We know about it," Cooper nodded. "And we're pretty sure you were deputized to mention the party to these nice people—just in passing—and make sure, in the pleasantest way possible, how sorry you are that they're not on the guest list."

"Yes," Stone said. "It would have started something like this: *say, don't I know you from somewhere?* And then when Greg said no, he didn't think so, you'd say *sure I do. I've seen you at Christopher Melendez-Greene's parties, haven't I? You going over there tonight? Really? You didn't hear about it? Well, he's gotten so popular lately he can't entertain everyone.* And that would have been that."

"You bastard," Franco chuckled. "Got it all figured out, haven't you?"

"Perhaps you'd like to ask your manager if he'll be so kind as to send someone else to wait on us," Cooper said.

"Yes," Stone smiled. "Please do."

"Sorry to eat and run," Stone said, "but Cooper has a date."

"And Stone has two," Cooper growled. "And counting."

"In my book, two hours plus of amusing conversation over a meal hardly constitutes eating and running," Maria said. "Especially since Cooper was so gracious about wrestling the check out of Greg's hand."

"He's like that," Stone said, "when there are ladies present. Usually we go dutch."

"I see," Maria laughed.

"Listen," Stone said, "now that it's stopped raining and the clouds have blown on out over East Bay, make Greg take you up to Coit Tower. We're right at the base of Telegraph Hill here, you know. It's less than five minutes by car. And the view of the city at night—you might never go back to New York."

"So that's what you haven't been telling your nearest and dearest about," Maria said, staring out at Alcatraz.

"I'm sorry, "Greg said, "I don't believe I follow you."

"Bullshit, boy," she said. "Christopher's gone over to the dark side, and you're embarrassed to talk about it. Athena will be fascinated. But what's really fascinating is those two monstrously hot bodybuilders. Not to mention charming and urbane. And you're fucking both of them, aren't you?"

"You say it like it's a good thing."

"What else would it be? Oh, I know. You think you want a husband. It's not just what you say, you know. We have the story of your travails from Penny's point of view as well. Every grisly detail. And she's a first-hand witness, isn't she?"

"Is it so much to ask?"

"When you're not emotionally or mentally ready for it, yes," Maria said. "And in a situation like that you really have no alternative but to get your ashes hauled as spectacularly as you can. Not to mention as frequently. And Stone and Cooper certainly look capable enough."

"If you say so," Greg said.

"Yes," Maria said. "It's exactly what I say. And Athena and Penny will agree once I explain the situation. But we heard this alarming rumor."

"What rumor? Who's been talking about me?"

"Patrick found out Christopher's living out here. Just a shout away from you, my dear. And there was no telling what he might do to interfere with your evolution. That's not Patrick's assessment, mind you. It's ours. Patrick's as brainless as always about such things. And Jeremy's worse. But it made us uneasy. Especially once we met Luke. So I was sent to investigate."

"And this is what you found," Greg said. "Poor, miserable Greg, still spinning his wheels, unable to make any progress getting his dreams to come true. Dream singular, that is."

"Nonsense," Maria snorted. "That's not what I found at all. I found our dear friend flourishing, sweet and handsome as ever and watched over by two ridiculously stalwart guardian angels."

JARED BARTOK: 1976

When Jared first came to San Francisco, he made the mistake of renting the wrong apartment in the wrong neighborhood. Nothing bad came of it, but nothing good did either. It provided him shelter, but beyond that it was a waste of time and money. It wasn't a mistake he intended to perpetuate, so when his lease was up, his buddies from the gym, Cooper and Nick, went apartment hunting with him. Or more accurately, they went apartment hunting and took Jared along. Cooper sold real estate and Nick was an attorney. In addition, they were two of the hottest and most sought after guys in the city, so Jared believed he was in the best possible hands. If anyone could find him the right apartment, it was those two. What they eventually chose for him was a newly redecorated basement apartment, the whole lower floor of a brightly painted Victorian. It featured a row of French doors leading out to the back garden. It was located, Cooper assured him, on the best block in the city for the money he was prepared to pay.

"If you don't rent it, I will," Nick said, in a tone of voice that nearly made Jared hard.

The landlady, who lived directly above, was one of those characters the city took enormous pride in, an eccentric of the old school who dressed like Isadora Duncan's more theatrical sister and cultivated her quirks as conscientiously as a surgeon would his suturing technique.

"Sun bathing?" she asked, when Cooper suggested that the seclusion of the back garden made it particularly appropriate for that activity. "I'm not sure I could allow a thing like that."

"Why not?" Nick asked, obviously prepared to argue landlord-tenant legalities with her until the cows came home.

"You young people these days lack commitment," she said. "That's your problem in a nutshell. I see it everywhere I go. Full of creative new ideas, but you don't stick with anything. You start out enthusiastic enough, but then you get distracted or simply bored and move on. My motto is *whatsoever thy hand findeth to do, do it with thy might*. That's in the book of *Ecclesiastes*, gentlemen. Holy Scripture, you understand. And as I read it, it means don't do anything half-assed. Unless Mr. Bartok here, whose celebrated relative's concertos and string quartets I'm extremely partial to by the way, is talking about stripping down to the altogether and giving his unmentionables a good airing, I'm not sure what the point of sunbathing in my back garden would be. There's Alamo Square not three blocks away for that other kind of sunbathing, understood?"

"I'm sure Mr. Bartok could be convinced to expose whatever parts of himself you'd prefer, Mrs. Bertelsen," Cooper said.

"Well," Jared said, breaking his silence, "not necessarily."

"It has nothing to do with my preferences," the landlady insisted. "What I've posed is a philosophical question, I believe. One none of you seems sufficiently engaged with. So I'm afraid. . ."

But by the time Jared had explained the medical necessity for keeping his lower leg covered below the knee and his preference for shielding his face as well, the spirit of compromise was in the air.

"Nothing else," Mrs. Bertelsen decreed, "should be hidden from the life giving rays of the sun. Thus saith the book of *Ecclesiastes*. Words to that effect, at least. Otherwise no dice to the so-called sunbathing. Makes about as much sense as taking a shower in your pajamas, if you ask me. Though come to think of it, one of my sisters was curiously partial to all manner of incomprehensible hygiene practices."

"And you are the landlady," Cooper nodded.

"None other," she nodded.

"I think the two of you understand each other perfectly," Nick suggested, though Jared had no idea why.

"You're right, Nick," Cooper said. "And I've got a blank lease agreement form right here in my briefcase."

The weather for the first several weeks after Jared moved in made the question academic. The garden held more promise as a training ground for arctic explorers than anything else. Jared would have forgotten the whole thing except Nick kept ribbing him about his landlady, the voyeur. But finally he got home from work one Friday afternoon half dead of heat prostration because the air conditioning on the Number 24 bus was broken and realized what a favor Cooper had done him in the course of those bizarre negotiations. He unfolded the chaise lounge he'd bought at Cost Plus, draped a towel over his calves and another over his face, and contemplated the weekend. It didn't seem to promise very much, and he soon dozed.

"I tell you it's him, Skip."

"You're kidding, Skip."

"No, I'm not."

"How can you be sure? His face is covered."

"I'd know that foreskin anywhere. Look."

"You know, Skip, now that you mention it, I believe you're right. And for that matter, those nipples are a dead giveaway."

"*Chacun a son gout*, as they say in the Greater Milwaukee Metropolitan Area. At least, they used to."

"And *ex post facto* to you, Skip."

"Besides, when have I ever been wrong about a foreskin? Does anybody we know ever remember a time?"

"If someone did, it would be time to alert the Guinness people. As far as that goes, when have I been wrong about nipples? Ever? I'm the Marlon Perkins of the male nipple."

"Too true."

"But just to make certain, I believe I'll step inside and get my field glasses. The ones I use for my ornithological expeditions."

"Good idea, Skip. Under magnification, we'll quickly be able to verify our findings."

"You can never see things too clearly, that's for sure."

"Things, no. Ideas, yes."

"Don't go metaphysical on me, please. But you're right as long as you're talking about observing wildlife in its native habitat."

"And when you're talking about foreskins."

Hearing this conversation, Jared thought he must be dreaming, and, concerned that he might be giving his junk an airing in excess of Mrs. Bertelsen's intentions, forced himself awake. But the voices went right on.

"On the other hand, in the time it would take you to focus those damn things, the specimen might bolt into the underbrush."

"That wouldn't do."

"There's a quicker way to find out for certain."

"Exactly. Shall I go for the hose, or would you rather do the honors?"

Jared had met Skip and Skip at the baths. Cooper and Nick deplored the baths in the most strident terms possible, and Jared's other friends, Tristan and Big Steve, who were a couple and ostentatiously monogamous, shook their heads in unison when the subject came up. But Jared's shyness and his still only partially eradicated stammering made the baths his first choice when cold showers couldn't suffice. He didn't think he'd ever master the art of barroom seduction and thus considered attempting it a waste of time and effort. That night the two Skips were operating as a team. One of them grabbed Jared's towel and ran and then the other one grabbed it from the first one and ran in the opposite direction and before Jared knew it they were all inexplicably in a cubicle together. The twosome's forte was competing to see which of them could be the most inventive and depraved bottom, and they'd apparently scoped Jared out as a combination top and arbiter. He wasn't really that into threeways. At least he didn't think he was. He'd never actually participated in one. But Skip and Skip were so damned insistent. They made his acquiescence well worth his while. He emerged from the experience happily satiated and more committed than ever to that establishment. Over a couple of months there were half a dozen or so rematches, all impromptu, but never so much as an exchange of names.

Now he knew who they were. They were Skip and Skip. As well as their first names, they shared the top floor apartment at his very own address, but they weren't boyfriends. They were defiantly single. They told everyone who would listen, and even people who obviously didn't want to know anything about them, that they were not a couple. That was the best news Jared had heard in quite a while. They were, they proclaimed, sisters. Skip number one was tall—almost

Jared's height—and had sandy hair that flopped around and looked boyishly cute without any apparent effort on his part. Skip number two was shorter and built like a gymnast. He had wavy chestnut hair and riveting green eyes. He was the brains of the operation. Their friends called Skip number one Skipper because his last name was Roberts. Skip number two's last name was Erikson, so they called him Skippy. They also had nicknames. Skip number one was "Miss Chatterbox". Skip number two was "Mr. Wizard". He was the experimenter. He was the first of their gang to get one of his nipples pierced, the first one to get a tattoo, the first one to shave his genitals, the first one to experiment with new drugs as they emerged onto the market and the first one to attempt the previously unknown sexual practices being introduced almost weekly into local currency. His discoveries along these lines were much discussed among their crew, sometimes as calls to action and sometimes as cautionary tales.

Before Jared knew it, he'd been adopted.

But not adopted in the manner he would have preferred, though he wouldn't have dreamed of complaining about it even if his stammering had been more thoroughly under control. The two Skips and their gang annexed him as a kind of sexual mascot, a go to guy when all else failed or went limp too quickly, or they were bored, or the weather was too bad for them to consider going out. He was just downstairs. What could be more convenient than that? A knock at his door and whatever disappointments or frustrations the night had left them with were banished. He was always sober, so no visitor ever found him incapacitated and went away unsatisfied. He was good for a quick blow job or an all-night session either vanilla or mildly rough, for a single buddy or a whole crew. Skippy and Skipper soon began hosting parties at which he was the main dish. Those gatherings made their reputation as hosts and his as a sexual athlete. Jared found this a little disturbing but he also found it very, very hot being the center of attention in a roomful of great looking guys all with one thing on their minds. He liked being recognized as the guy with the best body and the biggest equipment in the room. He hadn't felt good about himself in a long time and now he did, at least until everyone went home. He knew, or supposed he knew, that they found his prematurely silver hair objectionable and that when he wasn't around they talked about his scarred up calf muscle and his limp. But life had brought him to the point where any attention was better than no attention. And his solitary existence until the last year had left him with the belief that sexual fulfillment was worth whatever you had to endure to achieve it. It was all well and good for guys like Nick and Cooper, who had charisma and physical perfection and ready tongues going for them, to be more choosey. To think in terms of dates rather than tricks. The current situation, Jared sensed, was as good as it got for a guy like him. And Skippy and Skipper and their friends were so hot and so sexually uninhibited that lots of guys, he knew in his bones, would have been willing to trade places with him.

So he tried not to be too hurt when they didn't invite him out dancing, or when he got left off the guest list for someone's birthday party, or didn't get a call about brunch. He told himself being overlooked didn't matter, and he knew he wouldn't really enjoy those gatherings anyway. He just had to get over letting the feeling of being left out bother him. He hung on and held on and had lots and lots of sex and more than a few laughs even though he knew there wasn't one of Skippy and Skipper's gang who truly considered him a friend.

But always in the back of his mind he knew it wouldn't do. Not as a permanent arrangement. He wasn't that stupid. Or that desperate yet. And he never stopped dreaming about that—a permanent arrangement. That's what he really wanted someday. He could be up to the hilt of his cock in some pretty guy's ass, with someone else licking his armpit and somebody else chewing one of his nipples and still another guy deep kissing him and find himself thinking about that, a steady boyfriend who would stay around more or less forever.

"You know those guys are just using you," Big Steve said.

They were in the showers having just finished an early morning workout.

"Thank God somebody's interested enough in me to do that," Jared said. "At least."

"You don't mean that," Tristan said.

"You have no idea," Jared said.

"Ah, here he goes, tuning up for his aria," Tristan said.

"Let him sing it, T.," Big Steve said.

"I know you hate that crew because Christopher Melendez-Greene is their alpha dog. I've heard all the history, and I don't blame you. But they're nice to me."

"If you can call that nice," Tristan said.

"Believe me, I get what you're trying to say. I know I'm just a big piece of meat to them. But those guys, Big Steve. They're the best looking guys in the city. Present company excluded."

"If you like that type," Big Steve said.

"Who doesn't like that type?" Jared asked.

"All right, all right," Tristan said, "we can debate aesthetic theory until the end of time. Those guys may not be Big Steve's type. Or mine, for that matter. But they're lookers, there's no arguing that. They're very mainstream, Brooks Brothers, *Gentlemen's Quarterly* guys, very preppy-but-with-an-edge and just-moved-out-of-the-frathouse and all that stuff. Plenty of people look down their noses at vanilla ice cream, it's true. But Nick would not kick a single one of them out of bed, and Cooper wouldn't, either. That speaks for itself, I believe, so let's just move on."

"Thanks for understanding that, T.," Jared said. "It means a lot that you guys don't ridicule my taste."

"A true friend's taste is always above reproach," Big Steve said, "even when it changes."

"Oscar Wilde, right?"

"Betsy Ross, more like," Tristan said.

"Anyway, they're not just great looking. Those guys live in the nicest apartments and drive the coolest cars. They get into the best clubs without even trying. They wear the newest fashions before they even *are fashions*, right? They go to the opera. Gallery openings. Places like that. And they will do anything I ask them to—sexually, you understand? Absolutely anything. Sometimes I scare myself making them do the things I do. Just to see if they will, you know? Or what it feels like. But they never, ever say no to me. Not about anything sexual. Usually they fight over who gets to try it first. They worship me that way, Big Steve. You know what that feels like."

"Yes," Big Steve admitted.

"I know, I know," Jared said. "I'm not stupid. They may not be that crazy about being seen with me in public, but behind closed doors they tell me I'm a god. And they treat me like one. You want me to turn up my nose at that? You want me to set up checklists and compose a list of interview questions they have to answer before I'll let them suck my dick or worship my nipples?"

"I want you to do whatever makes you happy," Big Steve said.

"Yeah?" Jared said. "What's my second choice?"

"Do whatever doesn't get you hurt," Tristan said.

"Me? Hurt?" Jared grinned, making his pecs bounce.

"And never forget," Big Steve said, "what you're looking for is out there looking for you."

"God," Jared said, "if only."

One night about six months after Jared moved into Mrs. Bertelsen's basement, Skippy showed up on his doorstep alone.

"Good," he said, "you're home."

"Come on in," Jared said.

Skippy went to the refrigerator and pulled out a Heineken. Jared didn't drink but kept the refrigerator fully stocked for just such an eventuality. He knew it was Skippy's brand.

"Where's Skipper?" he asked.

"Sent him out dancing with some buddies," Skippy said.

Jared hardly dared to hope.

"I decided I didn't feel like sharing you. For once."

His wavy chestnut hair was so perfect and shiny and he smelled so good that Jared convinced himself God existed. It was real sex, not gymnastics. It went on for as long as Jared could make it last. The best thing about it was spooning Skippy afterwards. Backed up against Jared's chest he was the perfect size and shape. Jared dared to hope it was a sign.

"You want to be careful," Nick said. "It's like trying to domesticate a feral cat with a guy like that."

"What our friend means to say," Cooper panted, racking the bar, "is 'we wish you the best of luck'."

It was a dream Jared never wanted to wake up from. At least it was like that some of the time, though not nearly as much of the time as he would have hoped. Every week or so Skippy would make some excuse to Skipper or send him off on some adventure of his own and steal downstairs. These occasions were, Skippy said, "their little secret". Jared wanted to shout it from the rooftops, but he understood that his silence about these trysts was the price he had to pay for them. It was like taxes. You hated paying them, but you appreciated the protection you received from the United States Air Force and you liked the architecture of the Washington Monument, so you signed the check. The one thing Jared insisted on was that Skippy was no longer to be called that. He was just plain Skip. Skippy was peanut butter, or a terrier puppy, or a freckle-faced boy in your third grade class. Skip was the man he loved, for better or worse. Somehow the whole gang agreed to go along with that, at least when Jared's was around. And Jared was present exactly as before. Except for Skip's secret solo visits to his bed, it was business as usual. And business was booming. Any kind of attention is better than no attention at all. And nobody in the whole history of gay ever had too much sex.

"Christopher, you've got to go," Skip said. "He'll be here any minute."

"I'm not leaving until you promise me you're going to break it off with that big ape."

This was what Jared got for showing up early and then hanging out on the landing until it was time to knock on Skip's door. He had heard things out there before that he didn't particularly approve of, but this was like eavesdropping on Satan.

"Did you hear me, Skip? We've all been very patient with you, but it's gone on way too long."

"I can't break up with him."

There was a loud sound like a single clap.

"Ow. What the fuck did you do that for, Christopher?"

"Slap some sense into you," Christopher said. "And I'll do it again if you won't listen to reason. I'll do it all night long if that's what it takes."

"If you left a mark on my face I'll kill you. Or Jared will. He'll see it and he'll ask how I got it. He'll break your neck."

"Listen to me, you idiot. If you want a steady boyfriend, we'll get you a steady boyfriend. There are all kinds of great guys around right now."

"Yeah, right. Last year you set me up with Michael Sullivan."

"You and Michael would have been perfect together."

"He has the tiniest dick this side of Munchkin Land. And he's an even bigger bottom than I am. I have never been so bored with sex in my life. The minute you start thinking of a bed as someplace to sleep, you might as well just die."

"Time for you to figure out how to be a top," Christopher suggested.

"Like you have?"

"This isn't about me."

"Yeah, well, tops are born, not made. Ask your uncle about his pet gorilla if you don't believe me."

"O.K.," Christopher said. "We'll find you a top if that's what you think you have to have."

"I don't want you interfering. I want you to leave us alone. I'm in love with Jared."

"No, you're not. You're in love with the fact that he's in love with you. That's all it is. I know you, Skip."

"No, you don't," Skip said. "You don't know anything about me."

But Jared heard, to his horror, the slightest note of uncertainty in Skip's voice.

"You're not in love with him," Christopher said, "because it's impossible. Our set has an image to uphold. That depends on maintaining certain standards. You know that. You helped me formulate them in the first place. You're my second in command. You know the rules have to be enforced. Guys like us have love affairs, sure. But not with guys like him."

"I don't know what you're talking about," Skip said.

But Jared knew he did. Jared did himself.

"He's an oaf," Christopher said.

"No, he's not."

"He's an oaf and a troll. He may have muscles for years. He may have one of the biggest cocks in captivity. He may even know what to do with it. That's what everybody tells me. But he's too stupid to color his hair and he can't tell you what time it is without stuttering. You are not in love with him. Your friends won't stand for it. And you know what happens when someone lets down the team."

By then Jared had heard enough. He headed back down the stairs as quickly and as silently as was possible for a man of his size. When he got to his apartment, he practiced his breathing exercises until he could trust himself to pick up the phone.

"Hello."

"Skip, it's Jared. I'm sorry, but I'm going to have to give tonight a pass. I think I've got some stomach thing coming on."

Which was the truth as far as it went. Jared couldn't remember feeling that sick in a long time. He put down the phone. Then, after thinking about it for a minute, he unplugged it.

It was like waking up in that field hospital in excruciating pain not knowing for certain where he was and unable to speak. It was as if every minute of his life since that day had been a waste of time. He was right back there on that cot in post-op, weak and sick and in agony, unable to move, not sure he wanted to live. He called in sick at work for two days and spent them huddled in his apartment. When Skip knocked at his door, he ignored it. When the phone rang, he didn't answer it. He didn't eat. He stared at the walls and prayed that it would stop hurting. But it didn't.

He seriously considered packing a few clothes, emptying his bank account, and just going away. But he knew that what he wanted to escape couldn't be left behind that way. Wherever he went, he'd still be that guy that Christopher Melendez-Greene wouldn't let Skip be in love with. He'd never stop wanting what he wanted, and he'd never be allowed to have it.

On the third night Tristan showed up at his door. His hair was so resolutely greased into place that the rain hadn't disarranged it even slightly. If it had been anyone else, Jared would have tried to tough it out. Big Steve obviously understood that before issuing the assignment.

"You've been missed," Tristan said, "at the gym."

The next thing Jared knew he was in Tristan's arms, sobbing.

"It's O.K. if you don't want to talk about it," Tristan said. "Sometimes a good cry is the best thing."

Tristan spent three nights on Jared's sofa before clearing him to fly solo.

"Who do you think that blond was?" Skipper asked.

Jared could hear them in the garden, right outside his window.

"No idea," Skip said.

"Built like a brick wall," Skipper said. "And that Eagle Scout face. Wish we'd gotten to see that action. Bet it was hot as blazes."

"Sometimes you talk too much."

"Too bad about the guy's 1950's haircut," Skipper said. "Still, looks like the big boy is open for business again."

That night, when Skipper and a couple of his buddies showed up at the front door, Jared told them he had to get ready for a date. He didn't like the lie, because it meant he had to change clothes and actually go out, but he had no choice. He knew they'd insist on verification. He went to some nameless bar on Polk Street and spoke to no one. He stood around wishing he could disappear until it was finally late enough that he could go home without raising anyone's suspicions.

He sneaked in and out of his apartment like a burglar. His real friends learned how to knock on his door to get him to answer it. The telephone was still too threatening. Most of the time he left it unplugged. Eventually the two Skips figured out to leave him alone.

A couple of weeks later he met Skip for lunch at the Palace of Fine Arts. Jared brought the sandwiches and Skip brought the wine. They didn't talk about a conversation Jared might accidentally have overheard, though Jared was pretty sure Skip must have figured that part out. When Jared said he was sorry but he didn't believe things were working out between them, Skip cried a little. But he didn't argue. He seemed, Jared thought, kind of relieved.

"So that's the whole miserable story," Jared said, spotting Nick on his bench presses. Nick and Big Steve were the only men he knew of who bench pressed heavier poundages than he did. It was both humbling and inspirational to witness. It was incentive.

"Welcome to the club," Nick panted, finishing the set. "You were the only one in the gang who hadn't been burned by that bastard. Except Cooper."

"Please," Jared said. "Don't call Skip that. At least not in front of me. He may be weak, but he's not a bastard."

"He's not talking about Skip," Cooper smiled, "and by the way, your stammer keeps getting better. People have noticed. People are talking."

"Thanks," Jared said, "I guess."

"I'm referring to that arch fiend, Skip's frathouse paddle brother. Or whatever that gang has decided he is. The guy pulling all the strings."

"What?"

"Christopher Melendez-Greene," Cooper said.

"Now he's managed to screw every last one of us. Or at least try. Cooper's the only one who's been able to escape."

"He hasn't screwed Matt."

"He got close," Nick said. "He nearly fucked up Ashby's medical school. And anyway, Matt's never around."

"Well the only reason I got off clean was because I'm as heartless as he is," Cooper said, "and that's nothing to be proud of."

"It's like a baptism of fire," Nick said. "Once you've survived that, you can survive anything."

"It doesn't feel like it," Jared said.

"Of course not," Nick said. "Give it time."

"There's one odd place setting," Cooper said, helping Tristan in the dining room. "Who else is coming? Ashby minus Matt?"

"Nick's made a new friend," Tristan said.

"Lucky Nick."

"Big Steve doesn't think it's going to go that way," Tristan shook his head.

"Why not?" Jared asked. Between the two of them, Nick and Cooper always got first crack at the new guys. Sooner or later he hoped it would be his turn. It had never turned out that way so far.

"The usual. What else?"

"Maybe Nick should learn to be more flexible," Cooper suggested.

"Maybe you should, Cooper," Tristan said, giving Jared heavy eye contact. "But he's a very nice guy. We've both met him. He's got the Stefano Fabiani seal of approval. He'll be a good addition to the tribe."

"What's his name?" Jared asked.

"Scott," Tristan said.

GRIFFIN MACDONALD: 1977

At first Griffin thought someone had dumped an old rug on his doorstep. Despite his landlady's vigilance, passersby often used the entry to his basement apartment for inappropriate purposes. Then, as he unlatched the gate, the heap moved. It gave out a gruff sounding woof—not loud, not vicious, merely forthright. The animal, he decided, was announcing its presence, nothing more. It certainly meant him no harm. Griffin studied the face staring back at him intently before deciding *yes, a Newfoundland*. One of the English professors back at St. Gregory's, Dr. Boswell, had owned a Newfoundland named Beowulf, acquired from the aunt of a certain boy whose name Griffin could scarcely bring himself to whisper. She bred them. Which meant that Beowulf started out life with a name taken from Italian opera. That had been just the start of Aunt Olympia's eccentricities, but Griffin remembered her dogs as goofily benign. Amiable beyond belief, really. This one had that same expression. It had apparently been out in the rain all day.

It was late. Griffin was tired. Holiday hours at the record shop were long. But really, he had no alternative.

Drying the huge, hairy beast used up all his clean towels and one of the blankets off his bed. In addition, the process cleared up the question of the animal's gender. Griffin hated referring to any animal as "it", even if only in his head. It offended his farmboy sensibilities, which dictated that being reduced to employing neuter pronouns when speaking of livestock constituted an admission of incompetence. Ordinarily he wouldn't have considered making use of Millicent Peabody's washer and dryer in the garage, though she'd often assured him he was welcome to, but this could justifiably be deemed an emergency. There wasn't a laundromat within a mile, and he didn't have time to get there and wash and dry this load before it closed. And anyway, his landlady was gone until January. Somewhere in Europe, apparently. She had been remarkably unforthcoming as to the details of her itinerary. Usually she wouldn't shut up about such things. Griffin wondered what that meant. In any case, she'd never know he'd used her laundry equipment unless he told her about it. He tossed the load into the washer and started it running. The dog watched every move, its expression seeming to indicate that it understood the process perfectly and approved.

Griffin hated to shut the animal in the garage, even briefly, but didn't dare leave him in his apartment.

"Don't worry, boy," he said, securing the side door. "I won't be gone long."

It was only two blocks to the nearest pay phone. He called the number he'd found inscribed on the dog's collar. The person he spoke to answered in French. Griffin explained the situation as best he could. The dog's owners were not available, he was told. He left a message. At least he attempted to. Getting it across exhausted his schoolboy knowledge of the language. It was a lot to explain, giving the address of his apartment and the telephone number at the record shop. He did the best he could.

By the time Griffin got home, he knew he couldn't leave the dog in the garage overnight. It was far too cold. But before he dared let the animal into his apartment, he judged that he'd better take him for a walk. By then it was fairly dry outside. If he was careful, he wouldn't have to use the towels on the dog again before bringing him inside. He rummaged in Millicent's gardening things until he found a length of rope he could use as a leash. Seeing it and apparently understanding what it meant, the dog started to whimper with what Griffin hoped was excitement.

It was late enough that the neighborhood was almost deserted. The park was only a few blocks away. Once they got there, the dog didn't waste any time. It was a good thing because Griffin was freezing and dead on his feet.

Back home, he filled one of his mixing bowls with water from the kitchen tap and set it on the floor. The dog looked at him expectantly.

"It's O.K., boy," he said.

The dog drank greedily, almost emptying the bowl. Griffin refilled it.

"Bet you're hungry, too," Griffin said. He got out his other mixing bowl, filled it halfway with Cheerios, and hoped for the best.

The dog wolfed the cereal down. Wolfed in the manner of his undomesticated cousins.

"Sorry, boy," Griffin said, thinking of the morning, "that's all for now."

The dog's goofy grin said that right that minute Griffin was his best friend in the whole world.

Walking the dog, feeding the dog, leaving a bowl of water in the garage with the dog, and reassuring the dog as best he could exhausted Griffin and nearly made him late for work. On Christmas Eve, yet. The shop was packed. He was nearly run off his feet. He made lots of people happy and he made Kip Truman lots of money.

All day long his ears strained for the sound of the telephone. But when it rang it was never that call. All day long he scanned the faces of people walking in the door of the shop. But every last one of them, it turned out, was a bona fide classical music lover. Nobody was missing a huge black dog.

Just at closing, Kip came in and handed him his Christmas envelope.

His holiday affluence was short lived. By the time the guys had disappeared around the corner with his wallet, he was almost sorry it hadn't been a gay bashing. He'd been planning on a stop at the supermarket on the way home. In his head he'd already spent that money.

The dog had drunk all the water he left that morning. He'd been a perfect gentleman in the garage. Griffin fed him the last of the Cheerios. He followed Griffin around the house while Griffin ransacked the place for loose change.

He hated to go back out after walking the dog, but the stores would be closed the next day. He'd been mentally making his shopping list for weeks. A small-sized canned ham. The rest of the fixings for Grannie's cornbread stuffing. The cornbread was already made and "resting". Grannie always insisted on making her stuffing with four day old cornbread. She said it was the secret of perfect stuffing. Some sweet potatoes and some molasses for candying them. A few oranges and a package of shredded coconut for Grandpa's traditional ambrosia. It was Griffin's very first Christmas on his own. His very first here in San Francisco. These simple dishes had been intended to take the sting out of his solitary exile. But of course now all that was out of the question. The change tinkled as he funneled it into his pocket.

When he got to the supermarket, there was, as he'd suspected would be the case, just enough money for a small bag of dog food. He didn't think twice about it. His farmboy upbringing made that purchase imperative even if there was nothing left for him. Animals first.

He trudged home through the frigid streets. He mentally catalogued his remaining provisions. There were a couple of eggs in the refrigerator. He could have them for breakfast along with some of the cornbread. There was enough sliced bread—just barely—for some peanut butter sandwiches for tonight's now belated dinner and tomorrow's lunch. The holiday feast itself would have to consist of a box of macaroni and cheese and a small can of tuna.

That was all he had in the house except for half a box of Rice Krispies, which he might have to use to supplement the dog food. Somehow he would find a way to be grateful for every mouthful either he or the dog consumed.

Griffin rationed out the dog food. It had to last until the shop opened the morning after Christmas and he could borrow from Kip against his next paycheck.

Griffin hadn't been to church since coming to San Francisco, but as the holiday drew closer he sensed a hunger for those old tunes. The story he could tell himself, but the tunes needed more than his harsh sounding baritone to do them justice. Still, he hardly trusted himself to go inside.

The dog's presence suggested a compromise. He'd need a last walk before bedtime anyway. Why not a long one? With an extended rest stop outside the church three blocks away. Griffin could listen to the Christmas Eve service from outside. He could stare up at the glowing stained glass of the windows.

Griffin was half frozen by the time they turned the corner. As they drew in sight of the house, the dog started to tug at the leash. It was as if he already knew the way home.

Or maybe not, Griffin realized, seeing the large car stopped in the middle of the street, its headlights glowing.

"Are those your people, boy?" he asked.

The dog's whimper was unequivocal. He nearly jerked Griffin's shoulder out of joint in his excitement at the impending reunion.

There were two of them, dressed in tuxedos, sleek, black haired creatures, so handsome they seemed like models on a location shoot. They looked alike, but their ages differed too much, Griffin judged, for them to be brothers yet not enough for them to be father and son.

"Sorry," he panted, approaching them and dropping the leash so that the dog could greet them as it chose. "Sorry we weren't here. Hope you haven't been waiting too long. He needed a walk."

He was almost relieved that they ignored him in their excitement at seeing the dog.

"Thanks so much," the younger man finally said after they'd all greeted each other. "We'd have come sooner but we just got your message a little while ago. Mixup at the house."

"It's all right," Griffin said.

"He really likes you," the older man said in heavily accented English. "Dogs always know whom they can trust."

"Well," the younger man said, "we should really be on our way."

"Sure," Griffin said, "Merry Christmas."

"Christopher," the older man said.

"What?"

"You know."

Then, suddenly, they were speaking French.

"*Give him something,*" the older man said, "*for his trouble.*"

"*He's your dog, Rene. You give him something.*"

"*You know I have no money with me.*"

"*Neither do I.*"

"*Of course you do. I asked you if you had any money before we left the house. You said you had plenty.*"

"*I don't have anything smaller than a twenty.*"

"*So? Give him a twenty. It's a very expensive animal and he has obviously taken excellent care. . .*"

"*No,*" Griffin said, desperate to end their dispute before he could be humiliated any further, "*no. It's not necessary. Please, think nothing of it. Merry Christmas.*"

"You speak French," the young man said, looking faintly surprised.

"Not well," Griffin said. "Not well at all."

"Well enough, it would seem," the older man said, glowering at the younger one.

In the back seat of the Mercedes, the dog yelped.

"Merry Christmas," Griffin said, turning toward the house.

"Thanks again," the young man said.

Griffin listened as the car doors closed and the engine started. He looked back just for a moment. The dog was staring at him out of the rear window, wagging his tail and grinning that silly grin.

It didn't matter, Griffin told himself, entering the chilly apartment. It didn't matter. He had done what was required of him by the spirits of his farming ancestors. He had done right by the animal.

The apartment seemed strangely empty without that huge beast following him around. He stared for a moment at the bag of dog food on the kitchen counter, recalling the animal's blissful expression as it watched Griffin filling the bowl.

NICK ROMANOVSKY: 1978

I

Nick's building was a small, skinny one high on Nob Hill. There was only one passenger elevator—the freight elevator was too spartan to be used for anything else except in times of direst need—and the residents ended up knowing a great deal about each other by a kind of osmosis. They enjoyed or suffered from, depending on their individual perspectives, the kind of intimacy that riding up and down in that small, enclosed space with their pets and groceries and assorted paraphernalia inevitably enforced. Presumably at some point in the building's history at least one resident had found all this intolerable enough to use the emergency stair wells as a primary route of ingress and egress, because given long enough anything can occur, and San Francisco, as everyone recognized, was not only a city of eccentrics but a city where necessity brought forth all sorts of offspring. But during Nick's tenure in the building, no one had exhibited that particular aberration. In any case, the residents all knew each other's preferences in takeout, what dry cleaning establishments were utilized by which neighbors, the behavioral traits and emotional tendencies of the resident dogs from Chihuahua to St. Bernard, the yearly cycles of everyone's vacation travels, who shopped most frequently in Union Square and who by mail order, and myriad other mundane details of everyday existence to an extent that a private investigator would have taken pride in uncovering—and all more or less without conscious effort. Without curiosity, even. It was all simply there, available to be either observed or ignored during those slow but nevertheless brief journeys up or down, morning or night, fair weather or foul, workday or holiday. It was the urban equivalent, Nick supposed, of gossiping across the back yard fence or whatever it was that small town folk did to pass the time and mind each other's business.

It was impossible, in other words, to avoid knowing all sorts of things one would probably rather not have known, and equally impossible to move into or out of the building without being identified by one and all as a defector or a newbie. So when the newlyweds, Janie and Joey Archibald, moved in two floors below Nick, he'd have known about it more or less immediately even if Joey hadn't been Joey.

But Joey was Joey: an American archetype. Cornfed, boyish, aw shucks. What is an archetype after all but an accumulation of clichés? He'd been an Eagle Scout and second string quarterback and junior class vice president and had gotten straight B's, more or less, in college—a small, private, nominally but not devoutly religious institution with a picturesque campus located in a quaint Midwestern town set in the middle of farm country—and now had a good, if entry level, job in finance on California Street. This could be discerned with no more than a glance at him his first morning as a resident, spiffed up in his sober, nicely fitting but not anywhere near *au courant* suit and striped tie, toting his briefcase like it contained the Ark of the Covenant, on his way to work. Nick was already on the elevator when Joey got on. By a bizarre accident of timing they had it to themselves all the way to the lobby. When it arrived there and the doors crawled open, they said "have a nice day" in unison, and Joey grinned in embarrassment. He wasn't Nick's type. Though extremely cute after the manner of the all-American boy, he was a little awkward for Nick to be truly moved, and he lacked sufficient meat on his bones. Then there was the dress sense, which just barely passed muster even for a straight. None of that mattered, really, since Nick had a policy of not cruising on the property and Joey was more than attractive enough to ride on the elevator with, even such a glacially slow one. But despite his lukewarm appraisal that morning, Nick was neither so stringent with himself nor too much of a gym snob not to register the young man's fundamental adorableness. That was something he always approved of. He judged, watching Joey set off down the hill, that he must have married his high school sweetheart. He seemed exactly the type to have done that.

The most significant thing about being provided daily with so much information about one's neighbors, Nick often mused, was that one not only knew; one was known. The building was abuzz for a couple of weeks about that cute new couple on the eighth floor, which was certainly natural, but Nick thought it would be much more interesting if one could have been party to what Janie and Joey thought, or believed they thought, of their new neighbors.

He was reminded of this the next time he and Joey ended up alone on the elevator.

"You're Nick, aren't you?"

"That's right," Nick said. "And you're Joey."

Joey blushed a little, as if he found his name embarrassing. Nick wondered if he aspired to being known as just Joe, more adult and businesslike, or perhaps even Joseph. Whoever he dreamed of being, that morning he smelled of the new cologne television ads were currently promising possessed the potency to make young breeder men irresistible to women. It was a juvenile scent with no subtlety whatever, though Nick realized that such a description was redundant. He hadn't yet encountered it in any of the gay clubs, which he thought spoke for itself. He wondered if Joey thought wearing the scent truly instilled the promised confidence, or if it was only a coincidence that he was able to look Nick in the eye—just for an instant. Nick was generally an agnostic about coincidences, even when they involved breeders

"Nick," Joey said, and in his tone Nick sensed a prepared speech, "you look like the sort of man who knows his way around a gym."

"I do all right," Nick said.

"Thing is, I've been thinking about maybe trying to build myself up. Perhaps you'd be willing to give me some pointers."

"Sure."

"I hear there's a fitness room in the basement."

"There is," Nick said.

He never used it. Even if he'd been inclined to, the equipment was insufficient to his needs. But it would probably do for Joey. At least to start. And it had the advantage of privacy. To Nick's knowledge, nobody ever went down there.

"So maybe. . ."

By this time Joey was rapidly losing momentum and the elevator had nearly reached the lobby, so Nick took charge.

"I'll meet you down there tomorrow evening. Six p.m."

"Thanks, Nick," Joey stammered as the elevator doors opened. "Thanks a million."

"Slip that shirt off if you don't mind," Nick said. "Have a look at what we're working with."

Joey complied. It apparently required some effort on his part to appear casual about it, which Nick found endearing. It was the kind of physical shyness some guys never seemed to grow out of. Nick assumed it bespoke some locker room embarrassment of the distant past, but what did he know about the traumas of straight guys? Joey was sinewy and defined, apparently due to natural causes more than conscious effort. His shoulders were broader than the statistical average for his height, which was a good sign. He'd never be really big, but with concentration and diligence he might end up constructed like, say, Christopher Melendez-Greene, and that was nothing to sneeze at. Though Nick suspected that if Joey ever actually attained that sort of physique, young Janie would complain that her husband had become "grotesque".

His skin was even younger looking and more satiny that Nick had expected. His body was almost hairless. There was just that evocative little trail leading southward from the navel. The overall effect was so boyish it was hard for Nick to think of it as a man's body. Presumably, Janie would know more about that than he did.

Nick knew how the whole thing worked. His apprentices always started out enthusiastic enough, but when they realized how much hard work was actually involved they generally crapped out in a week or two. He was surprised one afternoon as he waited for Joey to show up in the fitness room to realize that they were at six weeks and counting.

"Sorry I'm late," Joey panted. "The bus was crazy this afternoon."

"It happens," Nick said.

"Listen," Joey said with that elaborately calibrated casualness of his, "your hair always looks so great. Where do you go to get it cut? Last guy really butchered me. Not going back there if I can help it."

Nick was reluctant to give out that information. Joey would run into some homosexuals of a particularly relentless type there. If he was going to live in San Francisco long term he'd have to get accustomed to such encounters, but Nick didn't want him spooked just yet.

"I don't think my hairdresser is taking any new clients right now," he said, "but I know of a little place in North Beach that does really nice work. I'll bring you their card next time."

"Thanks," Joey said, slipping off his t-shirt.

He was making progress more quickly than Nick would have predicted. The shoulders and chest were showing noticeable improvement, and his abdominals were emerging even more quickly.

"Hey, Nick," Joey said, stepping into the elevator. "Thanks for that tip about the barber. They're good guys there."

"Glad it worked out for you," Nick said.

"Janie really likes the way my hair turned out."

Nick looked more closely. Joey's hair was of a texture and growth pattern that wouldn't have presented a serious challenge to any halfway competent hairdresser. Nick couldn't discern any particular difference in its appearance since the last time he'd bothered to look. But obviously that wasn't what Joey wanted to be told. And Nick knew that for a certain kind of young guy, straight or gay, confidence was far more important than objective reality.

"I knew they'd take good care of you down there," he said.

"Finally threw out that cologne Janie bought me," Joey said a few days later as he came into the fitness room. "Everybody and his brother are wearing it lately. Smell it everywhere you go. Never really liked it on me. Too jazzy. Have to find something really classy. That's what seems to go in this town."

"Why don't you tell everyone about your new houseboy, Nick?" Cooper suggested.

Sunday brunch was at the Bailey-Bartoks' place that week, because now that Jared wasn't single any more he liked showing off. And anybody with a husband like Scott would have to be excused for succumbing to the impulse. Now that Jared was a hot guy with an incandescent husband, his stammer was all but nonexistent.

"Houseboy?" Nick asked. "What are you talking about? I don't have a houseboy."

"Last time I was at your apartment," Cooper explained, "there was a cutie in the kitchen changing your vacuum cleaner bag."

"Changing your vacuum cleaner bag?" Ashby asked. "Is that some new sex act I haven't heard about? I'd really like to surprise my husband next time he happens to show up in the Western Hemisphere."

"It is," Tristan said. "It involves a Hoover upright—your unit is an upright, isn't it, Nick?"

"Nick's unit is always upright," Jared said.

"I swear to God I don't know anything about a houseboy," Nick said.

"Then who did Cooper see in your kitchen?" Scott asked.

"Joey is my downstairs neighbor," Nick said. "He mentioned that he needed a new bag for his vacuum cleaner and I told him if he was going out for some, he should buy me a package as well. So he did. He's that kind of neighbor. That's the way people are in the Midwest."

"I'll buy that explanation," Big Steve said, "if anybody in the room can convincingly explain the difference between a downstairs neighbor and a fuck buddy."

"In Nick's case," Jared said, "the difference would be nonexistent. Or at the very least negligible."

"So what's he like?" Ashby asked.

"He's a nice young man who moved into the building three or four months ago with his wife," Nick said.

"Wife?" Cooper asked. "You didn't believe him when he fed you that line, did you?"

"I've met her," Nick said. "The whole building knows Janie and Joey, the cute married couple on the eighth floor."

"He may have a wife," Cooper said. "If you say he does, it might be true. But he's no more heterosexual than I am."

"You think everybody is gay, Cooper," Scott said.

"Not everybody," Cooper said. "Just every cute boy-next-door type I find hanging out in Nick's kitchen. With no shirt on, incidentally. I may have neglected to mention that detail before, though in a case like this it's crucial. Anyway, I believe statistics will bear me out."

"But what's he like?" Ashby asked.

"He's a newlywed who works in a big building on California Street," Nick said.

"He's an Eagle Scout playing hooky," Cooper said.

"You're so lucky, Nick," Joey said, cutting lengths of shelf paper for the weekend project he'd come up with: helping Nick spruce up his kitchen. "You have such terrific friends."

This had been a recurring theme ever since Janie and Joey held their belated housewarming party and insisted that Nick bring guests. He'd tried to get away with inviting Ashby only, figuring he was the least objectionable gay man he knew and perhaps even the least objectionable gay man on the planet, in addition to being a doctor. But somehow word of the event spread, which apparently made Ashby a little less of a paragon than Nick had believed, and the whole gang showed up. Two days earlier, Joey's comment had been, "that Cooper guy is really handsome, isn't he? And what pectoral development." The day before that, he said, "Tristan and Big Steve seemed really cool for police officers." He had met Jared a couple of weeks earlier, and the remark then was, "Gosh, I had no idea anybody was as big as you are, Nick."

"You're right," Nick said. "They're great guys."

"I had friends like that in college," Joey said. "We were really close, you know? Guys you could depend on for anything. But these days we're scattered all over the place. Back home in Minneapolis, the East Coast, I'm out here in California. And most of us are married now. That changes everything."

"I suppose it would," Nick said, remembering the trajectories of all his college and law school buddies.

"But you," Joey said, "you've got all those fantastic guys right here near you. It's so great."

"They liked you, too," Nick said. "And Janie."

Joey continued renovating himself. He needed new shirts and jackets to replace the ones he was outgrowing. Nick was surprised that he didn't want Janie helping him pick things out, but Joey was insistent on having Nick's assistance. So they went shopping. Or rather, Nick shopped, and Joey watched.

They were observed in the process, and this occasioned a new round of brunch table analysis.

"The Captain and I thought it was cute," Ashby said. "Like a guy helping out his kid brother."

"He is kind of like a kid brother," Nick said. "Only one you actually like."

"Which hardly ever happens," Cooper said. "Tolerate, yes. But you big brothers never really like the younger ones."

"I think I hear a story about to steam into range," Ashby said.

"Not tonight," Cooper said. "I have a headache."

"Nick, what is it that you like so much about Joey?" Jared asked.

"Yes," Cooper said. "Tell us, please. Is it the way his tight little rosebud opens up ever so slowly to your rampaging tongue?"

"Or the way he whimpers when you make him shoot?" Scott suggested. "Word is, you're a sucker for that."

"I don't understand why people find it so difficult to believe that a gay guy and a straight guy can have a platonic relationship," Nick complained.

"No, Niko," Cooper said. "We understand that. We've all had those relationships ourselves. What you don't understand is why people find it so difficult to believe that Joey's a straight guy. That's the only misunderstanding in this case."

"Besides," Tristan said, "you're not Plato. You're Zeus."

"And that makes him Ganymede," Ashby grinned. He loved playing off people's references.

"The opera was fantastic, Nick," Joey said, the Monday afterward at the gym.

"I'm glad you enjoyed it."

"Janie had the time of her life. I couldn't believe those seats. You sure I can't pay you for the tickets?"

"After you painted my living room? Absolutely not. I probably owe you my tickets to *La Traviata* as well."

"You're a great friend, big guy."

"Tell Janie it was my pleasure," Nick said. "Now, if you're warmed up, let's see some bench presses."

"Kind of need to ask you a question first," Joey said, looking, Nick thought, a little pensive.

"What's that?"

"I almost don't know where to start," Joey said.

"It's O.K." Nick said. "Take your time."

He hoped to God it wasn't marriage counseling. He really had no clue about that.

"I've been wondering lately," Joey said, "how you knew you were gay."

"I never thought it could be like this," Joey said. "Sex always seemed overrated to me. I couldn't see why it was such a big deal."

Nick melted. It had been a long time coming, like the iceberg that sank the *Titanic* finally succumbing to tropical waters.

"Can I take a shower before I go back downstairs?" Joey asked.

"Good idea," Nick said.

Nick couldn't help himself. He got into the shower with Joey. And nature took its course once again, as it inevitably will. Afterward, he toweled Joey off like he was a little kid.

"You're so good to me," Joey said, beginning to sob.

Nick held him until he settled down.

Nick wasn't used to having sex with the same guy repeatedly. Since that dire interlude with Christopher Melendez-Greene, his pattern had been that of a lion on the hunt. Once prey had been thoroughly devoured, he moved on. This didn't change noticeably. Joey and Janie were still very much newlyweds and Joey's visits were thus sporadic, leaving Nick free to come and go as he was accustomed to. But every few days Joey would find a way to work Nick into his schedule and into his surprisingly accommodating orifices, and the increasing familiarity of their two bodies together disoriented Nick.

He had been extremely careful at first, and not solely because Joey was a novice. It was not only bodily discomfort Nick felt bound to protect him from. But Joey was as avid a pupil as Nick had ever encountered, and he had deflowered a stunning number of virgins in his time. Much more quickly than Nick would have imagined he was operating at his accustomed level of intensity and sturdy young Joey didn't even hint that he might be playing too rough.

"I know it's not going to last," Nick said, contemplating an additional set of bench presses as a possible sedative.

"It's good that you understand that," Big Steve said, "because they never marry the guy who brings them out."

"I'm not sure that's even what I'm doing."

"What else would you call it?" Tristan asked, panting as he lay on the weight bench.

"I just can't be the one to end it," Nick said, ignoring the question. "I'm afraid it would destroy him."

"You know better than that," Tristan said. "Those young guys are as resilient as chimpanzees."

"I'm not sure in this case," Nick said.

"At any rate," Big Steve said, "his married name will not be Romanovsky. You can bet money on that."

Before Nick left the gym he made them promise not to tell the others. He didn't want to listen to smart remarks about Ganymede suddenly turning into Galatea, and he couldn't stand it when he was wrong and Cooper was right. Cooper of all people.

II

It was kind of a relief, Nick thought, each time Joey left his bed to go back downstairs to Janie. Perhaps Nick had been looking for the wrong kind of relationship all this time. Perhaps he'd always wanted to be the other woman. He knew men who made those sorts of arrangements. Their boyfriends came to see them when they could work it into their schedules. The rest of the time, there were the bars, the baths, the gyms, the parks. Nick had never seen the point of it. But the weeks since Joey had first come into his bed made him consider the subject from a different perspective.

"We can't afford to go to but one of the weddings."

From the kitchen, Nick listened to Joey explaining his domestic maneuvering to Jared. He could imagine them there in the living room, the warrior hanging on the words of the twinkie. Scott worked as a freelance literary translator and was in Germany meeting with authors for a couple weeks, and Jared, as always at such times, wandered in and out of Nick's place like a stray cat who had found a hole in a window screen. Joey seemed to think of him as some bizarre combination of uncle and sexual mentor. Nick suspected Joey of going to Jared with technical questions he was too embarrassed to ask Nick. Their relationship had entered that phase when Joey seemed to want pointers from someone other than the man he was sleeping with. Nick supposed that was inevitable. And he was glad Joey had settled on Jared. Jared knew everything there was to know about such matters and wouldn't steer him wrong.

"But there are three weddings on the calendar," Joey continued. "Three of Janie's closest friends. All in one summer. Like they planned it that way. I mean, I know women run those things, but can they actually do that?"

"I believe so," Jared said.

"So I told Janie that she should go without me. That way she could make all of them. The second two are only a week apart, so it's just a matter of staying at her parents' house. My mother-in-law loves having Janie to herself. Janie gets to be a bridesmaid three times and I don't have to go into debt over it."

"The wisdom of Solomon," Nick said, handing around the beers.

"What did Janie say?" Jared asked, avid as an opera queen during the intermission of an unfamiliar work.

"Nothing so far." Joey said. "She's mulling it over. Nick, does that expression have anything to do with the mulled cider they make at Christmas time?"

"I don't know," Nick said, "but it wouldn't surprise me."

"Yes," Joey nodded. "That's exactly what I thought."

"But how do you think it will turn out?" Jared asked.

"Generally if I don't push things too hard," Joey said, "Janie comes around."

It was the first time they had actually spent the night together as opposed to fucking energetically, showering together, and kissing goodbye at Nick's front door so Joey could sneak back downstairs. Joey kept saying how nice he thought it was, but it made Nick a little nervous. It was just for a weekend, of course, but later in the month Janie would be gone for a whole week—"and two weekends", as Joey kept putting it. It wasn't that Nick didn't like it. He liked it too much. That was the problem.

Spending a whole weekend with Joey meant bringing him along to Sunday brunch, which that week was at Matt and Ashby's. Joey hadn't met Matt before. Matt's schedule with the airline meant he was as elusive as Hamlet's Ghost or the Maltese Falcon. Joey seemed fascinated at the sight of the stalwart airline pilot and the sylphlike young medical resident in their native habitat. When Nick looked into Joey's eyes, he saw wheels turning.

"He acts like he's your boyfriend," Cooper observed as they walked to their vehicles after bunch the next Sunday.

"No he doesn't," Nick insisted.

"I don't mean all lovey-dovey," Cooper said. "It's more how natural he is around you."

"Please," Nick said, "whatever you do, don't share that observation with him. He doesn't need the encouragement."

"Perhaps you do."

"What? Are you trying to turn me into a homewrecker?"

"It's way too late for that," Cooper laughed. "You've wrecked more homes in your time than the Tokyo earthquake."

III

"I don't want to hurt you," Joey said.

For a moment, Nick thought Joey was talking about something he'd like to try once they caught their breath. He'd been wondering how long it would take Joey to get around to proposing it.

"What?"

"But I know I'm going to."

"Joey, exactly what are you trying to say?" Nick asked, staring into the dimness above the bed.

"I can't go on doing this," Joey said, nuzzling Nick's chest. "I like it too much. It's not fair to Janie."

"Oh, God. Did she say something? Does she know something?"

"She doesn't know about us," Joey said. "We've been too careful. If she was suspicious at all, it would be of the secretaries at my office. She brought me lunch once and you should have seen the way she looked at those poor girls. If she'd had a pistol in her purse I don't know what she might have done. Your husband with a guy? That's not what women worry about when they wake up in the middle of the night. But sooner or later it's going to come out. I know it is. I've thought about it a lot. You can't be that careful every time. You're eventually going to slip up. Accidents happen. And those times when she was out of town. It was too good between us, Nick. Just too good. It was the best thing that's ever happened to me, you know?"

"Hey," Nick said. "Don't cry."

"I'm sorry," Joey sobbed, struggling to control himself. "It was just so beautiful. Really just the most beautiful experience. I know Janie noticed something different about me when she got back. She never mentioned it, but I know she did. I've got to stop this before she starts getting ideas. Really, it's the only thing to do."

"It's your call," Nick sad.

"I hate it though," Joey said. "I know it seems unfair, hurting you now to keep from hurting her later. But it's what I have to do. You're a man. You're tough. Hell, Nick you're strong enough for anything. I'm her husband. I have to do what's best for her. It's my responsibility."

"It's all right," Nick said. "You don't have to justify anything to me."

"That's why I love you so much, Nick," Joey said. "Because of what a man you are. You always do the right thing. I'm about to go out of my mind worrying about this, but you're steady as a rock."

"Do whatever you have to do," Nick said, "but please, don't worry about me."

"I'm going to miss you so much," Joey said.

"I'll be right upstairs like always," Nick said, "if you need me."

"But you won't be right upstairs, is the thing," Joey said. "I know I'm not strong enough to do what I have to do with you right upstairs. There's just no way. I've found us a new apartment. We'll be moving out at the end of the month."

"Perhaps that's best," Nick said.

"I know it is," Joey nodded. "It'll just make things a whole lot easier if I know you understand."

"Of course I do."

"We'll always be friends, won't we Nick?"

"You know we will," Nick said. He doubted it. Post-affair friendships made great theory but never seemed to work out. But he knew what Joey wanted to hear.

"Yes," Joey said. "We'll always be very special friends. You're the best friend I've ever had. Probably the best friend I'll ever have."

"Let me know if there's anything I can do to help you with the move."

"God, Nick, that's so like you," Joey said with a sad little sigh. "Like I said, you're such a man. I wish I could be like you."

In the end, the whole gang helped Joey and Janie move into their new place. They made a day of it and finished up with pizza and beer. Janie claimed to be "overwhelmed" by their kindness, but Nick thought he could see the slightest tinge of relief in her expression as she kissed him goodbye. He didn't know if it was because she had some actual suspicion or if it was merely the natural relief any young married woman experienced when her husband finally gave in to domesticity.

They weren't invited to the housewarming. None of them.

"You never tried to talk him out of it, did you?" Tristan asked, putting his used clothing into his gym bag.

"Don't bug him," Big Steve said.

"Some homewrecker you are," Cooper said. "Flags are flying at half-staff all up and down Castro Street."

"Please, guys," Nick said, bending to tie his shoes. "Can we just not talk about this?"

"Probably not," Matt said, "is my guess. Knowing this crowd."

"I'm proud of you," Big Steve said.

That's when Nick had to excuse himself. Ordinarily, they left the gym together.

IV

"We're all meeting up at Cooper's place," Ashby said. He always sounded like a teenager over the phone. "We can leave our cars there and walk down the hill to Castro Street."

"You honestly think anybody's going to show up?" Nick asked.

"It's the biggest thing that's ever happened to our community," Ashby said. "Of course people will show up."

"It didn't happen to our community," Nick said, just to be argumentative. "It happened to Harvey. And Mayor Moscone, of course."

After hanging up, he checked his watch. Unless he was going to miss them, he had to get a move on.

Matt was on a long haul to Tokyo, and Tristan and Big Steve had to report for duty. In the wake of the shootings of Milk and the mayor, the city was a powder keg and all police had been called to their stations. But Ashby was there, bundled up like a seventh grader on his way to deliver newspapers to Eskimos and looking outrageously sexy in his new glasses. Scott and Jared were there as well. Jared always had that silly grin on his face these days. It couldn't have happened to a nicer guy. Cooper had a lanky blond with him. His name was Porter, and Nick thought he remembered having sex with him once or twice. They trooped down the hill together. As they neared Castro Street, Nick saw that the crowds were indeed gathering. It was like every gay in the whole city was there.

"Don't look now," Ashby muttered. "It's history."

"Thanks for not saying it," Nick told him.

"Saying what?"

"I told you so."

The procession moved slowly up Market Street. Nick hadn't had much use for Harvey, but he really admired Mayor Moscone. And there was no question that the whole thing was a tragedy. Or that Dan White represented everything that was wrong with San Francisco politics. He heard snatches of conversation around him. There were plenty of frightened people in the crowd. They expected the police to sweep down on the procession and do their worst. There were even rumors that they were bringing tanks. That was obviously ridiculous. Where were the police supposed to get tanks? On such short notice, at least? Nick didn't think the police would do anything as long as the march was peaceful, and he sensed that the crowd was in no mood to cause trouble. If he was afraid for anyone, it was Tristan and Big Steve. To be gay and a police officer at a time like this—anything might happen to them.

"I hope you don't mind me always doing this," Ashby said.

"What's that?"

"Making believe you're my husband when he's not around," Ashby said holding onto Nick's arm. "I know you've noticed. But you're too nice to mention it."

"Why would I mention it?" Nick asked. "If I don't mind?"

"You're the exact size and shape is the thing," Ashby said. "Far too young, of course."

"Thanks for that," Nick laughed.

"Matt thinks I take advantage of your good nature."

"The Captain is sadly mistaken if he thinks any such thing. I don't have a single good intention in my body."

"I'm not supposed to call him the Captain anymore," Ashby said. "At least not when you guys are around."

"Why not?"

"He believes you all think it's silly."

"Is it the name you call him in your heart of hearts?"

"Of course."

"Then it's not possible for it to be silly."

"For the love of God, Nick. Why are you still single?"

"Ah, yes," Nick said. "The riddle of the Sphinx."

"Nick! Nick! Over here."

He turned. All along the march, he'd been running into people he knew but hadn't seen lately. The occasion, solemn as it was, had turned into a grand reunion of his tribe. The larger tribe, that was.

"The other way," Ashby muttered.

There, weaving through the crowd. Nick could hardly believe it at first.

"Nick," Joey said, hugging him hard. Like a grown man. "Good to see you."

"Joey," Nick shook his head, dazed. "How have you been? How's Janie?"

"I'm great," Joey said.

His hair was shorter than Nick remembered. Really, he looked like a Castro clone. And his shoulders—well maybe it was just the bomber jacket, but they seemed pretty impressive. He hadn't answered the question about Janie.

"That's good."

"God, you look fantastic," Joey said. "It's been way too long, you know?"

Nick shrugged.

"Hey," Joey said, "there's somebody I'd like you to meet. This is my lover, Christopher."

"Nick," Christopher grinned. "How've you been?"

"You two know each other?" Joey asked,

"Oh, yes," Nick said.

SEAN EASTMAN: 1978

I

Sean had never believed in love at first sight until the big lug walked into the gym one afternoon. He was one of the densest, most massive bodybuilders Sean had ever seen. And that face—right out of his daydreams, with those cheek-bones and that cleft chin. His plastered hair glinted luridly in the fluorescent lighting and his eyes were like twin black holes. He looked as likely to strangle you as fuck you. Gazing at him, Sean knew his life would never be the same. Bo spoke next to no English. Sean, who grew up in Montreal and just been down from Toronto for a couple of months himself, found himself acting as Bo's translator. It was strangely like being a mad scientist's laboratory assistant.

"Tell him he has to pretend to strangle me just before I come," the man said. "I mean, I really have to feel like I can't breathe. I have to think I'm about to die. Only I'm not really, of course."

Sean relayed this information to Bo, who nodded. That was all Bo ever did, either nod or shake his head no. There was no affect at all to his communications. They consisted of pure information and not very much of that. Every time Sean thought about this it just made him love Bo even more.

"Tell him I want his chest freshly shaven," the man said. "No stubble. And a little oil on it. Just enough to give it a sheen. Not Johnson & Johnson. That smell ruins it."

"Right," Sean said.

"Tell him to make sure he does that thing he did with our foreskins last time," the next man said.

"Tell him he has to spank me until I bleed," the man after that said.

Sean translated, even though he had no idea what the man really meant. Bo nodded.

In the beginning, Sean hadn't anticipated the nature of the negotiations he'd be mediating. He'd taken Bo at his word. "Personal trainer" didn't seem ambiguous at all. He didn't object on moral grounds. People could make whatever arrangements they wanted with regard to sex. And Bo had to make a living. It only bothered Sean because he wanted Bo all to himself. It got in the way of that.

"Tell him he has to tie me up," one man said.

"Tell him I want him to come all over my face," another man said.

"Tell him he has to shoot all over my chest and then rub it into my hair," the sixth guy that week said.

Then one day everything changed.

"Tell him I want you to watch us," the man said. "Better yet, tell him I want to watch him fuck you first. Tell him I want to lick his come out of your ass while he's fucking me. I'll make it worth your while. I'll pay double his usual rate."

That's how it started. That's how Sean finally got Bo's attention sexually. He had been about to give up, after doing everything short of throwing himself at the big lug. But all it took was a customer's request. Sean knew it was his big chance, so he really put everything he had into the scene. He was devastated when he realized that Bo scarcely registered it. But word got around. The customer told all his friends and they told their friends. It had been as big an event as Sean hoped, but for the wrong audience. Still, there was a positive outcome. Before he knew it, he was part of Bo's repertoire.

Sean told himself that it was better than nothing. Really, what did he have to lose? Sex with Bo was the best thing that had ever happened to him. And if people were willing to pay to watch it and consequently make it keep happening, it must just be the universe's way of bringing Bo and Sean together.

II

"The doctor says we are to put on a show," Bo said.

Bo's new friend and benefactor, the doctor, seemed to be calling the shots all of a sudden. It made Sean nervous. The doctor wasn't some grizzly, middle aged creep who did Bo favors and then faded into the woodwork. His name was Christopher Melendez-Greene. He was their own age, more or less, and so handsome it hurt to look at him. He lived in a house the size of a small hotel and drove a Rolls-Royce convertible. It was an older Rolls-Royce, but its age didn't seem to matter. For that matter, the house didn't really belong to him. But that didn't seem to matter, either. He'd attended university in Paris, which meant he could speak to Bo in French. And that certainly did matter. The doctor made Sean feel expendable.

"What kind of show?"

"I fuck you," Bo said. "Like we do for customers. The doctor invites an audience to watch us. They all pay. We make even more money."

By that point there wasn't anything Sean wouldn't have agreed to.

Dr. Melendez-Greene was onto something. They had to give a repeat performance and then another. Bo's bookings skyrocketed. Sean hadn't paid much attention to the fee structure, but the sums he was suddenly negotiating took his breath away. It was like he had learned at school. Even in Canada they were familiar with the law of supply and demand. Before Sean knew it, they were a regular act. Even his mere ten percent cut was suddenly lots of money. Certainly more than he made waiting tables and working part time for Harris Crawford, the private investigator.

Occasionally a client would ask for something Bo and Sean had never done before. That didn't usually bother Sean, but once or twice people suggested things that scared him a little. Bo had no patience with Sean's misgivings. The customer was always right. That was the nature of the business they were in. And to be fair about it, things always worked out O.K. Except for that one trip to the emergency room. It hadn't really hurt that much. And Sean recovered sooner than he expected.

Dr. Melendez-Greene hosted their performances at the mansion where his uncle and his uncle's lover lived. He demanded variety. They couldn't do the same thing over and over. Even Bo wasn't that hot. The audiences got bored easily. They needed something different each time. What they really wanted was to be astounded. Each new spectacle demanded an even more spectacular sequel. Sometimes this meant adding one or two additional performers. That required rehearsals. Sean didn't mind that. More sex with Bo was always a good thing, even if other penises and orifices were involved. But Sean couldn't help worrying a little about Bo deciding he liked one of the new guys better than he liked him. Lots of their "assistants" were really hot. Christopher seemed to have an unlimited supply of amazing guys at his disposal. To Sean's relief, nobody who spoke French ever showed up.

One day the bottom fell out.

"It's no good," Bo said, watching Sean make an omelet.

"What do you mean?"

"You're too small. What do you weigh? Eighty kilos?"

"Eighty-five," Sean said, quickly doing the math in his head and then cheating a little.

"Really? Are you sure? You don't look it."

For a second, Sean was afraid Bo would insist on putting him on a scale for verification.

"Even if what you say is true," Bo continued, "it's not enough. You look too small. It's not impressive enough when I fuck you. You are handsome, yes. No one could complain about your looks. Your equipment is larger than average, and they appreciate that. And you are unquestionably an athlete. You struggle like a man fighting for his life. And when you arrive, it's a geyser, not a dribble. They all see those things and approve. But you aren't really big and strong looking."

"I'm as big as Christopher," Sean said.

"Exactly," Bo nodded.

"Has anyone complained?"

"Of course not," Bo said. "How can they? They don't know what they haven't yet seen. They lack the imagination for it. Only I know. I must have someone bigger than you to fuck for them. Some worthier opponent. Someone whose struggles against me will present a more believable and thus thrilling challenge. Only then can my triumphs astonish as they should."

III

Twenty pounds, Bo insisted. Sean had been working his ass off at the gym, and he'd managed to gain exactly five in the last six months. He was hard as a rock and his proportions couldn't be beat. But he saw it in Bo's eyes every time they fucked, whether for a client or in front of a large audience or on the rare occasions when they did it just because Bo felt like it. Sean wasn't big enough. And at this rate he never would be. There was only one thing left to do.

"You realize that these are very potent drugs," Christopher said. In his lab coat, he looked like a refugee from nighttime television. But the examination room was real enough. And chilly. Sean shivered in the hospital gown the nurse had insisted he put on.

"Seriously," Christopher insisted. "They can actually be dangerous for people whose systems don't tolerate them well."

Sean shrugged.

"I know you don't think you care about that," Christopher continued. "Right now it's all about the results. You want to look at your body in the mirror and see it substantially bigger and harder than it already is. That's all guys like you care about when you come to see me. But down the road when the side effects kick in you might have second thoughts. And by then it could be too late. In many cases they're not reversible."

"If you're not interested in helping me out," Sean said, "I get it. I just thought because you and Bo got along so well, I'd ask you first."

"You're really determined, aren't you?"

Sean shrugged again.

"You're going to get the meds somewhere," Christopher said. "I understand that. But I'm a professional, not a pusher. I have to make sure you're an appropriate candidate."

"Just tell me whether I'm wasting my time here," Sean suggested.

"I'll let you be the judge of that," Christopher said, "after I've finished the examination. Now, I'm going to step out of the room for a moment. I need to check something with my nurse. Don't go anywhere."

On his way back into the room, Christopher locked the door behind him.

"Don't want to be disturbed, do we?"

"What?"

"Main thing to watch out for with these medications," Christopher said, "is loss of sexual function."

"Oh?"

"It's the first thing to go. Other problems show up over time. Some of them can be quite serious. But as long as your sexual functioning shows no signs of deterioration, the likelihood of anything else doing wrong is pretty low."

Sean assumed this was some kind of sick joke, but he didn't dare object. He had no idea where else to get the meds he needed or how he would afford them at market prices.

"So we need to determine your baseline in that area," Christopher said, slipping out of his lab coat and loosening his tie. "There are lab tests that can give us the information, but I prefer something a little more existential. This won't hurt a bit. I promise."

"Let me get this straight," Sean said. "I have to fuck you before you'll write me a script?"

"There's no better proof of optimum sexual function than a good hard cock," Christopher said, "shooting a nice big load."

"If you say so."

"And I'll need to monitor you frequently to make sure there's no change in your condition," Christopher smiled. "Say every two weeks. The up side, from your point of view, is that the drugs won't cost you anything."

"You're not joking."

"If you pass the exam," Christopher said.

COOPER LUXEMBERG: 1979

The first present Cooper Luxemberg ever bought Griffin MacDonald was an answering machine. Relatively few people he knew owned them, but Cooper swore the one he had was perfectly reliable and far more discreet than a service would be. This wasn't a very romantic selection, especially considering what else he could have purchased for what the contraption cost, but as anyone who knew Cooper at all well could have explained, romance wasn't the issue. Control was. Cooper was the master of the grand gesture if that's what the situation required. When he walked down the street from his gym, for instance, pumped and fresh from the shower, it was pure theatre. But histrionically wasn't how he proposed to live his life. He liked things calm. He preferred the rational to the intuitive. Some would have said he didn't have feelings at all. At least not in any conventional sense. That was certainly the impression he gave, and he enjoyed giving it. In his career he was presented daily with the unexpected. He sometimes felt he was a firefighter by another name. So to the extent he was capable of it, he ran his life by routines. His morning ritual was as unvarying as the Mourner's Kaddish. His dogs relieved themselves on cue. The receptionist at his office knew to the minute when he would arrive and had preparations for the event completed accordingly. Cooper liked being in charge. He took pride in inhabiting the here and now. He had little patience for speculation and none at all for make believe. You would have thought that made him the worst possible boyfriend for an artist, and if you thought that you wouldn't have been alone.

But Griffin's routine of graduate school and two part time jobs made his schedule unavoidably chaotic. For Griffin's sake, Cooper could just about stand the chaos if he could keep track of it. But leaving messages for Griffin at Harry Gordini's piano bar and at Kip Truman's classical record shop, reliable as that might be, subjected the two of them to a level of scrutiny Cooper couldn't abide. Leaving messages for Griffin at the university was impractical. And there were always those unanticipated situations when another point of contact might make all the difference to his peace of mind. So, though Griffin was only at his own apartment a few times during the week and leaving messages for him there was likely to be as approximate as all Cooper's other alternatives, an answering machine on duty there was the only solution that would serve.

Really, he thought as he hooked it up, he wouldn't dream of walking his dogs off leash. This was the same thing.

"Are you sure you've got everything you need?" Cooper asked. "You won't be back here until late Monday."

"I'm sure," Griffin said. "Let's go."

"Aren't you forgetting something?"

"What's that?" Griffin asked.

"You haven't checked your messages."

"What do I need to check my messages for?" Griffin asked. "You're right here."

Griffin had asked this question with averted eyes. Something was up. That couldn't be tolerated.

"The blinking light tells me you have four messages," Cooper said. "I know for a fact I only left you three. Don't you want to know who left the other one?"

"Probably a wrong number," Griffin muttered.

Cooper was now certain he was hiding something. It wasn't that Cooper was jealous. He knew better. Still, he had to know.

"It'll just take a minute," he said, walking over and hitting the button.

"*Griff, it's Cooper. . .*"

He hit the button.

"*Griff, it's Cooper. . .*"

He hit the button again.

"*Hi there, Griffin. Or should I say 'ugly little troll'? Yes, it's me again. Your guardian angel. Ha, ha. Just wanted to remind you that we all know Cooper's only on a short break from reality. He'll come to his senses soon. Don't you worry. Or come to think of it, maybe worry is exactly what you should do. There's no way he's going to stay with a little nothing like you. Surely you realize that. You're smart enough that you don't need me telling you how it works. If you have any sense at all, you'll cut yourself loose right now. It'll only hurt worse if you try to hang on to him. The two of you obviously don't belong together. . .*"

Cooper recognized the voice. He'd gotten rid of that damned Chanel, but she was just the tip of the iceberg. Except for the guys from his gym, the whole city seemed determined to obstruct and/or sabotage him. He hit the button on the machine and a deafening silence crashed into the small room. Griffin was looking at the floor hard enough to bore a hole through it.

"Griffin," Cooper said.

"What?"

"How long have you been getting calls like that?"

Griffin gulped. He wouldn't look at Cooper.

"Griffin, tell me about the phone calls."

"Ever since we started dating. I used to just hang up, but then you got me that damned machine."

"How often does he call?"

"At least once a day," Griffin said.

"Is it always that voice? Or are there others?"

"At first there were half a dozen. Lately there's just that one."

"Why didn't you tell me?"

Griffin shook his head.

"Never mind," Cooper said. "I guess I know."

He picked up the phone. He still knew the number by heart. After all this time. Damn his memory for phone numbers. Maybe he could get hypnosis for it. The answering machine on the other end picked up on the fourth ring, and he listened to the greeting. Then he left his own message.

"Hello, Christopher. You know who this is. I've just been listening to a message you left on a certain answering machine. I'm going to be checking that machine daily from now on, and if you or anyone else leaves any other messages of that nature, I'm going to come over and break your neck. Got that? I hope so. Have a nice day."

He hung up.

"Did you hear that?"

"Yes," Griffin said.

"I meant it," Cooper said. "And you've got to promise you'll try not to let stuff bother you so much. Some people live to fuck around with other people's business. The way to beat them is ignore them."

CHANEL ROCOCO: 1980

"What we learn from history," Ned Westerleigh said to the handsome, much younger man standing next to him, "is that no one learns from history."

It was so like Ned to wax epigrammatic, Chanel thought, skulking behind a potted palm tree. Trust him to philosophize when the situation called for action. Pontificate instead of seduce. He might be as rich as God's baby brother and speak with that accent straight out of *Masterpiece Theatre,* but he had no idea how it was done. If it was true that God was an Englishman, Ned was what most people would expect Him to look and sound like. Which made him, even at his age, one of San Francisco's most desirable men. Yet he was still single. Some people spent their whole lives failing to take advantage of the opportunities the universe granted them. It was inexcusable. With his background and experiences Ned should know better. Chanel did. She was still *persona non grata* all over the city, but a girl couldn't sit at home forever. Invisible was equivalent to nonexistent. Surely if she minded her p's and q's and maintained a sufficiently demure demeanor—she knew "demure demeanor" was too precious and alliterative, but she found alliteration a great *aide-memoire*—they probably wouldn't throw her out of the gallery. One day at a time. That was what they said in those dreary twelve-step meetings Mona Lott used to drag her to for moral support, but there was no question it was relevant in this instance.

Chanel had miscalculated badly. She got that now. Worse than that, she'd burned her bridges. Cooper Luxemberg was a lost cause. She had to accept it. Even once he tired of that russet haired mouse—really, that silly little Griffin was like some sad-faced extra in an animated feature from the Disney studios—Cooper still wouldn't give her the time of day. She knew him better than that. She just had to face it. Face the reality of her failure, learn whatever she could from it, and move on. Move quickly, too. She had to find some other prey. In the final analysis, a queen without a consort was insignificant. Nobody took a dowager empress seriously, even if she was still comfortably under the age of thirty. And in the right light, Chanel could still pretend to be without anyone challenging her. Ned Westerleigh was right about one thing, however. She had to give him that. Most people were too stupid to learn from their mistakes. Well, nobody would ever be able to say that about her. She knew exactly where she'd gone wrong with Cooper. She wouldn't make that mistake again.

The art on display baffled her, though Ned and his protege seemed to be fascinated. Most art baffled her, however, so that didn't mean this opening was a bust. Her own work was of a relentlessly representational style. Anything else seemed pointless, no matter how the "experts" raved. Still, Chanel knew that the art itself was for all practical purposes beside the point. The success or failure of an evening such as this had nothing to do with the work on display and everything to do with the guests pretending to pay attention to it. The artist's reputation depended on who had been in attendance tonight and what they decided they thought of him. If someone influential considered him cute enough, charming enough, or at least intriguing enough, his fortune was made. If not, it didn't matter whether he had talent or not. In New York it might be different, but she doubted it. As far as she was concerned, New York was just San Francisco with worse weather and a funny accent.

She wondered idly about the young man with Ned. She'd look smashing with a man like that on her arm, no doubt about it. Half preppy and half international terrorist, from the look of him. But really, she shouldn't waste time on anyone Ned would bring to a function like this, regardless of those shoulders and that mustache. Ned was like her kryptonite. She'd never get anywhere near Mr. Tall, Dark, and Cryptic with Ned in the room.

Still, she was glad she had come. It was risky, but you had to get back on the bicycle sooner or later. You had to prove to yourself you could still pull it off, if only in a small way. She had done what she set out to do. She faced them all. She faced them but kept her mouth shut. She let the whispers and pointed glances go unacknowledged. She held her head high. She carried herself with dignity and grace. That was important when you were trying to get back into their esteem. There would be plenty of time to scintillate later. Her scintillating days were far from over—no worries there. And the crowd was impressive. Not just large. This was the once instance in which size truly was insignificant. The wine and cheese guaranteed the turnout. But the audience was sufficiently prominent to merit her efforts. She knew they'd gossip about her later, but there was no such thing as bad publicity.

Not a bad job for a Tuesday night. Weekends were probably still off limits. But if the gallery opening had been any indication, not for long.

What Chanel had done was so insignificant, really, that the consequences made no sense. Who hadn't tossed a drink in the face of an annoying nonentity? In a crowded club? At least once? Why, if you possessed any standards at all, the act was more or less obligatory. But from all the hubbub it occasioned you'd have thought she'd shoved a toddler out of the line to sit in Santa's lap or deployed a nuclear weapon against a Sunday School picnic. She'd been banned more or less immediately from Harry Gordini's piano bar, the site of her "atrocity" and one of her favorite watering holes. And that was just the start of it. She expected it to blow over more or less immediately, but it didn't. It ramified. The shock waves rippled outward with no indication they'd stop short of total annihilation. Wasn't the punishment supposed to fit the crime? So what the hell were people thinking?

Here, *eons* later, she was still a pariah.

As she considered it, she decided that being a queen without a consort was at least arguably preferable to being a queen with the wrong consort, as long as the situation could be made to appear temporary. Look at poor Rhoda Harley and that dwarf of hers. He might have muscles for days and his shoulders might be a mile wide, but he couldn't be more than five foot three. His thingie must be the size of a thimble. Whether it was or measured normal size didn't signify—it was what the gossips said and that made it the truth. When those two appeared in public they looked like a circus act. Cooper hadn't been the wrong consort, just an unwilling one toward the end. And willingness, though indispensable, was the tip of the iceberg. Cooper had been ideal in every other respect. More than ideal, actually, and that made her quest to replace him a daunting one. There weren't a lot of guys like that running around loose. Or even happily married for that matter, and dreaming—even if unconsciously—of liberation. While she certainly considered herself up to the challenge, the timing for such an operation was wrong. She couldn't afford any more scandal until much farther into the decade. Meanwhile, if she showed up attached to someone obviously inferior to Cooper, it would signal the world that she had lost her touch. The gossips would have a field day spreading news of her decline. But perhaps there were more men who met the desired standard than she thought, if she just approached the matter systematically.

She decided to make a list of prospects. As a strategy, making a list seemed the polar opposite of the impulsiveness that had served her so poorly in her past. Doing something like that would indicate that she truly had changed. The more she considered it, making a list seemed so promising a beginning to her quest that she bought a brand new steno pad and ballpoint. She refused to employ them for any other purpose, and she kept them under lock and key because her housemates were as curious, not to mention morally reprehensible, as they had ever been.

And, perhaps in response to her weakened state, they seemed more prone to displays of insufficiently slavish obedience than she could recall. The look in Holly Montezuma's eyes alone was a warning that couldn't be ignored, and some of the others had actually taken to muttering in shadowy corners of the house they all shared in Haight Ashbury.

Chanel made her list.

There was the guy with the shoulders and the one with the sexy eyes. There was the one with the glossy, luxuriant hair of that unusual shade of darkest gold and the one with the teeth so perfect it was hard to accept that they could be real. There was the one with that dreamy French accent, the one who sounded like he'd just flown in from Rome, and the one who spoke like someone you'd meet at the Queen's garden party at Buckingham Palace. There was the one with the mustache that made him look like a pirate—not a real pirate of course, but one played by a Hollywood glamourpuss. There was the guy with the apartment on Nob Hill and the guy who drove the vintage Aston-Martin and the guy who had a yacht—a small one, but it floated—anchored off Tiburon. There was the guy who was notorious on the squash court and in bed and the one who managed a bank branch and jetted off to Vegas on weekends to play high stakes roulette. There was the one who had won a bronze medal in the Olympics and the one whose mother was a member of Congress. There was the guy who had a Ph.D. in ontological systems and the one who wore size fourteen shoes. There was the one who wrote poetry that had been published in the *New Yorker* and the one who had a pair of Dobermans that he walked in Alamo Square. Really, it was like sitting down with a pitcher of martinis and the Hammacher-Schlemmer catalogue.

She spent several weeks on her list. She reviewed it whenever she had a spare moment and sufficient privacy, striking off and/or adding names as the mood took her. Some days as she moved here and there about the city there seemed to be a bumper crop of qualified candidates. Some days there seemed to be an inexplicable dearth of talent, as if a Biblical plague had come through during the night and swept them all away. She'd meet a new young man somewhere—at a club, at the theatre, on the street, even—and she'd think to herself *that's the one, he's perfect, I'd better not waste any time*, but she held back. Three months. Three months she had decided to devote to compiling her list, pondering it, and making her selection, and though her resolve frequently wavered, it never collapsed. Collapsed resolve was the forte of her third string lady-in-waiting, Holly Montezuma, whose lack of backbone was legendary. Chanel didn't dare indulge in it. Three months would be ample time to give the matter due consideration. A true queen never allowed herself to be rushed. Too much was at stake. A true queen was wise, and her wisdom was the result of painstaking deliberation. Chanel felt her character growing stronger and finer and truer by the day. This, undoubtedly, would be her apotheosis. As she basked in this happy prospect, she found, often as not, the need to strike a few more names from her list and spread her nets even wider in the search.

Meanwhile, she envisioned something elaborate and grand as the culminating event that would crown her labors. Some dramatic tournament in which all the aspirants would compete for her favor, proving their mettle and their worthiness in picturesque and endearing displays which would eventually sweep her off her feet and make evident to all her subjects which man she should declare the winner. It would end in a sublime moment indeed, when she accepted him and received the acclaim of the entire city. She very nearly discussed this vision with Holly Montezuma but stopped herself in the nick of time. Which turned out to be a good thing. Holly would have broadcast the plan to the world, or at least to Chanel's second-in-command, the increasingly restive Marina del Rey, and Chanel would then be committed to it for better or worse. Her detractors would immediately begin their attempts at sabotage. Mona Lott and Rhoda Harley would stop at nothing. And they were only the tip of the iceberg. There were others. So many others. Meanwhile, the rest of the city would prepare itself to witness her failure. Still further consideration convinced her that it was exactly the kind of thing Cooper would disapprove of. And if she wanted her new consort to at least equal her old one—though eclipsing him was her fondest dream—that objection had to be factored into the equation.

The longer she pondered the question, the more she was forced to acknowledge that the situation had moved beyond theatrical flourishes. She had arrived at a point where she must position herself above gaudy attention seeking. She had already risen as high as was possible by such means. It was time to graduate, to play her scenes for class rather than flash. She didn't need to make a statement. She simply needed to make an entrance with her chosen escort by her side and leave the statements to her onlookers. She needed to make her quest seem effortless rather than arduous, which meant conducting it as much as possible in private in order ultimately to present her public with a *fait accompli*. Less would have to become more.

She needed to get it over with. She'd been overthinking it, like Holly Montezuma shopping for shoes or Marina del Rey flossing her teeth. She needed to shit *and* get off the pot. There was only one answer. There had only ever been one, really, because despite all those sublime young men she'd placed on her list, there was only one young man in the entire city of similar caliber to Cooper Luxemberg. Everybody knew that. Dithering just made her look like an idiot.

The telephone number was ridiculously easy to acquire. The prince in question, Christopher Melendez-Greene, agreed to meet her for lunch.

It went beautifully at first. She expressed herself succinctly but eloquently, describing in vivid detail the mutual benefits of the arrangement she was proposing. At first he seemed interested though a little confused. Then sometime over the entrée he figured out what she was getting at.

"You do realize you're a drag queen," Christopher said, "because you're not talking like you get that."

"What's your point?" Chanel snapped.

"No, what's your point?' he asked. "Honestly, nothing about you makes sense to me. I get drag as a kind of performance. On stage, I mean. For instance, in a cabaret act. In performance, anything goes. Mime. Kabuki. *Swan Lake.* Tag team wrestling. Sword swallowing. Pulling rabbits out of hats. It's all valid. But that's not what you're talking about, apparently. You seem to believe that drag is just another variation of real life. And that's where I lose interest. Because there's nothing real about what you do. If a man wants to hang around with women, that would make him straight in my book. But you're not a real woman."

"Now see here. . ."

"Spare me the dramatics. Biologically, you're not a woman. That's all a straight man would care about. And I have no idea what a gay man would find intriguing about a caricature of the gender he has no reason to be interested in in the first place. Except maybe as a momentary diversion. Or some kind of crazy experiment. Guy who gets that itch will satisfy his curiosity and move on. Which, if I understand your proposition, is not what you have in mind. And a closet case—sorry, but you're not a good enough approximation of the real thing to make a convincing beard, so what's your value to him? You're worse than useless, really, because you only serve to call attention to what he's determined to keep anyone from finding out. Any way you look at it, you're pointless. From my perspective, you don't fit in anywhere. Except with your own kind. Forget this crazy idea about acquiring a consort. You'd be better off forming a coven."

"You arrogant prick."

"Absolutely," Christopher nodded. "I know I am. I've been called a lot worse than that. But I don't believe I'd toss that drink if I were you. Once is a scene. Twice is a reputation."

"I think I've had about enough of you."

"By the way," Christopher said, "before you stomp out of here, lay off my boys, too. I know you've had your eye on some of them. As fallbacks, if I didn't accept the role. Porter. Mikey. Aaron. Beck. The two Skips. They're off limits. Make that all my crew, really. Go hunting in some other forest."

PORTER WINSLOW: 1980

"You have no idea what you're talking about," Porter said. "You've been away for five years. The scene has changed radically. You'll see. I'll take you around and introduce you to all my friends."

"I'm holding you to that," Clancy said.

"Hold me any way you like," Porter laughed. "Gotta go."

"Who was that on the phone?"

"Old friend of mine," Porter said, hanging up and rolling onto his back. "We were roomies at St. Dunstan's. He's just finished his M.B.A. at Wharton and his old man is making him move back here to join the family firm."

"Tragic."

"Nothing's that tragic," Porter said, "when your old man is worth fifty million."

"I wouldn't know."

"Me neither," Porter said, tweaking a perky nipple.

"Ready for seconds, are we?"

"Dirty boy."

"You ain't seen nothin' yet."

"I certainly hope not," Porter said, climbing back on board.

"Whoa," Clancy said, walking up to Porter in the lobby bar at the Sir Francis Drake. "What happened to you? Enlist in the Marines? Hardly recognized you. Who even knows how to give a flattop these days? Other than military barbers?"

"I spend a lot of time at the gym," Porter said.

"I'll say," Clancy said. "Looks like to me you don't really need your own apartment. Since you've practically moved in there."

Porter pretended to ignore this last comment but he was secretly pleased by it. He wasn't pumping all that iron only to have people fail to notice the results.

"With a schedule like I have, I hate having to futz with my hair all the time."

"You always were the jock," Clancy said. "Got to admit, it's kind of a hot look on you."

"Thanks," Porter said. "What are you drinking?"

"Coors."

"Be right back."

Clancy had been the beauty of their graduating class at St. Dunstan's. But those days, apparently, represented his physical peak. Since then his features had coarsened, and the hair texture that had seemed bohemian back then just looked like a suicidal hairdresser's cry for help. He was still good looking, or would be for a straight boy, but he'd never again turn heads like he had in those days. Porter couldn't help feeling gratified by this. Better a hot man at twenty-seven, when there was a practical use for it, than a high school Adonis, where good looks were more or less wasted. Porter planned to be spectacular when he turned twenty-seven. He bought their drinks and made his way back to the table where Clancy was sitting.

"I see what you mean about the local talent," Clancy said.

"I told you."

"And this isn't a gay place," Clancy said.

That was the point. Porter wasn't about to let Clancy appear on the scene prematurely. He'd heard discouraging rumors, primarily from Clancy's sister, Olivia. He had lunch with Olivia regularly. When her calendar wasn't too crammed, they took in a movie. When they met, she pumped him for information, primarily with regard to the extracurricular activities of her boyfriends and the boyfriends of her friends. He got plenty of information from her as well, but he liked to think he was far more subtle. Regarding her brother, she had said enough to prompt Porter to make some observations of his own, and on neutral ground. His preliminary ones weren't encouraging. Eventually people would realize who Clancy was related to, and that would trump everything. But you only had one chance to make a first impression, and Porter wasn't inclined to leave that sort of thing to chance.

"Good looks don't discriminate," Porter said, hoping Clancy wouldn't ask the source of this quote.

"And there's no place like San Francisco. I get it. I really do. But I still hate the idea of working for Dad."

"He's not a bad boss," Porter said. He had joined the bank Clancy's father owned a year earlier, just out of Stanford.

"I'm sure that's true," Clancy said, "if he isn't your father."

"It'll work out."

"So what about this famous boyfriend of yours? Christian? Is that his name?"

"Christopher," Porter said, checking his watch. "He should be here by now."

"Uh oh."

"He's a doctor. Not the first one I've dated, as a matter of fact. They get held up all the time. Sometimes they don't show at all. It comes with the territory, but so do their nice cars and fancy wristwatches."

"I hope he's worth it."

"You have no idea."

"Jesus," Clancy said. "That is one gorgeous hunk of man."

"Glad you approve," Porter said, shifting the BMW into gear. They had just dropped Christopher at his place. Porter would go back there once he got rid of Clancy. "Have to say, looks aren't the half of it. He's the best sex ever."

"Better than me?" Clancy pouted.

"We were kids."

"One of us was, at least," Clancy said.

"What's that supposed to mean?"

"You were never a kid. You had hair on your balls when most of us didn't even know we had balls. You were the ass bandit of the whole school. Was there anybody you didn't nail?"

"Nobody cute enough to matter," Porter admitted.

"Who is he exactly?" Christopher asked, coming up for air.

"Clancy? He's just a simple boy whose great-grandpa started a bank once upon a time."

"Oh. That Styles," Christopher said, reaching for the glass of wine on the nightstand.

"Yes, that Styles," Porter said.

"I thought you said he was cute."

"He used to be," Porter said. "When we were at St. Dunstan's, boys followed him around with their tongues hanging out. Not to mention a few of the masters."

"It's sad when guys outgrow their looks," Christopher said.

"Yes."

"Not like you, Porter. You just get better and better. You should hear the things people are saying about you."

Porter actually had heard some of those things. It was nice to be appreciated, particularly when you knew you hadn't peaked yet.

"Flattery will get you everywhere."

"I'm not interested in where flattery might take me," Christopher said.

"No?"

"I'm interested in where it might take you."

"Huh?"

"Getting a little lonely in my you-know-where. Thought you might like to make a return visit."

"Already been in there twice tonight," Porter said. "What are we doing here? Trying to set a record?"

"I'm game."

"You really are spoiling me, you know."

"Come on, big boy. Doctor's orders."

It was an article of faith in Porter's crew that all the young men aspired to be like Christopher Melendez-Greene. It was not enough that he was so glamorous, so charismatic, so affluent; that he was their guru, their arbiter, their muse. They had as their collective imperative, really, to emulate him in all things. Porter wouldn't have dreamed of contradicting this notion aloud, and his friends would have been shocked to learn that he was an agnostic. But though he didn't dispute Christopher's pre-eminence in any regard, he found that he really wasn't interested in being like him. If you were looking for a role model, he thought, Cooper Luxemberg was really a much more satisfactory man to take look to.

Cooper was unambiguously masculine, for one thing. And that was something Porter valued highly. There was always something a little soft about Christopher. Something lightweight and insubstantial that Porter didn't object to in the least in an associate but at the same time could never have felt comfortable emulating. You could appreciate a Siamese cat, for instance, without wanting to become one. In addition, Cooper was self-made. He had a real fetish about achieving success in the world through his own efforts, having dumped Sonny Dallas like a bag of dirty laundry and gone on to make his fortune. Porter couldn't help but admire a guy his age who could have had everything given to him on a plate but nevertheless turned up his nose at it and put said bodily part to the grindstone instead. A man who did a thing like that was really a man. No one could dispute it, though more than one of Porter's acquaintances tried. Doing so only made a questionable comment about the person making the claim. It was true that Porter had accepted a position the minute Clancy's father had offered him one in his bank, but nobody could say he wasn't giving good value to his employer. There wasn't a harder working, more loyal man in the entire organization. Porter was determined to prove himself deserving of the opportunity. Exactly the way, he was certain, Cooper Luxemberg would have done in similar circumstances.

It wasn't that Porter was actually friends with Cooper. His relationship with Christopher and his position in their set made that impossible. For their gang, Cooper was a non-person. He became one by taking up with a crew of gym rats when he could have become Christopher's deputy. Still, Porter refused to go as far as the rest of the gang, who observed Christopher's standing order to ostracize and pretended to ignore Cooper whenever their paths happened to cross. For instance, Porter and Cooper greeted each other cordially enough but rather distantly when they met at the gym. Porter wasn't supposed to go to that gym because Christopher's crew didn't consider it chic enough, but he did anyway. The establishment might not be fashionable, but the biggest bodybuilders went there. He and Cooper only slept together a few times. That had been a while back and he wasn't sure Cooper even remembered it. Porter just had a sense of something solid about Cooper that he would like to believe he possessed himself. And so he worked silently to uncover and nurture it, fucking the living daylights out of Christopher all the while. Doing so in the fashion, he imagined, of Cooper Luxemberg himself.

Porter had become Christopher's official boyfriend almost by accident and certainly without any such aspiration. He'd been considering letting his membership in the gang lapse when the opportunity more or less forced itself on him. At the time, the only reason he hadn't already gone his own way was, from what he could discern, nothing more than a kind of social inertia. His continuing status as prince consort seemed to depend on the same degree of disinterestedness he had brought to the original negotiations. The minute he showed the least sign of possessiveness, he understood, would be the minute Christopher dropped him. Not that he had any inclination in that direction. When Christopher had first let it be known—only by way of rumor and innuendo, to be sure—that he was in the market for such a thing as a steady boyfriend, the competition was ferocious. Observing this frenzy from its remotest fringes, Porter suspected that Christopher's sole motivation was to foment just such a dire spectacle as ensued. Porter was aware of all the turbulence it generated. He couldn't have avoided it, because virtually all his friends were involved to some extent. He heard all the speculation. He was present when accusations were leveled, bets were made, and drinks were thrown. Sure, Christopher seemed like a catch, but what exactly was being caught?

Eventually Porter received his summons. They had long since slept together, so he knew that Christopher's reputation as a sexual athlete was well deserved. Really, he defined the term "power bottom". Porter had no curiosity on that score.

"What I like about you," Christopher said that night over an intimate dinner observed by literally dozens of their friends and/or their friends' trusted informants, "is that unlike everyone else we know, you really don't give a fuck about being my boyfriend."

"I don't," Porter admitted.

"As far as I'm concerned, that's the highest possible recommendation."

"I didn't know I needed one," Porter said.

"Then there are your shoulders, which give rise to extensive comment, and your equipment, which inspires awe and which you certainly know how to employ with skill and commitment. Your body is worthy of worship but you don't seem to consider yourself entitled to that sort of reverence."

"I thought we were living in an age which disapproves of objectification," Porter said. He had learned about objectification in a women's studies course he signed up for on a dare.

"The age may," Christopher said, "but in our small corner of the world only an idiot believes things like that don't matter."

"You sound like one of my college professors," Porter said. Which wasn't true, but he thought sounded sufficiently irrelevant.

"The thing is," Christopher said, "I have to have a steady boyfriend. The gang is in turmoil. All that petty jealously. All that jockeying for position. All that competing—*I'm Christopher's best friend. No, I am.* It's the only way to settle it. Declare myself coupled. Soon as I do they'll all fall back into line. One again peace will reign over our people."

"If you say so," Porter said. He thought it sounded too easy, but he wasn't sure why it should matter to him.

"What I really mean to say," Christopher said, "is you're hired."

"I didn't realize I had applied for the position."

"Don't you get it?" Christopher laughed. "That's the whole point."

Porter and Christopher weren't sexually exclusive. More often than not each of them was in the bed of someone else. "Christopher Melendez-Greene's boyfriend" was a title just like "homecoming king" or "state champion" or "assistant to the vice president", which was what Porter was at work. He knew it didn't entitle him to anything from Christopher or anyone else. Pretty much nothing changed. He worked his tail off for Cabot Styles. He had his flattop trimmed weekly by Mr. Chang, who was also Cooper Luxemberg's barber, and, as far as Porter was concerned, a closely guarded secret from everyone he knew. He went to the gym. He'd never have the bodybuilder's physique that Cooper had. He'd never be a gymnast like Christopher was. He was too tall and lanky to realize either of those images. Long ago he had settled on "hot lifeguard" as his avatar.

"Got to hand it to you, Porter," Clancy said, lounging in the passenger seat of Porter's BMW. He was wearing too much cologne and the wrong shirt. For the sake of their friendship, Porter really should say something. But more and more, he found himself observing the Castro Street corollary to the Prime Directive. In the long run, it wouldn't do to adjust Clancy's presentation when he'd just revert once he was allowed to fly solo. Let people see who he really was and draw their own conclusions. Besides, they were already late.

"Oh?"

"That Cooper Luxemberg's a wizard. Found me the perfect apartment. Got me a deal on it, too."

"Glad it worked out."

"Jesus, is he ever hot."

"You noticed, did you?"

"Pa was determined to set me up with some old guy looked like he helped God write an offer on the Garden of Eden."

"Sonny Dallas, I expect."

"Yeah, that was his name. What a creep. Could hardly keep his hands off me even when Pa was around. God knows what he'd have been like one on one. Glad you talked Pa out of it. God, Cooper Luxemberg. What a wet dream. Did you ever?"

"Don't get too excited," Porter said, ignoring the question.

"Why? Does he have a boyfriend?"

"As a matter of fact, yes."

"When did that ever stop either of us?" Clancy laughed.

"Well, even if he didn't have a boyfriend, he wouldn't so much as look at you that way until close of escrow."

"We'll see about that. By the way, Olivia has been asking about you. What do you want me to tell her?"

"I have a girlfriend in the Peace Corps."

"You're kidding."

"It's what I've told my family," Porter said. "I think it's best to be as consistent as possible when making explanations."

"That military haircut really has gone to your head," Clancy laughed.

"Very funny."

"It's going to be a really mixed crowd at this housewarming," Porter said, backing cautiously into the parking space. Cooper Luxemberg drove a vintage Jaguar, and from its pristine appearance it was clear he'd long since mastered the art of parallel parking. One more lesson Porter had learned from observing that icon: don't rush delicate procedures. In that regard, seduction and parking were two sides of the same coin. "Clancy's parents and sister will be there. At least for part of the evening. Then there will be the uncles, aunts, and cousins. Probably even his grandmother. And some people he and I both work with. I don't care on my account, but I don't think Clancy's parents know about him. I'm sure Olivia doesn't."

"What's wrong?" Christopher asked. "You don't think I can behave myself?"

"Just letting you know."

Porter's father was a firefighter and his mother taught kindergarten. As a scholarship boy at St. Dunstan's he had become a keen observer, first of the children of the rich and then of the rich themselves. One of the things he found so satisfactory about Cooper Luxemberg was that he gave every appearance of being rich but had the hunger for success Porter had never observed in a person who came from serious money. What he found intolerable about the children of the rich was their laziness, as if they expected to go through life having everything done for them. What he found so deplorable about the rich themselves was their lack of taste. If you had the kind of money that allowed you to surround yourself with fine things there was no excuse for surrounding yourself with trash.

Which was what he found himself pondering at the housewarming. The apartment itself—the apartment Cooper Luxemberg had found for Clancy—was fabulous. But everything in it was awful. Clancy's Aunt Carlene was in charge of "redecoration", bringing in furnishings, draperies, and rugs that looked like they had been looted from European slums. The fixtures and appliances were expensive but looked cheap. Most of Clancy's friends did too.

"It didn't look like this when we closed escrow."

"Oh, hi, Cooper," Porter said. "I'm sure it didn't. Clancy's family has never been known for their taste. Or perhaps it would be more accurate to say that they have always been known for a certain kind of taste."

"I always expect a lot from my wealthy clients," Cooper nodded, "and they nearly always disappoint me. You'd think by now I would have learned my lesson. By the way, keep up the good work on the upper body. Your legs were always great, but now the rest of you is catching up."

Porter really had to find out about that fragrance Cooper was wearing, but it wasn't something he could ask Cooper. It was the kind of thing he knew the guy he was trying to be was supposed to know.

Cooper had brought his recently acquired boyfriend with him. Porter knew the verdict the brunch table juries had handed down. It was still current gossip and Cooper was prominent enough that Porter heard about it everywhere he went. The guy was no match for Cooper and would disappear sooner or later. That was the consensus. But Porter quickly got the point of him. He was very cute, but you had to look at him several times to get that. More important, Porter recognized him as a son of the working classes. He was as real as a clod of dirt. There was a look in his eye that said he was well acquainted with hard work and was way tougher than he appeared.

They didn't stay long.

Porter spent the rest of the evening flirting with Clancy's mother, who was crazy enough to be entertaining. He could keep up a conversation with her without actually paying attention to what she was saying. He could observe everything going on around him without Mrs. Styles feeling neglected or anyone else in the room noting his interest. Thus, he saw Christopher flirting with Olivia right under the nose of her current boyfriend, Trip Miller. Christopher had her eating out of his hand, and that big galoot didn't even see what was going on. So Porter knew about Christopher's new scheme about the same time Christopher did himself. And spoiled, lazy, obnoxious Trip deserved whatever happened to his plans to marry a fortune even larger than the one his father had pissed away.

"It was very nice of Christopher to invite me to his party next weekend," Clancy said, watching Porter take money out of his wallet for the lunch check, "since you didn't bother to."

"I'm not the host."

"You're screwing the host," Clancy said, draining his wine glass, "which should count for something. But you didn't even mention it."

"Didn't you hear me? It wasn't my place."

"You've got him wrapped around your finger," Clancy said. "Anyone can see that."

"That just shows that you don't know a thing about him."

"Sure," Clancy said. "Keep on making excuses."

"It won't be like any party you've ever been to," Porter said.

"God, I hope not."

"That Olivia got all the looks in the family," Christopher said.

Being Christopher's official boyfriend meant, apparently, that Christopher was extra chatty between rounds when they were in bed. It meant having television banished from Porter's bedroom. Porter remembered that there was no television in Cooper Luxemberg's bedroom, either. He wondered if that had changed now that Cooper was attached. His guess was it hadn't.

"And all the intelligence and personality as well," Porter said, "It's a shame, really."

"What's so terrible about a girl being beautiful?"

"Oh, nothing," Porter said, staring at the ceiling. "It's more her other qualities. A girl in her position doesn't need to be smart. It'll probably only get her into difficulties."

"I don't understand," Christopher said. "I didn't find her intelligent at all."

"That's her genius," Porter said. "She never lets anyone see it. She's got her whole family snowed."

"Keep talking."

"Cabot Styles is a very old fashioned father. Clancy is pretty much expected to make his own way in the world. I mean, his folks paid for his education, which wasn't cheap. And Cabot bought him that apartment and gave him a job. But that's about the extent of what he can expect. Until he marries, at least. There'll be some money then. Especially when the babies start coming. But in Olivia's case, all she has to do is look pretty and go shopping. There's no question of her having a career. Cabot wouldn't think of his daughter making her own living. And he doesn't want her dependent on some man. She has a trust fund that pays her a hundred thousand a year. All because she's a girl."

It wasn't the huge bacchanal that Christopher's uncle and his lover usually hosted. The guest list was still extensive, but more exclusive than usual. Many of those in attendance were from out of town. They were an older crowd generally, and obviously affluent. A few familiar faces had managed to score invitations. Porter saw that cute Will Crawford, looking like a Cub Scout who had wandered off from his troop. Just like a young doctor, a young attorney could always be expected to pay off in the long run. That was the theory Porter heard expounded, but poor Will seemed too decent for this crowd.

The ballroom had been transformed into a kind of arena, with bleachers set up around a large rectangular space. There would be various "performances" during the course of the evening. The piece de resistance was to feature Sean Eastman, that handsome sidekick of Bo Armstrong, being tied down and then ferociously gang raped by the biggest, roughest batch of bodybuilders Christopher had been able to assemble, culminating with the formidable Mr. Armstrong himself. If Porter had been in the market for a husband, Sean would surely have been at the top of his list. He suspected Will Crawford of having a similar interest. But Will was more squeamish than Porter was. He couldn't help but find the action distressing. Porter hoped that he would leave before that scene came onto the stage.

"I can't believe it," Clancy enthused. "They were having real, honest to God sex while everyone watched. It wasn't pretend at all. That Christopher knows how to throw a party."

They were walking down the hill toward the next block, where Porter had parked. The sun was about to rise over the East Bay.

"That's how a live sex show works," Porter said.

"Live sex show," Clancy said. "I had no idea there was such a thing."

"You're kidding."

"Oh, I know all about those things in Mexico where you get to watch a woman with a donkey," Clancy said, "but this was completely different."

"Right," Porter said. "There were no women or donkeys."

"No, stupid," Clancy said. "This was classy. Very, very classy."

Porter wouldn't have used exactly that word to describe it but didn't bother to argue.

"And that one guy," Clancy said. "What I wouldn't give to run into him alone in a room at the Fairmount."

"Which guy?" Porter asked, though he knew perfectly well. Sean could have been selected especially to attract Clancy's notice. Porter would have suspected exactly that if he hadn't known that the arrangements had been made so far in advance, well before Christopher even knew Clancy existed.

"That bottom guy they were fucking so furiously. Hot as the dickens. What I wouldn't give. . ."

"Oh, hi, Christopher," Clancy said. "Come in."

"Just wanted to drop off this belated housewarming present."

"You weren't supposed to bring anything," Clancy said. "The invitation specifically said 'no gifts'."

"I've always had a problem keeping my 'no's' and 'yesses' straight," Christopher said.

"Get you something to drink?"

"Chardonnay, if you have it."

"It just so happens," Clancy said, "that I have a really excellent Chardonnay on hand."

"I thought you might," Christopher laughed.

Clancy emerged from the kitchen a moment later.

"Here you go, sir."

"Thanks."

"You know, if Pa insists on having me work for him, I don't see why he won't send me up to the vineyard. I do love living in the city, but, say, three days a week up in Napa and the rest of the time down here—doesn't that sound perfect?"

"Now that you mention it," Christopher nodded.

"Well," Clancy said, clinking his glass against Christopher's, "here's looking at you."

"Speaking of looking at people," Christopher said. "I understand that you're interested in Sean. From my party the other night."

"Sean? Is that his name?"

"Sean," Christopher nodded.

"What a guy," Clancy said, exhaling expressively. "Handsome devil. And that body. For my taste at least, he's as built as it's possible to be without looking grotesque."

"Funny," Christopher said. "I thought that was me."

"You? Oh, no, Christopher. With your proportions you could carry another twenty pounds just fine."

"I'll bear that in mind."

"But that Sean," Clancy said. "Absolutely perfect. And then, well, you don't expect a guy with that kind of build and that kind of equipment to be such a bottom, you know? Watching him take on all those big bruisers—it was so fucking hot. He was totally into it. You expected him to beg for mercy, but instead he yelled for more. I know what you're going to say."

"Oh? What am I going to say?"

"Something about stereotypes," Clancy said. "Why should I expect bottoms always to be skinny little guys? Why should I be surprised for a big muscle guy like Sean to love taking it up the ass?"

"Really," Christopher said. "I think those political types are starting to have way too much influence in the community. All that should matter is having lots of sex and a good time."

"Lots and lots of sex," Casey nodded.

"You know, I might be able to help you out with Sean," Christopher said.

"Really?"

"Yes," Christopher said. "I'm always happy to arrange for introductions between friends."

"God, Christopher. That would be terrific. I'd certainly owe you a favor in return."

"I'll see what I can do."

"Hey, what're you doing?"

"It's O.K.," Christopher said, starting to unbutton Clancy's shirt. "Porter and I have an understanding. And you're really very cute."

OLIVIA STYLES: 1981

"I know you don't think he's good enough for me, Daddy," Olivia said, spreading raspberry jam on one of Mrs. Washington's fresh biscuits. "You never think anybody's good enough for your little girl. But I'm in love with him. And Mummy thinks he's dreamy, so you're outvoted."

"Speaking of your mother. . ."

"She's sleeping in," Olivia giggled. "Casino night at the club really wore her out."

"Something I really hoped to speak to her about before leaving for the office this morning."

"Too bad," Olivia shrugged. "It'll just have to wait."

Cabot Styles was accustomed to being outmaneuvered by his wife and daughter. Generally he grumbled a little and then acquiesced, but this was an exceptional circumstance. Those other young men were just flings. When it came to romance, Olivia had a short attention span. Thank God for that. Her affairs petered out like dying fireworks on the Fourth of July. Each time she dumped one of those young men Cabot was pleased but never let on for fear she'd come down with second thoughts. But this wasn't an affair. This was an engagement. Somehow things had gone that far without him suspecting anything serious was in the offing. An engagement meant this was about his daughter's long term happiness and that of his wife's grandchildren to be. But Olivia's fiance simply wouldn't do. He wasn't any better than the others. He might be a doctor, but as far as Cabot was concerned he was way too handsome and way too slick. He'd gone to university in France, for Christ's sake. God only knew what kind of whorehouse a French university was. Cabot had seen the young man's type before. His nieces had married men like that and the result was disaster, misery, and expense for their long-suffering fathers. Cabot prided himself on being a good judge of character, and the young man set off various alarm bells. Still, he knew better than to make a frontal assault. That approach might work with a business rival or a competitor on the tennis court, but he had learned that where his womenfolk were concerned subtlety was required. Unless Olivia decided that breaking her engagement was her own idea, the wedding was on. He had no recourse but to pull strings from behind the scenes.

It was still six months until the date. That should be ample time.

"I can't get over how handsome he is, Selene," Margie Brooks said, digging into her crab stuffed avocado half as if she hadn't seen food in weeks. "He reminds me of that actor on *Until Daylight*. You know the one I mean?"

"The one who plays the dual role?" Bootsie Armatraud suggested. "That surgeon and his evil twin?"

"That's the one," Margie nodded. "Don't you think he's just the sexiest thing on two legs?"

"As opposed to sexy things on four legs?" Doreen Waterman hooted.

It was a predictable quip. Doreen fancied herself the consummate *equestrienne*. She had failed to make the Olympic dressage squad four times running, and if that didn't make a girl an expert, what did?

"The only ones I can be bothered with," Paulette Snell said, "are the three legged variety. If you get my drift."

Paulette was the gang's official bad girl. She had been ever since that affair with her tennis pro. The one the gang ended up passing around among themselves like a tray of *petits fours*.

Selene Pennebaker Styles smiled at her Cobb Salad. This conversation afforded her intense satisfaction. All her friends had daughters. None of the daughters had husbands or fiancés as attractive as her future son-in-law. And matters between Olivia and her intended were still at the stage where charm and physical perfection outweighed everything else. Later on there might be grumbling about his lack of family background or a trust fund or, heaven forbid, some bad habit or other, but right now none of that mattered. She really had to hand it to Olivia. Other girls fell in love with penniless artists who had bad skin and wore clothing that looked like it had been stolen from Tenderloin bums. Or they fell for boys with obvious criminal inclinations who looked at the floor and mumbled when concerned mothers tried to make conversation with them. But not Olivia.

A handsome young doctor who spoke fluent French—now there was a fiancé a doting mother could really take pride in. Selene knew Cabot was a little suspicious of Christopher, but it was Cabot's job to be suspicious of all his daughter's beaus. All Selene had to do, really, was allow herself to be charmed. And what a pleasure that was. The young man really did have the nicest manners. And listening to him order dinner in French was almost like being made love to.

"Let me see it, Livvie," Jeannine Forrester said. She had just returned from a year in Florence studying art history and being chased by Italian boys until she caught them. Thus she missed out on Olivia's entire courtship.

Olivia extended her left hand.

"My God."

Olivia nodded and smiled around the table. Even their waiter was impressed, and Sean was one of the most savvy and discriminating lunchtime waiters in the whole Bay Area.

"It's the style all the brides are wearing in Italy this season," Jeannine said.

"Christopher used to live in France," Olivia said.

"I heard. When Annabelle and MacKenzie came to stay with me for a week, they were just about suicidal with jealously."

"Good."

"So when do I get to meet him?"

"Mary Alice's birthday party next week," Olivia said.

"I can't wait," Jeannine said.

"No," Olivia said, "you can't."

"What are you talking about, dear?" Selene asked, looking up from her magazine. "Of course we'll use Mr. Sebastian for the photographs."

"No, Mummy, we won't," Olivia said, flopping down next to her on the sofa. "Nobody's using him anymore."

"Lucianne van Dyke did," Selene pointed out. "Just last June."

"And she still regrets it," Olivia said. "I've seen her album. It might as well be pictures of zombies. No life in them at all. That man is hopelessly old hat. All the fashionable brides are having Lance Garrison shoot them."

"Never heard of him."

"Well, you will," Olivia said. "You'll be writing him a very large check, as a matter of fact."

"I'm not sure about this, Livvie."

"Well, I am, Mummy. I've called and booked an appointment. Tuesday afternoon at three. Don't even think about forgetting it."

"I can't possibly make it. I have an appointment with my hatmaker."

"Well, I'm afraid you'll have to reschedule," Olivia said.

"Really, darling, that's going too far. . ."

"I mean it, Mummy," Olivia yawned.

"Oh, all right. I suppose we can at least interview him. But I can't imagine he'll meet with my approval."

"That's hardly the issue," Olivia said.

"What, dear?"

"His schedule is like the social calendar at Buckingham Palace. We're going to have to pull out all the stops to make sure he approves of us."

"Him approve of us? I never heard of such a thing. He's just a photographer."

"No, Mummy," Olivia shook her head in that way she had. "He is not *just* a photographer. He's *the* photographer. Don't forget it."

There was only one man Cabot believed might be able to help him: Arch Swenson. Several men he knew had employed private investigators in the past, with varying degrees of success. But Arch had not only found one who really got the job done, he got the job done discreetly. Arch had carried the whole thing off with dignity and class, and that was principally because of the man he used. It didn't matter if you were in the right if your private investigator made you look like a fool in the process of proving it.

"Miss Jordan," he spoke into the intercom.

"Yes, Mr. Styles?"

"I need a number for Archibald Swenson."

"Shall I put the call through for you?"

"No, Miss Jordan. Just get me the number. I'll call from my club."

"I suppose I really should stop fucking my sister's fiancé," Clancy mused.

"You really should," Porter said, pulling out and rolling off Clancy. "In some quarters it's considered extremely bad form to carry on an affair with your sister's fiancé this close to the wedding. After the wedding, of course, all bets are off."

"It's such a shame," Clancy said.

"Don't worry. You can hand him back over to me."

"You'd like that wouldn't you?"

Clancy didn't know that Porter had been sleeping with Christopher all along. Porter and Christopher agreed that it would only complicate things.

"He's certainly presentable," Porter said.

"Oh, hogwash," Clancy snorted. "You don't give a fuck about how presentable he is. You're just in love with that ass of his."

"It's magical, really," Porter admitted. "He does things with it that are generally considered humanly impossible."

"He's good with his mouth, of course," Clancy said, "but you're right. It's really his ass that sets him apart from the others."

"Well, Mr. Garrison," Selene said, staring at the photographer like a young girl sighting the Blessed Virgin in the skies over a French village, "this all seems satisfactory. Now on to weightier matters."

"What are you talking about, mummy?" Olivia sputtered. "Nothing's weightier than my wedding."

"Please excuse her, Mr. Garrison," Selene smiled. "She doesn't mean anything by it. She's a young girl, and every young girl thinks the world begins and ends with her wedding day. I certainly did, and look where it got me. She'll understand better when she's older. She's my daughter, after all. Now while we were talking, it occurred to me what a long time it's been since I last had my portrait taken. And I'd like for you to shoot me."

"I'll be happy to work with you, Mrs. Styles," Lance said. "If you're sure it's something you want to do."

"Why wouldn't I?"

"A certain kind of woman has a timeless beauty," Lance smiled. "Her portrait isn't something that really needs to be replaced very often."

"What you say is true of course," Selene agreed, "if you're only speaking of external appearances. But I sense that however little I may have changed in terms of my outward appearance, inwardly I continue to evolve in the most fascinating ways. And I believe you're the man to bring that out of me."

"Well, Mrs. Styles, you certainly put the case very charmingly. Fortunately, portrait sittings are much easier to schedule than weddings."

"Wonderful," Selene said. "I so look forward to my sittings. There will be several major functions in our home during the run up to the wedding, and I'd like to have the new portrait on display by then."

"I have to hand it to you," Selene said, climbing into the car after her daughter. "Mr. Garrison is most impressive."

She didn't know what she'd been expecting. Someone wispy and insubstantial, she supposed. There were so many men like that around the city these days. But what she encountered instead was that ridiculously handsome head atop those monumental shoulders. She imagined that having her portrait taken by him would be very much like being made love to. The prospect had her quite dizzy.

"I hate to say I told you so, Mummy."

"Actually, dear, that's one of your very favorite things to say. Your grandmother and Auntie Carlene and I were discussing it only the other day. But in this case, I can't really object. Talking with Mr. Garrison, you realize immediately how terribly outmoded Mr. Sebastian is."

"Cabot, there you are."

"Arch. Great to see you, old man. It's been too long."

"That it has."

"Take a load off," Cabot said. "The waiter will be around soon for our drink orders."

These old places around lower California Street were still the best, Cabot thought. Management knew how to treat a businessman and the staff knew how to keep their mouths shut. He knew men who actually met their mistresses here for lunch.

"Thanks, pal."

"You seem to be holding up."

"It was difficult at first," Arch said. "I can't tell you."

"I'm sure it must have been."

"But if you're going to end up getting a divorce anyway, getting one without having to pay alimony has certain consolations."

"Do you hear anything of Marjorie?" Cabot asked.

"Her sister insists on keeping me informed, damn her. It's so annoying. The Taggarts are apparently hoping I'll have mercy and take her back. But it'll be a cold day in hell."

"Marjorie behaved shamefully," Cabot said. "Everybody understands that. Everybody who matters, at least."

"The guy deserted her in Newport, from what I'm told. He didn't realize that he was going to have a penniless forty-nine year old on his hands. The two things you can depend on a woman to lie about. Money and her age."

"Those flash boys always think they're immune to real life," Cabot said. He'd seen his sister go through something similar. Pa bailed her out on condition she didn't come back to San Francisco. Selene and Olivia visited her in Santa Barbara from time to time, where she bred Pekingese. Nasty little beasts. He supposed it was her revenge on what she saw as a hostile universe.

"Yes," Arch said. "Imagining the expression on that pretty boy mug when he realized he'd been snookered was all that got me through it at first. Why any man would consider trading on his looks in the first place is beyond me."

"Any real man," Cabot said, thinking of his daughter's fiancé.

"Well," Arch said. "Water under the bridge, you know?"

"That man you used in the investigation was superb, wasn't he?"

"Worth every penny. I was so grateful, I paid him a gratuity equal to what the first year's alimony would have been. Tried to return it to me, but I wouldn't have it back. Real decent sort."

"What was his name?" Cabot asked.

"Crawford," Arch said. "Harris Crawford. He has an office on Greenwich Street. He's only been in San Francisco for a short while. That was one of the things that attracted me to him. All the others in that line are either so long in the tooth you can't be sure they won't kick off before they've closed the case, or they're such familiar faces they can't go about the work discreetly."

"What's his background?"

"That's the other thing about him," Arch said. "He's not sleazy like so many of the others. Top notch Philadelphia family. Ivy League graduate. Then worked at the State Department. Some hush-hush kind of work. That's his training, so to speak. Say, Cabot, you're not having some kind of difficulty with Selene, I hope."

"Olivia's gotten herself engaged, is all," Cabot said. "Just want to know if the young man has any kind of form."

"Good thinking," Arch said. "Jennifer is dating a young man I'm not sure I approve of, but I hadn't thought of bringing in an investigator. Let me know how it works out for you."

"So you think this Mr. Crawford is my best hope?"

"Sniffing around Olivia's fiancé is right up his alley, old man."

"Mummy," Olivia said, finding her mother in the potting shed. "I've been looking for you just everywhere."

"What's the matter, darling?"

"You have to talk to Daddy for me."

"About what?" Selene asked.

"It's those pearls from Great-Grandmother Styles."

"Oh."

"I know he wants me to wear them in the wedding. But they're just so old fashioned."

"Olivia," Selene said, "you know your father worships her memory. She very nearly died on the *Titanic*."

"She wasn't on the *Titanic*, Mummy."

"She almost was. She had a passage booked. And it was only a fluke that caused her to miss the sailing. Her maids were rescued, but those poor poodles. When I think of what she must have gone through, stranded in a foreign country like that."

"She was English," Olivia said. "It wasn't a foreign country."

"She was an American citizen by then, dear. It must have been terrible for her. Her luggage was all on board, and there she was on the dock at Southampton empty handed. Thank God Mason was able to bring the jewels with her when they abandoned ship. Otherwise we wouldn't have those pearls to argue about."

"Of course Daddy worships her memory," Olivia smiled. "We all do. But this is important. This is my wedding. He can't expect me to wear those horrid old things in my wedding. I don't care if they belonged to the Queen of Sheba."

"Those horrid old things were recently appraised for eighty thousand dollars," Selene said.

"Daddy probably bribed the appraiser," Olivia said. "For insurance purposes. Nobody in their right mind would pay even a tenth of that for them."

"I'm sorry, darling, but I'm afraid I'm not going to be able to help you with this one. Your father has been extremely cooperative up to now and I'm not doing anything to spoil it. We're still going to have to ask him for all kinds of things. We haven't even talked about your honeymoon yet. You just don't know how difficult it is for a woman who loves her daughter and wants the best for her but has a husband standing in the way. When I think about what your Auntie Rachel went through with Simon."

"Mummy, please."

"The answer is no," Selene said. "Your father has his heart set on seeing you come down the aisle wearing those pearls. And really, I don't know what the problem is. They're absolutely exquisite. I'd have killed to be able to wear them at my wedding."

"What a terrific idea," Olivia said.

"You can't expect me to kill your father. What a selfish girl."

"Nobody's talking about killing anyone, Mummy. But if you were to go to Daddy and tell him what you just told me—that you've never gotten over the disappointment of not getting to wear those pearls in your wedding, he'd have to let you wear them in mine. And he'd have to buy me something much nicer. Oh, you're a genius."

"What do you mean twelve bridesmaids?" Cabot demanded, staring the full length of the dining table. Quiche again. Why in blazes did Selene think quiche was dinner? Quiche was lunch for women determined to starve themselves.

"You heard me, Daddy. Twelve," Olivia said. "You're a businessman. You know now many twelve is. A dozen."

"The Queen of England didn't have a dozen bridesmaids at her wedding."

"You know that for a fact?" Olivia smiled. "You were there, I suppose?"

"You're both missing the point," Selene said. "It really doesn't matter how many bridesmaids the Queen of England had. What matters is that Ellie Capriati had twelve bridesmaids."

"Eleven," Olivia corrected her.

"Eleven," Selene nodded. "And you know better than to put me on the same level as Rae Capriati. Don't you, Cabot?"

Cabot had dated Rae O'Daugherty before Selene managed to grab his attention, and she never let him forget it. Rae married Junior Capriati on the rebound.

"Please, dear, let's not bring the Capriatis into this."

"I'm not planning to," Selene said. "If you agree to let Olivia have her twelve bridesmaids, we don't have to mention the Capriatis at all."

"It's not like it's going to cost you anything extra," Olivia pointed out. "They buy their own dresses."

"They don't buy their own corsages," Cabot pointed out, "or their brides-maid's gifts. The ones your mother told me you picked out at Tiffany. Or their own plates at the rehearsal dinner. Or the reception. And that many bridesmaids means at least three additional limousines. Perhaps four. So actually, it does cost me something."

"You'll pay to feed them in any case," Selene said, "because we'll be enter-taining them whether they're actually bridesmaids or not."

"You see, Daddy?"

"Oh, Livvie, you know it isn't a question of money, really," Cabot said. "It just seems so excessive. And twelve bridesmaids means twelve groomsmen, doesn't it? Does Christopher even have that many friends?"

"There are all kinds of cute boys still around from Clancy and Porter's gradu-ating class at St. Dunstan's, if worst comes to worst," Olivia said. "You see, I really am being practical about this."

"Thanks for stopping by to see me, son," Cabot said. Somehow, Clancy always seemed smaller and less imposing here in Cabot's office. Not that he was impos-ing anywhere, really. But still, the impression he gave of being insubstantial was always worst here. When Cabot engaged Harris Crawford, he never expected to have to have this particular discussion. He almost wished he had hired someone less efficient. But there was no turning back now.

"You say 'jump'," Clancy grinned, "and I ask 'how high'."

"I know that's the unofficial company slogan," Cabot said, "but I really wish you wouldn't use it with me."

"It's just a joke, Pa."

"I certainly hope so."

"What's wrong? Get up on the wrong side of the bed this morning?"

"I'm afraid I have something rather distressing to discuss with you, Clancy."

"Oh? Did Olivia decide she wants to ride up the aisle on horseback?"

"Don't be preposterous," Cabot said. "Though it is about the wedding, in a way. It's no secret that I've had my suspicions of your sister's young man."

"Right," Clancy said. "You've been so discreet that I think just about everybody in Northern California is aware of it."

"Well, as a matter of fact, I've had a man looking into the matter."

Really, it was as if Clancy had suddenly come face to face with a coiled rattlesnake, Cabot thought. He had been hoping that Mr. Crawford was mistaken, but that expression on his son's face, was, he thought, extremely revealing.

"A man?" Clancy said. "You mean you hired a private investigator to go after Christopher? Olivia's going to be furious when she finds out. I wouldn't be surprised if she never spoke to you again."

"Actually, I believe she's going to thank me," Cabot said. "Though not right away, perhaps."

"So what does your private dick think he's turned up?"

"Please don't be vulgar, son," Cabot said, heart sinking further. "This is difficult enough. Let's try to address the matter like men."

"What matter are we addressing?"

"My investigator has presented me with evidence that seems to lead to the conclusion that Christopher is a practicing homosexual."

"You're joking," Clancy said.

"I wish I were."

"Well, even if it's true, he's Olivia's fiancé," Clancy said. "I'm not sure what it has to do with me. I'd just as soon not discuss it."

By now, Cabot was certain. He was sorely tempted to cut the interview short and just leave the thing alone. It would be far easier, because if he went any further Selene would have to be involved. He wouldn't mention it to her. It wasn't a decent thing to discuss with a woman. But Clancy would go running to enlist her aid. Then there would be all sorts of domestic turbulence to deal with. Sometimes Cabot envied men like Arch Swenson the simplicity of their new existences, bitter as it had been achieving them. But that wasn't how Pa Styles had raised him. Clancy had to be confronted for his own good. At least as to his dishonesty. The other thing—Cabot had no idea how you even talked about that with your son. But the dishonesty he was clear on. A Styles always knew how to handle questions of integrity. It was their birthright. Except, apparently, in Clancy's instance.

"He has also presented me with evidence that seems to lead to the same conclusion about you," Cabot said.

"That's ridiculous."

How the hell had Clancy gotten to be so brazen? Was that what they learned at Yale these days? Bold-faced lying? Surely not at Wharton, though.

"Is it?" Cabot asked.

"Of course it is. How can you even ask a question like that?"

"Right now in San Francisco, Mr. Crawford is the best in the business. The very best. His inquiries have been thorough, and the evidence he presents is extremely convincing. Now, I'd hate to think that what he says is the truth."

"It isn't."

"But I'd also hate to think that you'd lie to me about it."

"I think it's all just a misunderstanding," Clancy said, barely skipping a beat.

Cabot felt he could see the wheels turning in his son's head. He dreaded what he might be about to hear. This corruption was far worse, he considered, than a sexual peccadillo. Those could be kept under wraps. People generally did. The world didn't come to an end over such a thing. But a dishonest nature made a man unfit for business.

"I mean, Porter's a homosexual, of course," Clancy said.

"Really?"

"But we've always known that," Clancy said.

"We have?"

"Of course we have. Why even back at St. Dunstan's he was pretty notorious for it. I think your Mr. Crawford has gotten his signals crossed. It's true that Christopher and I are both very friendly with Porter. That's where the misunderstanding probably started. Honestly, Dad, you wouldn't have wanted me to drop my best and oldest friend because of a thing like that, would you?"

"The dress costs how much?" Cabot asked, looking up from his *Wall Street Journal*.

"Don't pretend you didn't hear me the first time, dear," Selene said. "It makes you seem older than you are."

"I could buy her a Porsche for that."

"Your daughter would look very silly coming up the aisle in a Porsche. Mind you, I'm not saying she wouldn't enjoy it. But that kind of thing isn't done in our set. We leave it to the *nouveau riche* families."

"Well, I could buy myself one."

"How many Porsches does one man need, dear?"

"I don't have any Porsches at present. Not since Clancy totaled the 911."

"Dear, let's not get sidetracked," Selene said. "Accidents happen."

"Particularly when people have been drinking."

"He said he hadn't been," Selene said. "He swore to me."

"Selene, when I picked him up from the accident scene, he could hardly walk. It was all I could do to convince the officers to overlook his condition."

"He was in shock, dear," Selene said. "You would have been, too, if you'd been in a terrible accident like that. I'm sure I would have been comatose. But what happened to your precious Porsche is beside the point."

"I know it is, Selene," Cabot said. "I was just trying to put the wedding gown into perspective."

"Why don't you let me put it into perspective for you," Selene said. "We only have one daughter. That means I have only one chance to host a wedding. One chance, Cabot, to be the mother of the bride. Do I make myself clear?"

"Olivia, listen to me," Cabot said, closing his daughter's bedroom door behind him. "It's time we had a serious talk."

"I'm always serious," Olivia said. "My friends will tell you no one is more serious than I am when it comes to all kinds of things. Parties, shopping, planning vacations, the theatre. I'm like a five star general at the Pentagram. I don't know why you and Clancy give me such a hard time about being shallow."

"Sweetie, you know that there's nothing more important to your mother and me than your happiness."

"I should hope so," Olivia said. "That's what parents are for. To ensure the happiness of their children. It's important to me, too, you know."

"Of course. Now, I need you to remember that while I tell you what I have to tell you."

"Oh, Daddy, that's so sweet," Olivia beamed. "I love you, too."

"Um, yes. Now, sometimes when it comes to the people we love, we have to do certain things to protect them. Even if they may not agree with what you do, you know you have to do it for their own good. Because you love them, you see?"

"Oh, not this again," Olivia rolled her eyes. "That old 'this is going to hurt me more than it's going to hurt you' line. Because it never hurts you more than it hurts me. You should know that by now. I'm very, very sensitive. My friends will tell you that no one is more sensitive than I am."

"And that's why it's even more important that your mother and I look out for you. What I have to tell you is not something I'd ordinarily consider discussing with a decent young woman, but there's no getting around it. You're simply going to have to hear me out as an adult. If there was any way around this, believe me, I'd have taken it. So the thing is, I'm deeply sorry to have to tell you this, but I've learned that your Christopher is a homosexual."

"What?"

"A homosexual. A man who has sex with other men. Who prefers that to normal sex."

"Daddy, don't be ridiculous. Christopher is no more a homosexual than he is an Eskimo."

"I'm not being ridiculous. I have proof."

"Well I have proof that he's not."

"What do you mean?" Cabot asked.

"I don't know what it was like back in your and Mummy's day, but my friends and I wouldn't dream of agreeing to marry a man without taking him out for a long test drive. If you get my drift."

"Darling, it's not that simple."

"Silly Daddy," Olivia smiled. "Of course it is."

"Clancy, what the hell did you say to Daddy about Christopher?"

"Jesus," Clancy said, looking up at her through the eye he'd managed to open. "Where did you come from?"

"You know you gave me an extra key to your apartment. Did you think I wasn't going to use it?"

"Some people call," Clancy said, pulling up the sheet to make sure he was decent. "They let you know they're coming to see you. They don't just drop in on you in your sleep."

"You're a fine one to complain about someone else's manners," Olivia said. "And stop trying to change the subject."

"What subject?"

"Don't play innocent with me," Olivia said, stamping her foot. "You got Daddy all wound up about something, and he put a detective on Christopher's tail. Now he's got some crazy idea about Christopher being homosexual and he wants me to call off the wedding. This is all your fault."

"You stupid bitch," Clancy said. "I never said anything to Pa about your precious Christopher. I didn't need to. You know Pa's always been like the CIA when it came to your boyfriends. Even when you were in kindergarten. Remember your fifth birthday party, when he gave Marty Kavanagh the third degree after he found the two of you playing that kissing game in the butler's pantry? You didn't seriously believe he'd let you marry somebody without giving them a full going over, did you? Who do you think Pa is? The Cowardly Lion?"

"He does sound like that sometimes."

"And sometimes you sound just like a four year old. Now go away and leave me alone. I was up late."

"Honestly, Roberta, I don't know what I'm going to do," Selene said, eyeing the platinum brooch in the display case. "Olivia isn't speaking to her father or her brother. I have no idea what's going on. Nobody will talk to me about it. It's like living in an armed camp."

"I know exactly what you're talking about," Roberta Skinner smiled. "When my Lulu was getting married—her first wedding, I mean—it got so bad that she threatened to have me banned from the whole thing. Can you believe that? Weddings seem to turn young girls into mental patients who've escaped from the asylum."

"Is there anything you'd like me to show you?" the store attendant asked.

"No, dear," Selene smiled.

"We'll call you if we need you," Roberta said.

"You're certainly right about that," Selene said. "At our house lately, it's like scenes from Shakespeare's tragedies at mealtimes. And now it seems that Clancy isn't speaking to his father, either. If I had half a brain, I'd sit down with dear Christopher and take out my checkbook and give him a large sum of money just to elope with that girl of mine. It would serve them all right, and it would get the job done."

"You remember that's exactly what I did the third time Lulu got married. 'You're not putting me through all that again', I told her. 'Here's a nice check for you. Now leave me alone.' I believe the young man lost most of the money playing roulette in Aruba. I had to wire her more just so they could pay their hotel bill. It was worth it to have them out of the country for a few weeks."

"Dear Roberta," Selene said. "It's so nice to have a sympathetic ear to lean on."

"You remember, of course, that Olivia's trust is not revocable," Mason Robek said, voice booming out of the speaker.

"Of course," Cabot nodded. "I'm not trying to make her penniless, you know. That trust pays about a hundred thousand a year, depending on how the markets are doing. It won't be enough to keep her in the style to which she's accustomed, but she won't starve in the streets. But as to my estate, I insist on having her written right out of it. And Clancy as well."

"It's your will," Mason said. "As your attorney, I follow your directions absolutely. You can certainly do whatever you want. But as your friend rather than your attorney, I don't advise it. There are bound to be hard feelings."

"Hard feelings? You don't think I'm proposing to tell anyone about this? Selene will burn down the house if she hears a word of it. It's between me and my attorney, which is you. In any case it's just a temporary measure. Clancy is— well, Clancy is very confused right now, and if anything were to happen unexpectedly to me it wouldn't be a good thing at all for a young man in his addled state to have a lot of money at his disposal. Now, with regard to Olivia, this is just until she gets divorced from that young doctor of hers. California is a community property state, after all."

"Divorced? They're not even married yet."

"No," Cabot said, "but I don't see any way of preventing it. Once she's free of that scoundrel I won't have any qualms at all about putting her back in the will. And as for Clancy, he already hates me. It would be hypocritical of him to accept another cent from me under the circumstances, and I have no intention of placing that kind of temptation in front of him. If worst comes to worst, he's just going to have to take it like a man and make his own fortune."

"Porter, sweetie," Olivia said, looking up from her menu. "How tan you are."

"Just back from Acapulco," he said, bending to kiss her cheek.

"Oh? How long were you there?"

"Only a few days," he said, sitting down across from her.

"That's funny," Olivia said.

"What is?"

"Everybody seems to be going on trips but me."

"Who else do you know who's been out of town?" Porter asked.

"Well, Christopher for one," she said. "He had that medical convention in Denver. Or Dallas. Or was it Detroit? Some D place. Is it just me, or does every state have one?"

"I can't think of one here in California," Porter said.

"Downey," Olivia said.

"Right."

"Of course that's really just Los Angeles, isn't it? Like Daly City is really just San Francisco. Christopher was gone nearly a week, and he came back with a tan, too. Not as dark as yours, of course. He doesn't have the complexion for it. You know, Nancy Boswell was just talking about you the other day."

"Was she?"

"Something about how wide your shoulders have gotten."

"Oh."

"But Christopher going away like that here just a month before the wedding. It didn't seem fair at all, me up to my eyeballs in wedding plans and him off learning about—whatever his convention was about. He explained it to me, but it didn't make any sense."

"Yes," Porter said, "I'm sure you're very busy these days."

"You don't know the half of it," Olivia said.

"Should we look at the menu?"

"Oh, I already know what I want."

"Good," Porter said. "I'll just signal the waiter."

"Listen, darling, before you do, I really need to ask you something."

"What's that?"

"Well, it's been bothering me, you see. I've never understood why Clancy dislikes Christopher so much, and I'm hoping you can clear that up for me."

"Clancy dislikes Christopher?" Porter asked. "First I've heard of it."

"Oh, surely you've noticed how stiff he is whenever Christopher's in the room."

"Stiff, huh?" Porter said, trying not to grin, "now that you mention it, I may have noticed something like that."

"I don't care about tradition," Olivia pouted.

It was bad enough that Jeannine's apartment had better views than the one Olivia and Christopher had signed a lease on. Jeannine's new decorator had just done a refresh that made it look like a flat in Paris. And Olivia wouldn't be able to use him because Jeannine already had. Marriage was shaping up to be full of challenges.

"I'm a modern bride. Everybody knows that. Probably the most modern bride in history. We are going to crash the bachelor party. Nobody better try to stop me. And you're going to help me do it, Jeannine. You and Annabelle and MacKenzie."

"Not Mary Anne?"

"Not Mary Anne," Olivia said. "Definitely not Mary Anne."

"I just don't see the point," Jeannine said.

"The point is, I think it will be fun. Plus, I won't have my Christopher in a smoky room full of strippers, hookers, drunk fraternity boys and God knows what other lowlife without me there to defend him."

"Porter and Clancy will look out for him."

"Porter will do his best," Olivia nodded. "I know I can depend on him to keep Christopher out of trouble. But that snake in the grass brother of mine will do everything he can to sabotage things. Sometimes I think he doesn't really want me to marry Christopher."

"I'm sure you're imagining that, Livvie."

"And I'm quite sure I'm not."

"Well, all I know is, whenever I see the two of them out and about, they seem like the best of friends."

"The two of who out and about?"

"Clancy and Christopher, of course. Who did you think I was talking about?"

"Clancy and Christopher out and about?"

"I've run into them several times just in the last couple of weeks."

"Damn that Clancy," Olivia fumed. "Pretending to be Christopher's friend. Worming his way into his confidence. I'll kill him. I swear to God I will."

"You're not going to believe this," Christopher said, rolling off Porter and landing on his back next to him.

"What?" Porter asked, squinting at the ceiling and panting slightly. Once again, he pondered the question of who the true bottom was when the guy taking it up the ass was really the one in control of the situation.

"Cabot Styles has offered me money to go away."

"Really? How much?"

"A hundred fifty thousand dollars."

"Not bad," Porter said. "He only offered me twenty-five thousand to leave Clancy alone."

"When did he do that?"

"Last week. Twenty-five thousand in cash and a transfer to the San Diego branch. Promised me a promotion when I get down there. It's really quite a generous offer. Especially considering that I'm not actually having an affair with Clancy."

"Yes," Christopher said. "Especially considering that."

"At least not twenty-five thousand dollars' worth of an affair. By any stretch of the imagination. It was only a couple of blow jobs. Which he's no good at. Those teeth of his. I was afraid I might have suffered permanent damage. Somebody needs to give him lessons."

"Are you going to take the offer?"

"Well, first of all I talked him up to fifty. It means leaving my family behind. And everybody knows how close we are. I practically sang 'I left my heart in San Francisco' to him."

"Did you? Good man. And did you close the deal?"

"I'd have been pretty stupid not to," Porter said. "Wouldn't I? I mean with you marrying Olivia, I'll pretty much be at loose ends."

"Who says I'm going to go through with it?" Christopher asked. "A hundred fifty thousand is a lot of money."

"It's a drop in the bucket," Porter snorted. "Don't try and make me believe that you engineered all this for a measly hundred fifty thousand."

"Just checking," Christopher laughed.

BO ARMSTRONG: 1981

I

When Bo first arrived in San Francisco, he required only two things: a gym to conduct business out of and a doctor to write his prescriptions. The first gym he chose was perfectly located and had exactly the right atmosphere. The reigning muscle gods there, two men named Stefano and Nikolai, seemed friendly at first. But before long they made the owner ban him from the place for entertaining his clients on the premises. The second gym was in a more fashionable neighborhood but lacked the spartan atmosphere he preferred. He feared these conditions might adversely affect business. But contrary to what he would have expected given its décor, it was run on a *laissez-faire* basis more in keeping with the requirements of his profession. And to his good fortune, once he'd set up operations there the doctor he had been looking for found him. This gentleman was so helpful that he not only was willing to write the prescriptions, he arranged for Bo to have them filled for free.

But the best thing about the doctor was that he was as handsome as a cinema idol and sexually accommodating almost beyond imagining. Sometimes, after a long day servicing the trolls, because since he was new in the city Bo made a policy of taking everyone's money indiscriminately, he ached in his bones to fuck someone truly beautiful. And the good doctor was exactly the right medicine for that. Bo couldn't fuck little Sean every time he was in that mood. Little Sean was beautiful enough, it was true. But he was too lovesick already. It wouldn't do to encourage him any more than necessary. On the other hand, the doctor didn't seem to know what being lovesick meant.

"Bo Armstrong" wasn't his real name. It was a pun. He had come up with it on his way south, and he was really very proud of it. "Bo" sounded like "beau", which meant handsome in French. Which he certainly and absolutely was. And "Armstrong" was even simpler. With his twenty inch biceps, he unquestionably was "Armstrong". These silly Americans—it all went right over their heads. Which he thought was extremely funny, considering that coming up with the name had for all practical purposes exhausted his knowledge of their language.

Little Sean got it, of course. Though he was Anglophone by birth and education, he spoke French as well as anyone Bo had known in Montreal. Little Sean was somewhat annoying. He didn't mean to be. Bo understood it was simply that Sean was friendly and lovesick. And those emotions were understandable. In Bo's presence, lots of people became friendly and lovesick. He had long ago accustomed himself to it. Indeed, it was, to be quite honest about it, what put food on his table and kept someone or other's roof over his head. Still, it was awkward having little Sean so very present morning, noon, and night. Because little Sean had no money to speak of and no influential friends that Bo might be able to exploit and not even an apartment of his own that Bo could have made use of when he was in a pinch or merely not in the mood to depend on the hospitality of trolls. But little Sean was faithful and understood Bo's French almost better than Bo did himself. So until Bo was more securely established in the city or perfected his English, little Sean was indispensable. And his ass was so hospitable whenever Bo desired to repose his organ there, which made a very agreeable bonus.

Little Sean wasn't that little, really—only in comparison with Bo. And little Sean didn't do sex for a living like Bo did. He did it for favors mostly, generating his real income from odd jobs: posing for photographers, dancing in clubs, but other, more mundane activities as well. Sometimes he didn't take off his clothing at all but nevertheless got paid. Bo found this almost impossible to fathom, because Sean was certainly attractive enough not to have to work in actual jobs. In addition to his skills as a translator, little Sean was valuable to Bo for his boyish face and friendly demeanor. People who found Bo too imposing or actually frightening to approach thought little Sean was adorable. With a young man like that looking on, could anything terrible happen to them? Would a young man who looked like that allow them to be cheated? He acted as a kind of mediator.

Bo lost count of the deals that would never have been closed without little Sean there to make everything seem just possible enough. It was a perfect arrangement, because little Sean wanted nothing in return except for a good hard fuck every now and then.

San Francisco was everything Bo had been led to expect of it. Having succeeded spectacularly in Montreal and Toronto, he nevertheless failed to find in either city the pot of gold at the end of the rainbow. Here on the edge of the Pacific, a different outcome seemed possible. He wouldn't have to service all comers forever. Before he knew it he would have accumulated a client list of sufficient eminence that he'd be able to stop servicing the trolls almost completely except for a handful of unbelievably wealthy ones who paid so well that he couldn't in faithfulness to his dreams cut them off. There was a surprising number of reasonably good looking, sufficiently affluent men around the city prepared to pay for his services. He saw them everywhere. That they knew he was available to them was due to the doctor, who, it turned out, possessed a genius for just the right sort of publicity. It wasn't enough to lurk at the gym and rely on word of mouth, he said. Things in San Francisco didn't work that way.

What Dr. Melendez-Greene had proposed was that unless Bo was working out or actually on a call, he should place himself on public display. Hanging out in a club. Shopping, preferably for underwear though he wore none, or at the very least for things to work out in. Eating in a restaurant. Attending a party. Anything, really, as long as he could be seen doing it. Being seen ensured being talked about by the ever present gossips. If he could have his picture taken performing whatever activity he was engaged in, that was even better. Pictures could be published. Pictures could go home clutched in the fists of prospective clients, to be retrieved and gazed at longingly whenever the mood struck. Dr. Melendez-Greene knew of a photographer who was only too willing to help. The doctor had at his disposal a whole army of hairdressers, dermatologists, chiropractors, health food purveyors, and assorted other artisans and vendors willing to do their part in keeping Bo looking his best. Most of them agreed to work for free—just for the privilege of having him in their hands for even the briefest encounters and the most innocuous of purposes. It all meant that the market never forgot about him. Word of mouth was fine and good, but visuals trumped everything.

Dr. Melendez-Greene suggested a few modifications to Bo's business practices as well. Bo wasn't to allow himself to be picked up impromptu. He had to insist on prior bookings. And to insure that, he should not on any account fly solo on any of his excursions. He must always have at least one buddy present.

Little Sean was only too willing.

Dr. Melendez-Greene was right. Bookings soared. Bo increased his fees, increased his fees, and increased them again. There was still more work than he could, um, handle. And the customers got younger and better looking all the time. As he had anticipated, there were a few older men whose bank accounts were so bottomless that their business couldn't be turned away, but he was able to minimize that. His work, which he had regarded as a necessary evil, a means to an end, became something he almost looked forward to.

What Dr. Melendez-Greene didn't understand, though Bo sensed that little Sean was starting to, was that he didn't actually need dozens of clients. He only needed one—the right one. He had long ago realized that his goal was not to earn lots of money with his muscles and equipment and technique so that he ended up financially independent. That would take far too long. His plan was much more efficient than that. Someday one of his encounters would bring him face to face with the one man he sought. The right man. He would be handsome, sexually accommodating, and rich. He would set Bo up in his own apartment. If you moved in with a man he could always throw you back out, but if he bought you your own place, you were set for life. In addition, he would buy Bo a Ferrari. He would provide Bo with a trust fund. He would be available when Bo wanted him, but the rest of the time he would leave Bo alone.

Bo wasn't looking for a man like that because he absolutely had to have a man. He wasn't certain a man was even his first choice. It was a question of practicalities. Bo had been on the market long enough to conclude that he'd never achieve the kind of arrangement he was so intent on with a woman. Very few women possessed the sort of resources required, and the ones who did tended to be so old and unattractive that Bo would have been embarrassed to be kept by them. Such an arrangement might well destroy his mystique. But the real problem was that in his experience women were invariably possessive. Regardless of the terms of the agreement, their possessiveness made it impossible for them to live up to their end. That ruined everything. He required the freedom to come and go as he pleased. A man would understand that. The kind of man who would want Bo enough to pay the price required would accept it as a matter of course.

Before long, Dr. Christopher came up with an innovation that Bo considered extremely valuable. It was all well and good for potential clients to be constantly reminded of his magnificence. Keeping the merchandise on view was nothing more than good common sense. But the doctor showed Bo how to take things further. The men weren't just buying the company of arguably the hottest man in the city. They were buying an experience. It wasn't like they were just going to sit around looking at him when he came into their homes. Things would happen. Acts would take place. Physical contact would be made. So why not give them a clear understanding of what that would be like? What better advertisement could there be for his services but a presentation of those services themselves?

Dr. Christopher took him to a certain "theatre" in the Tenderloin where patrons paid to sit in the audience and watch while men on stage jerked off. Bo got the idea immediately. But it wasn't enough. He wasn't a skinny twenty year old with big eyes and floppy hair. Propping himself on a stool—the very same stool as all the others—and performing the same act? No. It placed him on the same level as the other performers. Pretty as they were, those young men were pygmies. He was a god. He had to manifest himself in a more spectacular fashion.

II

"The idea is," Dr. Christopher explained to little Sean, "that Bo is going to fuck you in front of a live audience."

Sean blushed as he translated this for Bo.

"*Tu comprends?*" Bo asked.

"Yes," Sean nodded. "*Oui.*"

"*Tout va bien.*"

Their performance was a sensation. The first of many.

After one of their bigger successes, Dr. Christopher's uncle gave Bo free run of the big house in Pacific Heights. The servants were instructed not to interfere with him. He had his own keys. He had a suite of rooms on the third floor. Because the doctor's uncle was the lover of a famous, semi-retired film director, Bo assumed there were hidden cameras in the house and behaved accordingly. He never wore any clothing when he was there, except, on occasion, something fetishistic. He didn't tell little Sean about the cameras. Little Sean didn't need to know about them. Little Sean didn't need to do anything but open his mouth or spread his legs as Bo's whim dictated, and little Sean never needed any encouragement to do either of those things. Bo still needed little Sean's translation skills from time to time, though his English had improved to the extent this wasn't necessary except with new clients. The rest of the time little Sean disappeared. Bo honestly had no idea where little Sean went when they weren't together and didn't especially care. Little Sean would outlive his usefulness sooner or later, but until then Bo appreciated his pliant nature.

Bo helped himself in the kitchen. Bo used the pool whenever he felt like it. The one thing Bo never did was entertain clients at the big house. Clients didn't need to know he more or less lived there. His living arrangements needed to be a mystery, as so much about him remained mysterious. Bo was very careful about concealing things. What people didn't know about him gave him power, almost as much as his physique, beauty, and sexual prowess gave him power.

He fucked the doctor's uncle a few times. Just enough to satisfy his curiosity. Not enough to dampen the desire he saw raging in the man's eyes.

Before long he came to understand that the position the doctor's uncle occupied in the household was analogous to the one he aspired to. Though he appeared to run the whole show it was actually the film director who did. Uncle Rene was merely the mouthpiece. The film director himself rarely appeared. There was a suite of rooms on the second floor that Bo's keys wouldn't admit him to, and he assumed this was the man's private apartment. Bo was introduced to him and congratulated on his achievements. Jules apparently knew as much about him as he had allowed anyone to know and seemed to approve. Bo was prepared to fuck Jules if necessary, but the occasion never arose.

Bo continued to fuck Dr. Christopher from time to time. He didn't have to fuck Christopher as much as he had initially expected to. Christopher was young and really very beautiful. He never lacked for admirers. When he did come to Bo, however, he never failed to assert that Bo was absolutely the pinnacle. Bo didn't need to be told that, but it was good to know that the doctor understood it.

III

"There's no doubt about it. The specialists say the tumor is inoperable. And there isn't any way of knowing how quickly it will develop. I may have six more months. I may have two or three years. Long before the end comes, I'll be helpless."

"I see."

It was the servants' night off. The big house was empty. Bo was certain Uncle Rene and Jules thought they were alone. He stood still on the stairs. He barely allowed himself to breathe.

"You must do as you wish," Jules said.

"I'll stay as long as you need me," Rene said.

"That was never our agreement."

"I know. Still."

"I never planned to make you my heir," Jules said. "That hasn't changed. You said you understood that."

"I did. I do. I don't need your money."

"I will leave you provided for," Jules said. "A trust fund. About fifty thousand a year."

"Very generous."

"The same as I'm providing for Volk. I don't know what your arrangement with him is."

"I have no arrangement with Volk," Rene said. "He's just a diversion."

"What will you do?"

"Go back to Paris, I expect. This city is lovely, but I don't find the people very sympathetic."

"No," Jules said. "You've never been happy here."

"I expect I'll find a place with Graciella."

"Ah yes," Jules said. "Christopher's mother. Lovely woman. Speaking of Christopher."

"You don't have to tell me," Rene said.

"I feel I should," Jules said. "Everything is to go to him. This house. The apartment in Paris. The villa on the Cote d'Azur. The furnishings, of course. And the art."

"Certainly," Rene said. "And the money."

"And the money," Jules said.

"He'll be rich."

"Extremely."

"It won't make him love you."

"No," Jules said. "It won't. It didn't make you love me, a million years ago. It didn't make Volk love me. In my whole life I have never been truly loved by anyone. Really, money is the most futile thing in the world."

"Not for those who don't have it."

"I made my peace with the powerlessness of wealth a long time ago."

"Have you spoken to Christopher?" Rene asked.

"He doesn't need to know," Jules said, "until the time comes. You won't say anything, I hope."

"What would be the point?"

"Exactly," Jules said. "The fewer who know anything of this, the better."

It was, Bo thought as he sneaked back up the stairs to his room, the answer to everything.

It required, however, a shift in strategy. From now on, pleasing Christopher must be Bo's highest priority. Everything he did must somehow further the goal of making himself indispensable to that exquisite young man. Which meant no more extracurricular fucking with little Sean. Unless he was with a client or performing in a live show, all Bo's energy had to be saved until it could be expended between the doctor's perfect thighs. Little Sean had just about outlived his usefulness anyway, except as a performer. He would always be good for that. So he'd have to be encouraged sufficiently to ensure his willingness, but no more.

Meanwhile, Bo must make the doctor his slave.

On the day when that crazy man on the second floor breathed his last and the doctor became rich almost beyond reckoning, Bo must be the one standing at his side. More than that, Bo must be the one holding the whip and the reins.

IV

When Christopher first announced his engagement to an heiress, Bo took no notice. Men of every conceivable proclivity got married all the time. He didn't see how it altered matters in the least. He had never disqualified married men from his list of prospects. Christopher's fiancée had money of her own. Even after marrying, he would be just as able to support Bo as he had been before. But one day when little Sean and he were having lunch in a small bistro in North Beach, Bo overheard two gentlemen at the next table talking about Christopher. They were speaking quickly and they weren't talking about sex, so his English wasn't up to the task. But he was always curious when Christopher was being spoken about.

"What are they saying?"

"That he's getting married for money," Sean answered.

"Obviously."

"No," Sean said. "It's actually very interesting. It seems that here in California there's a thing called community property. The minute he marries that girl, half of everything she owns is his, legally speaking."

"Really?"

"She comes from a very wealthy family. She stands to inherit over twenty million. That means if she and Christopher were to get a divorce, he would walk away with ten million."

"Only if they were still married when her father died and she inherited," Bo said. "If I understand correctly."

"Yes," little Sean nodded.

"That might be years," Bo said. "And rich men sometimes change their wills. The doctor will have to be careful and patient if he's ever to enjoy that payday."

The questions which had been raised by this new information were of such a sensitive nature that Bo didn't dare confide them to little Sean. They were of such a technical nature that little Sean couldn't have answered them even if he had. What Bo required was an attorney who spoke French. But even that request was one he couldn't allow himself to make. Little Sean couldn't be given any opportunity to form suspicions. But there was someone who could help.

"Professor Schein," Bo smiled, calling on the manners of his French boyhood.

The professor's studio at the conservatory reminded Bo of a room in Montreal.

"*Monsieur*," Professor Schein nodded.

"I find myself in need of assistance," Bo explained. "And I thought perhaps, as a fellow Frenchman, you might be agreeable."

"That would depend," Professor Schein said, "on what sort of assistance you refer to."

Bo's reputation had preceded him. He didn't blame the professor for being dubious.

"An introduction only," Bo said.

"May one ask for what purpose the introduction would be made?"

"I seek professional services," Bo said, as disarmingly as he could.

The attorney's office reeked of Gitanes, which, Bo thought, was a good sign. The attorney himself spoke the French of upper-class Paris, which was even better. Bo laid out his questions, taking care to couch them in hypothetical terms. What he learned in from the attorney's responses confirmed his fears. The laws regarding community property were essentially as little Sean had explained them, and they applied to wives accessing the wealth of their husbands as well as vice versa.

It was a question of timing. Timing in combination with that crazy old man's ridiculous fetish for secrecy. If Christopher had decided to get married after Bo's future was assured, he would have had no objection. It would have been a relief, really, to have Christopher distracted by a wife and, presumably at some point, children. Bo could then have gone about his business undisturbed, servicing Christopher at his own convenience. Christopher was beautiful and charming and as good in bed as one could possibly want. Christopher was generous to a fault. All that was certainly true. But Christopher was unpredictable in the extreme. You could never be certain when he wouldn't go off on some strange tangent, become fascinated with some new person. He was ripe for exploitation. Bo had seen it over and over. He had always come back to his senses, but that was no guarantee for the future. And worst of all, Christopher was a narcissist, and Bo had no patience with narcissists. They were extremely difficult to manipulate. They lacked sufficient reverence for what he represented. They thought they could have whatever they wanted without having to earn it and that made them lose sight of the value of what they already had and squander it. All that explained Christopher's engagement to the heiress.

And if that crazy old man had only made his plans known, Christopher wouldn't have considered getting married in the first place. Bo knew as well as anyone that the marriage was only a plot to assure Christopher's own future. An unnecessary plot, but apparently Bo was the only one aware of it. Rene would never talk. More than once Bo had been on the point of telling Christopher what he knew. But Christopher would demand proof, and how was he to provide that? How could he guarantee that the crazy old man wouldn't take it into his head to change his will? And if he told, how could he be assured that his own solicitude for Christopher wouldn't then be viewed in a somewhat different light?

But still, the timing was the real problem. The wedding was only a few weeks away. And it looked as though Jules wouldn't live for more than a few months after that. A year at most. At that point, Christopher would inherit, and his wife would be eligible for half of what Jules had left him. Knowing Christopher as he did, Bo couldn't imagine the marriage lasting very long. A divorce within a few years seemed inevitable. At the very least, it was a contingency that had to be allowed for. Meanwhile, Cabot Styles was a vigorous man in the best of health. It didn't seem likely that Olivia would inherit her share of his estate until long after her marriage to Christopher had ended. But by then, she might already have taken half of Christopher's fortune.

It was maddening. Bo had invested so much. He had literally drained his manhood over and over in his efforts to secure his future, and this stupid girl had put it all at risk.

"How many times do I have to tell you?" Christopher asked, slowly expelling Bo with a determined contraction of his muscles that Bo thought of as the ultimate caress. Sometimes he stolidly stood his ground, remaining in place despite Christopher's efforts. But not this time. He was simply too fatigued. Not sexually fatigued—that would never happen. But intellectually fatigued by this infernal cat and mouse game Christopher insisted on playing. "My marriage won't change anything. You'll still have me as often as you like."

"You say that," Bo growled, "but what assurance do I have?"

"This assurance," Christopher said, grasping Bo's penis, which immediately started to firm back up. "This right here. You know as well as I do that nobody else on the planet is capable of doing to me what you do to me with this. Surely you know I'd never allow anything to prevent me from having this. This is what I live for."

"You expect me to accept that as a promise?" Bo asked, as Christopher kissed the tip.

"A solemn oath sworn on your own manhood?" Christopher laughed. "What better promise could you possibly need?"

Ever since Bo's days, all too brief, in the Paris *gendarmerie,* he had abhorred violence. It was a ridiculous waste, ruining things which couldn't be replaced or repaired. Worse than that, violence was nothing less than a failure to get one's way by other means. It was the ultimate indictment of one's manhood. If one's physique and looks and virility weren't sufficiently convincing to others that they did your bidding, you simply weren't a man. Violence was a symptom of impotence, nothing less. A man who was forced to resort to it would be better off dead.

But the threat of violence—that was something else altogether.

"Not one of those little popgun things women carry in their purses," Bo said. "You understand? A man's weapon. And some ammunition."

"*Mais, certainment*," Sean said.

"Here," Bo said, handing him a roll of bills. "No paperwork. No permits. No serial numbers."

"*Je comprends.*"

DARIO COVARRUBIAS: 1981

I

The boy they sent with Cody's letter should have been Dario's first clue. From halfway down the corridor he was a dead ringer for Cody at that age. Or, for that matter, Nick at that age: Dario had seen photos. Dario hadn't known Nick at twenty-two, but he remembered Cody at twenty-two, sometimes so vividly it took his breath away. Someone, anyone really, determined to get Dario's immediate attention couldn't have devised a method more assured of success. And it wouldn't have taken a mind reader to figure it out. Dario had all too often been accused of being a sucker for a pretty face. It was a charge he wouldn't attempt to refute. He'd only make himself ridiculous. In addition, his oldest and dearest friends would unanimously attest to his perennial and tragic weakness for blonds. Finally, anyone even casually aware of his antics over the last decade and a half would be forced to conclude that Dario was the consummate afficionado and connoisseur of lats, pecs, biceps, deltoids, triceps, abs, quads, intercostals—the whole beefcake, protein powder, and sweat litany of the bodybuilding cult. And the young man they sent was the complete package. The briefest glimpse of him standing outside the door of the department office was more than enough to confirm the impression.

In retrospect, it seemed all too obvious they must have thought that by making the medium the message in such an unmistakable, even ostentatious, fashion they could in turn depend on eliciting the classic Pavlovian response Dario exhibited every time he caught sight of that particular kind of spectacle. Cody had described it to them in lurid detail long before that afternoon, in addition to God only knew what else he had revealed. Everything, Dario supposed. He blushed whenever he imagined it. But in spite of all their careful planning, the boy's appearance there might easily have failed to have the anticipated effect. After all, Dario wasn't nineteen any more. Or even twenty-nine. And though they couldn't have known it from anything Cody might have told them, of all the changes Dario had undergone in the years since they had parted ways his advancing age was the least important one. The absolute bottom of the list, as a matter of fact. Perhaps they did know this, or at least suspect it in spite of what Cody had to say on the subject, and that young man was just a shot in the dark. But given everything that eventually transpired, Dario had no reason to think so. Nor would anyone else with half a brain.

In any event, tall, golden haired, Nordic-looking bodybuilder that the young man was, clad that afternoon in black gym shorts and a deeply scooped tank top which exactly matched his eyes and featured the thinnest imaginable of straps, Dario had been briefly married to one of those once upon a time and subsequently and more permanently to another. So though it certainly wasn't the most common of types and Dario didn't expect he'd ever become immune, at least not in this life, to the positively mythic appeal of its extravagant, masculine beauty, he had one just like it at home. Thus, such an arresting vision simply didn't affect him the way it would have in the past, with an array of physical and emotional manifestations that would make him sound like the heroine of one of those pulp romances on sale row after row in racks at the supermarket, their cover art glimmering luridly in the fluorescent lighting, were he to catalogue and describe them all, each and every one predicated not only on the physical appeal of the specimen in question but also on the challenge posed by his apparent unavailability.

Dario had no inkling that afternoon that anything out of the ordinary was going on. No reason to think that the boy's presence in the corridor had anything to do with him at all, much less that he had been sent for the express purpose of being seen by Dario as he stood by the drinking fountain and a few moments later as he smiled in at the door of Dario's office. Realistically, Dario had no reason to think of the people who had sent that young man. Particularly as anyone he would ever have any sort of dealings with. There were the bare facts of his biography, of course, which might seem to lead in one direction, while on the other hand there were the actual experiences of his life, which led in another. Though he'd arrived in the States only recently, in his heart he was as American as apple pie and 'Fifty-seven Chevys. All-American boyhood had always been his aspiration, and like just about every American of his generation he had heard, read, and been told enough over the years that he thought he knew all there was to know, or at least all that was worth knowing, about those shadowy people behind the affair, including the crucially important fact that they would never bother themselves with someone so obscure and unimportant as he was. His mistake, obviously. And a big one as it turned out. It was only sheer dumb luck that the consequences weren't horrendous. He really should have paid more attention on those endless evenings when his parents and their friends sat at the kitchen table drinking wine and talking politics—the politics of their homeland, that was, not Dario's. He hardly remembered the place, and their new home didn't interest him, either. Nor the place his parents sent him for school. All he cared about was America as he knew it from movies and television. No, he hadn't paid attention to his parents' politics any more than he would have if they'd been opera fanatics or Satan worshippers. Perhaps rather less. But he didn't know if it would have made any difference in any case. Show him anyone, any non-professional at least, who wouldn't have made a similar miscalculation under the circumstances. After all, the full might and energy of the United States Government had been bent for his entire lifetime on keeping everyone, even young expatriate Argentine boys growing up in Geneva, safe from just such eventualities. Right thinking individuals were perfectly secure, and others, like Dario's parents, who barely deserved that description, huddled under the umbrella alongside them. With J. Edgar Hoover's minions and the invisible men of the CIA looking out for them, not to mention their proxies all over Western Europe, the oblivious masses had nothing to fear. They had been told as much over and over. And like his friends, Dario grew up thinking of people who looked under their beds every night for communist agents as hopelessly paranoid. Who knew that just this once Dario would have been right to look under his own? But under the circumstances, Dario had no reason to be suspicious of that blond, sinewy vision. Spectacular as he was, he wasn't the least bit out of place. Lots of afternoons the corridors of that building and every other one on campus resembled those of a modeling agency or fashionable gym more than those of a university. Ask anyone who has anything even remotely to do with higher education and they would tell you. The most beautiful men on the planet were on American college and university campuses. If you didn't find them there it was only because they had graduated recently enough that they were able to maintain the illusion they still belonged there: children of the North American middle and upper classes, with the sons of the *crème de la crème* of five other continents mixed in for piquancy. So he was just one of hundreds of beauties Dario had sighted in that corridor over the last couple of years, and except for a momentary pang, he didn't think anything about the young man at all. Dario merely registered his appearance, which made him think about Cody of course but at the same time, and much more to the point, about Nick, who was, since Mondays were his early afternoons when he wasn't actually in court, most likely leaving the office that very minute on his way to the gym. There was always something to look at in that corridor, even if not quite so stunning and so exactly Dario's type. Far more often than not those visions had absolutely nothing to do with him. Almost never, in fact. And a few moments later, when there was a soft knock on his office door and Dario opened it to find the young man there, he still didn't sense anything out of the ordinary. There was an obvious explanation. There always was. That day's explanation was that the seminar in modern fiction he was scheduled to teach in the fall semester was full, and the waiting list had gotten so long that he had asked the department secretaries to stop taking names several days earlier. It looked like he was going to have to go through the whole spiel again.

"Dr. Covarrubias?"

The look in the boy's cornflower blue eyes made the question mark superfluous. There was no doubt he knew who he was talking to, and it wasn't knowledge he'd just gleaned from reading the card posted beside the office door. He had known who Dario was when he'd seen him in the corridor. He would later learn that the young man's handlers had given him pictures they had taken on the street just outside the building where Nick and Dario lived. The young man was probably carrying them in his gym bag at that very moment. And he was there at Dario's office because they'd been tracking Dario ever since he left home that morning. Really, the young man couldn't have missed Dario. That the young man so obviously recognized him should have been Dario's second clue. God knows,

Dario wouldn't have forgotten a previous encounter. And in addition, the young man was too self-possessed by half. Students presented themselves in all kinds of ways, but somehow he didn't fit any of the patterns Dario was accustomed to. The distinction was a tiny one, however, and it didn't strike Dario until later. So much later, in fact, that when it finally did Dario couldn't be certain he hadn't imagined it. In his defense, Dario explained afterward that it was his last afternoon of office hours that term. And he had been up late the night before grading final exams. And he had a long list of errands to do on the way home. Most important, though Dario wouldn't have admitted to it, Nick had turned him every which way but loose that morning before either of their alarms rang and hours later he was still woozy and reeling from that onslaught. So to say he was preoccupied right that minute would be a massive understatement.

"Yes," he smiled. It was that automatic smile he had learned to flash students when he would really prefer not to be dealing with them but couldn't quite figure out how to make them go away. "What can I do for you?"

He was already turning away, heading back to his desk in the expectation that he'd be followed into the office; that the young man would sit down and present his petition. Dario even knew what that was going to sound like. He was familiar with all the approaches. In his experience, boys who looked like that one almost invariably flirted. And nobody could flirt like a student trying to get into a closed section.

"A friend asked me to drop by," he said, and the accent, though faint, was unmistakable. Which should have been Dario's third clue, because Eastern Europeans were about as common at Berkeley that year as giraffes.

"What friend?"

"He sent you this," the young man said by way of an answer and held out the envelope. Just a simple white standard sized envelope. Though there certainly should have been ominous sounding music in the background at that point, the office and the corridor outside remained silent. By the time Dario had stopped staring at his name written on the envelope in handwriting he'd given up hope of ever seeing again, the young man was gone. It didn't occur to Dario until later that he could have tried to chase the young man down in the corridor. There was only one elevator working in the building that day. Dario had waited for it for ten minutes before taking the stairs up that morning. The young man would probably have been held up waiting for it for long enough that Dario might have caught up with him.

Thinking back on the incident afterwards, Dario was absolutely certain that asking the first question that came to his mind, where and how the young man had gotten that letter in the first place, wouldn't have elicited the information he really wanted. For one thing, the young man's handlers would have told him as little as possible before sending him on his errand. And that wouldn't have included any of the things Dario wanted so desperately to know that afternoon as he stood clutching Cody's letter in his trembling, suddenly sweat-drenched, hand. Even in the unlikely event that the young man knew anything, he wouldn't have divulged it.

In retrospect, Dario would readily admit that the eventual outcome would have been the same no matter how the letter had come into his possession. They really didn't have to have it hand delivered, much less send a boy like that as their messenger. He read Cody's letter, which he would have done regardless of how it had arrived. He couldn't have resisted the lure of Cody's handwriting indefinitely. For although he had never admitted it to anyone before that afternoon, he had been waiting a long time for just such an opportunity as that envelope so tantalizingly seemed to promise. So he would have done the same thing in any event. But even afterward he continued to suppose they couldn't have been absolutely certain of that when they sat down to formulate their plan, despite everything he later learned Cody had told them about him and the additional information they had from their own investigations. After all the time that had passed and considering everything they were able to tell him about Dario's life after he left, Cody couldn't have been that certain of it himself. So the fact that they sent that boy instead of anybody else, or instead of using any other means of getting the message delivered—well, when Dario looked back on the whole thing, that seemed to indicate more than anything else just how serious they were. How determined. How obsessed with detail and how unwilling to leave anything up to chance. It was astounding, when he considered it, that they should have been willing to go to such lengths when there wasn't anything in it for them. That it was purely personal. There were no governments teetering on the brink of collapse, no advanced technology to be acquired, no economic shift in the balance, not a geo-political advantage that could possibly be foreseen. In no way could the affair have been expected to alter, even minutely, the course of history. They were not playing for any of the stakes they were perennially ready to fight and even kill for.

At least as far as Dario ever knew. Nick always said that even questioning that was paranoid. When a hotshot lawyer talked about paranoia he had to be listened to. If anybody was an expert in abnormal psychology it would have to be a former prosecutor turned defense attorney. Even so, it was astounding to consider how important Cody was to them. That never stopped being scary. So was the faint but ever-present possibility that the whole thing wasn't really over yet. Perhaps it would never be over. Maybe some morning Nick and Dario would wake up and find that they'd been left holding the bag. That what they'd experienced so far was only the tip of the iceberg and that the hull had suddenly been ripped to smithereens and the steel gray, freezing Atlantic was gushing into the holds. It was a risk that never occurred to Dario when he agreed to Cody's proposal. But Nick had his eyes open. Nick always had his eyes open, even when he was fast asleep. And Nick hadn't raised a single objection. At least not seriously.

It was the first letter Dario had gotten from Cody in a long time. For the first several years after Cody joined the Peace Corps he had written Dario regularly. Long, chatty letters came from him every week. Reading them, it was as if they had never been lovers and would always be the best of friends. Tantamount to fiction, in other words. In spite of himself, Dario answered every one of them. He suspected Cody knew he would because according to the tenets of his upbring-ing one of the cardinal sins was failing to respond to correspondence, no matter how little appreciated, in a timely manner. The possible consequences of such an infraction were too grave to contemplate, much less risk. Going straight to hell, even the Marxist-Leninist one his parents subscribed to, paled in compari-son. There was another reason, too, a much more compelling one, for answering Cody's letters, though Dario wouldn't have admitted it to anyone, not even under torture, and never alluded to it in any of his painstakingly composed replies. He could hardly bear to think of the weakness that it seemed to signify on his part. He knew Cody recognized it for what it was. Concealing it would have been impossible. Dario knew that he read it between every line despite his obsessive care to keep the words themselves as neutral as the ones Cody wrote to him. Cody was no fool, while Dario undoubtedly still was. He finally stopped answering Cody's letters not long after meeting Nick, though his friends had been trying to convince him to do it for a long time. When he stopped answering Cody's letters, Cody stopped writing them, completely without recrimination and apparently without regret. Not another word passed between them, and the total lack of curiosity on Cody's part this seemed to indicate would have been devastating if not for the fact that at the time Dario was so completely distracted by Nick's totally unexpected attentions that he was incapable of thinking of anything else.

So he had to consider long and hard whether he truly wanted to open that letter. Because until the moment the young man handed it to him, the brilliant eyes and shy little smile all but irresistible, Dario had believed that it was all over. He had spent years telling himself that this was so, insisting that even if the opportunity arose through some all too easily imagined miracle to turn the clock back to that earlier time he wouldn't avail himself of it. One glance at that handwriting was all it took. He sat in the silence of his office cringing at how wrong he'd been to think he had ever actually stopped caring about Cody. Everybody else in San Francisco thought he was the luckiest man in the world because he'd landed a prize like Nick. But here he was, about to burst into tears over someone else.

Even as Dario opened the letter, part of him couldn't help wondering why he was doing it. Just because it had been delivered and was in his hands? That didn't signify any responsibility on his part. He could toss it into the trash. He could lay it on top of his desk with other correspondence he intended to leave until September. Why open it? Why now? He certainly knew the risk it represented. And why wasn't he resisting harder? Then again, why had Cody written after all that time? And why had he insisted on having his letter hand delivered by a young man who was, at least physically, his unmistakable avatar? Cody had to have known how reluctant Dario would be. But he had also known, or at least been willing to bet, that curiosity would eventually win out over that reluctance. In retrospect, Dario decided that they must have had a contingency plan in case Cody had miscalculated. But that afternoon, such a thing was beyond his comprehension. Since the outcome depended not only on what he did but how quickly he did it, they must have made alternative plans. Nick once suggested that these might well have entailed kidnapping. And he was only half joking when he said it.

By the time Dario got home that afternoon he knew what he wanted to do. His next step was to face Nick, who was certain to have an opinion about it and to express that opinion with as much force as he considered necessary. Considering the circumstances, and knowing how much force Nick had historically brought to bear in discussing matters of far less magnitude, this threatened to be an outburst that registered somewhere well up on the Richter scale. He was already home from the gym. Dario heard him clattering around in the kitchen as he walked in the front door. It was Nick's turn to fix dinner. Dario went in, clutching the letter in a sweaty hand, nervous as a cat.

Still pumped from the gym and chopping vegetables bare-chested, Nick was dazzling as always. Seeing him like that made Dario a little weak in the knees. But that wasn't all that had gone limp. His resolve flagged as well.

"What's wrong?"

Dario handed over the letter.

"What is it? Mash note from one of your students? You should be used to that by now. Besides, nobody's ever going to top the ones I sent you."

That was undoubtedly true. As far as it went.

"Read it."

Then, because he suddenly had a blinding headache, Dario went to the bathroom for some aspirin and on to the bedroom to lie down. Nick didn't follow him.

"You realize it's a completely irrational request."

It was Nick's courtroom voice. Dario looked up from his dinner plate almost expecting to see him in his charcoal suit and three hundred dollar shoes. That's the impression Nick's courtroom voice always gave.

"Yes."

"About par for the course for him, isn't it?"

Dario nodded.

"But you'll go anyway."

It was a statement of fact, not a question. Dario knew Nick was framing it like that because he had understood his intentions from that first moment in the kitchen. Dario could have protested that he'd made no such decision yet, that he wouldn't dream of doing such a thing without consulting his husband, but he knew that Nick would realize it wasn't true. He would only seem ridiculous. And it would be stupid to add to Nick's annoyance that way.

"I suppose," he said. "Yes, I'll go."

"Why?" Nick riveted him to his chair with those eyes.

"You read it. He says he needs my help."

"Yes," Nick nodded. "*Your* help specifically. I wonder what it is he thinks you can do for him that no one else can."

"Right."

"Because I would have thought that sometime over the last several years he'd find someone else to bail him out."

"I know," Dario admitted. "That makes me especially curious."

"So your motives aren't purely altruistic."

"God, Nick, whose ever are?"

"Point taken," Nick grinned. Nobody enjoyed taking something simple and complicating it more than he did.

"You don't think I should go."

Actually, Dario didn't have any idea what Nick was thinking at that point. He simply assumed it. He knew how he would feel if Nick got a letter like that. He also knew that if Nick voiced the least objection, he'd forget the whole thing. He sat there halfway hoping that's exactly what would happen and he could start to breathe again. *My husband won't let me*—the perfect excuse.

"I didn't say that."

"What then?"

"You know," Nick said, pretending he was thinking through it as he spoke, "maybe it's something you need to get out of your system."

"What's that supposed to mean?"

"Come on, Dario, don't get all defensive. Nobody's accusing anybody of anything. I'm just trying to put myself in your position. To understand why you'd even consider going off on this wild goose chase. And it seems to me that after the way he left you—well, let's face it: there's just so much you can resolve without a confrontation of some kind. And you never really have confronted him, have you?"

"No."

"I wasn't there, babe, but I know how it was. Hell, I could probably quote your side of the conversation verbatim. You'd rather kill yourself than make a scene. So I expect you mostly kept your mouth shut and gritted your teeth and acted all patient and understanding. You were probably hoping that if you were enough of a gentleman about it he'd suddenly turn into one too and forget the whole thing. Sooner or later he'd have to come to his senses, and as long as you hadn't burnt any bridges he'd be able to crawl across them on his way back to you."

Dario shrugged. Nick's unerring instincts again.

"When I met you," Nick continued, "he still hadn't given you any encouragement along those lines. But at least you could finally stop waiting for him to. I know how arrogant that sounds on my part. But it wasn't really about me. It could have been anybody. You were finally ready to move on, that's all. But, and here's what's crucial, you hadn't really resolved anything. That's what you still need from him. That's why you want to do this."

So Nick had it all worked out. Nice and logical. Nothing to worry about. Dario knew it was supposed to make him feel better. But Nick's reasonableness made the whole thing seem even more illicit.

"But it's still irrational," Nick said. "On his part, I mean. Asking you for this after so long. Getting in contact with you that way. Giving you no way of responding except to just show up. Or not. Talk about manipulation."

"Exactly. So you think I shouldn't go."

"Don't put words in my mouth."

"You think I should go."

"I didn't say that, either."

"Then what?"

"Do what you need to do, sweetheart. Only you know what that is."

"But I honestly have no idea."

"Is that the truth, or are you afraid you still can't say no to him?"

"Of course I can say no to him."

"I know that," Nick said. "But do you know it? Really?"

II

Anyone observing Dario would have thought he was a traveling horticulturist from the painstaking way he examined the stock in the hotel florist's shop the morning after his arrival. There were long stemmed red roses, extravagant sprays of orchids, exotic looking birds of paradise, strange, presumably tropical, things he couldn't identify, and banks of mixed bouquets. But he was only killing time, nervously checking his watch every couple of minutes or so, anxious to get on with things. And, as usual, ready far too early. One of his major character flaws. He was constitutionally incapable of unpunctuality. God knows he had tried. But too many generations of schoolmasters in his pedigree made it impossible. He had spotted what he wanted the minute he stepped into the shop. He'd known what to look for the night before, as soon as he'd read Cody's second letter.

He had always been a nervous flyer, even at the best of times. And this couldn't possibly be thought of as deserving such a designation. All the way to Mexico City on the plane, Dario pondered what Nick had told him when they first discussed the trip and repeated just before he boarded the flight. Nick instructed him to tell Cody all about their perfect life. Dario knew this was Nick's way of telling him that no matter what passed between Cody and him, he mustn't forget his life back in San Francisco. It was Nick's warning shot. Nick's signal that as supportive as he appeared, he didn't trust Cody and he'd stand for no nonsense. Dario could only wonder if Nick thought he'd already crossed the line.

Contemplating this possibility generated a level of internal disturbance that was even greater than the turbulence caused by the thunderstorms they flew through. By the time he stepped into the terminal in Mexico City, Dario was ready to crawl out of his skin. He very nearly went straight from baggage claim to ticketing to book an immediate flight back home. No request Cody might make was worth putting Dario's relationship with Nick at risk.

But Nick would never have let him leave in the first place if there had really been any danger. At least that's what Dario believed. Or wanted to believe.

The taxi ride to the hotel settled him a little. Not that it was soothing in itself. Not even close. It was more a case of being distracted from his anxiety by the noise, filth, and chaos that clamored at the car from all directions. He recalled Cody once describing Mexico City as being a modern equivalent of Dante's Inferno, circle on circle of misery, and that old quip came back full force that late afternoon. It was Dario's first trip there in nearly a decade. The city was still recovering from the great earthquake. Signs of the devastation were everywhere. Other than that, the only differences he could see were thicker traffic, dirtier air, and larger numbers of beggars on the streets. He knew it was inexcusably bourgeois of him, but all he could think of, surveying the surroundings, was that he was glad he didn't have to live in a place like that. He cringed at what he knew his mother would have said.

Contrary to the expectations and apparent intentions of at least half the motorists they shared the streets with, the taxi driver got them without incident to the hotel Cody had recommended in his letter, though there was what seemed like a close brush with disaster about every eight seconds. It was the hotel where he and Cody had spent what they always referred to as their honeymoon. This was a detail Dario had kept to himself, rationalizing that it had no bearing on current circumstances and gun shy of Nick's reaction. Dario's honeymoon with Nick was in Paris. That hotel was exquisite, and meeting some of Nick's French-speaking cousins was unexpectedly entertaining. This hotel looked the same as Dario remembered it, a gracefully aging structure with rain-stained pink stucco walls, sun bleached clay tiles on the roof, and statuary and babbling fountains clotting the gardens. It looked like it had been there for a thousand years and would be for a thousand more, a fitting accommodation for minor royalty and princes of the church. Much of the older part of Mexico City gave that impression.

Dario honestly couldn't have said what he was expecting. After all, Cody hadn't said anything specific in his letter about when and where they'd actually meet. And with no way of contacting Cody about his travel plans, it would have been unreasonable of Dario to expect him to be waiting at the airport or in the hotel lobby on his arrival. At least that's what Dario told himself in an attempt to rationalize away the sense of anticlimax and disappointment he felt on entering the lobby to see it empty except for the employees, feelings compounded by his increasing discomfort as he considered how totally in the dark he was. If he had known that the people involved were familiar with his travel plans down to the last detail, from the amount of luggage he had brought and the appearance of every piece of it to the exact second the wheels of his plane had touched the tarmac to the license number of the taxi that had brought him to the hotel—that, indeed, he'd been accompanied every step of the way, from the car that followed unseen from their own block on Nob Hill to the airport to the couple sitting four rows ahead of him on the airplane to the man behind him in the customs line to the one who helped him flag down that particular taxi outside the terminal—he might have felt differently.

As it was, a letter waiting for him with the concierge, even one addressed to him in Cody's handwriting, only emphasized his feelings of being alone, far away from home, confused and anxious. He didn't open it until he was alone in his room, a room at the rear of the hotel which looked out and down at immaculately manicured gardens and a swimming pool that wouldn't have looked out of place in front of the Taj Mahal. The letter welcomed him to Mexico City, expressed the hope that he'd find his accommodations comfortable, suggested some likely selections from the menu in the hotel dining room for his dinner, wished him a restful night, and told him that he'd be picked up in front of the hotel at nine o'clock sharp the next morning by a taxi driver he'd identify himself to by carrying a bunch of flowers he'd buy from the shop in the hotel lobby.

Dario checked his watch a last time and picked out a bunch of daisies. That's what Cody had brought the first and only time he ever bought Dario flowers, and he was pretty sure someone involved knew it. He paid the proprietress, a woman who looked like she'd be a stockbroker if she lived in New York or a member of parliament if she lived in London. She obviously disapproved of his selection. Her smile, though gracious, betrayed a telltale glimmer of disdain, presumably at Dario's miserliness. He could obviously afford something more elaborate and she apparently considered it a kind of insult that he hadn't spent more money. Dario smiled back at her, took the flowers, and stepped out the grand front doors of the hotel just as the bells in the church tower across the square were beginning to strike the hour.

There were well over a dozen taxis lined up in front of the hotel, but Dario only hesitated for a moment before a tall young driver nodded at him in a particularly authoritative fashion and gestured toward the daisies. As he shut Dario into the back seat of the light blue Volkswagen he handed over another envelope. Dario was still fumbling with it when the driver pulled into the street, making a violent 180 degree turn against traffic. The force of the maneuver nearly gave Dario whiplash.

Cody's unmistakable handwriting again. More instructions. It had already been arranged that the driver would drop him at a park. He was to wander around there looking touristy for exactly thirty-seven minutes. He should buy a copy of that morning's *El Imparcial* from a street vendor and carry it folded in the crook of his left arm with the second half of the headline showing. He should carry his flowers in his right hand. A young man wearing a navy blue sweater and wheeling a Peugeot bicycle would speak to him, but he should pretend not to speak Spanish. He would be picked up by another taxi at the northeast corner of the park at precisely nine forty-eight.

Just like in the movies or on T.V. As far as Dario was concerned it was too elaborate even for one of Cody's practical jokes. By that time the driver's erratic maneuvering had him completely disoriented, and though Dario had been in the car less than five minutes he had no idea where they were or how far they had come from the hotel. He knew he could get back simply by getting out, hailing another cab, and giving the driver the name of his hotel, so he wasn't actually concerned about that. But he had to get out of this taxi first. And alive, more to the point. Which seemed less and less likely with each gear shift, each lurching change of direction, each squeal of the tires as they rounded another corner. Each second, each foot they traveled, added to his alarm. He was just about to demand that the driver stop the car and let him out when they screeched to a stop and his eyes focused long enough for him to see grass and trees surrounding an operatic looking statue of a man astride a rearing horse.

Before he could fumble in his wallet for the fare, the driver told him in perfect, unaccented English that it had already been paid and that Dario wouldn't need to pay for the next cab either. As Dario stepped out of the car, the young man apologized for his driving, astounding Dario nearly into unconsciousness by ending his speech with "but when in Rome" a split second before roaring back into traffic.

Dario was more relieved than he could ever remember just to be standing still. He gripped the daisies in a sweaty palm and wiped his forehead with the back of his other hand, which still clutched Cody's letter. It occurred to him that he didn't recall the instructions very well and it was apparently crucial not to make any mistakes in following them, so he found a bench and sat down for a brief review.

He didn't much like the way things were going. He had promised Nick that he'd bail out the minute anything happened that made him uneasy. There was no question that he'd reached that point. What kept him from hailing another cab and heading back to his hotel, or even to the airport, was his certainty that things hadn't yet reached the point where Nick would have been uneasy himself. And as he stood there clutching the daisies it occurred to him that Nick's discomfort was the standard by which the situation should be judged. The more Dario considered it, the more convinced he was that he'd just been momentarily spooked. By the time he worked that out and reread his instructions it was time to move. Time to make like a tourist, time to buy that morning's El Imparcial, time to figure out, without being conspicuous about it, which was the northwest corner of the park.

The second cab ride was identical to the first except that it was almost over before Dario had time to skim the next letter from Cody and panic again and decide that whatever Nick's limits were, Dario had so totally exceeded his own that for the sake of his sanity he'd better curl his tail between his legs and head for home. But the moment he stepped from the taxi, sweating profusely despite the cool breezes off the mountains surrounding the city, he saw the church, the market stalls, and the street photographer just as the letter had described them. And almost without thinking about it he took a couple of deep breaths and began to follow his instructions. He meandered across the shabby little square in the general direction of the church, consciously attempting not to give the impression that it was his objective, and further, that he was in no hurry to get anywhere. He stopped at a few of the stalls, even going so far as to bargain half-heartedly for a small painting of fishing boats in a harbor overlooked by rows of white stucco cottages on a terraced hillside.

He absent mindedly inspected a few more items in a few more stalls. He tossed his copy of *El Imparcial* into a trash can outside a small shop. He stood looking at the old church from across the square, raising a hand to shade his eyes from the sun. He pretended to study its Romanesque dome and twin towers. He concentrated on not checking his wristwatch every three minutes as he charted a meandering course toward it. Eventually he sauntered toward the wide steps in front of the church, stopping just before he reached them to speak to the photographer stationed there and pat his flea bitten little burro. He pretended not to speak any Spanish as he negotiated. He posed awkwardly. He paid the man for the polaroids even though he knew he looked terrible in them. Haunted, he thought. Pursued by demons. Or perhaps just ghosts.

He didn't open the letter he'd received from the photographer until he was inside the church.

Once again, a Volkswagen. This one was yellow. It was equipped with an amazing assortment of dents and lacked a muffler. Once again, a letter. Dario barely bothered to skim it. He didn't even look out the windows as the car rattled along the bumpy pavement, just folded the letter and slid it back into the envelope. Cody was making it too hard. He was asking too much putting Dario through all this cloak and dagger stuff. He had to have known that when he wrote all the letters. Dario was furious. He just wanted to go home and forget the whole thing. But he hated the thought of Cody sitting somewhere shaking his head about how Dario had let him down because he was a wimp who couldn't cut it and how he should have known it all along.

It made no sense. If Cody needed Dario's help bad enough to drag him here from San Francisco, why put him through all this? Why piss him off and frighten him? What was the point? He couldn't begin to fathom it. He was so preoccupied he didn't notice it when the car stopped. The driver had to speak to him twice. There was no telling what he'd have done left to his own devices, but the minute he climbed out of the car the red haired woman he'd been told to expect took his arm and led him toward the sidewalk café he could see, just as the latest letter had described it, halfway down the block.

The woman spoke in French, talking to him as if he were her lover or husband, and as though no reply was necessary to anything she said. They found a table in the café and she ordered *café au lait* for both of them and a basket of *pan dulces*. Dario sat back in his chair and tried to get his bearings. His temples were throbbing, his guts churning, his knees shaky.

"I know you have a great many questions," the woman said quietly in English once the waiter had left them alone. "They'll all be answered. Very soon. There's just one more short ride."

"Not another taxi," Dario groaned in spite of himself.

"No," she laughed, running a hand through her thick, lustrous hair in a gesture that looked quintessentially European. "No, Dear Dr. Covarrubias. No more taxis for you today."

"Thank God."

"I can't stand them myself."

"I'm used to the taxis in San Francisco," he said. "The drivers there are only partially insane. And the cabs themselves don't seem like quite such deathtraps. Though I have to admit the drivers speak better English here."

"I know," she nodded. "Every time I'm here, I have to get used to it all over again. Ordinarily I make it a point never to use taxis outside Europe."

"Probably a good plan," Dario said. "So this isn't home for you?"

"No," she said in a manner that politely but firmly communicated that no additional personal questions would be answered. "Please listen carefully, Dr. Covarrubias. Your friend told us that by now you might be starting to get cold feet. Which would be perfectly understandable. God knows I would be in your place. So please let me assure you that although this roundabout is absolutely necessary, it doesn't signify that anything illegal is involved or that you are in any danger whatever. I wish I could explain more, but I'm not allowed to. I hope you'll trust me enough to stay with us for just a little while longer."

"Could I at least know your name?" Dario asked. "You know mine."

"Call me Daisy," she smiled.

Ingesting some sugar and caffeine provided only momentarily relief. It was startlingly obvious to Dario, sitting across from that elegant woman and recalling everything that had taken place since he left the hotel, that this was a good sized operation. Lots of people were involved, and he had an unmistakable impression of careful, detailed planning. It could only mean one thing. The people behind it were professionals. It was fascinating and it was scary, but above all it was puzzling. Because what did it all—what could it possibly—have to do with Cody? And if these people were so good at this kind of thing, whatever it was, what did they need Dario for? And who the hell were they anyway?

Daisy glanced at her watch, making it look like a casual, unthinking gesture, and Dario was shocked to notice that it was a Rolex. It was in character for her role, but it told him still more about the resources these people had at their disposal, whoever they were.

"Almost time to go," she said. "Are you up to one more ride?"

"Why not?"

She took a final sip of *café au lait*, opened her purse, took out a compact and lipstick, and spent several moments carefully touching herself up.

"The car is halfway up the block," she said. "You can't miss it. A red Alfa-Romeo 2600 Spider. I hope you don't mind traveling with the top down."

Just like the one Nick had recently bought, Dario mused. He didn't even bother being surprised.

"Is there a driver?"

"I'm coming with you. I'm your driver."

"Thank God."

"Ready?"

Dario heard it as a statement of fact. Or perhaps a command. He shrugged. He fished his wallet out of his jacket pocket. He was beginning to feel in character himself—at least a little. Whoever he was at that point would undoubtedly just leave a wad of that ridiculous looking money on the table without bothering to count it.

Then they were off down the sidewalk arm in arm, chatting in French that suddenly felt as normal to him as breathing just as he remembered doing on his Paris honeymoon with Nick. The French of his boyhood on the shores of Lake

Geneva, for that matter. They talked about things that caught their eyes in the shop windows and what kind of weather the day promised. Despite its age, the car was gleaming, as spotless as if it had just rolled out of the showroom. It truly was a twin of Nick's pride and joy. Daisy was no demented taxi driver. She handled the car exactly as you would have expected a woman who looked like that and lived in that place and owned a car like that to drive. Not slowly but not recklessly, either. Smoothly and competently. It was almost soothing riding along with the fresh breeze slipstreaming past and Vivaldi—another signal from Cody—on the stereo.

Their destination was a high rise apartment building. It reminded Dario of something out of a 1930's magazine feature about what life in the future would be like. Daisy steered the Alfa-Romeo into an underground parking garage. In the elevator Dario got nervous again. After the elevator there was a long, plush carpeted, silent corridor. He clutched the daisies, unable to imagine how Cody had ended up in a place like that. The prospect of him waiting on the other side of that anonymous door brought a lump to Dario's throat. At the same time he thought about Nick and wondered if what he was feeling constituted some new, advanced state of emotional infidelity.

Daisy ushered him down a narrow entry hall into a living room bathed with sunlight which streamed in through an entire wall of floor to ceiling windows— acres of glass with half Mexico City stretching into the distance beyond. Dario hadn't paid attention in the elevator and couldn't begin to guess what floor they were on, but it was obviously a number well into two digits.

The man standing with his back to that view wasn't Cody.

"Your friend said you'd bring daisies," he smiled. His heavily accented English reminded Dario of his father and uncles. "Welcome."

"Thank you," Dario said. "I think."

"Indeed," the man said, still smiling. "You've been an extremely good sport, Dr. Covarrubias. Please accept my apologies for all the drama. I can only excuse it by assuring you that it was necessary."

"I suppose I'll have to take your word on that."

"Oh, I assure you. And please allow me to introduce myself. I am Col. Alvarez."

The rank threw Dario. The man was sleekly handsome and roughly Dario's own age. He was wearing a suit that had to have come straight from Paris or Milan and made him look like a banker. But it wasn't only the clothing that Dario found disorienting. He'd have expected a Latin American colonel to be much older than this, to look dissipated and lethargic, to reek of cigar smoke and corruption and a thinly veiled propensity for a particularly sadistic form of violence. There was none of that stereotypical iconography about this man. If anything, its absence frightened Dario more than the B-movie variation could have. No mistake about it. This was someone to take very seriously indeed. And what was there about Cody's current predicament that called for the involvement of someone like this?

"Cody calls me Andre," he said. "Perhaps you'll do the same."

"I suppose you should call me Dario."

"Very well. Why don't we sit down, Dario?" He indicated a pair of Barcelona chairs in the far corner of the room. "It's a magnificent view, isn't it? One of the world's great cities."

"Yes."

"Cody told me you'd be a good sport about all this. He said you'd be very patient. But I can tell that your patience is wearing thin. And for good reason. So I won't presume on it any longer. I'm prepared to answer your questions. Now, Dario. This minute. Anything at all you wish to know about this business."

Being given *carte blanche* like that, or at least the appearance of it, served only to inhibit Dario. For a long moment he sat trying to find a comfortable position in his chair and wondering where to start.

"It's all right," Alvarez said. "You're perfectly safe here. No one intends to harm you in any way."

Time would tell. Interesting, though, that Alvarez would even raise the issue. Dario wondered if he looked that anxious. Or was the mere mention of the possibility a threat in itself?

"Cody isn't here, is he?" Dario asked, feeling his heart sink.

"No, he is not. And please believe me when I tell you how much I regret the misrepresentation. It was to insure his safety as well as your own. If we could have guaranteed that without deceiving you in this way, I assure you we would have. But bringing you directly to him was, unfortunately, out of the question."

Alvarez was as smooth and sincere, not to mention as well groomed, as any soap opera villain. Or any big screen Mafioso.

"What kind of trouble is he in?"

"No trouble of any kind," Alvarez said, his voice betraying not a single false vibration.

"You'll forgive me if I'm a little skeptical."

"Under the circumstances I'd be surprised if you weren't," Alvarez laughed, eyes glinting like polished stones.

"All right," Dario said. "Well, assuming that's true, why would he need my help? And why all this?"

"Once again, Dario, everything you have been through this morning, the arrangements for your trip to Mexico City, and even the manner in which you were originally contacted, were planned for the purpose of guaranteeing the safety of all parties involved. Including not only yourself but Mr. Romanovsky, I might add. Please believe me that your safety is as important to us in this matter as our own. None of the precautions we have taken has any bearing except on the request that Cody wishes to make of you, which is of a purely personal nature."

"And you can't tell me what that is?"

"That's not entirely true. I could. It might even make all this easier for you. But Cody asked me not to."

"I see," Dario said, but of course he didn't. He wasn't even sure what to ask next. Nick was the attorney in the household, and Dario scrambled to formulate his probable line of questioning.

"You say you're a colonel?"

"Correct."

"Exactly what kind of colonel? If you don't mind my asking."

"Not at all. I am a colonel in the Nicaraguan Army. My present posting is Assistant Military Attache with my country's mission here in Mexico City."

"The Sandinistas?"

"Yes. Cody didn't think that would be a problem for you. Considering your family connections."

"I see."

"You seem dubious."

"I've applied for U.S. citizenship," Dario said. "I'd be extremely reluctant to do anything that might jeopardize that. And there's Nick to think of."

"Of course," Alvarez said. "I warned Cody about all that. However, it's not insurmountable."

"No?"

"Certainly not."

"But you're not prepared to explain what makes you able to say that," Dario said.

"Alas, no," Alvarez chuckled.

The man's confidence forced Dario's hand.

"Military Attache," he said. "Isn't that just a euphemism for spy?"

"The term my colleagues and I prefer is intelligence officer," Alvarez chuckled. "But please, don't get the wrong idea. I'm no James Bond."

So Dario's suspicion had been correct. This confirmation might be either good or bad news. It all depended.

"Is this official business for you?"

"That's not so easy to say. My superiors are aware of what I'm involved in. And they approve of it. But it's not a matter of state business. Quite the contrary. In fact, part of my job is to make certain that it doesn't become a matter of state business."

"I don't think I understand."

"I'm not surprised. It's a complicated situation, to say the least. The story is a long one. Perhaps it would be simplest for me to tell it from the beginning. Would you like some refreshment while you hear it?"

"No, thank you."

"Very well. This business started some years ago, when Cody joined the United States Peace Corps."

"I already know that part," Dario said.

"Indeed," Alvarez smiled. "The two of you had been lovers for several years at that time. You had just finished your Ph.D., and he had just finished his M.A."

"That's right."

Incidentally, I've read your dissertation. The influence of Edward Carpenter on Christopher Isherwood. Most original. I see you think I'm flattering you.

Not at all. You have a fine intellect and a novel way of looking at things. Truly, I couldn't have initiated this operation just on Cody's whim. I had to have some objective measure of you to present to my superiors. They knew of your parents' work, of course. That was helpful testimony. But it was more a historical artifact than anything. It didn't tell us anything about you. Apples sometimes fall quite far from the tree. I'm happy to say that once I shared the results of my investigations, my superiors were as impressed with you as I had become."

"Really."

"Maintain your skepticism to whatever extent you choose," Alvarez laughed. "It only reinforces our original impression of you. I hope eventually to persuade you of the sincerity of our regard. Now, back to our story. Would you tell me what you thought of our friend's joining the Peace Corps? Aside from the personal considerations, which you may not wish to discuss with me, and which aren't really germane to my narrative."

"I guess I thought he was crazy."

"Why was that?"

"Well, he was such a commie, if you'll pardon the expression. I didn't see how he'd stand it out there. I was sure that sooner or later he'd find it intolerable fronting for the U.S. Government. Not to mention far too restrictive. I expected him to become frustrated because his bosses wouldn't let him do the things necessary to truly help the people he was working with. He'd eventually end up doing or saying the wrong thing and getting sent home. Either that, or he'd quit."

"And you were right to think all that," Alvarez nodded. "More or less. He did find his situation too restrictive. There was some difficulty with his superiors over it. And they did send him home. Or at least they thought they had. But before the blowup he'd made certain contacts."

"What contacts?" Dario didn't like the sound of it. The word itself called to mind shadowy figures skulking around in East Berlin or someplace like it, smoking too much, speaking in cryptic sounding epigrams, and greeting each other with arcane passwords and secret handshakes.

"Well, as I'm sure you're aware there were many different groups active in Central America at the time. The local regimes were extremely corrupt and becoming more unpopular by the day. It doesn't really matter which group Cody approached. It doesn't exist anymore. In Nicaragua, the Somozas are gone now. I played my own small part in making that happen. Let's just say Cody ended up working with what the Americans would have referred to at the time as a leftist guerilla organization. You look surprised."

"I am surprised."

"Why?"

"I know what you're thinking."

"You do?"

"Sure," Dario said. "I should have figured it out long before now. I mean, it's exactly the kind of thing Cody would have done. But you see, middle class Americans don't actually ever do anything like that. Talk about it, fantasize a little—sure. But that's all. They leave it up to the guys in the movies or on T.V. to actually get their hands dirty."

"And of course they look so good doing it," Alvarez laughed.

"That, too."

"I see your point, of course. But for the sake of argument, you do agree, don't you, that he had—how shall I put it? A predisposition?—to do just such a thing?"

"Maybe," Dario said, then wilted under the gaze. "All right. Certainly he did. If I've ever known anybody who actually could have gone and done something like that, it's Cody."

"Good," Alvarez nodded. "It makes the rest of what I have to tell you that much simpler."

"Are you trying to tell me that he's in Nicaragua?"

"Yes."

"And next you're going to say that I have to go there if I want to see him."

"Yes."

"This is too crazy," Dario said, starting to panic. "I don't see how I could do that."

"Dario, just listen to the rest of the story before you make up your mind."

Dario didn't speak. He was imagining Nick's reaction to this proposal, and it wasn't a pleasant thing to contemplate. Mexico City was one thing. But Managua was something else altogether. There were all kinds of possible consequences. With Reagan in the White House, travel to Nicaragua was problematic at best.

"Please, Dario, hear me out."

"All right," Dario said. "It can't hurt to listen."

"In those days I was a young agent with what eventually became Sandinista Intelligence. My mission was to help coordinate activities among various smaller groups in the countryside. That's how I met Cody. What's the matter?"

"I didn't realize you'd known him before all this."

"Oh, yes. I remember, for instance, how sad he was when you stopped answering his letters. I was able to do certain things that helped put his mind at rest."

"What do you mean?"

"I arranged to have you observed."

"Observed?"

"Don't be alarmed. It was a very low level operation. In a matter of a few days, I was able to provide him with enough information about your new situation to explain the lack of correspondence."

"You found out about Nick. You told him about Nick."

"Correct. He agreed that under the circumstances it was to be expected that you had stopped writing. He saw that there was no cause for alarm, and he realized that in fairness he should have been expecting it. He was fine after that."

As Alvarez explained it, Dario heard a note creep into his voice that made him curious about the nature of his relationship with Cody. A Sandinista agent investigating the ex-lover of a Peace Corps volunteer turned leftist guerilla was an unusual scenario to say the least. And to conduct such an investigation from the wilds of revolution-torn Central America had taken some doing. Suddenly he knew his next question.

"Were you and Cody lovers?"

"Not at that point," Alvarez said, smiling sheepishly. "That was earlier, and only for a short while. We weren't really suited. And the circumstances couldn't have been worse. Though I have to admit that it's one of my fonder memories."

"I see."

"Cody was—well, I don't have to explain him to you. You knew him better than anyone."

"I'm not so sure of that."

"But you did. Truly. How could you doubt it? Now tell me, what would you expect Cody to have done as a part of a leftist guerilla group?"

"I don't know. Probably end up running the whole show."

"Exactly."

"You're joking, of course."

"Not at all. Exaggerating, perhaps. But only a little. Not so much at all. Eventually he became extremely important in the opposition movement. Important enough that the CIA tried more than once to neutralize him. You're familiar with that terminology?"

"Yes," Dario said, a chill running down his spine.

"I've always found it a particularly obnoxious euphemism."

"You're going to have to forgive me, but this whole thing is getting to be too much to swallow."

"I understand. But let me assure you, it's all true. And I'm afraid it's quite likely that although my organization went to great lengths recently to make it appear that he had died at the hands of a right wing death squad, the CIA may still be after him. That's the main reason for all the precautions we've taken in this matter—all that silliness we put you through this morning. Quite elementary tradecraft to be sure, but in a city such as this enormously effective. We couldn't take any chances, you see. We had to make sure they weren't observing you. It wasn't easy. Cody insisted that he had described you to us quite thoroughly, but he'd left out the most important detail. When I realized how exactly you resemble a certain famous Mexican film star and how difficult that would make staging your disappearance, I almost aborted the entire operation."

"I don't suppose Cody's ever heard of Jorge Rivero."

"No," Alvarez said, "probably not."

"But your response was ingenious," Dario said. "Dr. Dario Covarrubias leaves his hotel for a day of sightseeing, and the next thing anyone knows, a certain Mexican actor meets a glamorous woman for coffee and pastries."

"Of course the real Mr. Rivero isn't even in the country right now."

"I'm sure you know exactly where he is," Dario said. "And how long he's gone for."

"Timing is everything in matters such as these."

"All right," Dario said, "I get the picture. But I still don't understand why I'm here."

"It's very simple really," Alvarez said. "Cody is considered a great hero of our revolutionary movement, albeit a little known one. And this matter is very important to him. So my people and I are expediting it."

"You're very good at not telling me what I want to know," Dario said.

"I'm sorry. But Cody wishes to explain it all himself."

"In Nicaragua."

"In Managua," Alvarez said. "You'll be perfectly safe. You'll only be away from your hotel for twenty-four hours or so. You'll travel as a guest of the Nicaraguan Government and under its protection. I will accompany you. Officially, of course, you will never have been there. You will never have left Mexico City. Your passport won't be stamped. There'll be no visa issued. As far as anyone will ever know or be able to discover, you will simply have spent a night away from your hotel. You'll be able to call your Mr. Romanovsky from your accommodations in Managua and assure him of your continued safety."

Dario was preparing to state his objections when Alvarez pulled a familiar looking envelope out of his chest pocket.

III

Time seemed to stand still that afternoon, as if they were suspended in it as well as space aboard the small aircraft. It had taken what seemed like an eternity to climb over the mountains surrounding Mexico City. The noise and vibration from the engines and propellers made Dario feel like he was trapped inside a washing machine on a spin cycle without end. It was all he could do not to scream. The only thing that kept his mouth shut was his fear that once he started he'd never stop. He forced himself think about Cody. How would he be able to help Cody if he went to pieces?

Eventually they crossed the coast, filmy and insubstantial below them in the haze. After that there was nothing to see outside the cramped cabin but the endless sky and the endless water, which met at some indiscernible point in the tropical distance. There was nothing out there Dario could identify with certainty as the horizon, just an infinity of sky and water. A landless planet. Inside the plane, though it was quieter once they stopped climbing, it still felt like taking a long trip crammed into the back seat of a clapped out, twenty year old Volkswagen. Soon after takeoff, Alvarez explained that their flight path would describe an arc, not the shortest distance between Mexico City and Managua but one that wouldn't overfly any neighboring countries, unfortunately but necessarily adding several hours to their flying time. Just another of his precautions, he said, and Dario didn't think any more about it at the time. Later, of course, he understood the true nature of the precaution Alvarez had taken and just whose suspicions and objections it was intended to neutralize. But in spite of the colonel's explanation, Dario wasn't at all prepared for the length of that flight or the sheer, mind-numbing tedium of it.

They seemed to have nothing more to say to each other. It was the kind of uneasy silence that inevitably follows too much intimacy—involuntary intimacy on Dario's part—between people who have just met, and the slightest pressure of his companion's shoulder against his in that confined space was excruciating, as if in the process of their negotiations Dario had been stripped down to one raw nerve. Worst of all, the neatly combed backs of the two blond pilots' heads were a constant, disquieting reminder of the blond he had left back home and the one he was on the last leg of his journey to see, though their soft murmuring in Russian gradually seemed less sinister than at first. Eventually, the droning of the engines and the hissing of the slipstream outside the comically flimsy plexiglass windows lulled him to sleep.

Earlier they had driven to the airport in a dark blue Mercedes with windows so deeply tinted no one could possibly have seen inside short of an x-ray technician. Instead of dropping them at any of the main terminal entrances, the driver, whom Dario recognized as the handsome young cabby who'd picked him up at the hotel that morning, took them around to a private entrance, pulling up so close to the unmarked metal door that they were only exposed to view for a few seconds. Given what Dario had seen of the layout of the terminal buildings, any onlooker would have had to have binoculars. Anyone close enough to distinguish them without such assistance would have been totally exposed to their own view. But unless Dario missed his guess, Alvarez had already made sure that there would be no one positioned to observe them even for so brief a time.

Inside the building, there were none of the usual airport formalities. A dark haired, dark eyed beauty in a business suit only slightly less chic than the one Alvarez was wearing nodded as they entered a spartan little room. He handed Alvarez a walkie-talkie. Alvarez spoke only his name into the device. Dario couldn't decipher anything he overheard through the crackling in its speaker. The exchange didn't take place in English or Spanish. Could Alvarez be fluent in Russian? Dario supposed it made sense for a Nicaraguan intelligence officer, but this explanation didn't ease his anxiety. After handing the radio back to the young man, Alvarez smiled.

"The plane's been refueled and they're doing final flight checks. We'll board in about five minutes. If you need to use the facilities, you'd better go now. There's no toilet on the plane. Ricardo will show you the way."

Dario followed Ricardo out of the tiny room and into a dim corridor. He realized he had seen Ricardo in the park earlier, wearing a navy blue sweater and wheeling a Peugeot bicycle. There was no one in sight in the corridor. That seemed awfully unlikely. It was hard to imagine that Alvarez had enough influence with the local authorities to secure an entire wing of the airport, but that was the only explanation that came to mind. Ricardo motioned him through an unmarked door. The cubicle was tiny and hadn't been painted in at least a decade, but it was clean and didn't smell. The face that looked back at Dario from the mirror over the small wash basin almost looked like the face of a man who could do what he was about to. But he wasn't convinced.

"Ready?" Alvarez smiled at Dario. "These are our pilots, Misha and Yuri."

Not certain of the etiquette when embarking on a clandestine flight into a developing nation, Dario offered each man his hand. Their palms were cool and dry, and their grips were firm. He saw himself mirrored in the lenses of their sunglasses, but whether they thought that reflection matched up with what they had been told about him, if they'd been told anything at all, was anybody's guess. Ricardo opened the door for them and Alvarez led the way across the tarmac to the twin engine plane. Dario had never been aboard a plane that small before and wasn't crazy about the idea, but there was no turning back. He clambered onto the wing behind Alvarez, crawled into the rear seat beside him, and fastened his seat belt.

He awoke in a panic with sweat trickling into his eyes. The muscles in his neck and shoulders were cramping, and his stomach churned threateningly. In the dream, Cody had been drowning and Dario was unable to pull him from the water. Cody was swept away by a current more powerful than their combined strengths. Even a psych 101 student could have deciphered it. Nick would have laughed his head off. But Dario's symptoms of distress were real enough and they persisted as the tiny plane lurched dizzyingly and the engines roared. He was certain they were about to crash. The Russians in front muttered unintelligibly but with unmistakable tension, and if he could have fit through the window beside him, Dario would surely have jumped out.

"What's happening?" he croaked.

"Relax," Alvarez said. "Nothing's wrong. Just a little ground turbulence. We're on final approach."

"Oh."

"Are you all right?"

"No," Dario said. "I'm not all right. I have no idea what the hell I'm doing here or why I let you talk me into coming."

Alvarez chuckled softly.

"We're almost there. And if you really want it, I'll put you on the next commercial flight back to Mexico City. I'll even pay for your ticket. First class. You're not being abducted, you know."

Just then there was a chirp from the tires and a bounce as the plane touched down. Which should have made Dario feel better. But he had eyes, and outside the cabin windows was a nasty surprise.

"Not abducted, huh? What about that sign on the terminal building? Don't tell me your flyboys can't navigate any better than that. Nobody ends up landing in Havana these days by mistake."

"Easy, Dario."

"Lying bastard."

"Listen to me. I had to lie to you. I had to get you onto this plane. If you had panicked at the last minute and refused to come along, you might have said anything to anybody about where we were planning to take you. I couldn't risk that. No one must ever know that Cody is here in Cuba."

Dario didn't want to admit it, but it made sense. By that time, the pilots had taxied up to a small, dimly lit building. Away from the lights of the main terminal, the deep evening shadows made them practically invisible.

"So is he here? Tell the truth."

"I am telling you the truth, Dario. So help me God."

"I thought you guys were all atheists."

"A figure of speech, if you wish. And you shouldn't believe everything you hear about us. Some of our strongest support comes from within the church."

"Don't let the pope hear that."

"Cody is here. In a house in one of the suburbs. It's about a thirty minute drive from the airport."

"Are you coming?"

"Of course."

"Maybe you'd better tell me who you really are first. You can't expect me to believe that story about Col. Alvarez of the Nicaraguan Army. Not now."

"That was no lie."

"Perhaps not," Dario said, "but I'd bet anything that it wasn't the whole truth. I'm not going anywhere else with you unless you tell me the rest."

"All right."

The Russians had clambered out of the plane and were standing beside the wings. They were no longer wearing their sunglasses, of course, but it was too dark to make out their features any better than before.

"I am Colonel Alvarez of the Nicaraguan Army. But I'm also Colonel Enriquez, Cuban State Security. Everything else I've told you is true. Can we get out of the plane now?"

He began climbing out of the plane, and Dario followed. He didn't like this turn of events but he had no idea what to do. It felt indescribably good to have his feet on solid ground, even though the solid ground in question was a long way from where he'd expected to put them down. It was a cool evening. The smell of the ocean was on the breeze. A light drizzle was beginning to fall. He stood face to face with Alvarez in the gloom, the Russians hovering behind. He wondered how much they understood of what was going on. He wondered, more to the point, if they were carrying guns.

"Dario, the main terminal is to your right." Alvarez reached into this jacket and pulled something out of the pocket. "This is a diplomatic passport. It has your picture in it. Or rather, a picture of our friend Jorge Rivero is. No one will know the difference, I guarantee it. Your name is Anastasio Beltran. There's one thousand dollars American inside. All you have to do is walk up to any ticket window and buy a ticket back to Mexico City."

"Just like that?"

"Just like that. You walk away from us here and you don't look back. No one is going to shoot you in the back. Or call airport security before you reach the terminal. You're free to go. All I ask is that you don't speak to anyone of this. Not for my sake, you understand. For Cody."

He handed over the passport. Dario looked inside. It was too dark to see anything but the money. Perhaps it was counterfeit but it felt like the real thing. And perhaps the passport was exactly what Alvarez said it was. Or Enriquez, or whoever else he might yet turn out to be. Dario was just about ready to trust him on it. But if he could trust the man on that, didn't it mean that he could trust him on everything else? Dario looked over his shoulder at the terminal building. No more than two minutes' walk. But it was still too far.

"You win." He handed the passport back to Alvarez.

"Are you sure?"

"No," Dario said.

"It's understandable. You've had too much to deal with today. Please try to relax. The car will be here in a moment. It will take you to the house where you'll be staying. You can rest there and have a shower and change clothes."

"Into what? I don't have a thing with me except what I'm wearing."

"Don't worry. We know all your sizes."

"I just bet you do," Dario snapped.

"Please. I'm not the bad guy. There are no bad guys here."

"All right."

"Don't worry. You'll feel better soon. And I'm sure you'll find the clothing Martin picked out for you suitable. By the time you get to the house, it'll be nearly nine. You'll need a rest, you'll need dinner, and you'll want to call Nick."

"I can call Nick?"

"Surely. Why not? I do ask that you don't tell him you're not in Mexico City. But you can certainly tell him you're all right. And there's no reason you can't be back in San Francisco by the day after tomorrow. Your business here won't take long. We've already rebooked your reservation."

The sound of Nick's voice over long distance almost brought Dario to tears.

"You sound funny."

"Speaking Spanish all day," Dario lied. "I'm not used to it any more. I didn't know it would be so tiring."

"You've seen Cody?"

"Yes," Dario said, regretting another lie and hoping it wouldn't matter in the long run. "We spent the afternoon together. I'm back at the hotel now, and I'm meeting him for dinner in a little while."

"And what about the big favor he wants you to do?"

"We haven't talked about it yet."

"Well, don't have too much wine with that dinner. Just remember, the Mexican jails are hellholes. And whatever you do, hold onto your checkbook."

"I'm sure it isn't anything like that."

"Just joking, sweetheart."

"In that case, ha, ha."

"Jeez, you really must be tired."

"Exhausted."

"Well, relax and try to enjoy yourself. I'll be waiting when you come home."

"Oh. I almost forgot. It looks like that'll be sooner than we planned."

"Really?"

"Day after tomorrow. Same time, same flight number. And believe me, I'm counting the minutes."

IV

Cody's room was a single one on the top floor. Alvarez was waiting in the dimly lit corridor. In Havana, even hospitals had to make do with as little electricity as possible.

"I'm sorry," Alvarez said. "I wanted to tell you. Cody and I argued about it quite a bit. I thought you should know, but he was insistent. You know how stubborn he can be. He said I should only tell you if it began to look like you were going to turn back."

"He's dying, isn't he?"

"I didn't say that."

For a moment, he sounded exactly like Nick despite his accent. His expression confirmed what Dario had been fearing on his way up all those flights of stairs, rationed electricity not only meaning little light but also that elevators were reserved for emergency use.

"But you haven't said he isn't, I notice."

"You can go in," Alvarez said. "He slept all afternoon so he could wait up for you."

It seemed to take Dario forever to walk through the doorway into the shadowy room. There was only one bed, a night table, and a chair, every piece looking like it dated from well before the revolution. The linoleum on the floor showed heavy wear even in the meager light. The bedding bore the marks of many launderings and much mending. An electric fan—what luxury!—droned in the open window, drawing clammy air into the room. There had been a shower earlier and the air smelled of damp vegetation.

And there was Cody, sitting up in the bed, his head and upper body visible in a small circle of light cast by a lamp on the night table. But it wasn't the Cody Dario remembered. He looked old enough to be Dario's grandfather.

"Hello, stranger." At least the voice was the same. It took Dario back all those years and all those miles, and only then did he comprehend that he was actually face to face with Cody after that harrowing journey. Cody had obviously been on a journey of his own, a much more arduous one.

"Hi yourself," Dario said. His voice, husky and tenuous, didn't sound like his own.

"Come closer. I can hardly see you over there in the dark."

Dario wasn't sure he wanted to move any closer, to see or be seen any better.

"It's O.K., Dario. I'm not contagious."

"I know."

"And stop crying."

"I don't know if I can."

"Sooner or later you'll have to."

"I suppose."

"Eventually we all do."

By then Dario was standing next to the bed, staring at thin, wispy hair of no discernable color, mottled skin that looked thin and fragile and nearly transparent, at prominent bones where once there had been hard young muscular flesh, at the cadaverous lines and planes of a face that barely hinted at the shapes he recalled. Only the eyes were the same, huge and sky blue in that shrunken and ruined head.

"I look like hell," Cody said.

"No."

"No bullshit,"

"All right," Dario said, struggling for composure. "You do look like hell."

"Now we're getting somewhere. You, on the other hand, look fantastic. How was your trip?"

"Surreal."

"I bet. What did you think of those flyboys? Hot as pistols, huh?"

"I guess."

"Come on. Don't pretend you didn't notice. You must have. I know they're your type. Hell, they're almost enough to convert me. And you know I never was much for blonds."

"O.K. I noticed."

"They're lovers. They moonlight making porn videos together. You should see one. So hot. I'll bet Alvarez has one lying around somewhere. You really should ask him to show it to you. Those guys are all the rage in Eastern Europe."

"You're joking."

"Not me. Not anymore. Just one more thing there isn't time for."

"How long have you been sick?"

"I was diagnosed a few months ago," Cody said. "Pancreatic cancer. And before you start, there's nothing more anyone can do. They've had specialists in from Leningrad, the whole catastrophe. There's no question about it. Alvarez pulled out all the stops. You can rest assured."

"Who is he, anyhow?"

"Who did he tell you he is?"

"Well, first he was Colonel Alvarez of the Nicaraguan Army. Later on he said he's Colonel Enriquez of Cuban State Security."

"That's who he is," Cody said, "but that's not all he is."

"Go on."

"Who he really is," Cody said, "is KGB. What did you think?"

"You're joking. You have to be."

"No. His father is Cuban, but his mother is Russian. He was raised in Leningrad, where his father was sent to attend university. The KGB was active all over the Caribbean and Central America during the years before and during World War II, recruiting men and women they thought might be useful. The parents came back to Cuba right after the revolution, but the Russians kept him in Leningrad. They sent him to special schools and finally Moscow State University. When he eventually got back to Cuba, ostensibly as assistant to the director of Cuban State Security, his job was really to be the Kremlin's agent in place. Later they sent him to Nicaragua to coordinate operations against the Somozas."

"He told me that's where he met you."

"That's right."

"Is he still KGB?"

"Nobody resigns from those guys, Dario."

"Cody, they're killers."

"We're all killers, sweetheart. One way or another. Every last one of us. You. Me. Nancy Reagan. Especially Nancy Reagan. All of us have blood on our hands. More than we're comfortable thinking about even though we accept it as a necessary evil. We kill because we believe we have to in order to survive. Don't tell me you don't know that."

"We're not discussing hypotheticals here. I know I'm guilty of all kinds of things just because I'm a middle class male living in America. I don't even have to leave my living room to be told that. But I've never literally taken a human life. You know what I mean, Cody—with my own hands. But Alvarez. . ."

"Not as many as you might think. It's not like in the movies. Mostly it's in self- defense, as far as that goes."

"Perhaps." Dario didn't argue the point, but he didn't buy Cody's defense of Alvarez for a minute. How could he be any use to an organization as ruthless as that one unless he had ice water running through his veins?

"Oh, come on," Cody laughed. "I know he didn't spook you that badly."

"He didn't have to," Dario said. "The circumstances themselves were enough to do that."

"Granted. But his status as a KGB agent doesn't have anything to do with why you're here."

"I would have thought the opposite," Dario said.

"Not why," Cody said. "How you got here, yes. But not why."

"So why am I here?"

"Not yet," Cody shook his head. "I want to hear about you. Tell me all about you and Nick."

Alvarez was still sitting in the corridor when Dario left Cody's room. He still looked like he'd just stepped out of a layout in a men's fashion magazine. Didn't he ever get tired? Didn't his hair ever get the tiniest bit mussed or his clothing even slightly wrinkled? Dario was quite certain he looked like an unmade bed in a fleabag hotel himself.

"How was your visit?"

"Enlightening. Surprising."

"I wanted to tell you the whole story up front. I felt we owed it to you. And it would have made things far easier logistically. It was Cody's idea to string you along like this was some amateurish television script. I want you to know that this is not the way I usually operate."

"It's not, huh?"

"Absolutely not."

"Where are we going?"

"Back to the house. At least I assume we're through here for the night. Unless you want to make a short visit to the nursery?"

"I don't think I can handle that right now."

"I think that's a good call on your part," Alvarez said. "Back to the house it is, then. You found your room comfortable, I hope."

"Yes."

"And dinner was satisfactory?"

"Delicious."

"I must say, Martin did a fine job of shopping for you. That shirt is extremely becoming."

"Thanks."

"Are you always this terse, Dario? I know that you're very tired, but you seem extremely terse."

"Cody thinks you can do just about anything. Walk on water, I wouldn't be surprised."

"Hardly that."

"Sorry. Wrong church. But you get my drift."

"Cody exaggerates."

"Not in my experience. But still. I mean from what I've observed. I know I'm not the best of observers. A lay person, after all. But you do seem terrifyingly competent."

"As long as that's the only way in which I terrify you," Alvarez smiled, "I'll accept the characterization. Yes, I have a few skills. And I have many friends and associates."

"Who presumably have skills of their own."

"It would be fair to say that. They are thorough and dependable. All one could ask for in one's associates, really."

By that time they were stepping out of the hospital lobby into the tropical night and as if choreographed by a Hollywood director the black Mercedes-Benz glided to the foot of the steps and the handsome young driver got out and opened the rear door.

"You know," Alvarez said, settling himself in the seat next to Dario, "you may speak freely in front of Martin. He is second in command of this operation."

"I see."

"He was on the flight from San Francisco with you. Two rows behind you and to the left of the aisle. Did you know that?"

"No," Dario said. "I don't remember seeing him."

"It's true. Right, Martin?"

"Yes, Colonel."

"He made all our arrangements on that end."

"My congratulations," Dario said. He didn't know if he was being sarcastic or not.

"Now. What is it that you're trying to ask me?"

"This business is more complicated than Cody realizes," Dario said. "Way more. I can't just show up at the airport with a three month old child. I might get him out of Mexico, but I certainly won't get him into the States without complete adoption paperwork."

"Of course not," Alvarez said. "We've taken the liberty of preparing as much of that as we were able prior to your arrival. So you're going to agree to Cody's request? You're going to take the boy?"

"I don't know what I'm going to do," Dario said. "I can't even consider it without talking to Nick. And as you know, Nick's an attorney. He's going to want to know all about the legal side of things."

"Certainly," Alvarez said. "We've got everything well in hand. I realized the moment I heard of Birgitta's death that arrangements would have to be made. Cody was already gravely ill. I know he told you that we've done everything in our power for him."

"Yes," Dario said. "Tell me. You're his friend. Is this what you want? For me to take Cody's son to America? Or would you rather handle it your own way?'

"I want whatever Cody wants. I want him to die peaceful and unconcerned on any account. I could, as you say, handle the matter in many different ways. I could adopt the child myself. I could find him a good family either here or in Eastern Europe. Perhaps even Canada. But I didn't suggest any of those things to Cody. I simply told him that whatever he wished I would do all in my power to bring about. I may have sounded pessimistic or reluctant in some of our conversations, Dario, but please believe me: it wasn't because I disapprove of the arrangement Cody wishes to make. I just understand the difficulties better than he does. And in some ways, I flatter myself that I understand you better than he does. That's why this matter has never been as simple as he believes."

"So I have your assurances that if Nick and I decide against this. . ."

"The child will want for nothing. Ever in his life. You have my promise. Cody has it as well. Now, when we arrive back at the house, Martin will contact his people in San Francisco to determine whether your telephone line there is still secure. If it is, you'll be able to speak with Mr. Romanovsky immediately."

As it happened, Martin was able to put the call through to San Francisco in a matter of minutes. Just long enough for Alvarez to go over the documents with Dario. As far as he could tell Alvarez's people had done their homework, and he felt confident the he could field any question Nick came up with. If not, Alvarez and Martin would be in the next room, available for consultation. But actually speaking to Nick was another matter. One a.m. in San Francisco, and all Dario got was the answering machine. He stood stunned, listening to Nick's recorded voice on the other end, imagining the sound emerging from the speaker in their kitchen. Terrified of what Nick's absence from home might mean, he slammed down the handset.

"Get San Francisco," Alvarez barked to Martin, sizing up the situation without a word from Dario. "Have our people find out where he his."

★ ★ ★

"Dario?" Alvarez said, stepping into the room, "are you asleep?"

"No."

"We've found Nick."

Dario sat up in bed.

"I'm turning the light on. O.K?"

"All right."

"I'm sorry it took us so long," Alvarez continued. "The man who's been doing surveillance simply neglected to check in. It's not unusual this time of day. He's just a low level watcher. He had no way of knowing the urgency of the situation. He was told it was merely routine surveillance. That's my mistake, and I hope you'll accept my apologies."

"Do I want to know where you found him?" Dario asked. "No. I don't think so. Let's just forget the whole thing."

"It's all right," Alvarez said. "You're just overwrought. In fact, I've sent out for some valium. I think you could use a dose or two."

"I'm sure I could. But would you please stop tap dancing around this?"

"All right. Nick arrived home from work at the usual hour. He had no visitors. He stayed in all evening until he was seen leaving your building just after eleven. That's San Francisco time. He drove to an address in Pacific Heights."

"Our friends Morgan and Forrest," Dario nodded. Perhaps it wasn't what he'd originally assumed.

"Morgan and Forrest?"

"Morgan Lundquist and Forrest Reynolds," Dario said. "I'm sorry, I can't remember their address. They live on Octavia Street."

There was a knock on the door. Alvarez opened it. Martin handed in a tray. On it were a pill bottle, a carafe of water with lemon slices floating in it, and a glass. Alvarez set it down on the dresser. "I want you to take one of these," he said, removing the cap from the bottle and shaking a tablet into his palm. "It will help you rest. I'm off to see what else I can find out."

Martin brought his breakfast. Not that Dario was in the mood to eat. He pushed the food around the plate with his fork until he got tired of it. Then he took it to the bathroom and flushed it down. He went back to bed thinking about starving children. He had just taken another valium when Alvarez came in.

"The gentleman Nick went to see last night is a Dr. Christopher Melendez-Greene," he said.

"Oh, great."

"You've heard of him."

"I have," Dario said, his blood running cold.

Christopher was the biggest homewrecker in all San Francisco. But actually it was worse than that. Dario cursed himself silently for ever walking out their front door. He had to have known better. In the years before Dario met Nick, literally hundreds of men had enjoyed Nick's company. Dario hadn't been celibate himself by any means, but the scale of Nick's activities dwarfed his. In fact, the scale of Nick's activities had dwarfed almost everyone's. It wouldn't be going too far to describe Nick's sexual history as belonging in a category all its own. And the sheer volume of Nick's conquests wasn't its only defining characteristic. His prowess was a Castro Street legend. It was that history that had been behind Dario's refusals the first several times Nick asked him out. He had no intention of becoming just another face in that crowd. His reluctance drove Nick to desperate measures. After they began to date, that history continued to be an issue for Dario. Not because he couldn't get past what was past, but because he wasn't at all convinced it actually was past. You couldn't expect a man like Nick to call that sort of rampage to a halt as easily as turning off a light switch.

You couldn't drive yourself crazy thinking about it, either. Dario got that. Most of those men—all but a handful, really—had been no more significant to Nick than the meals he'd eaten on the nights he'd slept with them or the newspaper articles he read on the MUNI on his way to or from their apartments. But there had been a few who mattered. And chief among them was Christopher Melendez-Greene. Nick's encounter with him had come fairly early in Christopher's career. In some ways it actually defined his career. It certainly put Christopher on the map in a way he hadn't been before. After Nick, his notoriety grew by leaps and bounds, while before Nick, Christopher had been noteworthy more in terms of his potential. All that was peripheral, however. What mattered to Dario was that to this day there were still people in San Francisco who insisted that between the two men there was unfinished business, that Nick had never truly "let go" or "moved on", and that eventually and inevitably matters between Dario's husband and the notorious young doctor demanded resolution of a highly dramatic nature. For all he knew, those gossip mongers were correct. Just because something was an item of gossip didn't automatically signify that it wasn't true.

Dario knew all that, yet he'd come on this fool's errand anyway.

"You don't look like you're feeling well," Alvarez said.

"Christopher Melendez-Greene, you said?"

"I believe that was the name," Alvarez nodded. "I'll try to get confirmation. And some additional details."

So here he was, facing the most important decision of his life so far, one he couldn't, or wouldn't, dare make on his own. And Nick was unavailable. Perhaps indefinitely.

It didn't take long in objective terms, but it managed to feel like the longest forty minutes of Dario's life. Which he was pretty certain was over at that point. At least life as he'd known it the last few years. What else could it mean that at the earliest opportunity, Nick had flown in that particular direction?

"There was a shooting at Dr. Melendez-Greene's place last night," Alvarez said. "He's in police custody and another man is dead. We don't have many details at this point. But from what we've managed to find out, Dr. Melendez-Greene apparently called Nick. As of twenty minutes ago they were still at police headquarters."

"Where the hell have you been?" Nick's voice couldn't have been clearer if he'd been in the next room.

"I could ask you the same question," Dario said.

"If you'd been at your hotel when I called I could have explained the whole thing."

"I hear it's something to do with a shooting involving Christopher Melendez-Greene," Dario said. "I can't believe you'd agree to defend him."

"I didn't," Nick said. "I've already handed him off. And the look on his face when I told him I was doing it was priceless."

"Who did he shoot?"

"Some hustler. He's claiming self-defense."

"Do you believe him?"

"Hell no," Nick said, "but the police just might. That's enough about him. Start talking."

Nick's explanation was just a little too neat, Dario thought. But in his position nothing could help but a leap of faith.

"That's about the craziest thing I've ever heard of," Nick said.

"I know."

"And you're going to do it."

"I didn't say that."

"But you're going to."

"Only if you agree to it, Nick."

"And if I say no?"

"I'm on the next plane home."

"It means you'll never be free of him."

"He's dying, Nick."

"Just saying."

"Who's ever free of anybody they really love?"

"Spare me the rhetorical questions," Nick said. "We have to be practical about this."

"That's why we're having this discussion," Dario said. "So you can talk me out of it."

"Is that what you want? For me to talk you out of it?"

"I want you to try."

V

In daylight, Cody looked worse than he had the night before. Even though Dario thought he knew what to expect, he was shocked.

"Worse than the part when the Phantom of the Opera is unmasked," Cody laughed, the broad grin on his face making him even more grotesque. "Worse even than the late, late, latest show."

"Cody," Dario choked, gulping at the lump in his throat.

"Come on, Dario," Cody said. "What else is there to do but laugh?"

"All kinds of things, I'd think."

"Name one," Cody said. "And don't you dare tell me to start dictating my memoirs."

"Hell," Dario shrugged. "I don't have a clue."

"You always took things too seriously."

"If Nick were here he'd give you an earful on that subject."

"Speaking of which," Cody said, "what did he say?"

"All systems go," Dario said. He could hardly believe it, but Nick had consented to the plan.

"God, Dario, you have no idea what this means to me."

Finally Cody permitted himself the luxury of tears. They came slowly, rolling down both ruined cheeks and dropping onto the threadbare bedding. The hours Dario remembered just staring at those cheekbones.

"Sweetheart," Dario said. "It's all right."

He reached for Cody's hand. Cody gripped him like a drowning man holding onto a life preserver.

Alvarez came into the room.

"Sorry to disturb you two," he said. "Dario, the fax arrived from San Francisco. I want you to take a look at it. I've got my handwriting people downstairs with all the documents."

He handed over the fax. On it were three examples of Nick's signature.

"That's it," Dario said, surprised at how relieved he felt. It was almost as good as having Nick walk into the room with a grin on his face and not a sign of care in his eyes.

"What's all this?" Cody asked.

"Mr. Romanovsky insists on having his signature on all the documents as joint adoptive parent," Alvarez said. "God knows what the American authorities will make of it."

"Our counsel says it will be fine," Dario said.

"Jesus," Cody sobbed.

"I'll just run these downstairs," Alvarez said. "Is there anything else you two need?"

"I can take care of things here," Dario said.

He sat back down beside the bed. Cody sobbed quietly. Dario stroked his wispy hair. There had been a time when one of his greatest pleasures had been running his fingers through Cody's luxuriant, straw colored hair. He knew Cody remembered.

"It's going to be all right," Dario said. It sounded stupid, but it was the best he could do.

There was a small metal bowl of water on the night table. Dario dampened a wash cloth and gently wiped Cody's face.

"Do you need to rest?"

"No, Dario. Stay. There isn't much time. Once Alvarez's people finish with those documents, he's going to want to get you out of here and back to Mexico City. The longer you're away from your hotel the more he worries. He may not look like it, but he's just millimeters away from blowing a head gasket. I'll have plenty of time to rest when you're gone."

"How much time is there?"

"No one can tell for sure. Probably somewhere between three and six weeks."

"And there's really no hope of recovery?"

"Absolutely none."

"I just wish I could be here for you."

"Alvarez and Martin will take good care of me."

"All right."

"There is one more thing I'd like you to do."

"All right."

"There are a few things of Birgitta's. Personal things. Not much. Most of it went to her parents in Leipzig. But I kept a few things I want him to have when he's older. Alvarez will send them on to you. He says he can organize it."

"All right."

"There'll be a few things of mine, too. You'll know when he's ready for them."

And as if on cue, Martin came into the room carrying the baby.

"Give him to Dario," Cody said.

The baby wriggled momentarily, then settled into the crook of Dario's arm like he'd been born there. He looked up at Dario with terrifying solemnity. He had Cody's eyes and would probably have his chin, too. Dario felt like a fraud holding him like that and pretending to be his father.

The slightly stockier of the two Russians handed the baby to Dario in the back seat of the plane. Alvarez sat next to him holding the packet of documents and a diaper bag. His grin said he was thoroughly conscious of the incongruity. He actually seemed to relish it. The flyboys closed the doors of the craft and situated themselves at the controls. The engines roared to life. The baby stirred a little at the sound and then went limp again. The plane taxied to the end of the runway and then left Havana in the dust of the June afternoon, climbing just moments after takeoff into a cloud bank that obliterated the island.

NELSON LUNDQUIST: 1981

When Nelson stepped into the bar, his quarry was leaning against the back wall watching a couple of lesbians shoot pool. He was the exact height and build as Nelson's brother Morgan. Even the face, a boy scout all grown up, was the same basic type. Only the dark brown hair, glistening like an oil slick, distinguished him from Nelson's twin.

"Five nine. Two hundred pounds. Twenty-nine inch waist," Nelson muttered. It was like he was repeating a phrase from the Eucharistic prayer. He headed toward the bar.

He ordered a beer and started the dance.

"Hi," he said, arriving at his quarry's side.

The guy turned to look at him. Exactly as he'd hoped, the gray eyes were as cold and empty as an arctic midnight.

"Whose little boy are you?"

"That depends," the guy said.

"On what?" Nelson asked.

"The next words out of your mouth."

"In that case," Nelson said, "how about having breakfast with me?"

Sean's left nipple was pierced. He had a sunburst tattoo on his right shoulder. Every inch of his body was clean shaven. Every single inch. There wasn't a hair anywhere except what grew so slick and fragrant on his head. Sean's penis was average length but well above average in girth. Nelson had known that already. He lacked only the existential experience of it slowly but inexorably entering him and bestowing on him all those sensations, all that ecstasy and all that hurt, everything he had anticipated so perfectly. Now he could check that off his list. He had always known someone like this was out there. Always. It must simply be karma that had made the search so tortuous.

Nelson had been curious about the apartment. He hadn't known anything about it at all except the location. It was neater than he expected. Tiny and very neat, like the cabin of a junior officer on a ship.

"I'm afraid I lied to you," Sean said.

"Oh?"

"About breakfast. I've got to go back out."

"Another date?" Nelson asked.

"Kind of," Sean said.

"Don't forget to take your gun."

"What?"

"Your .45, Sean. The one you don't have a permit for. The one with no serial number. You bought it last week. Eureka Park. That sleazy Mexican in the custom '49 Lincoln. Not that Mexicans are sleazy as a group. I'd never say a thing like that. No, in terms of absolute sleaziness, we white guys have everybody else on the planet beat. But that guy—sheesh. Anyway, that's the gun I'm referring to."

"You've been following me?"

"Maybe."

"Who are you anyway? Some kind of weirdo?"

"Your guardian angel, Sean." Nelson said, pulling on his jeans. "I know you didn't think you had one, but you do. And please accept my apologies for my belated arrival. I'm here now. At long last, I'm on the case. In fact, I think it would be a good idea for me to drive you to your appointment."

"No," Sean said, "it isn't a good idea at all."

"You can drop me off here," Sean said.

Nelson steered the car to the curb and cut the ignition and headlights. He didn't own a car. After an extensive search in the vicinity of Lafayette Park he had found a Volvo with keys in its ignition. The owners were probably looking for it. They might already have called the police. Nelson certainly hoped so.

"What are you doing?"

"Whither thou goest," Nelson said, quoting the Book of Ruth.

"You're crazy."

"I'll carry the rope," Nelson said.

"This has nothing to do with you."

"Like you know that," Nelson said. "You have no idea who I am, so how can you know that? I'll carry the rope. Do we need duct tape as well? There's some in the trunk."

"We don't need any duct tape."

"Maybe I'll bring a roll anyway," Nelson said. "Just in case."

"You carry duct tape around in your trunk?"

"Somebody does," Nelson said.

They were somewhere in Pacific Heights. What a coincidence it would be if they were headed to his brother's house. How hilarious if Morgan and his millionaire boyfriend, Forrest, were somehow tangled up with the man of Nelson's dreams. They trudged up the block, turned a corner, walked some more, and then they were on the very block where those two lived. Nelson felt almost giddy. His brother's perfectly manicured blond flattop and this guy's greased down chestnut mop. Their two pairs of perfectly matched, musclebound shoulders. Nelson was hard as a rock inside his jeans. He knew that if he looked down he'd see the damp spot.

But it wasn't Morgan and Forrest's place they were headed to. It was the white mausoleum across the street. Nelson should have figured. He'd been to parties there. Lots of them. It was where he'd first seen Sean.

They rounded the corner. The high stucco wall of the mansion glinted spectrally in the fog diffused light from the streetlamps. Around the corner, almost at the rear of the property, there was a small service gate almost totally concealed by overgrown shrubbery. He shouldn't have been surprised that Sean knew how to pick the padlock. The mansion was dark and silent. No guard dogs accosted them when they stepped through the gate. No lights flashed on. No bells or buzzers sounded. It was almost as if they were expected. Or as if no one was home, or cared. They headed away from the big house, past the swimming pool and toward the garage. There must be an apartment upstairs. Nelson saw lights in the windows.

"Hello, Sean."

"Christopher," Sean said, flashing the pistol at him. "Good to see you. Yes, thanks, we would like to come in. And in case you're wondering, this thing is loaded."

"Sean what the fuck?"

"Oh, don't tell me you haven't been expecting this visit," Sean said, closing the door and throwing the dead bolt.

"Actually, I wasn't," Christopher said. "Who's your friend?"

"His name is none of your fucking business," Sean said, "but you can call him Bob."

"He looks familiar," Christopher said. "Have we met somewhere, Bob?"

"Bob won't be answering any of your questions," Sean said. "He's a mute."

"Really?"

"Well, for now he is. Do me a favor and pull that chair over here in the middle of the room, please."

"You know I really don't appreciate having that .45 waved in my face," Christopher said.

"You have a good eye for firearms," Sean said, "but we already knew that."

"I don't know what you're talking about."

"The chair, Christopher? Now? Please?" Sean waved the gun at him again. Just enough to get his point across.

Christopher fetched the chair.

"Bob's going to tie you up now," Sean said. "We won't bother with a gag. You have some explaining to do, and that's difficult with a gag on. Bob's hearing is extremely acute, I'll give him that. But nobody can really enunciate through a gag. And besides, it's the servants' night off and Rene is at the hospital with Jules. So even if you did decide to yell for help you'd be just like that tree falling in the forest. You remember that tree, don't you?"

"Nice job on those knots, Bob," Sean said.

Nelson mimed *thanks*.

"As you see," Sean said, "Bob was in the Boy Scouts. After that he joined the Merchant Marine. Then he ran away with pirates. Bob knows his knots."

"And you were a Mountie," Christopher said. "Isn't that the story Bo always told about you?"

"Funny you should mention Bo," Sean said.

"Oh, don't play dense. We both know that's why you're here."

"Do we?"

"Please."

"All right then," Sean said. "Let's talk about Bo."

"What about him?"

"I'd like you to tell me the real story," Sean said. "Not that bullshit you gave the police about how he showed up that night demanding drugs and a blank prescription pad and wouldn't believe that you didn't keep anything like that around here, so he pulled a gun on you and the two of you struggled over it and it went off and just happened to kill him with that one accidental shot. None of that bullshit about how you were terrified and thought you were about to die. You're going to tell me the real story."

"That is the real story," Christopher said.

"Fuck you, Christopher," Sean said. "That is not what happened. The real story is you were terrified that Bo was going to mess up your plan to marry Olivia Styles and get filthy rich. He was probably blackmailing you, but I don't know anything about that. And neither does Bob. Anyway you lured Bo over here. You let him fuck you. Probably more than once, so he'd be good and relaxed. Afterwards you went into the bathroom to clean up. Everybody knows how particular you are about that. When you came back out, surprise, surprise. You were carrying a gun. A .45, by a strange coincidence. No registration. No serial numbers—they'd been filed off. Something Volk taught you how to do between sessions worshipping that anaconda of his, no doubt. So no identifying marks, just a shiny piece of metal with bullets packed inside. Bo was dozing. He never dozed off around clients, but with you he was safe. You moved very quietly. You made sure he didn't hear you coming. He didn't know a thing until you put the barrel of that gun against his head. And you didn't waste any time. You couldn't. A second too long and he'd have yanked that gun out of your hand and broken your

JACKSON PEOPLES-ROSENBLATT

neck. It wasn't an accident and it wasn't self-defense. It was cold blooded murder. Murder with malice aforethought, just like this is going to be."

"You're not going to shoot me, Sean," Christopher laughed.

"Not yet, anyhow," Sean said. "I haven't heard your confession. If I shoot you now, I never will. And that's what I came for—as Bob is my witness."

"Very funny," Christopher said.

"Now is when you start telling me the real story," Sean said.

"The real story is the one I told the police."

"Try again," Sean said, cocking the gun.

"You really don't want to shoot me."

"Oh, but I really do. Even if I didn't, I owe my buddy Bo."

The way Sean spoke the name "Bo" each time wasn't a surprise. Nelson had figured out that part of the story. He had smelled it on Sean when they fucked.

"I repeat. The real story is not the one you told the police."

"Yes, Sean. It is."

The gunshot was deafening in the small room. But it wasn't loud enough to drown out Christopher's scream. Nelson nearly jumped out of his skin.

"Jesus, Sean, you shot him in the crotch."

"Relax," Sean said. "That's not blood. Mr. Wonderful here just peed himself. I put the bullet into the wall over his left shoulder. Wouldn't be surprised if he felt the slipstream."

"Sean," Christopher panted, "I swear to God, I never meant to kill Bo. It all happened exactly the way I told it to the police."

There was something electrifying, Nelson thought, about the sight of an extremely beautiful man stripped to the waist, tied up, and weeping with terror. He had already known Sean was sexy. Now that Sean had accomplished that feat, Nelson wasn't sure he'd ever escape Sean's appeal. It was better than anything he could have imagined. He had always wanted to be a slave for life.

"Sorry," Sean said, "but Bob here doesn't believe you. Do you, Bob?"

"Having weighed the evidence, I have to say I don't," Nelson heard himself growl.

"You seem like a nice guy," Christopher said. "You don't want to let Sean get you mixed up in something that could send you to prison."

"Oh, dear," Nelson said. "The man thinks I'm a nice guy. You ought to shoot him just for being stupid, Sean."

"You think so?" Sean asked. "It wasn't in the original plan, but I don't see why not."

The second gunshot was as loud as the first. Christopher screamed again, and a stench permeated the room.

"Bob?"

"Yes, Sean?"

"Did you just shit your pants?"

"No, Sean, I don't believe I did. Did you?"

"No, but someone must have."

"Please, Sean," Christopher sobbed. "Don't do this. Bob, you have to make him listen to reason."

"Reason?" Nelson mused. "What's that? Some new cologne you get at Nordstrom's?"

"I have plenty of bullets left," Sean said. "And that story about me in the Mounties: did Bo tell you the part about how I was a sharpshooter? See, with my training, I can kill you immediately with one shot or I can empty the gun into you in such a way that it will take you several hours to bleed out. Several long, excruciating hours. While Bob and I watch. Bob will probably want to sing to you. French art songs are his specialty. What do you think?"

"I think you're fucking crazy," Christopher said, "if you believe you can get away with killing me."

"About as crazy as you were," Sean said, "thinking you could get away with killing Bo. Everybody knows the cops are stupid enough to believe anything a rich man tells them. But the cops aren't the only interested parties, as you're coming to realize. Now really, I'm starting to run out of patience. Talk. Tell me the story."

"There is no story."

Another gunshot. Another scream from Christopher.

"Oops," Sean said. "Missed again. Sorry about those Lalique cats. Or maybe I'm not. Bo always said he hated them. It must have been karma insisting that they die before you do."

"Sean, I swear to God."

"Leave God out of it, please. She doesn't want to hear your mealy-mouthed lies. She knows what you did. And She is a deity of vengeance."

"You crazy fucker."

"Plenty more bullets in the gun," Sean said, "and Bob's got several spare rounds in his pocket. Show him, Bob."

"Goodbye, Christopher," Sean smiled. "This certainly has been a pleasure. A magical evening, I have to say. I know I won't ever forget it. I don't suppose you will, either. For the rest of your life, however long that may or may not be, I'll always be the guy who made you piss and shit yourself. Oh, and the guy who knows what really happened that night. Let's not forget that."

"You're not leaving me tied up like this."

"Somebody will eventually come along," Sean said. "Somebody always does."

"Nice meeting you," Nelson said, running his hand through Christopher's sweat soaked hair. He couldn't leave without doing it. He'd been itching to. He sniffed his slimy fingers.

As they slipped out the gate, the neighborhood was as silent as if they had never been there. There were no worried looking neighbors milling around on the sidewalks. There were no sirens in the distance drawing ever nearer. Nelson looked across the street. Lights were on at Morgan and Forrest's house, but he knew nobody was home. He had remembered they were on a cruise in the Caribbean.

Sean didn't speak as they walked back to the car.

Nelson started the engine.

"Call me Goel," Sean said.

"The avenger," Nelson said. "You went to a very good school. Either that or you're Jewish."

"I went to school in Canada," Sean said. "I was a Mountie."

"I thought that was just a story."

"Maybe it was."

"You didn't kill Christopher," Nelson said, shifting into first. "Is that vengeance?"

"I never intended to kill him," Sean said.

"You could have fooled me."

"No, I couldn't. Nobody fools the guardian angel."

"Well, Christopher apparently thought you meant to kill him," Nelson said.

"Apparently."

"You didn't even rape him," Nelson said.

"That would have been exactly how he wanted the scene to go," Sean said. "He could have retreated into the fantasy that no one is immune to his charms."

"The question of vengeance still stands."

"I loved Bo," Sean said. "I didn't know what love was until I met him. I don't know if I'll ever love anyone else the way I loved him. He was one of the most spectacular looking men alive. There wasn't anything I wouldn't have done for him. I have no idea what to do with myself now that he's gone."

"Go on," Nelson said.

"He was a male prostitute. He was a narcissist. He was probably a sociopath. Except for the prostitution he wasn't a criminal, but he certainly had criminal tendencies. I'm not sure there was anything he wouldn't have done under the right circumstances. He used people. Constantly. He used me. He used me and used me and used me, and he gave very little back. Basically nothing except his cock. Sooner or later something bad was going to happen to him. He was exactly the type of guy to get himself shot. Or drive too fast and go over a cliff. Or play too rough with some client and end up in prison and get killed in a fight there. There was no way of telling how it would eventually happen, but there was one thing you could be sure of. He was never going to live to a ripe old age. And if by some miracle he had, he'd have hated it the minute his looks and body started to go and he couldn't get whatever he wanted from people anymore. How do you even talk about revenge in the case of a guy like that?"

"Is that a rhetorical question?" Nelson asked.

"Can you answer it?"

"Probably not."

"I can't either," Sean said. "I guess that makes it rhetorical."

"So how do you explain tonight?"

"Tonight wasn't about Bo," Sean said.

"Sounded like it to me."

"Tonight was about Christopher," Sean said. "About the way he treats people. About the way he treated me. He needed to be taught a lesson about that. He needed to understand that if it could happen to Bo it could happen to him. Killing him would have been pointless. This way, it's never over. This way he has to live with what he did."

"That was true before we ever got there."

"Fair enough," Sean said, "but now he has to think about it differently. Now he knows he didn't get away with anything."

"Huh?"

"Now he knows that a little nobody like Sean can scare him so bad he'll piss and shit himself. Now he knows he'll say anything just to save his life. Now he knows what it feels like to look down the barrel of a gun into the eyes of a man who hates him and beg not to die. He isn't special at all. He's just like everybody else. And he can never forget it."

"And you finally made him tell the truth about what he did to Bo."

"I have no idea what the truth is," Sean said. "A man looking down the barrel of a gun into the eyes of a man who hates him will tell that man whatever he wants to hear. But on the other hand it might have happened the way he originally told it to the police. I know that. I'm the one who bought Bo that gun."

"What gun?"

"A gun. From that same Mexican in the park that I got mine from. Maybe the one I bought for Bo was the one that killed him. Maybe it wasn't. Maybe Christopher already had a gun. Maybe he didn't. 45's with their serial numbers filed off are all alike. Ballistics tests are meaningless without a sample to test against. I'll never know for sure if the gun I bought for Bo was the gun Christopher used to kill him. That's what I have to live with."

"What did Christopher do to you, anyway?"

"All kinds of things," Sean said.

"For instance."

"All right," Sean said. "At one point Bo threatened to cut me loose. We made a lot of money doing sex shows."

"I saw one of them," Nelson said. "Actually, I saw more than one of them."

That's when Nelson fell in love, but he didn't say so.

"Bo said I wasn't big enough to impress our audiences. I looked small and weak. I had to do something about it. So I went to Christopher for a prescription. Bo was always on juice. Lots of guys at our gym were. And they all got it from Christopher. Christopher didn't bother writing me a script. He supplied me the pills direct. Acted like he was happy to do it. Made me suspicious. So I had the pills tested. He'd given me a placebo. He didn't want me getting bigger. He wanted Bo to tell me to get lost. It wasn't because he wanted Bo for himself. It was only because he knew how bad it would make me feel if I couldn't have Bo anymore."

"What happened?"

"His trick made me so mad that I really worked my ass off at the gym. I put on fifteen pounds in less than a year. And I did it clean. It got Bo off my back about it. It made me the man I am today. Whoever that is."

"What's with those photos you grabbed?"

"What photos?" Sean asked.

"The ones in the envelope you didn't think I saw you take out of that safe in the bedroom I wasn't supposed to know you were going through. How did you know about that safe?"

"Bo gave me the combination."

"Did he tell you about the photos?"

"Just a guess."

"I assume there were negatives."

"The pictures aren't anything special," Sean said. "Family snapshots. That kind of stuff."

"If your family is the Borgias," Nelson snorted. "Try again."

"Bo," Sean said.

"You don't have photos of him already?"

"Bo," Sean said, "with someone holding a gun to his head and the biggest bodybuilder in the history of the planet fucking him in the ass. I swear I never thought a man or a cock could be that big until Bo and I met him. If I hadn't met Volk, I'd think it was trick photography."

"Oh."

"Bo never took it up the ass in his life. They'd have had to tie him up and hold a gun to his head. Just like in the pictures."

"You think that's what happened that night? Before he was killed?"

"I don't think anything. I either know things about this or I don't. There's no way of proving the pictures have anything to do with his death. Even with photographs of Christopher holding the gun to his head, it's just circumstantial. The police wouldn't do anything based on them. But they might be enough to make him lose his license to practice medicine. I'm sending the photos to a man I know who's a private investigator. Insurance. Christopher will figure out I've taken them as soon as somebody cuts him free. They're the first thing he'll look for when he sees that the door of the safe is open. He'll know I took them. He'll have a pretty good idea what I've done with them. He'll leave us both alone."

There was very little traffic as they headed down toward the Marina District. Nelson pulled over on a particularly dark street corner. There was a bus stop a few yards away. The route ran all night. Sean wouldn't be stranded.

"Get out of the car, Sean," Nelson said. "Leave the gun with me."

"I don't understand."

"Mission accomplished. Now I take over. We haven't been followed. I'm absolutely certain of it. If Christopher thinks he recognized me it's because my twin brother lives across the street from him. By the time Morgan gets back from cruising in the Caribbean and Christopher notices him over there, he'll think it was just a weird coincidence. And anyway, by then the scent will have gone cold. Now I'm going to get rid of the gun for you. Don't ask me where I'm taking it because I won't tell you. Just rest assured it won't ever be found. Not in an alley. Not in either of those dumpsters we passed. Not in your nightstand tomorrow afternoon when the police come by your apartment to ask you a few questions. If they don't find a gun, it's just Christopher's word against yours."

"The police won't come," Sean said. "He won't call them. The pictures aren't the half of it. He's got every possible reason not to get them involved. He's a weasely little coward, but he isn't stupid."

"You're probably right about all that," Nelson said, "but supposing he did go to the police. He could still make things very uncomfortable for you. No, Sean, let me take care of this. No loose ends. That's a rule in the Merchant Marines. And probably the Mounties too. Certainly the pirates subscribe to it. I told you I'm your guardian angel."

"You're crazy," Sean said.

"I am," Nelson nodded. "As the man said, 'about as crazy as you are'."

"Jesus."

"Here," Nelson said, grabbing a handful of change out of the ash tray. In his experience, people who drove Volvos always kept change in the ash tray. People who drove Peugeots did, too. He really preferred Peugeots, but beggars—and car thieves—couldn't be choosers. "For bus fare."

"Thanks. I've got plenty."

"Don't forget," Nelson said. "You're meeting me for breakfast. The Bottomless Mug. On Market. I know you know the place. I've seen you in there. Veggie omelette, no cheese. Fruit cup instead of home fries. Rye toast, dry. Black coffee."

"How long have you been following me? Or should I say stalking?"

"Guardian angels don't follow," Nelson said. "Nor do we stalk. We hover."

The visitor's center was closed. The parking area was empty. He steered the car into a space in the darkest corner. He got out, leaving the key in the ignition. This was as good a place as any to ditch it. He moved to the rear of the car and pulled his things out of the trunk. He closed the lid softly. He moved slowly. The mistake people made when they had something to hide was hurrying. Hurrying made them conspicuous. When they hurried they got clumsy. They made mistakes. He sauntered across the parking lot and toward the bridge like he was a straight guy without a thought in his head and all the time in the world. The south tower of the bridge loomed out of the low hanging fog. The far tower was invisible. There was only a little bit of traffic whispering past, headlight glare diffusing in the damp air like the landing lights of UFO's. He didn't see any other pedestrians. Under his feet, the bridge was like a living thing. Its barely perceptible movements were the breathing of a huge, sleeping animal. Behind him, the city snuggled under its damp blanket. By the time he had reached the middle of the bridge the fog was so thick that he couldn't see to either end.

He pulled the pistol, still wrapped in Sean's t-shirt, out of the paper sack. He sniffed the t-shirt. He'd have to leave it in a trash barrel just to be safe. That was a shame. It would have made a nice souvenir. He took another sniff, a good long one. Soap, aftershave, that hair stuff. He wasn't sure he'd ever get enough of Sean. But he was sure as hell going to find out. A man as true as his own penis. That was as rare a thing as could be imagined.

But first things first. Holding the pistol gingerly by the tips of his gloved fingers, he tossed it over the rail. It was out of sight immediately. It was undoubtedly toxic to marine life, but it was even more dangerous on shore. As he walked back past the Volvo it was shiny with damp.

He headed for the nearest bus stop that would take him back into the city. As he walked, he whistled "*Un bel di.*"

Rene Melendez: 1982

"It won't be long now."

Rene turned. He hadn't heard Christopher come into the room.

"I didn't know you were back from Montreal."

"I got in last night," Christopher said. "Very late. I spoke to the nurse."

Rene turned back toward the bed. Jules already looked like a corpse. He'd been on the morphine drip for a week.

"He isn't suffering," Christopher said.

"So they tell me," Rene muttered. But how could one know such a thing? Jules couldn't speak for himself. Anything might be going on inside that ravaged head. And no one knew better than Rene that nightmares were invariably worse than reality. That chaos in your head—how could one escape that?

"The nurse said you were here all night," Christopher said.

"I suppose I was."

"Why don't you go rest? I'll sit with him for a while."

Rene couldn't sleep. He went out to sit by the pool. In a little while the cook brought him a tray. He didn't bother lifting the cover. He wasn't hungry. He didn't even sip the coffee. He wasn't hungry and he wasn't sad. He just wanted it to be over. He couldn't be certain that this was a selfless impulse, a wish that Jules' suffering would be at an end, or merely that he didn't want to witness it any more.

"I thought you were going to rest," Christopher said, settling into the neighboring chaise lounge.

"I thought you were going to sit with him," Rene said. He hadn't been away from Jules for more than an hour. But that had been too much to ask of Christopher.

"He's completely unresponsive, Rene. He doesn't know if anyone's with him or not."

"He does," Rene insisted.

"You can't stay with him twenty-four hours a day."

"He shouldn't be alone."

"You've done everything you can," Christopher said. "It's going to be what it's going to be."

"Yes," Rene said, "but meantime he's still here. He needs to be properly cared for."

"That's what we have full time nursing care for," Christopher said. "And the servants."

He simply refused to understand. What Rene wouldn't give to be such a narcissist himself. The horrors he would have been spared.

The cook came with the coffeepot and a cup for Christopher.

"Have you thought about what you're going to do?" Christopher asked.

"I must be the only gay man on earth who doesn't think of San Francisco as heaven," Rene grunted.

"Paris then?"

"He'd like to be buried there," Rene nodded. "He bought the plot ages ago. He even designed a headstone. I'll find a flat near Graciela."

"Have you spoken to her? How is she?"

"She's fine. She'd like to see you."

"I'll come for the funeral," Christopher said.

"She'll like that. She didn't think much of Jules but she'll be there if she knows you're coming."

"I'm sure you'll enjoy living in Paris," Christopher said.

"It won't be on the scale I'm accustomed to, certainly," Rene said. He was tempted to leave this part to the attorneys, but Jules had demanded it of him. He owed the man that much. He might as well get it over with.

"What do you mean?" Christopher said. "With forty million or so to work with, I'd expect you to live like a prince."

"You'd expect that, would you?" Rene asked. The figure was actually higher, closer to sixty million, but it would be clarified soon enough.

"Sure."

"Well, you'd be mistaken," Rene said. "I'm not the heir."

"What are you talking about?"

"Will you understand better if we discuss this in English?"

"No," Christopher laughed. "I just can't imagine—I mean, if you're not his heir. What? Did Volk squeeze you out?"

"Volk is provided for exactly as I am," Rene said. "A modest trust fund. I'll be comfortable enough, as will Volk. And God knows, he's a resourceful man. He'll flourish, I expect. As for me, eventually there'll be some money from your grandfather, as well. If his mistress doesn't go through all of it."

"Well," Christopher said. "If it's not you and it's not Volk, then who is it?"

Rene couldn't believe Christopher didn't already know. Perhaps this scene was a sick charade.

"Who else?" Rene asked.

"You're joking."

"Oh, I'm not. It's been his intention since he first saw you."

It wasn't that Rene had expected or even wanted Jules' money. Honestly, that wasn't why he was against Jules making Christopher his heir. Rene knew his nephew in a way he was quite certain Jules didn't. Jules simply worshipped the iconic figure he saw when he looked at Christopher. Rene knew Christopher the man, and he couldn't imagine anything good coming of his nephew having that much money. That's why Jules should have left it to him instead. Or Volk. Or split it between the two of them. That would have been the thing to do. But Christopher? No. It wouldn't do.

But the last few months had given Rene cause to reconsider.

Not that Christopher had improved. Certainly not. Anything but, when you came right down to it. Because those events had proven irrefutably that Christopher was much worse than even Rene had previously understood. Trying to marry that heiress? That had been the work of an amateur. Every Tom, Dick, and Harry went down that road at some point. Rene had. More than once, actually. No, it had been murdering that bodybuilder when he tried to interfere in Christopher's plans that changed Rene's mind about the inheritance.

If Christopher was willing to kill to preserve his shot at the Styles fortune, then he'd be willing to kill for the de Croteau estate as well. If he was willing to kill his own lover, because for all practical purposes that's what the bodybuilder was, why not his uncle? Rene didn't want money—even that much of it—badly enough to put a target on his own back for it. Let Christopher have it all and let him destroy himself with it.

Rene planned to wash his hands of the whole thing.

"The situation is this," Dr. Sternberg said. He spoke the French of Jewish Montreal, and the accent always made Rene self-conscious of his own Mexican inflected version of the language. "The tumor is a very slow growing one. It has almost totally destroyed the brain centers responsible for cognitive functioning, but the parts of the brain which control basic bodily processes are untouched. Respiration, heartbeat, digestion—all those and more are undisturbed. And his organs are apparently very strong. You know better than anyone what a vigorous man he has always been. I know it is a terrible strain for you, but you must prepare yourself for this phase of the illness to go on for some time."

"How long?" Rene asked.

"Weeks certainly. But I would be surprised if it didn't take several months. I've known patients in similar circumstances to hang on for as much as a year. It's unfortunate but there's nothing that can be done."

Not legally, Rene thought. But he didn't dare say it aloud. Not to Dr. Sternberg, who might become suspicious. And not to Christopher, either. As a doctor, he surely understood the situation already.

Rene found that he was curious about only one thing. How long would Christopher wait? Rene judged that he was too greedy to let nature take its course. Yet he couldn't do anything too soon after learning of the inheritance. He was smart enough to know it might raise Rene's suspicions. But Rene didn't believe he'd delay very long before acting. He considered giving some sort of follow up signal but decided against it. Christopher might feasibly find a way of using it against him.

Rene didn't care much one way or another. At least for his own sake. But he did hate to think of Jules lying there in limbo.

The prospect of delay troubled Rene in one respect. With so much at stake, Christopher might grow extremely impatient. Rene acquired a pistol and began sleeping with it under his pillow. As a doctor of medicine Christopher surely had knowledge of poisons, so Rene began taking all his meals out of the house. He was not, he knew, the primary target. But being the secondary one, even theoretically, was a dangerous enough position for him. He considered leaving the city, but his loyalty to Jules prevented him.

"Monsieur Melendez."

"Yes? Who is it?" Rene woke from a dream whose details had been indistinct but unmistakably disturbing.

"Suzette."

The night nurse.

"Yes, Suzette. What is it?"

"You need to come, monsieur."

"Jules?"

"I'm afraid so."

She closed the door behind her, leaving him privacy to get out of bed. He pulled on his clothing and headed upstairs.

"I can hardly credit it," Dr. Sternberg said. "I was certain he'd hang on for a good while yet. His last electrocardiogram showed no signs of heart trouble."

His last electrocardiogram. Yes. Taken a week or two before Rene told Christopher about Jules' will.

"You're sure that's what it was?" Rene asked. "His heart gave out?"

"Almost certainly. We can do a post mortem to confirm it if you wish."

"I hardly think that's necessary," Rene said. "His condition was terminal, after all. There is ample documentation of it in his charts. And as he was under your daily care, there should be no problems about the death certificate."

"As you say," Dr. Sternberg nodded.

Christopher wasn't the only corrupt physician in San Francisco, Rene thought. All the more reason to pack up and leave.

As soon as the cabin attendants permitted it, Rene adjusted his seatback to full recline. In first class on Air France, that nearly made a bed. For the first time in weeks he expected to be able to sleep. Christopher had been the soul and body of tasteful mourning during the days since Jules' departure. Rene was certain that all Paris would rave about his decorum at the funeral. What they would really be wild over was his beauty, of course.

Rene had flown on ahead. Christopher would follow in a few days. There was very little for either of them to do. Most of the arrangements had already been made by transatlantic telephone. Really, there was only one matter yet unresolved. A tiny, irregular matter involving the hardly significant sum of five million or so that was to be split between Rene and Volk. Christopher would be inheriting plenty. But Rene was not at all certain that Christopher saw it that way. Sometime during the next few days, Rene had to find a way of ensuring his own safety. A young man who had killed twice in the space of a few months might do anything. And a will, though Rene had been told his own was bulletproof, could be forged. A replacement document could be prepared and substituted for the real one. A man with all those millions in the bank could see to such a thing easily.

Rene had no particular concerns about Volk. If ever a man had been capable of taking care of himself, Volk was it. But Rene had no experience of such things. He'd have to learn fast.

EVAN WHITNEY: 1983

I

"Jules had the worst taste in the world," Christopher laughed. "In everything but men, that is. Look at all this. There's no getting around it. It's too embarrassing. I can't consider entertaining with the place looking like a vampire's wet dream. Everyone will think I'm the offspring of some bizarre liaison between Eva Peron and Bela Lugosi. And the rumors about my parentage are bad enough already. I know it'll be expensive, but every inch of the place has to be redone. I don't want to keep anything. Not a scrap of it."

"It's a designer's nightmare," Evan nodded. It was true that the place was deplorable. But the furnishings, tasteless as they were, had originally been expensive. An antique dealer would swoon at the opportunity it all presented. He was pretty lightheaded himself.

"So what do you say?" Christopher asked.

"I'd love to have a crack at it," Evan said, thinking of all the designers in the city that would be peeing themselves when they heard about the commission.

"Just what I was hoping," Christopher nodded.

Evan wasn't exaggerating. It was a dream commission. From the street, Dr. Christopher Melendez-Greene's house was one of the most impressive in Pacific Heights. The architecture, a rhapsody in ornately sculpted white stucco which recalled Paris, or perhaps more accurately Paris as interpreted by the plutocrats of Buenos Aires, wasn't to Evan's taste, but that wasn't the point. Plenty of people considered such buildings beautiful. And Christopher wasn't exaggerating the hideousness of its décor. The previous owner, the man Christopher had inherited the property from, furnished it in the style of a medieval castle. Everything was gothic, ornate, heavy, dark, and looked like it had been plundered from a real castle or at least a previous century. Jules was an award winning film director and thought of the place not as a home so much as a film set. Evan's friends in the business in Los Angeles assured him this was typical of people in movies.

Evan recognized Christopher as a kindred spirit, a man whose good looks and charm garnered him so much admiration that his professional accomplishments were obscured. Evan's career in modeling had certainly smoothed the pathway as he'd begun his new one in interior design. He hardly had to show up at meetings to receive commissions. He slaved away preparing pitches that would never seriously be attended to. And lots of clients of both genders barely looked at the renderings he presented, staring raptly at him instead. He knew how it felt to have his success attributed to appearance rather than ability. Bitter—that's how it felt. The success itself became tainted. He could hardly take pride in any of his work because of the public skepticism occasioned by his physical attributes. He realized that in the grand scheme of things this wasn't such a terrible cross to bear. He wouldn't have dreamed of complaining about it to any but his closest and most trusted friends. He knew exactly how self-indulgent he would have sounded doing so. But he had always wanted to be taken seriously as a professional and as a human being. And the apparent impossibility of this still rankled. He knew the queens who believed they ran the city would advise him to shut up and keep cashing the checks. Much as he hated them as a type, he recognized the pragmatism behind that sentiment. But Evan wasn't the sort of man who could put a price on his self-respect. At least, he didn't want to think of himself that way. And there was Will to consider. More and more, Will's good opinion of him mattered to Evan. In the beginning of their relationship this had been the last thing on Evan's mind. He was shocked to realize how much he had changed. He had become more than just a pretty fact and arresting collection of muscles in order to win Will's authentic regard and be the man Will could proudly introduce as his husband.

Evan sensed the same sort of impulse in Christopher, and the same struggle against public expectations. Being a medical doctor certainly wasn't the same as being a designer. The general public held certain assumptions about the rigors of medical school, internship, and residency programs. But there was still a whiff of suspicion surrounding Christopher Melendez-Greene that Evan recognized and related to.

"I know Big Steve and company don't like him much," Evan said at dinner a few nights after signing the contract. It was his turn to cook, and he whipped up a Salad Nicoise. Will didn't consider the dish real cooking, but he was certainly happy to be off kitchen duty. To be fair about it, Will did more than his fair share of the cooking. Anyway, Salad Nicoise was good for you. One of Evan's gym buddies said so. Evan had forgotten the details. But Dale's abdominals were fast becoming a local legend, and if Salad Nicoise facilitated results like those, so be it.

"It's not really that they don't like him," Will said. "He's likeable enough, God knows. That's part of the problem. Perhaps the crux of it, really. It's more that they don't trust him. And they have ample reason."

"I know," Evan nodded. "I've heard all the stories. But he seemed completely reasonable to me. He was fine with the details of the contract."

"Well," Will said, spreading herbed butter on a slice of baguette, "just be careful, that's all. Contracts are made to be broken. I can't tell you. . ."

"Are all attorneys as suspicious as you?" Evan laughed.

"You should have a chat with Nick Romanovsky on that topic," Will said, rolling his eyes. "He makes me look like a schoolgirl."

"What I like best about these," Christopher said, leafing back through the renderings, "is that you really listened to me. You got what I was asking for even though I couldn't envision it myself. Or even describe it very clearly. It's almost uncanny—like you were reading my mind."

"Good designers have to be mind-readers," Evan laughed. "Or at least make their clients believe they are."

"I bet you can make people believe just about anything you want do," Christopher said.

Evan chose to ignore the innuendo, which had been much more apparent in Christopher's body language than in the actual words. He'd known of too many guys who'd made the mistake of mixing the professional with the personal. And besides, Evan's life was complicated enough. Will's feelings were so easily hurt.

The project itself veered almost daily—and some days practically hourly—between sublime dream and hideous nightmare. This was true of nearly all Evan's jobs, of course. But the immense scale and complexity of the Melendez-Greene project guaranteed that those extremes were more extreme than usual. It was the difference between an earthquake measuring seven on the Richter Scale and one measuring nine. Or a Fugita 4 tornado and a Fugita 5 one. If you had the choice you wouldn't experience either one, but if there was no escaping the fate, you knew darned well which one you'd choose. Thus, the challenges Evan faced both exhilarated and horrified him. He found himself fantasizing frequently about minor renovations to bungalows in Berkeley, jobs he could leave on site in the evening when he headed home instead of obsessing over well into the wee hours.

II

"Oh, sweetheart," Will sighed, wiping tears out of his eyes. "It's unbelievable. You must be so proud."

Evan had just finished taking him on a tour of the completed project. He always wanted to impress Will. Will was an attorney and a published poet, and in the back of his mind Evan always wondered if Will considered him a lightweight. He knew much of gay San Francisco looked at their marriage as a charade. Or an exercise in the strong exploiting the weak, at the very least. Evan hated this, but recognized that directly addressing the innuendos would be viewed widely as a confirmation of them. He couldn't imagine how such talk made Will feel, though he never mentioned it. It forced Evan to be ridiculously conscientious as a husband, and what was wrong with that? Making Will happy turned out to be its own reward.

And there was no mistaking his reaction to this project.

"I'll certainly be happy for people to see this and know it was my work," Evan nodded.

He led his client through the last walk-through. Christopher's satisfaction couldn't have been more apparent.

Christopher scrawled something across the invoice Evan had just presented to him and slid it across the desk.

"If you'll just sign and date this," he said.

Evan looked down at what Christopher had written. It said "paid in full."

"I don't understand," he said.

"Oh, I think you do," Christopher smiled.

Christopher's parting shot was a note, unsigned, which Evan received in the mail a week or so later. It said "it didn't have to be this way. I gave you plenty of chances to play nice."

"Certainly you could sue him," Will said, "but he was absolutely right when he said that it wouldn't be in your best interest. Failing that, you could have a lien placed on the property. But God knows when he might get around to selling it. It could be years before you got the money. Decades, even."

"Bastard," Evan fumed.

"Me, or him?"

"Him of course," Evan said. "You're just the messenger. You know one of the things I depend on you for is telling me the truth. God knows nobody else ever does."

"Every guy who ever tries to pick you up is telling you the truth," Will laughed. "At least a variety of it. But I get your point."

"Not everything is about sex," Evan protested.

"Can I quote you?"

"Come on, Will."

"Sorry, hon," Will said. "You know, he's actually been very astute about it. He gave you no trouble about paying the first two installments. As a result, all the contractors got their money. All the materials and furnishings got paid for. It's not like you're actually losing money on the job. You're just not making any. Isn't that right?"

"More or less."

"I know working for free doesn't feel good," Will said, "but everybody who ever walks into that house will know that it was decorated by a serious talent. And half the city already knows you were the designer on the project. So you'll at least get the exposure. I know that's not much consolation. But before you got the contract you were complaining that nobody seemed willing to trust you with a really big commission. That's certainly won't be true anymore."

"You're right," Evan said.

"But you're still not happy about it."

"If word gets around that I let him do that to me," Evan said, "every client I ever work with will expect to do the same thing."

"That's a risk, I suppose," Will nodded, "but I happen to believe it isn't going to go that way."

"Why?"

"First of all, because as big an asshole as he is, he's really trying to go legit these days. So I don't think he's going to be talking to anybody about having stiffed you. As long as you keep your mouth shut, he will."

"Please," Evan snorted. "You don't really believe that."

"That business a year or so ago was really nasty. The police bought his story about self-defense, or at least the prosecutor's office chose to pretend they did. But plenty of damage had been done. Bottom line: there was a dead hustler in his bedroom and no explanation that didn't leave him looking like a sleazy character at best. Olivia Styles dumped him and his cover as a heterosexual was blown and none of those society types will have anything to do with him now. Not to mention, the nice folks over at the medical association talked seriously about suspending his license to practice in California. So I really don't think he's going to be telling people any stories that reflect badly on him. You could choose to believe he's bluffing, and he certainly might be, but the thing you have to remember is he's smarter than he is crazy. Word is, he's worth upward of fifty million since Jules de Croteau died, so the money isn't any object to him. But all that money can't buy him respectability if he keeps on being a bad boy."

"I wouldn't think respectability mattered to a guy like that."

"There aren't as many true outlaws in the world as TV and the movies want us to believe," Will said. "Now, he might just let you take him down over this because in the process you'd be taking yourself down as well. He's certainly that spiteful. Especially about our crew. You've heard the stories."

"Mutually assured destruction," Evan said. "You make it sound like Reagan versus the Russkies."

"It's not quite that serious," Will said. "And in this case, there are no drag queens involved."

"Ha, ha."

"But the real reason I don't think you have anything to worry about," Will said, "is that most of your clients aren't anything like Christopher. Most of them will do anything they can think of to keep the hottest decorator in the Bay Area happy. That's not going to stop. Trust me on it."

At dinner the next Saturday evening, Kirk reminded him that nobody ever won a fight with an evil queen, and Yvette delivered a lengthy homily on the workings of karma in the world. It was almost as if Will had written their dialogue.

Evan supposed that settled it.

He was used to the three of them ganging up on him. He kind of depended on it.

"Mr. Whitney?"

The voice crackled over the line. Evan couldn't decide if it sounded familiar or not.

"This is Evan."

"Sonny Dallas here."

Sonny Dallas was one of the city's most celebrated real estate agents and notorious queens. He was Cooper Luxemberg's former sugar daddy and a previous business partner (and rumor hinted at more than that) of Ned Westerleigh.

"Hello, Mr. Dallas."

"Reason I'm calling—been talking to all kinds of designers and none of them get me. But people keep telling me you're the man to redecorate my place in Hillsborough. And now that I've seen what you did at Dr. Melendez-Greene's house, I have to agree with them. So when can we meet?"

Ned Westerleigh had told Evan to expect this call. Ned assured him there would be no difficulty about payment in Sonny's case.

MORGAN LUNDQUIST: 1984

I

Bobby Lee came up the jetway looking like the fifth horseman of the apocalypse.

"God, no," Forrest muttered.

But Morgan wasn't surprised. He had heard it in Bobby's voice the last time they talked on the phone and was dreading Bobby's arrival. He'd spent the last week bracing himself for it. As much as Forrest pretended to disapprove of his cousin, he would be devastated. The real surprise, as far as Morgan was concerned, was that Bobby had been allowed on the plane in that condition. The general public was in on it these days, and their paranoia appeared to have no limits.

"Wait here," he told Forrest. "I'm going to go call Jamie Altman. I'll get him to meet us at the house."

"Right," Forrest grunted. "I guess you'll be able to find us in baggage claim."

"You know," Morgan said as Bobby stumbled into the departure lounge, "you probably should commandeer a wheelchair. I'm not sure he'll make it to baggage claim on his own feet."

"Is there a phone I can use?"

"Sure, Jamie," Morgan said. "Right this way."

"I'm arranging to have him admitted," Jamie said, following Morgan into the study. "Sick as he is, the air on that plane was really bad for him. I'm surprised he got here without going into full-on respiratory collapse."

"So it's that pneumonia?"

"It could be anything," Jamie said. "We won't know for certain until we do some tests."

"Oh, please," Morgan said. "Do we have to play it that way?"

"I know I'm your friend," Jamie said, "but this doctor stuff has to be done by the book."

"All right," Morgan said. "Sorry."

"No apology necessary."

"Will we need an ambulance?"

"It'll be a lot faster if you and Forrest drive him over," Jamie said. "And cheaper."

Morgan looked in on Forrest and Bobby Lee in the guest room and then went to bring the car around to the front door. Despite Jamie Altman's reluctance to name it, there was no mistaking what it was. Bobby was the closest one so far. First there had been faceless names spoken—or more accurately, muttered—at brunches or in the locker room at his gym. Later, it was people he actually knew by sight. Friends of friends of friends. It seemed inexorable. It kept coming closer. Last week, Reggie Newton's funeral. Morgan had seriously considered having the gym fumigated. Not that he didn't know better, but some of the members were truly rattled and he couldn't afford to lose their business. Now it had come to this. Forrest's cousin, Bobby Lee. Forrest's double first cousin, to be technical about it. Morgan hadn't known such a thing existed until he met them. How many times had he cringed listening to them explain what it was that made them double first cousins to befuddled "yankees", who, they asserted, were ignorant of the nuances of kinship?

"There's nothing more for you to do here," Jamie told them. "You might as well go home."

They were in the corridor outside Bobby Lee's room. The nightmarish paraphernalia had already been set up outside the door. No one was supposed to enter without first donning cap, gown, mask, gloves. Like Bobby Lee was hazardous waste or something. Officially, of course, it was all for Bobby Lee's protection. But the theatricality of the scene made that assertion seem ridiculous.

"I don't want to leave him alone," Forrest sobbed.

"He's in good hands," Jamie said. "This ward is the best in the city."

"I'll take care of it, Jamie," Morgan said, stroking the back of Forrest's neck and reminding himself he wasn't supposed to care who might be watching.

"I can't believe this is happening," Forrest said, bleary-eyed across the breakfast table the next morning. "I simply can't."

"Of course you can," Morgan said. "Not a week ago you were predicting all sorts of dire consequences as a result of Bobby Lee's refusal, and I quote, 'ever to listen to good advice from the one person in this world who really and truly loves him'. You spend half your life complaining about that. You believe this is happening, all right. You just don't want to."

"You bastard," Forrest muttered, staring into the distance over Morgan's left shoulder. "You god damned bastard. Making sense at a time like this. Can't you ever just let go and feel anything? Like normal people do?"

"That's not fair," Morgan protested.

"You know what? I don't care if it's fair or not."

"Of course you don't," Morgan said, "but one or the other of us has to keep his wits about him. Bobby Lee needs that. Fall apart all you want to. Throw something. For that matter, there are far worse things you could call me than bastard. So do it. Seriously. Do the grand opera thing for both of us. I'm going to call the hospital."

Bobby Lee rallied over the next few days. Morgan had known he would. Let a handsome man smile at Bobby Lee, and there was very little he couldn't bring himself to endure. And though Bobby Lee couldn't see anything but the eyes of the people caring for and visiting him, he convinced himself that he was surrounded by adonises and their female equivalents. The power of suggestion was enough. He responded to his treatments. He looked better every day. Still, the news wasn't good. He had pneumocystis pneumonia. The lesions on his arms and chest were Kaposi's sarcoma. And he'd been battling a toxoplasmosis infection. He was, Jamie Altman finally admitted, a textbook case.

"I know he has no insurance," Forrest told the hospital administrator. "You're just going to have to bill me personally for everything. Anything he needs. I mean it."

"I appreciate that, Mr. Reynolds," the administrator said, "but our situation is very difficult with regard to these patients. I hope you can understand that."

"Perfectly well," Forrest said, pulling his checkbook out of his briefcase. "Now I'm prepared to write you a check for twenty thousand this minute. Surely that's enough for——how shall we say?——a down payment?"

This was the kind of thing Forrest was exceptionally good at. Throwing money around in a good cause. He could whine and complain to beat the band, and he tended to dither rather than act decisively. But when it was a question of money he just put his head down and went for the goal line. Morgan, whose father was a successful cardiac surgeon who'd grown up in a family of successful cardiac surgeons, pinched every penny until it screamed and then, likely as not, shoved said penny back into his pocket instead of spending it, so Morgan appreciated good, old-fashioned, no-holds-barred profligacy, even when its object was a little questionable. In this case, of course, he had no misgivings about it whatever.

"And don't worry, Mr. Overbeck," Forrest said, sliding the check across the desk top. "I'm not going to run off to my bank the minute we're through here and stop payment."

"Steady, Forrest," Morgan muttered.

"Anything he needs," Forrest said. "You know I'm serious now."

Bobby Lee continued to improve, and on the tenth day Jamie Altman agreed to let him come home. Bobby Lee had only planned on a two week visit to San

Francisco and immediately started agitating about his return flight to Nashville, but Forrest put his foot down. The hands would have to run the farm without him. He wouldn't be going back to Tennessee any time soon. For once, Bobby Lee didn't protest. He seemed to accept Forrest's order in the spirit in which it had been issued.

Every day Bobby Lee got a little better, though anyone could see he was still a very sick man. Morgan wondered how much time he had left but didn't raise the matter with Forrest, who was bent on Bobby Lee's full recovery in time to take him on a trip to Hawaii in eight more weeks. Morgan couldn't see it as a reasonable possibility but sat silent and trying to smile during the daily discussions of their travel arrangements. Indeed, Morgan was the one who stopped in at Bart Correa's office and added Bobby Lee to their airline and hotel reservations.

"He's out of his mind, of course," Bobby Lee said. "You know it as well as I do."

"I know that he loves you very much," Morgan said.

"The only reason I'm letting him do all this is because once it's over he'll never forgive himself if he didn't do everything possible. Not that it'll change anything."

"You don't know that," Morgan protested.

"Of course I do," Bobby Lee said. "You do, too."

"They're coming up with new treatments all the time," Morgan said.

"I'll just about be able to get through this," Bobby Lee said, "as long as you don't start sounding like him."

"All right," Morgan said.

"Once I'm gone," Bobby Lee said, "you'll be all he has."

"Our friends. . ."

"Are terrific guys," Bobby Lee said. "I know. I've met them all. But you're the only one he's ever allowed to see his imperfections, while I've known about them since we were toddlers. He's going to see an unhappy ending as a personal failure."

"That's what I'm afraid of," Morgan agreed.

"Perfectionism to the extent Forrest suffers from it is a form of mental illness," Bobby Lee said.

Morgan certainly couldn't argue with that.

"You're going to have to watch out for yourself," Bobby Lee said. "When he needs someone to blame, any target will do."

The respite was all too brief. It wasn't nearly as simple as lots of rest and ample, wholesome meals. Inside three weeks Bobby Lee was back in the hospital and Forrest was inconsolable.

Then the unthinkable happened. Jamie Altman had a heart attack. He was ridiculously young for it, but it happened nonetheless. He felt a little unsteady on rounds but ignored it. One of the ward nurses didn't like the look of him and called the cardiologist on duty who convinced him to have an EKG done as a precaution. It was a mild attack. He was expected to make a complete recovery. But he'd be off work for six to eight weeks. His patients had to be farmed out to other doctors. The ones with HIV/AIDS were assigned to Dr. Christopher Melendez-Greene.

"I believe it will turn out to be a blessing in disguise," Forrest said.

The Luxemberg-MacDonalds were hosting brunch that Sunday. Griffin was a wizard in the kitchen, and, since Cooper's day to day diet was extremely stringent, he welcomed occasions such as this as opportunities to show off his skills. Morgan was a bodybuilder himself but wasn't sure he'd be able to exercise Cooper's degree of self-control if Forrest had been so inspired in the kitchen. Sometimes he wasn't sure if Forrest knew they had a kitchen and the rest of the time he was pretty sure Forrest didn't know what their kitchen was for.

"You know you're going to have to explain that," Tristan said.

"Sure are," Jared said. "Look who you're talking to."

"Jamie Altman is a fine doctor," Forrest said. "Everybody at this table knows that. We all use him as our personal physician."

"And with good reason," Big Steve grunted.

"Right," Morgan ventured, hoping he wouldn't pay for expressing even that meager skepticism when they got back home.

"You'll get no argument from me," Forrest assured them. "But Christopher Melendez-Greene has all but shut down the rest of his practice so he can devote himself full time to treating AIDS. This is well known. And I believe that a man with the kind of expertise that implies is more likely to be able to help someone like Bobby Lee."

"You're making an assumption that increased specialization automatically equals greater expertise," Cooper said, "and I have to tell you, I'm skeptical of that."

"Yes," Forrest said. "I understand what you're saying. You're absolutely right. But I sat in on Christopher's first consultation with Bobby Lee. And he was asking questions that Dr. Altman had never asked. He shared information about the disease and its treatments that neither of us had heard before. He was confident. He didn't pull any punches. He certainly inspired Bobby Lee's trust, and that isn't easy."

"It's none of our business, Forrest," Griffin said, bustling in from the kitchen and setting more dishes on the already crowded table. "Keep eating, everybody. We're nowhere near exhausting the provisions."

"I know none of you guys like him," Forrest said. "I've heard all your stories, and I certainly understand your reasons. But isn't it possible for a man to be really good at his job without being a likeable person?"

"It goes way beyond whether or not he's likeable," Scott said. "It's a question of character."

"Understood," Forrest said. "But my question stands. Does professional expertise really require good character?"

"To an extent it has to," Big Steve said. "Genuine expertise can only develop as a result of certain personal qualities—self-discipline comes to mind but it's not the only one—that are generally thought of as aspects of good character. But I'll be the first to admit it's not clear cut by any means. I can certainly accept the possibility that a man like Christopher could be very, very good at his profession and at the same time be a truly sleazy individual."

"There are thousands of examples," Tristan admitted.

"Maybe millions," Ashby said

"You're a doctor, Ash," Jared said. "What's your take on it?"

"I'd rather not discuss it," Ashby said, "but I certainly don't think being Christopher's patient will do Bobby any harm."

Dr. Melendez-Greene was good at what he did. No question about it. But he was no miracle worker. There were, Morgan mused, no miracles in the offing. Medical science might produce them in time, but Bobby Lee's time was running out. Not even Christopher's charm and amazing looks would be enough to pull him through.

II

"I was just so certain he would beat it," Forrest sobbed.

"I know you were, sweetheart," Morgan said, stroking his hair. They were in the corridor outside Bobby Lee's hospital room. Ordinarily, Forrest detested public displays of affection, but he was too distraught to object.

"And now it's over."

"You wouldn't want him to go on suffering like that," Morgan pointed out.

"Stop making sense."

The day of the memorial service was perversely beautiful. The actual funeral would be in Tennessee, but Forrest arranged for a ceremony in San Francisco. In his last days, Bobby Lee had relented and decreed it his spiritual home.

"I beg your pardon," Morgan said, as quietly as he could.

"You heard me," Christopher grinned.

Not twenty feet away from them, on the front steps of the chapel, Forrest was being consoled by Tristan and Big Steve.

"I don't believe it. And at a time like this."

"Why not?" Christopher. "It's not like you're my patient. My patient is dead, poor fucker. Life has to go on. And I bet you're a real tiger in the sack."

"I have a husband," Morgan said.

"And I bet he hasn't let you touch him in months," Christopher said.

Which, Morgan had to admit, was true. But it wasn't the point.

"Believe me. I see it all the time. All the happy couples, and none of them having sex any more. Everybody's too terrified to get off. Well, I say fuck that. What's the point of being gay if there's no more sex?"

"Sorry, doc," Morgan said. "You've got the wrong guy."

"You know where to find me," Christopher smiled. "When you change your mind."

BUZZ MONTGOMERY: 1984

"You're not wearing that," Trevor complained.

"Why not?" Buzz asked. "What's wrong with it?"

"This is a party and that makes you look like you're going to work," Trevor said. "And anyway, everybody's seen that sweater. Several times."

"I like this sweater," Buzz said.

"Buzz."

"I feel good in this sweater."

"It makes you look like an English teacher," Trevor said. "In fact, that's how long you've had it. I remember the first time you wore that sweater to school. I was in eleventh grade, dreaming of being a senior and finally getting to take your class."

"Seriously," Buzz said, "it's just the guys. There's not going to be anybody there to impress."

"That's not the point," Trevor said.

"What is the point?"

"Oh, God," Trevor said. "Sometimes I just don't get you at all."

Yes, Buzz thought. That was certainly true.

They were arguing a lot lately. Always about little things. Insignificant things. Not what was really on their minds. That couldn't be a good sign. But what was he supposed to do? The idea of sitting down with Trevor to talk about their "issues" made Buzz feel sick to his stomach, and counseling, if they could find anybody who wasn't a charlatan or a homophobe, seemed like an admission of failure. For his part, Buzz felt that Trevor was going out of his way to find fault with him these days. It was a one hundred eighty degree turn from the way their relationship had always worked. He had hated the way Trevor always put him on a pedestal until Trevor pulled the pedestal out from under him. He had no idea what had prompted the change. Which was another thing that was his fault, he supposed.

He knew who his friends all blamed, however.

"You're not wearing that, either," Trevor said, pulling things out of the closet. "They may be our best friends, but this is a very special occasion."

"It's a dress rehearsal," Buzz said. "The real housewarming is next week. I'll rent a tux for that, if you want."

"A tux?" Trevor said. "A tux? Nobody wears a tux to a housewarming. And anyway, when your friend the famous architect is hosting a party to show off his new house, the one he designed, the one custom built especially for him and his husband, it's more than a housewarming. It's a major event. Here. Change into this. It's really hot looking and you've never worn it."

"A jump suit? You're crazy. Where did that thing even come from? I don't remember buying it."

"You'll be sexy in it."

"I'll look like I'm there to fix the furnace."

"You'll look fabulous," Trevor insisted.

"It's too young for me," Buzz said. "And Halloween was over a month ago."

"Stop arguing," Trevor said. "We're already late."

Jared heard them coming up the walk. As always, they were the last to arrive. As was typical lately, they were in the middle of an argument. He couldn't make out any of the words, but the edge to their voices was unmistakable. Their body language as he swung open the front door for them called to mind two murderers being interrupted as they ransacked the victim's pockets.

"Hey guys," he said. "Let me take your coats."

Buzz had been wearing the same black leather bomber jacket since Jared first met him. Jared had one just like it. So did Tristan and Nick. Sometimes when they all met for dinner on a chilly evening they looked like the crew of a B-17 just back from bombing Hanover. Jared thought of that jacket as iconic but recently he had overheard Scott telling Morgan it was a cliché. Trevor's Burberry tweed overcoat looked brand new and had probably cost as much as a used Civic.

"Go on in," Jared told them. "Everyone's here."

"Three guesses what they were fighting about," Jared said to Scott, who was putting the finishing touches on a chafing dish of meatballs to refill the buffet table. "And the first two don't count."

"Who they were fighting about," Scott corrected him. "Not what."

"Right."

"Buzz," Forrest grinned, lounging beside the fireplace, "look at that outfit. When did you start shopping the *International Male* catalogue?"

"I didn't," Buzz said. "It was a gift, apparently. Please don't tell my husband you like this look. Please. Whatever you do."

"So, sweetheart," Scott said, returning to the kitchen. "Want to make a bet on who'll bring it up first?"

"In this crowd?" Jared scoffed, "I'm sure it's too late for that."

"Love the haircut, Trev," Cooper said, pouring himself a glass of pinot noir.

"Thanks, dude," Trevor said. "The hair and makeup guy at the station wanted to try something different."

"Very cutting edge," Cooper said. "Very *au courant*."

"I'll tell him you liked it," Trevor said. "I think you know him. Jonnie Maxwell."

"Sure do," Cooper said. "Sold him and Jack their place in Noe Valley."

Griffin had decided long ago that there were only three kinds of men in the world. It wasn't about sexual orientation, religious preference, ethnic background, social class, or any of the usual markers that determined the categories. It was about their relationship with their hair. The first group consisted of the bald guys, the guys with tragic hair texture, and the guys who it seemed just didn't give a fuck, tonsorially speaking. He felt sorry for them and envied them in equal proportions. For whatever reason, they were on the sidelines. They never gave that aspect of their presentation a thought. At worst, they jammed a baseball cap on their heads and were good to go. The second group consisted of guys like himself. They wanted to look neat and well groomed, but most of all they didn't want to call attention to themselves, at least in that way. This group included most of the men in the room. The final group included the individuals whose hair, either their own, God given hair or the hair they had purchased, was used to make statement. Like his husband. How many different cuts and styles had Cooper been through in the five years plus that they'd been together? How much time and money had been devoted to maintaining that admittedly magnificent, all but indescribable coif, which was recognizably one of the best of his many remarkable features? Cooper's bathroom testified to the seriousness with which he took this aspect of his regimen. There were shampoos, rinses, and conditioners, each in multiple varieties depending on the climatic conditions, the length of Cooper's current cut, and all sorts of other parameters Griffin could hardly guess at. And to style it there were oils, creams, pomades, waxes, pastes, clays, sprays, and mousses. These products Griffin knew intimately if existentially—their smells, their touch against his fingertips, their various and arcane manners of application. Regardless of the length or style or grooming agent in use in any given situation and thus the over- or understatement of its impact on his overall appearance, Cooper's hair made a consistent claim to the effect that not only was he drop dead gorgeous, he was probably the classiest guy you'd encounter that week. Whoever you were.

Trevor, who seemed determined in almost all things to emulate Griffin's husband, still hadn't mastered the nuances, which, apparently, were many and esoteric in the extreme. His hair didn't make a statement. It orated. Tonight, it was deafening.

"It's a magnificent house, my boy," Ned Westerleigh enthused. "Truly magnificent. Every inch of it. What a coup. I wouldn't have missed seeing it for the world. I'm so sorry Harris and I are double booked for the evening. But we'll be here next Saturday, with bells on."

"Thanks for coming, Ned," Jared said.

"You know, I have a few small parcels here and there," Ned said. "You, Cooper, and I should sit down next week and talk about building on one or two of them. I'm sure there's a market in this city for your aesthetic."

"That would be great," Jared said.

Good old Ned. Jared hadn't wanted to invite him tonight, feeling he was too grand for the gathering, but Scott insisted. That's all Jared had ever needed. Just the right contacts and a little push now and then from Scott. And now there was the prospect of more commissions.

"Sean. Great to see you," Cooper said.

"Hey, Coop."

"Great placing at the Californias," Cooper said. "Griffin and I were there. Congratulations."

"Thanks, man."

"You'd have won the light-heavies if Judge #3 hadn't hated your tattoo so much."

"And if Judge #4 wasn't such a homophobe," Big Steve said. "Guy's afraid if he doesn't score the good looking contestants down everybody will think he's gay. Fact is everybody already knows he's gay. That paranoia just makes him an asshole."

"So all things considered," Cooper said, "second place in the class was a great result."

"Thanks," Sean muttered. "Appreciate it."

"Nelson with you?" Big Steve asked.

It was a loaded question. No, it was a warning. Sean knew this, but walked into the trap anyway.

"Supposed to be meeting me here," Sean said, looking around the room.

"I ran into an old friend the other day," Cooper said.

"Who?" Jared asked.

"Remember Porter Winslow?"

"God," Jared said. "I haven't thought of him in ages. That was one hot young man. How's he doing?"

"All grown up," Cooper said. "Hasn't given up the gym. Very impressive."

"I guess San Diego agrees with him."

"He said he likes it there," Cooper said. "He was in town for a funeral. What else?"

"The airlines are making a fortune out of this disease," Jared winced. "Fucking vampires."

"It was Skip Erikson," Cooper said.

"Oh, God."

"Yeah."

"Oh, jeez. I'm sure sorry to hear that."

"Me too," Cooper said.

"He was so. . ." Jared shrugged, surprised to find himself at a loss for words. He'd gotten over Skip, but somehow the hurt feelings could still sneak up on him.

"Yes," Cooper said. "I always thought he'd have been a really decent guy if he'd had different friends."

"That's it exactly."

"Porter told me a funny story," Cooper said.

"Funny ha, ha? Or funny tragic?"

"Both, I guess you'd say. It seems that Skip's last name wasn't really Erikson. He was really Skip Eisenberg."

"No kidding?"

"Guess who made him change it."

"Every time I think I know about every shitty thing that bastard has done in his time, I get a nasty surprise," Jared said.

"We brought in just enough furniture for this evening," Evan told Will. "The real work starts Monday morning. You won't believe what this place looks like next Saturday."

"I'm sure it'll be amazing," Will said, "but it seems like such a lot of work. You'll just have to pull it all back out again so that Jared and Scott can move their own stuff in."

"I know. But it'll be worth it. You won't believe the guest list for next Saturday. Ned and Cooper have pulled out all the stops. And we've got photographers coming in after that. It's not just a big deal for Jared. It's going to be great for me, too."

Sean hadn't seen Morgan for several months. There was bad blood between the twins. It wasn't that Sean took Nelson's side in their dispute. He guessed he just suffered from guilt by association. Morgan never said anything about it, but Forrest always looked like he'd stepped in dog shit when he saw Sean. Then he tried to cover it up with that sickly sweet southern charm which wasn't a bit charming—or convincing. It wasn't particularly pleasant. Not that Sean could blame him. Nelson's picture could have been used in the dictionary as an illustration of "black sheep". The last time Sean and Morgan had run into each other was at the California Championships. Morgan had placed third in the light-heavies, just behind Sean. They were the same height and same weight. Their proportions were almost identical. Sean was still surprised that Morgan hadn't placed higher than him.

"Seen Nelson?" he asked, though he already knew the answer.

"I didn't know he was invited," Morgan said.

"Supposed to be meeting him here," Sean said. "Just thought you might have heard from him."

"I wouldn't have thought this was his kind of party."

Sean shrugged. But Morgan was right. When it came to Nelson, Morgan was always right. Had Sean misunderstood when Nelson talked about his plans for tonight? Had he really meant they should meet at that party over in Pacific Heights?

"Will," Griffin said. "I know it's none of my business, but are Ned and your Uncle Harris an item?"

"No," Will said. "Though they certainly give that impression. More kindred spirits than anything else. You know how it is when two people share a hobby. One they're really passionate about. It ends up a lot like a marriage."

"Yes," Griffin said, "I've noticed that. I just wouldn't have thought of anything Ned does as a hobby."

"It's the wrong word for it, of course," Will agreed. "Avocation would be a better term. Apparently you never really retire from the line of work they were in."

"I suppose not," Griffin agreed.

"Ned's way too diplomatic to have mentioned it," Will said, "but they're invited to a certain party in Pacific Heights tonight."

"Really?"

"Somebody's under the mistaken impression that Uncle Harris is a Republican."

"You're joking."

"That's how good he and Ned are at their little games."

It was as if Jared had been channeling the Bauhaus, Cooper thought. It was like getting to walk through the Barcelona Pavilion or one of those other buildings he'd only ever seen black and white photos of in architecture books. And the finishes: the marble, the chrome, the plate glass, were exquisite. His mind whirled. If he could get his landlord to sell Griffin and him the property their cottage sat on, could they afford to have it bulldozed and get Jared to design them something like this?

"Somewhere between here and Frankfurt," Ashby said, consulting his Breitling.

"I don't know how you stand it," Evan said.

"It would be just as bad for him," Ashby said, "if he had a regular job here in the city."

"I know," Evan nodded. "You doctors. I don't see how you guys have any kind of personal life at all."

"And yet some manage to," Tristan said.

"Yes," Ashby said. "Well, it all depends on what kind of practice you have. If I'd had the contacts and the interest for it and set myself up as a high society doctor, things might have been different."

"You mean, like. . ." Evan nodded.

"He whose name shall never pass the lips of the righteous," Tristan suggested, with a meaningful glance in the direction of Trevor and Buzz, who were conversing quietly but intensely in the far corner of the living room. Pretending not to be arguing, it looked like.

"Why don't any of these people want to talk about that series of interviews I did last week with Christopher?" Trevor fumed.

"Sweetheart," Buzz said, fearing a serious eruption was imminent, "tonight's supposed to be about Jared and this house."

"Oh, please," Trevor said, "since when did any of these queens turn their noses up at a chance to dish Christopher?"

"Keep your voice down, please."

"What if I don't?"

"Trevor, I promise you," Buzz said, "if you cause a scene, we'll leave."

"What if I won't come with you?"

"Then I'll go home by myself."

"You won't," Trevor smiled. "You say you will but you never do. You know what? I'm just about tired of your bluffing."

"Please, sweetie. Please just try to be nice."

"Nice? I'm always nice. It's these so-called friends of yours who aren't nice."

"Of course they are," Buzz said. "They've always been perfectly nice to you."

"They've always looked down their noses at me. And now that I'm not an intern anymore but a real reporter doing regular features at the station they're jealous that I'm so successful. That's what Christopher says it is. I'm younger and hotter than they are and they can't stand to see a guy like me getting ahead."

"Listen to me," Buzz said, "regardless of what you choose to think, none of that is true. Nobody here means to snub you. They just really are focused on Jared and this amazing house he's designed. It's his big night."

"It's about as appealing as a shoebox," Trevor sneered. "Pretty much the same size, too."

"What people haven't figured out yet," Big Steve said, "is that it's not only about their personal circumstances. Just because your own bank account is healthy and your own job is secure doesn't mean you shouldn't care about anything else. That's what enlightened self-interest really means, but the 'Great Communicator' hasn't really done a very good job of enlightening his followers. How could he? He doesn't write the scripts, he only performs them. He's like a puppet. Meanwhile, it actually does matter what happens to the people around you. It's a question, really, of what kind of country we all want to live in."

"The Social Contract," Dario nodded.

"Yes," Nick said. "The Gipper has convinced everyone that our new avatar needs to be the rugged individualist."

"'Who is John Galt?'" Dario laughed.

"Idiot woman should have been sent back to Russia," Big Steve grumbled. "She was as bad in her own way as Stalin. But for gay men to go down that road is nauseating. Our very existence is threatened and no one man is capable of standing up to it on his own, so what do those nitwits do? Ally themselves with the group of people most likely to shove them into the crematoria."

"Calm down," Tristan said, sauntering over from the buffet table.

"Don't tell me to calm down," Big Steve fumed.

"I only meant," Tristan said, "that if you get any louder, you could shatter glass. And there's so much of it around here that people might die."

"They're out and about quite a bit," Ashby said. "Mostly lunch dates, from what I hear."

"It's true," Sean said. "I've waited on them three times in the last month. I'm not supposed to say so, but the doctor is a shitty tipper. I suppose that's due to some questionable history between us."

"I bet it's not," Will said. "I bet he'd be a shitty tipper if Nancy Reagan herself was waiting on his table."

"You know," Ashby said, "I've always believed that the way a man tips is a sure indication of his character in general."

"I wonder if Buzz knows about it," Will mused.

"That his husband's boyfriend is a shitty tipper?" Ashby grinned.

"No, you idiot," Will laughed. "That his husband has a boyfriend."

"I don't think it's quite gotten to that stage yet," Sean said.

"You'd be a better judge of that than either of us," Will said. In spite of being happily married to Evan, he was still more than a little bit in awe of Sean. What he didn't know was that the feeling was mutual.

"But it could get there any time," Sean said. "And everybody in this room knows how determined Christopher can be."

Griffin wished that Scott and Jared had brought their dogs over from the old house for the party. He always felt more at ease with a dog or two in the room. He had pretty much convinced himself that he was better with dogs than with people. He suspected everyone he and Cooper knew sensed that about him. The people here tonight were his tribe—his own familiar people. Yet even among them he was often socially awkward. Not that they did or said anything

to make him feel that way. That was one of the biggest surprises of his married life to date. How downright nice all their close friends were. Though to
be completely accurate about it, they were all Cooper's friends that he simply
inherited. He was pretty sure they wouldn't have been his friends on his own.
But that said, there wasn't one of them he'd be too timid to ask for help from
if he ever really needed it. Still, he didn't drink and he'd eaten as much as he
comfortably could, at least for the moment, and when his hands were empty his
anxiety seemed impossible to control. A dog would have instinctively understood his predicament and would have pitched in immediately to occupy him
and put him at his ease.

"What did the babysitter say?" Nick asked.

"Everything's fine," Dario grinned.

"I told you," Nick grunted. "So much for your maternal instincts. People
leave their children with babysitters and go out for the evening all the time."

"Right," Dario said.

"Just not you."

"Great party," Cooper said.

"Yes," Evan said. "Great party. Everybody pretending not to talk about who's
sick or whose funeral they just went to and not a word about you know who."

"Who?"

"Exactly."

"Don't worry," Cooper laughed. "The night is young."

Scott couldn't remember ever seeing Jared this happy. Well, he should be
happy. Or at least proud. The house was a masterpiece. Not huge, of course.

Not grand or particularly impressive, as those things went. But the aesthetic statement was clear and true, and, though achieving it had driven both of them to distraction, the execution of Jared's original intentions was demonstrably of a very high level.

Whether they'd actually be comfortable living in the house remained to be seen. But as an advertisement, an endorsement of Jared's talents, it couldn't have been more perfect, even with a budget fifty or a hundred per cent higher. That was a sign of true genius as far as Scott was concerned. The ability to say what you needed to say regardless of the availability of resources.

What Ash had finally realized about really attractive men was that they were no better off, really, than everybody else. Observing them as a schoolboy, he had assumed the opposite, that their looks entitled them to some special dispensation under which they were fated to lead charmed lives. Even in his tiny hometown there had been plenty of examples to the contrary, but in each and every case there had been a clear disqualifying factor that made them exceptions to the rule. This one was stupid, that one was lazy, another one was morally dissolute to the extent that it was inevitable his life be ruined sooner or later. But in general, the default setting for all truly beautiful men seemed to be a condition of what could only be labeled grace. Looking around the room with his adult eyes, he knew better. Magnificent as they might be, they were as capable of making themselves, and as likely to actually be, as miserable as any other man. Life itself was the equalizer. And now, of course, it wasn't just the daily vicissitudes that degraded their ordained bliss, it was the virus.

It was never spoken of, or at most referred to obliquely, during their gatherings. There was some kind of unwritten rule. Presumably a *diktat* had come down from Big Steve to the effect that it wasn't an acceptable topic for general discussion. Still, Ashby knew it could never have been far from their awareness, individually or collectively. So far, no one in their inner circle was sick, though it had struck as close as Forrest's cousin Bobby Lee. But it would be shocking indeed if that didn't change. The statistics almost guaranteed it. It might be anyone. It might feasibly be all of them. That, presumably, was the reality that lay behind Big Steve's "thou shalt not". Group discussions could only lead to orgies of despair and God only knew what kinds of nihilistic acting out. The reality, Big Steve seemed to believe, was better examined and dealt with individually or in smaller groups. Each of them knew his own sexual history best. Each of them knew his own body best, not to mention his own psychological state.

One thing Ashby was certain of. When the time came, this group would behave differently from so many sets of friends he knew of. This group would exhibit the kind of solidarity that the community in general had lacked. Sure, the straights had behaved, continued to behave, reprehensibly. That went all the way to the White House, the Vatican, and the palaces of the media and high finance. Ashby sensed that history's eventual indictment of those institutions would be fairly damning. But at first gays hadn't done a great deal better themselves, though matters seemed to be improving. Still, there was an alarming lack of consistency abroad in their world. Unpredictability still prevailed among them.

But not here. Not in this house or the houses of his other closest friends. With a glance here and a gesture there, Big Steve and his deputies wordlessly ensured it.

"Well," Tristan said. "I don't think she's a bit funny. Not anymore. I know I'm supposed to because everyone insists she's a 'gay icon', whatever that means. And everyone swoons over her and repeats her *mots* over brunch. You can't *not* know what she said about such and such. And I'll admit that some of it is clever. Her self-deprecation is obviously very simpatico with a community like ours. And the irony, of course. Gay men do seem to have a special gene for the appreciation of irony. And then there's no question but that she's inspired a whole generation of drag queens. And we all revere them—whether we truly do or not. It's obligatory reverence that we all recognize and at least pretend to observe. God knows, nobody dares speak a critical word on that subject except behind closed doors with the lights off. But she lost me forever when she sat there on national television and defended Nancy Reagan. You might as well nominate Eva Braun for sainthood. No, she can't do a thing like that and claim to be a friend of our community. She can't tell us to eat cake and then gobble it all up herself. The friend of my enemy is not my friend. It can't work that way. Not in a world with any rationality at all."

"You realize, of course," Cooper said, "that yours is a minority opinion."

"He doesn't care," Nick said. "If anything, it makes him more entrenched in his position. You know, sometimes I think that the social glue that holds our gang together isn't the gym or our veneration of Big Steve but our collective reverence for contrarianism. It's not that we share opinions, though in many cases we do. It's that we share the impulse to contrary positions no matter how outrageous they are. And we honor them in each other. The more untenable they are, the more we admire one another for holding to them."

"My position with regard to that cow isn't untenable," Tristan insisted. "It's the only one with any integrity to it at all."

"Integrity?" Cooper laughed. "In our community?"

"'A man's reach should always exceed his grasp'," Nick nodded.

"He fought me on it tooth and nail," Trevor told Dario. "He threatened to come here in the nude instead of wearing it."

"It certainly is striking," Dario nodded, thankful that Nick had no particular interest in fashion.

"If I let him," Trevor said, "he'd turn into an old fuddy-duddy overnight."

"Surely not."

"Sometimes I think it would serve him right."

Griffin's favorite room was the tiny office Jared had created for Scott at the very top of the house, accessible only by way of the roof deck. Not more than eight feet square, it was an almost perfect glass box. Everything was built in. The desk top was a slab of onyx running the entire width of the room with filing cabinets situated underneath, and it only required the addition of a single piece of furniture, a chair, to be a fully functioning work space. He could imagine the divine Scott, secret avatar of his own long regretted Brock, toiling away here in magnificent solitude. The views, he imagined, must be ravishing.

"I'd ask you for the recipe," Buzz said, "but. . ."

"I know," Scott laughed, "there aren't enough hours in the day to work it back off at the gym. It isn't safe making a batch of it unless you're planning to feed at least a dozen guests."

"It's easy to forget that we're not typical," Big Steve said. "I mean look at us. We all have good jobs. We all live in nice homes. We're all coupled. It's what we're used to, so it's inevitable that we take it for granted. But for most people, the way we live isn't what it means to be gay. If it were, society in general might—might, you hear?—be a little less inclined to accept what's being done to us."

"That's assuming," Will said, "that society's attitudes were based on rational thought. I still believe it's not about our so-called lifestyles at all. It's all about the fact that we're so forthright about having penises. Not to mention where we insist on putting them."

"You're probably right," Big Steve said. "The homophobia of the masses is probably much more existential than I think. Ned Westerleigh was just taking me to task the other day for what he called my 'unfortunate utopian tendencies'."

"Utopian?"

"Yes," Big Steve laughed. "Of all people. And utopian? A police officer—utopian? Talk about oxymorons."

"But still," Will said, "you're right about one thing. We're not typical. Not at all, yet unlike that noxious crew over in Pacific Heights tonight, we're not elitist about it. And it's not just the straights who find us difficult to comprehend. The bars and shops and restaurants are full of young men who don't share our aspirations. Castro Street is almost a monument to our non-existence."

"It's not just that those young men don't share our aspirations," Big Steve said. "It's almost as if they don't know aspirations like that exist. Or, and here's the real tragedy, they've been brainwashed into believing they don't deserve to have such aspirations."

"Why won't any of these people let bygones be bygones?" Trevor moaned. "I know they've all got history with Christopher. But he's not like that anymore. He's really changed. He told me all about it."

"It's not just personal history," Buzz said. "He may have let go of all that baggage, but he picked up a whole new set in exchange. He supports closing the bathhouses. He supports mandatory testing and reporting—in the event a test ever becomes available. He supports quarantines. These guys hear him say all that stuff on the television, they see themselves behind barbed wire."

"He's just trying to save lives," Trevor protested.

"It doesn't help that he aligns himself with all the people who are dead set against giving us any rights," Buzz said. "He had his photo taken with Nancy Reagan. He used that shot for his Christmas card. What are people supposed to think?"

"That's all such bullshit," Trevor said. "It's a free country. He can have his picture taken with anybody he wants to. It doesn't make him Hitler's grandson."

"That's where you're wrong," Buzz said. "It's hardly a free country for people like us. And as bad as it already is, if the fundies get their way it'll be just like what happened to Wulf von Riedel back during World War II. You interviewed him for the station. You know his story."

"Oh, hogwash," Trevor said. "That was about a million years ago. You're just as bad as all these other dinosaurs."

Sean had to face it. He'd come to the wrong party. He should have left the minute Morgan raised the possibility. There had been plenty of time then to catch up with Nelson over at the wedding cake house. But he'd known what he'd see there. And, to be absolutely accurate, he wasn't completely certain that Nelson meant for him to show up. Nelson was so damned indirect. Or addled. Or disorganized. Or duplicitous. It hardly mattered which. Each explanation was as likely and as frustrating as any other. Nelson would have been happy to see him there, of course. Nelson was always happy to see him when he showed up, or at least pretended he was. But Nelson would be just as happy to tell him all about the party after the fact. Maybe even happier.

Looking around the room, Sean saw the kind of couples he wished he was part of. They made it look so easy, but of course it wasn't. If it had been, Sean would have been happily married long since. Instead, he was batting a thousand. He always ended up involved with psychos. It had never failed and it showed no signs it ever would. It was enough to turn a guy straight, except he was quite certain that the world had an endless supply of female psychos, too. And anyway, he'd probably get sick soon. Really, there was no way it wouldn't happen. Then it wouldn't matter.

What he'd do if he had the balls was throw himself on Big Steve's mercy. *Help me, Big Steve,* he'd say. *I just want a nice guy to settle down with. I'm sorry about all that shit—the prostitution, the porn, all of it. Just help me out and I'll be an upright citizen, a card-carrying member of your gaygeoisie.* He'd spent years imagining the scene. But he'd never gone through with it. He never would. He was sure that at the mention of finding him a husband Big Steve would look at him and give him the thumbs down. Big Steve's standards were high. Some guys just didn't deserve his help.

"So what do you think?" Morgan asked. "Should I agree to have Lance Garrison shoot me?"

"Last time I saw you without your sweats on," Cooper said, "you'd never looked better. So what if you're pushing thirty? It's been a couple of years since your last sessions with him, after all. I think you'll regret it later if you don't get some documentation of yourself in your current condition."

"You see, sweetie," Forrest said. "What did I tell you?"

"Better start tanning," Morgan said. "And dieting. Carrying about five extra pounds."

"Or seven," Cooper laughed, "after tonight."

Every party Griffin went to got the better of him sooner or later. Too many people, too much noise, the wrong music—that was a particularly sensitive issue, with his classical training—yes, all that, but his own self-consciousness was what really did it. He got to a certain point where he felt that if he stayed in the room another minute he'd start screaming. Which, given his upbringing and general demeanor, was anathema. Invariably things reached critical mass long before it was time by any reasonable standard to leave. And what did reasonable standards matter? Cooper liked to be the last guest, or at least nearly the last, to leave a party. Cooper loved parties, adored the crowds, found the noise and chaos exhilarating. Griffin would have chewed off his own leg before he'd have attempted, almost certainly without success, to drag Cooper away from any party before his appointed time.

Griffin wasn't a drinker. In earlier times he'd tried observing a strict two drink limit, but that had proven ineffective. It wasn't enough to relieve his anxiety, yet it was more than enough to leave him miserable the next day—headachy, dyspeptic, short-tempered, generally out of sorts. There was no liquid solution. At some parties there was food, but that didn't work, either. He nibbled, he gorged. The result was the same. He inevitably ruined his outfit, and his bowel, already under assault by his nerves, behaved unpredictably.

Years of trial and error had finally revealed the solution. Within minutes of his arrival at any social gathering, he identified his escape route. There was always a back garden, a balcony, a stair landing, a lobby, or in a pinch a doorstep where he could take refuge. He could disappear, commune with his thoughts, regain his all too easily dissipated comfort in his own skin. This had all taken place B.C.— before Cooper—but he relied on the strategy still. And they were barely in the door tonight before Evan Whitney insisted on taking Cooper out into the garden to get his opinion of the twin chaise lounges he had caused to be installed there, so Griffin hardly had to look for his emergency exit.

In his imagination, someone came looking for him. Someone noticed he was no longer in sight or earshot, wondered where he'd gone, became concerned, and actually came in search. Every time that's what he halfway expected, even after all these years. Nobody ever had, and he sensed that nobody ever would. Eventually he always grew tired of the solitude he had craved, or cold and uncomfortable, and would slink back inside, where, it inevitably turned out, nobody had missed him. He chalked it up to his general insignificance, but in that he was mistaken. Their crowd had taken note of his habit almost immediately. The first time it was mentioned, Cooper assured them that it was just one of Griffin's little quirks, completely harmless, not to be fretted over. *He likes a little fresh air during a party*, he told them when the subject came up. *It helps him relax. It gives him ideas. Besides, he's very sensitive to noise.*

It would, Griffin thought as he tried to find a comfortable position on one of those astonishingly expensive chaise lounges, have been an ideal time to encounter a nice dog or maybe two.

"I know," Ashby nodded. "I couldn't believe it the first time around. Why the Democratic National Committee didn't spend a million dollars or so paying the networks to air *Bedtime for Bonzo* in prime time the night before the election is something I've never understood. If he couldn't out act a chimp, how could anyone seriously expect him to lead the free world? Yet here we are, looking at four more years."

"Gentlemen," Nick grinned, raising his glass, "I give you the primate who presented with the opportunity might have changed the course of history."

"For that matter," Will said, "chimps live a long time. Bonzo may still be alive somewhere. In Palm Springs, presumably. So where's the tell-all book about his experiences backstage with the Gipper? It's as if the Democratic establishment hated Carter so much that they actually wanted him to lose four years ago. And now we're all stuck with that idiot. The Republicans are probably plotting to repeal the Twenty-second Amendment as we speak."

"Nancy in an ermine stole and a tiara," Tristan laughed. "Could you die?"

"Unfortunately," Nick said, "it's no joke. We're looking at four more years of a very bad time to be gay."

"Thank God you're out here," Trevor said, stumbling toward Griffin in the shadows of the garden. "I felt like if I had to stay in there a minute longer I'd start screaming. Do you ever feel that way at parties?"

"Yes," Griffin said.

"I knew it," Trevor gloated. "We're a lot alike, you and I."

This seemed such an absurd proposition that Griffin couldn't begin to formulate a response. It was like comparing a wallaby with a cheetah, and he was in no mood to be eaten.

"Is that chaise lounge as uncomfortable as it looks?"

"'Fraid so," Griffin said.

"Damn," Trevor said, sitting down in the chaise next to Griffin's. "Well, beggars can't be choosers."

"Right."

"Cold out here, too. Should have grabbed my coat."

"It's not that bad once you get used to it," Griffin said, though his teeth were on the point of chattering. Sometimes he couldn't help being contrary.

"This is nice," Trevor said. "Just the two of us. Chance to get to know each other a little better."

It sounded to Griffin like dialogue from a particularly badly written screenplay. He wondered if Trevor was working on one. It seemed like the kind of thing he'd do.

"I can't wait for Kirk and Yvette to see this place," Evan said.

"I'm sure they'll be impressed," Will said, trying to sound suitably enthusiastic. Encountering Sean always made him pensive. Not because of anything that actually passed between them, because nothing ever did.

"It's exactly the kind of house they should build," Evan said. "Cooper will help us find a site."

"It's too small," Will pointed out. "With three boys, I mean."

"You're right, of course," Evan said, "I mean architecturally."

"I can see Yvette in a place like this," Will nodded, "but won't Kirk find it too stark? He seems more the hunting lodge kind of guy."

"The three of us will just have to talk him around."

"I can't help it," Trevor sobbed. "It just hurts so much, you know? He says he loves me, but how can I believe it when he treats me this way?"

During the course of Trevor's monologue, which grew increasingly incoherent, Griffin sat revising Monday's lesson plans in his head. It was dark enough there in the garden that he didn't feel the need even to pretend he was listening. Every once in a while, Trevor's volume reached a level high enough that it pulled Griffin back into the present, and he'd interject something like "uh huh", or "you're not serious," but it really felt like being an extra caught accidentally on stage during one of Hamlet's more intense soliloquies. He had suspected almost since meeting Trevor that he was more than usually self-absorbed even for a guy that spectacularly attractive, and here, finally, was his proof. He got no satisfaction from knowing it. Buzz was one of the most notable figures in Griffin's pantheon, and thinking of him held hostage by such ridiculous notions as he was listening to was terrible.

What was more and more clear to him as he tried in vain not to listen was that Trevor hadn't actually jumped to any of his ridiculous conclusions about his marriage. He'd been pushed.

"I'm at my wit's end," Buzz said. "Everything I say is wrong. Everything I think is wrong. He says if I really loved him, I'd change for him."

"You can't let him get away with that kind of emotional blackmail," Big Steve said. "Once you give in to it, it never stops. Men have burned through their whole lives that way."

"I know," Buzz nodded, "but I've got to do something. He's convinced himself that he's miserable and it's my fault."

"He's had help," Nick said, "coming to that conclusion."

"That may be," Buzz said, "but I'm still his husband. I'm still the one who has to fix it."

"Just what is it that he wants from you?" Big Steve asked.

"He won't come right out and say it," Buzz said, "but he keeps mentioning things he's heard and things he's read about open relationships. He thinks he's being subtle."

"About as subtle as underground nuclear testing," Nick said.

"Who knows?" Buzz shrugged. "Maybe he's right."

"No, Buzz," Tristan said. "He isn't right. There may be issues in your marriage, but opening it up to sex with outsiders won't resolve anything. Open relationships are for couples who have already worked through their shit."

"If they're for anybody," Nick said. "Nobody's convinced me yet that they're a good idea under any circumstances. What he's really asking for is your permission to have an affair with you know who."

"But in his defense," Tristan quickly added, "Trevor may not know that's what he's asking for. Christopher's so convincing with that propaganda of his about open relationships that Trevor may not even recognize the ulterior motive at work."

"How could he not see that?" Buzz asked.

"Trevor's a hot young guy," Big Steve said, "who thinks that he should be able to have whatever he wants just because he's a hot young guy. And that's the kind of individual who's an easy target for the doctor. He knows exactly what to say to them because that's the kind of young guy he was not so long ago. And now that he's a media darling, thanks, ironically, to your husband's efforts, he's got a weird kind of credibility on all kinds of subjects that people ought to realize he's not qualified to talk about."

"Yes, yes," Buzz said, "I get all that. But what am I supposed to do?"

"Where is the boy prince anyway?" Nick asked, scanning the room.

"Hell if I know," Buzz said, "he told me he was stepping outside for some fresh air. My bet is he went off in search of a pay phone."

"Oh, hell no," Tristan muttered. "Shit, piss, fuck."

"What?" Big Steve asked.

"Time to call the cavalry," Tristan said. "Griffin's out in the garden."

"Try not to be too obvious about it," Big Steve said.

"What's that mean?"

"Griffin is already suspicious that we think of him as a mascot rather than a friend."

"Trevor," Tristan called from the doorway. "Trevor, you out here? Buzz is looking for you."

"Uh, hi," Trevor answered. "Just out here talking to my buddy Griffin."

"Go find your husband," Tristan said, walking toward them.

"If he wants me he can come find me himself," Trevor protested.

He sounded, Griffin thought, like a student of his at St. Dunstan's. One of the more annoying ones.

"Trevor," Tristan barked, "go."

So that's what he sounded like when he was on duty.

"All right, all right," Trevor said. "Keep your shirt on."

He moved toward Griffin like he was going to hug him, but then apparently thought better of it.

"I guess I'm going now. Talk to you soon."

"Right," Griffin said. The next thing he knew, Tristan's hand was on his shoulder.

"You O.K.?"

"Sure," he said, "but that one's not."

"No," Tristan agreed.

"He must have lost his mind," Griffin said. "It's unbelievable. If you can't be happy with a husband like Buzz, there's something seriously wrong with you."

"How long was he out here with you?"

"Seemed like hours," Griffin said, "but it probably wasn't more than twenty minutes. After a while I just stopped listening. I mean, what can you say to somebody who's not making any sense?"

"Bad, huh?"

"Fucking crazy," Griffin laughed. "Just fucking crazy. Thanks for rescuing me."

"Thought I'd better. You know how your husband gets when somebody upsets you."

"He does? Funny, he never mentioned it to me."

"Right," Tristan said. "Forget I said anything about it."

"Jesus," Griffin said. "Poor Buzz."

"Come on," Tristan said, "let's go inside."

"Nick, darling," Dario said, "It's time to go. We have to relieve the babysitter."

"Is that some new sex game I don't know about?" Ashby asked.

"No," Dario said.

"Yes," Tristan contradicted him.

"Nick, please, we should have been home half an hour ago."

"I'll slip the babysitter a little extra," Nick grinned.

"I'll just bet," Ashby laughed.

"I felt so stupid," Griffin said. "I didn't have any idea what to say to him."

"You have the right to remain silent," Will said. "Anything you choose to say can and will be used against you the next time you go to brunch. Or, more likely, behind your back."

"Exactly what I thought," Griffin said. "Sure could have used you out there, counselor."

"Poor Buzz."

"Yes," Griffin said. "It's very sad. I don't think I'll ever understand boys like Trevor. Not even if I live to be thirty."

One of the things Cooper liked most about his life, and there were a great many things he liked about his life—indeed, if there had been an award titled Most Self-Satisfied Gay Man in San Francisco he'd have been a shoe-in to win it—was that he could go to any party anywhere in town and be assured that no matter what drama erupted, it would have nothing to do with him. That's the gift Griffin had brought into their marriage. Unlikely as it had seemed in prospect, Griffin proved to be exactly as imperturbable as Cooper himself. They were polar opposites, of course. That's how all the pundits had finally come to explain their relationship. So Griffin must have come to his almost supernatural equanimity by some route completely different from Cooper's. But in this one instance and despite all the psychobabble to the contrary, it wasn't the journey that mattered but the destination. Griffin, for all his apparent fragility, was nevertheless the emotional equivalent of a Sherman tank. And something about his southern upbringing made it impossible for him to participate in airing their dirty laundry in public. Hell, Cooper could barely get him to fight things out in the privacy of their own home. His abhorrence of public scenes was downright pathological. What irony then, that Griffin had been the one Trevor unloaded on in the back yard. That in itself was inexcusable on Trevor's part. It was his stupid miscalculation that Griffin, mousy and nondescript as a spoiled young beauty like Trevor was likely to consider him, was someone safe to unburden himself to. Letting go like that in front of an individual more obviously impressive would have threatened too great a loss of face, but little Griffin was basically a nonentity and thus no such consequence need be feared. It was the equivalent of crying into your drink in front of a strange bartender in a town you were visiting briefly on business. Which meant this was the last straw. Really. Cooper had always been Trevor's biggest fan, defending him against all and sundry, excusing him of everything under the sun. But treating Griffin like that, as if he were insignificant—it was an insult that couldn't be abided. If Griffin was good enough to be Cooper's husband, and there was no argument about that, he was good enough for anything or anybody, and Trevor had been so far out of line that he'd never get back on the right side of it.

Poor Buzz. Nobody deserved what he was going through. And Cooper was convinced that he and Trevor hadn't gotten to the truly bad part yet. Poor Buzz. What Cooper wouldn't do to protect him from the baptism of abject misery that seemed inevitable. If ever Cooper had witnessed a couple fated not to succeed. There was nothing to do about it, however. Nature would have to take its course. Cooper promised himself he would make sure that Buzz's next husband deserved him. And he might as well start the search for likely candidates now. Buzz might not be able to recognize the inevitable, but Cooper did. And while Buzz would assume the end of his relationship with Trevor meant he'd be single for life, Cooper was damned if he'd see that happen.

Meanwhile, after tonight's debacle Griffin would be in need of reassurance, though he might well not have realized it yet. He was cerebral enough and sensitive enough that by morning he'd understand exactly how thoroughly he'd been demeaned, but Cooper would see to it that long before that Griffin's ego would be properly reinforced. Nobody was better at keeping a husband impregnable to the indignities perpetrated by thoughtless men than Cooper.

Sean headed up the hill toward the bus stop he'd seen earlier. It probably wasn't too late to catch up with Nelson at Christopher's place, but it would take the best part of an hour to get there. He wasn't sure he saw the point. Halfway up the curving block, he heard a car coming up behind him and stepped to the curb to let it pass.

"Sean? Need a ride?"

Sean looked over his shoulder. It was Ashby.

"It's just a few blocks," Sean lied. "I'm O.K."

"Get in," Ashby insisted. "It's cold out there."

Why punish himself? Why insist on chasing after Nelson, when all they were, if they were anything, was fuck buddies? It was just more of the same old insanity. What was it Einstein had said about that? But you never knew who you'd run into at one of Christopher's parties. His parties nowadays weren't anything like the ones in the old days. That was for sure. Still, you never knew who you might meet.

But Ashby was right. It was cold. It reminded Sean of back home. Montreal in winter. How did anyone survive it? He climbed into the car and they were off up the hill with a kind of roaring whine.

"Thanks, man," Sean said.

"You still have that place in Haight-Ashbury?"

"*Plus ca change*," Sean laughed, knowing how Ashby loved foreign phrases.

The Porsche was at least fifteen years old, perhaps closer to twenty, but immaculate. Typical. Sean had noticed two guys at the party sporting vintage Rolexes and Nick Romanovsky's shoes had just been re-soled. Even with a husband working only part time and three young sons in the household, Nick could afford new shoes if that's what he wanted. Big Steve's crew was that way about everything. Acquire the very best item you could, maintain it properly, hang onto it more or less forever. They were apparently that way about husbands, too. There was a lesson for you.

Except, it seemed, in the case of Buzz and Trevor. All the signs pointed to Buzz being a single man again soon. All because that fucking lunatic Trevor was fixated on some bullshit of Christopher's. It wasn't the first time Sean wondered why he hadn't made the world a better place by shooting Christopher between the eyes when he had the chance. That was what came of trying to be a nice guy: everybody suffered. He had it on good authority—there was a priest he occasionally fucked—that "no good deed goes unpunished" wasn't from scripture, but he was beginning to believe that it was only an oversight on God's part. Damned shame about Buzz, of course, but there wasn't anything Sean could do to prevent it. And if it was inevitable anyway, Sean should seriously consider focusing his efforts in Buzz's direction. That's what anyone in his situation who had half a brain would do. It would be a long-term project. Buzz wasn't the type to marry, or even date, on the rebound. Sean wasn't sure he had the patience. Or the time. He had no symptoms, but that could change by morning.

"Great party, guys," Big Steve said, slapping Jared on the back. As usual, he and Tristan were the last to leave. "Terrific house. May have to have you design one for us. Probably ought to bulldoze our whole street and put up a row of them."

It was the ultimate validation for Jared, who thought of Big Steve as the big brother he'd never had, as opposed to the one he did have who refused to be in the same county with him. This was, after all, the man who'd kept Jared on the trail despite Scott's initial fickleness and was thus ultimately responsible for their marriage and tonight's triumph. Was there a word in the dictionary for "platonic ideal of best friend and mentor?" Big Steve didn't mean to pontificate, to be revered by all who knew him as if he were an oracle. He was just a big, hot guy. With, as it happened, opinions. And impeccable taste.

"And you," he said, folding Scott into a bear hug. "Behind every great man."

"Thanks for everything, Big Steve."

"I feel terrible for Buzz," Tristan said.

"It's a damned shame," Big Steve said, the steam of his breath puffing out ahead of them as they walked down the hill to the Land Rover.

"I wish there was something we could do."

"There is," Big Steve said. "Leave him alone to work it out."

"But. . ."

"It's the only way he can get through it and hold on to his dignity."

"What's going to happen?"

"What's going to happen is what's going to happen," Big Steve said.

"It isn't love," Tristan said, "it's destiny. I know. But what if their destiny is to be together and Trevor just doesn't get it?"

"Please," Big Steve said, "look around you. The cosmos invented the concept of second chances. Whatever happens won't be the end of the world unless Buzz decides it is."

"And if he does decide that?"

"Then we'll do something," Big Steve said. "Then it will be time for us to intervene. And if and when that time comes, there's nothing we won't do, you see?"

"If you say so," Tristan said.

"For God's sake, don't go all Griffin on me."

"What the fuck does that mean?"

"Like a boy who lost his puppy."

"Maybe he gives that impression," Tristan said, "but somehow he never truly succumbs to despair."

"No, he doesn't," Big Steve said. "Fragile as he looks, he never does. Our friends are men. Real men. And that's your lesson for this evening."

"You looked very cute tonight," Cooper said, shifting into third.

"Did not," Griffin said, squirming with his usual cocktail of two parts embarrassment and one part pleasure. He'd never learned to take a compliment on his appearance seriously but fantasized more or less constantly about being considered truly hot by a truly hot man. And who was hotter than his husband, whose nickname, "World's Handsomest Man" was only partially ironic?

"Did so," Cooper growled. "I can't wait to get you home."

Cooper was always unusually horny after spending an evening in the company of his friends. Griffin had finally come to terms with it, deciding that it didn't matter who Cooper was thinking of when they were in bed together as long as the performance was up to standard. So far, Cooper had never let him down in that regard.

If he could just have put that afternoon's encounter with Jeff Curtiss out of his mind, Scott knew he'd have enjoyed the party. The house, Jared's masterpiece, was truly magnificent, and their friends had properly appreciated it. And the food, the flowers, all Scott's preparations really, had done the occasion justice. Even Buzz and Trevor's ongoing drama hadn't been enough of a disturbance to spoil the evening. True, that kind of turbulence was pretty much unheard of among their tribe, but they were all adults, all capable of giving it exactly the amount of attention it deserved—very little—and staying focused on the real reason for the gathering. They had done Jared proud. Scott would never be able to thank them enough for the attention they had paid Jared and their effusions over the house.

It was hard to see how things could have been more perfect.

But though his distraction had been sporadic at most, from time to time during the event he found himself recollecting his surprise the instant he recognized the panhandler there on Market Street as his old friend, O.K., fuck-buddy, Jeff. There were panhandlers everywhere these days. It was hard to go anywhere in the city without running across one. Many of them were sick, of course, which was unspeakably sad, and which invariably filled Scott with that noxious combination of gratitude and guilt over his own good fortune mixed with the nagging fear that it might run out at any time that had become the universal subtext of gay life in the city. But though he occasionally recognized men he had seen on the streets and in the clubs standing here and there rattling their tin cans and mumbling their beseeching mantras as he passed, he'd never before seen anyone in that condition that he actually knew by name.

Or had slept with.

And in that initial moment of recognition, it almost seemed that Jeff was as shocked as he was. Scott had to park the car several blocks from the bakery, and was headed up Market Street to pick up the desserts he had ordered for the party.

He noticed the man out of the corner of his eye, and he barely slowed down as he strode past. It was how he always armed himself against the sight and the distress it brought with it. He still didn't know what had made him turn to look the man full in the face. And the man himself seemed intent on the retreating backside of a young hustler who, apparently, had just insulted him in some vague way. But for whatever reason their eyes met, and though nothing about Jeff's appearance seemed at all familiar, changed as he was by his illness and bad fortune, the eyes were—well, the eyes were the first thing Scott had ever noticed about him. And they hadn't changed.

"Jeff?"

"Scottie. Fancy running into you."

"Jeff. I can't believe it."

"Lookin' great, Scott."

Which of course Scott couldn't respond to with any degree of authenticity. All he could do was stare. And a moment later, stifle a sob.

"Hey, buddy," Jeff said, "none of that."

"Oh, God, Jeff."

"So you're one of the lucky ones," Jeff said.

All Scott seemed to be able to do was stare at the grimy fingers grasping the tin can.

"So far," Scott grunted.

"Thank God."

"Who knows?" Scott said, trying to master his rioting emotions. "Probably not for much longer, as far as that goes."

"One day at a time, Scottie."

Those fingers. That tin can. Scott patted his jeans pocket and realized he'd left his wallet in the car.

"God, Jeff," he said. "I feel awful. I don't have anything with me."

"Don't sweat it," Jeff said. "Wouldn't take your money anyway."

"If you'll wait here," Scott insisted.

"Forget it," Jeff said. "I'll just get rolled by some gang banger or druggie on my way home. Honest to God, I don't know why I bother. It's probably just to provide local color for the tourists."

"Where are you living?"

"No, Scottie," Jeff shook his head. "I know how this works. You guys always swoop down wanting to help. Which is great for about fifteen minutes until you realize how filthy the place is and how sick I am and how bad the whole thing bums you out and you get all embarrassed about how bad you hate it and I end up having to throw you out."

"Isn't anyone helping you?"

"I get my welfare checks," Jeff shrugged, "and the soup kitchen at St. Andrew's is the most hospitable."

"What about your family?"

"They don't know about this," Jeff said, "and it's staying that way."

"And Sonny?"

"I broke up with him," Jeff laughed. "Don't you remember? Christopher and his gang up in Pacific Heights took a shine to me and I never looked back."

"They're not helping you?"

"That crowd of snobs," Jeff snorted. "The minute you get sick or even look like you might get sick they're through with you. Bad for the image. Those guys aren't the sort to get sick."

"That's bullshit, Jeff," Scott said. "Anybody can get it."

"They really hate being reminded of that. It's like that story by Poe when the black plague shows up in the middle of the prince's costume party or however the fuck it went."

"Jeff, please," Scott said, "if you'll just give me three minutes to get to the car and grab my wallet. . ."

"I won't be here," Jeff said. "I told you."

When Scott got back, he was gone.

"Who was that you were talking to out front?" Scott asked when Jared came in from taking out the last of the trash.

"One of our new neighbors," Jared said. "Lives three doors up, apparently. Kip Truman."

"Kip Truman? He's the guy who took over *Gay by the Bay* back a few months ago."

"Really."

"Some kind of crusader. Wants to make the paper relevant. Not just a rag for the drag queens and go-go boys. You read it lately?"

"Who has time to read?"

"Heavy political stuff."

"Well, he's no go-go boy," Jared said. "That's for sure."

"So? He was out walking his dog? Trolling for twinkies?"

"Looked like he'd been to a party," Jared said. "Or maybe the opera."

"The opera's not on this weekend."

"Party then," Jared said.

"If he publishes a paper, we should invite him for next Saturday."

"If he's a muckraker, he'll hate it."

"Half of our friends are muckrakers," Scott said. "At least would-be ones."

"I don't think so."

"There's no such thing as bad publicity."

"Yes, there is," Jared said. "In my line of work, there definitely is."

"For some reason," Scott mused, "the name seems familiar in a different connection."

"Isn't he the guy who owns that used bookstore?"

"God, yes," Scott said. "Griffin used to work for him. Back when dinosaurs ruled the earth and we rented that place from Millicent Peabody. Kip Truman. Now you really have to invite him for next Saturday. It'll be like a reunion."

"Seriously, Scottie, I don't think so."

"Why not?"

"Well, to be quite frank he kind of gave me the creeps."

"Can't have that," Scott laughed.

"Come on," Jared said. "Let's lock this place up and go home."

It had been one of the best nights of Jared's life, right up there with his second date with Scott. Like that night, this one had been a culmination, the realization of a long cherished dream. The only appropriate emotion, he thought as he rinsed his toothbrush, was gratitude. And he was grateful, all right.

Sad about Skip, though. Poor guy. And that crazy story about him changing his name. As if it hadn't been as plain as the nose on your face that he was Jewish, and as if that was something to be ashamed of. That bastard Christopher. There didn't seem to be any limit to his determination to make people miserable.

It wasn't losing Skip, Jared eventually realized, that had hurt him so badly at the time. It was the way the loss made him feel about himself. It had exacerbated his self-doubt until it became intolerable—until he wanted to die. Thank God for Tristan and Big Steve. For Nick and Cooper. They hadn't tried to talk him out of his feelings like so many "friends" would have done. They simply stood with him as he figured out how to fight those feelings off for himself. Thank God for them. And thank God for Scott.

"I do love you, you know," Buzz said, wishing there was some way of making Trevor see how much without leaving him feeling he'd just committed suicide.

"What I know is that's a really shitty way to try and win an argument," Trevor said.

"What are you talking about?"

"Arguments are supposed to be based on reason and logic," Trevor said, "and there you go trying to get around me with sweet talk."

"I wasn't," Buzz said. "I just felt like telling you I love you."

"Christopher says it's not about the utterance," Trevor said. "It's about the context within which the utterance takes place."

"Oh," Buzz said, heart sinking.

The End

Also by Jackson Peoples-Rosenblatt:

The Navigators
Lodestar
The Current
Intersections
Voyages

Directory of Recurring Characters

Armstrong, Bo: born, 1955. French citizen, former gendarme. Bodybuilder. Hustler. (*Voyages*)

Bailey, Scott: born, 1953. Son of an American professor and the daughter of a German Field Marshal executed for his role in Count von Stauffenberg's 1944 plot to assassinate Hitler. She survived the fall of Berlin in 1945, later marrying Scott's father and coming to the U.S. Scott has built a career translating literary works from German. (*The Navigators; The Current; Voyages*)

Bartok, Jared "J.B.": born, 1950. Wounded during a tour in Viet Nam, nearly losing his left leg below the knee. This injury discouraged him from entering bodybuilding competitions, though his mentors, Big Steve Fabiani and Matthew Duckworth, insisted he try anyway. An architect specializing in Mid-Century Modern style. (*The Navigators; The Current; Voyages*)

Bentley, Tristan: born, 1947. Graduated from NYU, where he was involved with a student radical cell. Served as a combat medic during one tour in Viet Nam. Joined the San Francisco Police Department subsequent to his military service. A competitive bodybuilder. (*The Navigators; Lodestar; The Current; Voyages*)

Crawford, Will: born, 1952. Published poet. Attorney. (*The Navigators; Voyages*)

Danziger, Eli: born, 1950. Financial analyst. (*Intersections*)

De Croteau, Jules: born, c. 1925. Acclaimed French film director, later pornographer. (*The Current***)**

De Havilland, Kirk: born, 1955. Trust fund baby. Bodybuilding competitor. (*The Navigators; Voyages*)

De Havilland, Yvette (nee Grossman): born, 1952. Corporate attorney. Mother of three sons. (*The Navigators; Voyages*)

Del Rey, Marina (aka Bartolomeo "Bart" Correa): born, 1951. Travel agent. Drag queen. Chanel Rococo's second-in-command. (*The Current; Voyages*)

Duckworth, Matthew: born, 1933. Airline pilot, husband, father. Successful bodybuilding competitor. (*The Navigators; The Current; Voyages*)

Eastman, Sean: born, 1952. Former CBC child star. Former member of the Royal Canadian Mounted Police. Former professional rugby player. Bodybuilder, waiter, sometime hustler. (*The Navigators: Voyages*)

Fabiani, Stefano "Big Steve": born, 1935. Joined the military while under-aged. Served in Korea and Viet Nam. On retirement from the army, joined the San Francisco Police Department. A guru of local bodybuilders. (*The Navigators; Lodestar; The Current; Voyages*)

Garrison, Lance: born, 1950. Collegiate and later Olympic wrestler. Physique photographer. (*The Navigators; The Current; Voyages*)

Krakowiak, Michael: born, 1935. Professor of piano performance at San Francisco State University. Cousin of Nick Romanovsky. (*The Current; Voyages*)

Lundquist, Morgan: born, 1956. Gym owner. (*The Navigators; Voyages*)

Lundquist, Nelson: born, 1956. Twin brother of **Morgan Lundquist** (see previous entry). Individual with no visible means of support. (*The Navigators*)

Luxemberg, Cooper: born, 1955. Realtor; partner with Ned Westerleigh and Elizabeth Montefiore in the Luxemberg-Montefiore Realty. (*The Navigators; The Current; Intersections; Voyages*)

MacDonald, Griffin: born, 1956. Graduate student in classical piano performance and local piano bar performer. (*The Navigators; The Current; Intersections; Voyages*)

Melendez-Greene, Christopher: born, 1950. Medical student. (*The Current**)**

Melendez, Rene: born, 1933. Former actor and model. (*The Current*)

Montezuma, Holly (aka Enrique "Henry" Sandoval): born, 1953. Travel agent. Drag Queen. Chanel Rococo's court jester and enforcer. (*The Current; Voyages*)

Montgomery, Burton "Buzz": born, 1947. Former high school English teacher. (*The Navigators; The Current; Voyages*)

Powell, Evan: born, 1955. Stanford roommate of Kirk deHavilland. Male model, later designer. (*Voyages*)

Rococo, Chanel (aka Johnnie Miller): born, 1950. Graphic artist, painter, empress. (*The Current; Voyages*)

Romanovsky, Nikolai "Nick" aka "Niko": born, 1940. Attorney. Big Steve Fabiani's second in command. Legendary Castro Street sexual athlete and bad boy. (*The Navigators; The Current; Voyages*)

Sainte-Claire, Ashby: born, 1950. Medical student. (*The Navigators; Voyages*)

Schein, Jean-Pierre: born, 1940. Frenchman. Professor of piano at the San Francisco Conservatory. (*The Current; Voyages*)

Stone: born, 1955. Bodybuilder. Hustler. (*The Current; Voyages*)

Weitzmann, Trevor: born, 1960. High school athlete. University student. (*The Navigators; The Current; Voyages*)

Westerleigh, Ned: born, 1918. Youngest son of a minor British aristocrat and a cousin of Czar Nicholas II. Attended Winchester College and Oxford. Served in MI6 during and after World War II. "Deactivated" at an unspecified time during the Sixties or Seventies. Resettled in the United States, where he began a career in real estate. A partner of Cooper Luxemberg's, in the Luxemberg-Montefiore agency. (*The Navigators; The Current; Intersections; Voyages*)

Yates, Gregory: born, 1951. Cooper Luxemberg's freshman composition teaching assistant at San Francisco State. Subsequent career as a high school English teacher. (*The Current; Voyages*)

www.ingramcontent.com/pod-product-compliance
Lightning Source LLC
Chambersburg PA
CBHW071330020726
47502CB00001B/39